Praise for *The Devil of Nanking*

"There is a terrible beauty to both narratives as they unfold toward an agonizing but inevitable conclusion, with the two stories dovetailing exquisitely. . . . *The Devil of Nanking* just may be one of the best books of the year." —*The Denver Post*

"A literary thriller that examines violence on a grander scale: the infamous 'rape of Nanking' in 1937 . . . Throughout, Hayder's prose is striking . . . Beautifully written and often fascinating, and it has a powerful historical hook." —Patrick Anderson, *The Washington Post*

"A perfectly sinister novel . . . Hayder creates such a threatening environment that when the novel gains its strength, every page evokes a shudder . . . A thoroughly satisfying thriller." —*New York Daily News*

"Terrifying, compelling . . . Hayder expertly piles suspense upon suspense. [*The Devil of Nanking*] is both a fascinating and moving historical novel and a thriller so fast paced I had to sit up until the early hours to finish it, lest my sleep be disturbed by its chilling vision." —*Daily Telegraph* (UK)

"A real page-turner, full of suspense, with a terrifying, gritty edge that turns the blood cold." —Minette Walters

"Confirms a major talent that transcends thriller writing." —*Time Out New York*

"With *The Treatment* Mo Hayder cemented her reputation as one of Britain's pre-eminent crime writers. *The Devil of Nanking* jackhammers her to the top of the field. This is the epic thriller of the year."   —Karin Slaughter

"History, folklore, and ancient taboos are interwoven seamlessly with the modern-day mystery . . . By any measure, *The Devil of Nanking* is a novel that resonates long after the last page is turned."
                                    —Mystery of the Month, *Bookpage*

"What a story—what a storyteller!"   —Colin Dexter

"Hayder's novel moves beyond the mystery and suspense angles into larger issues of history, memory and power . . . [A] powerfully written, haunting thriller."   Beth Lindsay, *Library Journal*

"Mo Hayder writes hauntingly of hidden Tokyo, where the past lies only just below the surface."   —*Literary Review* (UK)

"You won't read a more frightening and shocking novel this year. Mo Hayder knows how to keep you on the edge of your seat right up until the moment she pushes you off screaming. *The Devil of Nanking* . . . is an intense and consuming book that steadily builds in tension and thrills."
                            —Peter Mergendahl, *Rocky Mountain News*

The Devil of Nanking

MO HAYDER

The Devil of Nanking

GROVE PRESS
New York

First published in Great Britain in 2004 by Bantam Press/Transworld Publishers,
a division of The Random House Group Ltd., London

Printed in the United States of America

Library of Congress Cataloging-in-Publication Data
Hayder, Mo.
    The devil of Nanking / Mo Hayder.
       p. cm.
    ISBN 978-0-8021-2219-3
    eBook ISBN: 978-0-8021-9960-7

1. Young women—Fiction.   2. Nanking Massacre, Nanjing, Jiangsu Sheng,
China, 1937—Fiction.   3. Sino-Japanese Conflict, 1937–1945—Fiction.
4. British—Japan—Fiction.   5. College teachers—Fiction. 6. Tokyo
(Japan)—Fiction.   7. Nightclubs—Fiction.   8. Criminals—Fiction.   I. Title.
PR6058.A688594D48 2005
813'.54—dc22   2005040302

Grove Press
an imprint of Grove/Atlantic, Inc.
154 West 14th Street
New York, NY 10011

Distributed by Publishers Group West

www.groveatlantic.com

14 15 16 17   10 9 8 7 6 5 4 3 2 1

For Iris Chang, 1968–2004,
whose bravery and scholarship
first lifted the name *Nanking*
out of obscurity

Prologue

史 **Nanking, China: 21 December 1937**

To those who fight and rage against superstition, I say only this: why? Why admit to such pride and vanity that you carelessly disregard years of tradition? When the peasant tells you that the great mountains of ancient China were destroyed by the angry gods, that thousands of years ago the skies were torn down, the country set out of kilter, why not believe him? Are you so much cleverer than he is? Are you cleverer than all his generations taken together?

I believe him. Now, at last, I believe. I tremble to write it, but I do, I believe all that superstition tells us. And why? Because there is nothing else to explain the vagaries of this world, no other tool to translate this disaster. So I turn to folklore for my comfort, and I trust the peasant when he says that the wrath of the gods has caused the land to slope downwards to the east. Yes, I trust him when he tells me that everything, river, mud and towns, must eventually slide into the sea. Nanking too. One day Nanking too will slide away to the sea. Her journey may be the slowest, for she is no longer quite like other cities. These last few days have changed her beyond recognition and when she begins to move it will be slowly, for she is tethered to the land by her unburied citizens, and by the ghosts that will pursue her to the coast and back.

Maybe I should consider myself privileged to see her as she is now. From this tiny window I can peer out through the lattice and see what the Japanese have left of her: her blackened buildings, the empty streets, the corpses piling up in the canals and rivers. Then I look down at my shaking hands and wonder why I have survived. The blood is dry now. If I rub my palms together it flakes off, the black scales scatter on the paper, darker than the words I write because my ink is watery: the pine soot inkstick is finished and I haven't the strength or the courage or the will to go out and find more.

If I were to lay down my pen, lean sideways against the cold wall and adopt an awkward position with my nose squashed against the shutters, I would be able to see Purple Mountain, snow-covered, rising up beyond the shattered roofs. But I will not. There is no call to push my body into an unnatural place because I will never again look upon Purple Mountain. When this diary entry is finished I will have no desire to recall myself, up on those slopes, a ragged and uneven figure, keeping desperate pace with the Japanese soldier, tracking him like a wolf, through frozen streams and snowdrifts . . .

It is less than two hours. Two hours since I caught up with him. We were in a small grove near the mausoleum gates. He was standing with his back to me next to a tree, the melting snow in the branches dripping down on to his shoulders. His head was bent forward a little to peer into the forest ahead, because the mountain slopes are still a dangerous place to be. The cine-camera dangled at his side.

I had been following him for so long that I was bruised and limping, my lungs stinging in the cold air. I came forward slowly. I can't, now, imagine how I was able to remain so controlled because I was trembling from head to toe. When he heard me he whirled round, falling instinctively to a crouch. But I am not much of a man, not strong, and a full head shorter than he was, and when he saw it was me, he relaxed a little. He straightened slowly, watching me come a few steps nearer until we were only feet apart, and he could see the tears on my face.

'It will mean nothing to you,' he said, with something like pity in his voice, 'but I want you to know that I am sorry. I am very sorry. Do you understand my Japanese?'

'Yes, I do.'

He sighed and rubbed his forehead with his cracked pigskin glove. 'It wasn't as I would have wished it. It never is. Please believe this.' He raised his hand in the vague direction of the Linggu Temple. 'It is true that – that *he* enjoyed it. He always does. But I don't. I watch them. I make films of what they do, but I take no pleasure from it. Please trust me in this, *I take no pleasure.*'

I wiped my face with my sleeve, pushing away the tears. I stepped forward and put a trembling hand on his shoulder. He didn't flinch – he stood his ground, searching my face, puzzled. There was no fear in his expression: he thought of me as a defenceless civilian. He knew nothing about the small fruit knife hidden in my hand.

'Give me the camera,' I said.

'I can't. Don't believe I make these films for their recreation, for the soldiers. I have far greater intentions than that.'

'Give me the camera.'

He shook his head. 'Absolutely not.'

With those words the world around us seemed to me to slow down abruptly. Somewhere on the distant slopes below, the Japanese *sampohei* artillery were laying down heavy mortar fire, chasing renegade Nationalist units off the mountains, rounding them up and forcing them back down to the city, but up on the higher slopes I was aware of no sound at all, save the thudding of our hearts, the ice melting in the trees around us.

'I said give me the camera.'

'And I repeat no. Absolutely not.'

I opened my mouth then, canted forward a little and released a howl directly into his mouth. It had been building in me all the time I'd been chasing him through the snow, and now I screamed, like a wounded animal. I lunged, twisting the little knife into him, through the khaki uniform, grinding through the lucky *senninbari* belt. He didn't make a sound. His face moved, his head jerked up so fast that his army cap fell off, and we both stumbled back a pace in surprise, staring down at what I'd done. Gouts of blood fell into the snow and the inside of his stomach folded out like creamy fruit through the rip in his uniform.

He stared at it for a moment, as if puzzled. Then the pain reached him. He dropped his rifle and grabbed at his stomach, trying to push it back inside. '*Kuso!*' he said. 'What have you done?'

I staggered back, dropping the knife into the snow, groping blindly for a tree to lean against. The soldier turned away from me and lurched into the forest. One hand clutching his belly, the other still holding the camera, he went unsteadily, his head held up with a peculiar dignity, as if he was heading somewhere important, as if a better, safer world lay somewhere out in the trees. I went after him, stumbling in the snow, my breath coming fast and hot. After about ten yards he tripped, almost lost his balance and cried out something: a woman's name in Japanese, his mother's maybe, or his wife's. He raised his arm and the movement must have loosened things inside because some dark and long part of him slithered out of the wound, dropping into the snow. He slipped in it and tried to regain his balance, but now he was very weak and he could only stagger, in a hazy circle, a long red cord trailing from him, as if this was a birth and not a death.

'Give it to me. Give me the camera.'

He couldn't answer. He had lost all ability to reason: he was no longer aware of what was happening. He sank to his knees, his arms raised slightly, and rolled softly on to his side. I was next to him in a second. His lips were blue and there was blood coating his teeth. 'No,' he whispered, as I prised his gloved fingers from the camera. His eyes were already blind, but he could sense where I was. He groped for my face. 'Don't take it. If you take it who will tell the world?'

If you take it who will tell the world?

Those words have stayed with me. They will be with me for the rest of my life. Who will tell? I stare for a long time at the sky above the house, at the black smoke drifting across the moon. Who will tell? The answer is, no one. No one will tell. It is all over. This will be the last entry in my journal. I will never write again. The rest of my story will stay on the film inside the camera, and what happened today will remain a secret.

8

tokyo

史

1

Tokyo, summer 1990

Sometimes you have to really make an effort. Even when you're
tired and hungry and you find yourself somewhere completely
strange. That was me in Tokyo that summer, standing in front of
Professor Shi Chongming's door and shaking with anxiety. I had
pressed my hair down so it lay as neatly as possible, and I'd spent
a long time trying to straighten my old Oxfam skirt, brushing the
dust off and ironing out the travel creases with my palms. I'd
kicked the battered holdall I'd brought with me on the plane behind
my feet so it wouldn't be the first thing he saw, because it was so
important to look normal. I had to count to twenty-five and take
very deep, very careful breaths before I had the courage to speak.

'Hello?' I said tentatively, my face close to the door. 'Are you
there?'

I waited for a moment, listening hard. I could hear vague
shufflings inside, but no one came to the door. I waited a few
more moments, my heart getting louder and louder in my ears,
then I knocked. 'Can you hear me?'

The door opened and I took a step back in surprise. Shi
Chongming stood in the doorway, very smart and correct, looking at me in silence, his hands at his sides as if he was waiting to
be inspected. He was incredibly tiny, like a doll, and around the
delicate triangle of his face hung shoulder-length hair, perfectly
white, as if he had a snow shawl draped across his shoulders. I
stood speechless, my mouth open a little.

11

He placed his palms flat on his thighs and bowed to me. 'Good afternoon,' he said, in a soft, almost accentless English. 'I am Professor Shi Chongming. Who are you?'

'I – I'm—' I swallowed. 'I'm a student. Sort of.' I fumbled my cardigan sleeve up and pushed out my hand to him. I hoped he didn't notice my bitten nails. 'From the University of London.'

He eyed me thoughtfully, taking in my white face, my limp hair, the cardigan and the big shapeless holdall. Everyone does this the first time they meet me, and the truth is, no matter how much you pretend, you never really get used to being stared at.

'I've been needing to meet you for almost half my life,' I said. 'I've been waiting for this for nine years, seven months and eighteen days.'

'Nine years, seven months and eighteen days?' He raised an eyebrow, amused. 'So long? In that case you had better come in.'

I'm not very good at knowing what other people are thinking, but I do know that you can see tragedy, real tragedy, sitting just inside a person's gaze. You can almost always see where a person has been if you look hard enough. It had taken me such a long time to track down Shi Chongming. He was in his seventies, and it was amazing to me that, in spite of his age and in spite of what he must feel about the Japanese, he was here, a visiting professor at Todai, the greatest university in Japan. His office overlooked the university archery hall, where dark trees gathered round the complex tiled roofs, where the only sound was crows calling as they hopped between the evergreen oaks. The room was hot and breathless, dusty air stirred by three electric fans that whirred back and forward. I crept in, awed that I was really there at last.

Shi Chongming shifted piles of paper from a chair. 'Sit. Sit. I'll make tea.'

I sat with a bump, my heavy shoes pressed rigidly together, my bag on my lap, clutched tightly to my stomach. Shi Chongming limped around, filled an electric Thermos from a sink, oblivious to the water that sprayed out and darkened his mandarin-style tunic. The fan gently shifted the stacks of papers and crumbling old volumes that were piled on the floor-to-ceiling shelves. As soon as I walked in I'd seen, in the corner of the room, a projector. A dusty 16mm projector, only just visible where it had been pushed up in the corner among the towering piles of paper. I wanted to turn and stare at it, but I knew I shouldn't. I bit my lip and fixed my eyes on Shi Chongming. He was delivering a long monologue about his research.

'Few have a concept of when Chinese medicine first came to Japan, but you can even look at the Tang era and see evidence of its existence here. Did you know that?' He made me tea and rustled up a wrapped biscuit from somewhere. 'The priest Jian Zhen was preaching it, right here, in the eighth century. Now there are *kampo* shops everywhere you look. Only step outside the campus and you'll see them. Fascinating, isn't it?'

I blinked at him. 'I thought you were a linguist.'

'A linguist? No, no. Once, maybe, but everything has changed. Do you want to know what I am? I'll tell you – if you take a microscope and carefully study the nexus where the bio-technologist and the sociologist meet . . .' He smiled, giving me a glimpse of long yellow teeth. 'There you'll find me: Shi Chongming, a very little man with a grand title. The university tells me I'm quite a catch. What I'm interested in is just how much of all this . . .' he swooped his hand round the room to indicate the books, colour plates of mummified animals, a wall-chart labelled *Entomology of Hunan* '. . . how much of this came with Jian Zhen, and how much was brought back to Japan by the troops in 1945. For example, let me see . . .' He ran his hands over the familiar texts, pulled out a dusty old volume and put it down in front of me, opened at a bewildering diagram of a bear, dissected to show its internal organs coloured in printer's pastel shades of pink and mint. 'For example, the Asiatic black bear. Was it after the Pacific war that they decided to use the gall bladder of their Karuizawa bear for stomach ailments?' He put his hands on the table and peered at me. 'I expect that's where you come in, isn't it? The black bear is one of my interests. It's the question that brings most people to my door. Are you a conservationist?'

'No,' I said, surprised by how steady my voice was. 'Actually, no. It's not where I come in. I've never heard of the – the Karuizawa bear.' And then I couldn't help it. I turned and glanced at the projector in the corner. 'I . . .' I dragged my eyes back to Shi Chongming. 'I mean that Chinese medicine isn't what I want to talk about.'

'No?' He lowered his spectacles and looked at me with great curiosity. 'Is it not?'

'No.' I shook my head precisely. 'No. Not at all.'

'Then . . .' He paused. 'Then you're here because . . . ?'

'Because of Nanking.'

He sat down at the table with a frown. 'I'm sorry. Who did you say you were?'

'I'm a student at London University. At least, I was. But I wasn't studying Chinese medicine. I was studying war atrocities.'

'Stop.' He held up his hand. 'You have come to the wrong man. I am of no interest to you.'

He started to get up from the desk but I unzipped my holdall hastily and pulled out the battered pile of notes secured in an elastic band, dropping some in my nervousness, picking them up and putting them all untidily on the desk between us.

'I've spent half my life researching the war in China.' I undid the band and spread out my notes. There were sheets of translations in my tiny handwriting, photocopies of testimonies from library books, sketches I'd done to help me visualize what had happened. 'Especially Nanking. Look,' I held up a crumpled paper covered in tiny characters, 'this is about the invasion – it's a family tree of the Japanese chain of command, it's all written in Japanese, see? I did it when I was sixteen. I can write some Japanese and some Chinese.'

Shi Chongming looked at it all in silence, sinking slowly into his chair, a strange look on his face. My sketches and diagrams aren't very good, but I don't mind it any more when people laugh at them – each one means something important to me, each one helps me order my thoughts, each one reminds me that every day I'm getting nearer the truth of something that happened in Nanking in 1937. 'And this . . .' I unfolded a sketch and held it up. It was on a sheet of A3 and over the years

14

transparent lines had worn into it where it had been folded for storage. '. . . this is supposed to be the city at the end of the invasion. It took me a whole month to finish. That's a pile of bodies. See?' I looked up at him eagerly. 'If you look carefully you can see I've got it exactly right. You can check it now, if you want. There are exactly *three hundred thousand* corpses in this picture and—'

Shi Chongming got abruptly to his feet and moved from behind the desk. He closed the door, crossed to the window overlooking the archery hall and lowered the blinds. He walked with a slight tow to the left and his hair was so thin that the back of his head seemed almost bald, the skin corrugated, as if there was no skull there and you could see the folds and crevices of his brain. 'Do you know how sensitive this country is to mention of Nanking?' He came back and sat down at his desk with arthritic slowness, leaning across to me and talking in a low whisper. 'Do you know how powerful the right wing is in Japan? Do you know the people who have been attacked for talking about it? The Americans –' he pointed a shaky finger at me, as if I was the nearest representation of America '– the Americans, *MacArthur*, ensured that the right wing are the fear-mongers they are today. It is quite simple – we do not talk about it.'

I lowered my voice to a whisper. 'But I've come all this way to see you.'

'Then you'll have to turn round and go back,' he answered. 'This is my past you're talking about. I am not here, in *Japan* of all places, to discuss the mistakes of the past.'

'You don't understand. You've got to help me.'

'Got to?'

'It's about one particular thing the Japanese did. I know about most of the atrocities, the killing competitions, the rapes. But I'm talking about something specific, something you witnessed. No one believes it actually happened, they all think I made it up.'

Shi Chongming sat forward and stared at me directly. Usually when I tell them what I'm trying to find out about, people give me a distressed, pitying look, a look that says, 'You must have invented it. And why? Why would you make up a dreadful thing like that?' But this look was different. This look was hard and angry. When he spoke his voice had changed to a low, bitter note: '*What* did you say?'

'There was a testimony about it. I read it years ago, but I haven't been able to find the book again, and everyone says I made that up too, that the book never really existed. But that's okay, because apparently there's a film, too, shot in Nanking in 1937. I found out about it six months ago. And *you* know all about it.'

'Preposterous. There is not a film.'

'But – but your name was in an academic journal. It was, honestly, I saw it. It said you had been in Nanking. It said you had seen the massacre, that you'd seen this kind of torture. It said when that you were at Jiangsu University in 1957 there were rumours that you had a film of it. And that's why I'm here. I need to hear about . . . I need to hear about what the soldiers did. Just *one detail* of what they did, so I know I didn't imagine it. I need to know whether, when they took the women and—'

'Please!' Shi Chongming slammed his hands on the desk and got to his feet. 'Have you no compassion? This is not a *kaffeeklatsch*!' He hooked up a cane from the back of his chair and limped across the room, unlocking the door and taking his nameplate off the hooks. 'See?' he said, using the cane to close the door. He held up the nameplate to me, tapping it to make his point. 'Professor of Sociology. *Sociology*. My field is Chinese medicine. I am no longer defined by Nanking. There is no film. It is finished. Now, I'm very busy and—'

'Please.' I gripped the sides of the desk, my face flushing. 'Please. There *is* a film. There *is*. It was in the journal, I saw it. Magee's film doesn't show it, but yours does. It's the *only* film *anywhere in the world* and—'

'Ssssh,' he said, waving the cane in my direction. 'Enough.' His teeth were long and discoloured, like old fossils prised from the Gobi – polished yellow on rice husk and goat meat. 'Now, I have absolute respect for you. I have respect for you and for your unique institute. Quite unique. But let me put this quite simply: *there is no film*.'

*

16

When you're in the business of trying to prove that you're not crazy, people like Shi Chongming really don't help. To read something, in black and white, only to be told the next minute that you've imagined it – well, that's the kind of thing that can make you as mad as they all say you are. It was the same story all over again, exactly the same as what had happened with my parents and the hospital when I was thirteen. Everyone there said that the torture was all in my imagination, all part of my madness – that there could never have been such terrible cruelty. That the Japanese soldiers were barbarous and ruthless, but they could not have done something like *that*, something so unspeakable that even the doctors and nurses, who reckoned they'd seen everything in their time, lowered their voices when they talked about it. 'I'm sure you *believe* you read it. I'm sure it's very real to you.'

'It is real,' I'd say, looking at the floor, my face burning with embarrassment. 'I did read it. In a book.' It had been a book with an orange cover and a photograph of bodies piling up in the Meitan harbour. It was full of stories of what had happened in Nanking. Until I read it I'd never even heard of Nanking. 'I found it at my parents' house.'

One of the nurses, who really didn't like me at all, used to come to my bed when the lights were off, when she thought no one was listening. I'd lie, stiff and still, and pretend to be asleep, but she'd crouch down next to my bed anyway, and whisper into my ear, her breath hot and yeasty. 'Let me tell you this,' she would murmur, night after night, when the flower shadows of the curtains were motionless on the ward ceiling. 'You have got the sickest imagination I've ever known in ten years in this fucked-up job. You really are insane. Not just insane, but evil too.'

But I didn't make it up . . .

I was afraid of my parents, especially of my mother, but when no one in the hospital would believe that the book existed, when I was starting to worry that maybe they were right, that I *had* imagined it, that I *was* mad, I got up my courage and wrote home, asking them to look among all the piles of paperbacks for a book with an orange cover, called, I was almost sure, *The Massacre of Nanking*.

A letter came back almost immediately: '*I am sure you believe this book exists, but let me promise you this, you didn't read such rubbish in my house.'*

My mother had always been so certain that she was in control of what I knew and thought about. She wouldn't trust a school not to fill my head with the wrong things, so for years I was educated at home. But if you're going to take on a responsibility like that, if you are so afraid (for whatever private, anguished reason) of your children learning about life that you vet every book that comes through the door, sometimes ripping offending pages from novels, well, one thing's for sure: you have to be thorough. At least a little more thorough than my mother was. She didn't see the laxity creeping into her home, coming through the weed-choked windows, slinking past the damp piles of paperbacks. Somehow she missed the book on Nanking.

'We have searched high and low, with the greatest of intention of helping you, our only child, but I am sorry to say, in this instance you are mistaken. We have written to your Responsible Medical Officer to tell him so.'

I remember dropping the letter on to the floor of the ward, a horrible idea occurring to me. What if, I thought, they were right? What if the book didn't exist? What if I really had made it all up in my head? That, I thought, a low thumping ache starting in my stomach, would be the worst thing that could ever happen.

Sometimes you have to go a long way to prove things. Even if it turns out that you're only proving things to yourself.

When I was at last discharged from hospital, I knew exactly what I had to do next. In hospital I got all my exams through the teaching unit (I got As for most of them, and that surprised everyone – they all acted as if they thought ignorance equalled stupidity) and out in the real world there were charities for people like me, to help us apply to college. They took me through all the stuff I found difficult – phone calls and bus journeys. I'd studied Chinese and Japanese on my own, from library books, and pretty soon I got a place doing Asian Studies at London University. Suddenly, on the outside at least, I appeared almost normal: I had a rented room, a part-time job handing out leaflets, a student rail pass and a tutor who collected Yoruba sculptures and Pre-Raphaelite post-cards. ('I've got a fetish for pale women,' he'd once said, eyeing me thoughtfully. Then he'd added, under his breath, 'As long as they're not crazy, of course.') But while the other students were picturing a graduation, maybe postgraduate study, I was thinking about Nanking. If there was ever going to be peace in my life I had to know if I'd remembered the details in the orange book properly.

I spent hours in the library, sifting through books and journals, trying to find another copy of the book or, failing that, another publication of the same witness testimony. There had been a book called *The Horror of Nanking* published in 1980, but it was out of print. No library, not even the Library of Congress, held a copy and, anyway, I wasn't even sure if it was the same book. But that didn't matter, because I had found something else. To my amazement I discovered that there was film footage of the massacre.

In total there were two films. The first was Reverend Magee's. Magee had been a missionary in China in the 1930s and his film had been smuggled out by a colleague, who was so terrified by what he'd seen that he'd sewn it into the lining of his camel-hair coat on his way to Shanghai. From there the film lay forgotten in a hot southern California basement for several years, disintegrating, becoming sticky and distorted, until it was rediscovered and given to the Library of Congress film collection. I'd seen the video copy at London University library. I'd watched it over and over again, peered at it, studied every frame. It showed the horror of Nanking – it showed things I don't like to think about even in the light of day – but it didn't show the torture I'd read about all those years ago.

The second, or rather the mention of it, was Shi Chongming's. The instant I heard about it I forgot everything else.

It was my second year at university. One spring morning, when Russell Square was full of tourists and daffodils, I was in the library, seated at a low-lit table behind the Humanities abstracts stacks, cramped over an obscure journal. My heart was thumping – at last I'd found a reference to the torture. It was an oblique reference, vague, really, and without the crucial detail, but one sentence sent me bolt upright in my chair: 'Certainly in Jiangsu in the late 1950s, there was mention of the existence of a 16mm film of this torture. Unlike Magee's film, this film has not, to date, surfaced outside China.'

I grabbed the journal and pulled the Anglepoise low over the page, not quite believing what I was seeing. It was incredible to think there was a visual record of it – imagine that! They could say I was insane, they could say I was ignorant, but no one could say that I'd made it all up – not if it was there in black and white.

'The film was said to have belonged to one Shi Chongming, a young research assistant from Jiangsu University who had been in Nanking at the time of the great 1937 massacre . . .'

I reread the paragraph over and over again. A feeling was coming over me that I'd never had before, a feeling that had been packed tight and solid by years of disbelieving hospital staff. It was only when the student at the neighbouring desk sighed impatiently, that I realized I was on my feet, clenching and unclenching my hands and muttering to myself. The hair on my arms was standing on end. *It has not yet surfaced outside China . . .*

I should have stolen that journal. If I had really learned my lesson in hospital, I'd have put the journal inside my cardigan and walked straight out of the library with it. Then I'd have had something to show Shi Chongming, proof that I hadn't made things up from a diseased imagination. He couldn't have denied it then, and set me questioning my sanity all over again.

2

Opposite the huge red-lacquered *Akamon* gate at the entrance to Todai University there was a small place called the Bambi café. When Shi Chongming asked me to leave his office I did, obediently gathering up all my notes and stuffing them back into the holdall. But I hadn't given up. Not yet. I went to the café and chose a seat in the window, overlooking the gate so that I could see everyone coming and going.

Above me, as far as the eye could see, the skyscrapers of Tokyo rose glittering into the sky, reflecting the sun back from a million windows. I sat hunched forward, staring up at this incredible sight. I knew a lot about this phoenix city, about how Tokyo had risen from the ashes of war, but here, in the flesh, it didn't seem quite real to me. Where, I thought, is all of wartime Tokyo? Where is the city that those soldiers came from? Is it all buried under *this*? It was so different from the dark images I'd had all these years, of an old charcoal-stained relic, bombed streets and rickshaws – I decided I would think of the steel and roaring ferroconcrete as an incarnation of Tokyo, something superimposed over the authentic city, the real beating heart of Japan.

The waitress was staring at me. I picked up the menu and pretended to be studying it, my face colouring. I didn't have any money, because I really hadn't thought this far. For my plane ticket I'd worked packing frozen peas in a factory, wearing away the skin on my fingers. When I told the university that I wanted

21

to come out here and find Shi Chongming they said it was the last straw. That I could stay in London and finish my failed courses, or leave the university entirely. Apparently I was 'destructively preoccupied with certain events in Nanking': they pointed to the unfinished modules, the law department core courses I hadn't even turned up for, the times I'd been caught in the lecture hall doing sketches of Nanking instead of making notes on the economic dynamics of the Asia–Pacific region. There was no point in asking them for research funds to travel, so I sold my belongings, some CDs, a coffee-table, the old black bike that had got me around London for years. After the plane ticket there wasn't much left – just a grubby fistful of yen shoved into one of the side pockets of my holdall.

I kept glancing up at the waitress, wondering how long it would be before I'd have to order something. She was starting to look upset, so I chose the cheapest thing on the menu – a melon 'Danish' covered in damp sugar grains. Five hundred yen. When the food arrived I counted out the money carefully and placed it on the little saucer the way I could see all the other customers doing.

There was a little food in my holdall. Maybe no one would notice if I got some of it out now. I had packed eight packets of Rich Tea biscuits. There was also a wool skirt, two blouses, two pairs of tights, a pair of lace-up leather shoes, three Japanese language books, seven textbooks on the Pacific war, a dictionary and three paintbrushes. I'd been vague about what was going to come after I'd got Shi Chongming's film, I hadn't really thought about the practicalities. There you go, Grey, I thought. What were the doctors always telling you? *You'll have to discover ways of thinking ahead – there are rules in society that you will always have to consider.*

Grey.

Obviously it isn't my real name. Even my parents, tucked away in the crumbling cottage, where no roads came and no cars passed, even they weren't that odd. No. It was in hospital that I got the name.

It came from the girl in the bed next to me, a pale girl with a ring in the side of her nose and matted hair that she'd spend all day scratching: 'Trying to dred it up, just want to dred it up a bit.' She had scabs around her mouth from where she'd sniffed too much glue, and once she'd untwisted a coat hanger, locked herself in the toilets and pushed the sharp end up under her skin from her wrist all the way to her armpit. (The hospital tried to keep people like us together, I'll never know why. We were the 'self-harm' ward.) The girl in the dreds always seemed to have a confident smirk on her face and I never thought she would speak to me of all people. Then one day we were in the breakfast queue and she sensed me waiting behind her. She turned and looked at me and gave a sudden laugh of recognition. 'Oh, I get it. I've just sussed what you look like.'

I blinked. 'What?'

'A grey. You remind me of a grey.'

'A *what*?'

'Yeah. When you first got in here you were still alive. But,' she grinned and pointed a finger at my face, 'you're not now, are you? You're a ghost, Grey, like all of us.'

A grey. In the end she had to find a drawing of a grey to explain what she was talking about: it was an extra-terrestrial with a big head, blank, insect-like eyes set high and even, and strange, bleached-out skin. I remember sitting on my bed, staring at the magazine, my hands getting colder and colder, my blood slowing to a crawl. I was a grey. Thin and white and a little bit see-through. Nothing at all left alive in me. A ghost.

I knew why. It was because I didn't know what to believe any more. My parents wouldn't back me up, and there were other things that made the professionals think I was crazy – all the stuff about sex to start with. And then there was my weird ignorance about the world.

Most of the staff thought secretly that my story was a little outrageous: brought up with books, but no radio or TV. They'd laugh when I jumped in shock when a Hoover started up, or a bus rumbled by on the street. I didn't know how to use a Walkman or a channel-changer and they'd sometimes find me stranded in odd places, blinking, forgetting how I'd got there. They wouldn't believe it was because I'd grown up in isolation, cut off from the real world. Instead they decided it was all part of my madness.

'I suppose you think ignorance is some sort of excuse.' The nurse who used to come in the middle of the night and hiss all her opinions in my ear thought my being ignorant was the biggest of sins. 'It's not an excuse, you know, it's not an excuse. No. In fact, in my book ignorance is no different from pure, straight evil. And what you done was just that – pure, straight evil.'

When the waitress had gone, I unzipped my holdall and took out my Japanese dictionary. There are three alphabets in Japan. Two are phonetic and they're easy to understand. But there's a third one, too, evolved centuries ago from the pictorial characters used in China, and it's far more complex and far, far more beautiful. *Kanji*, it's called. I've been studying it for years, but sometimes when I see *kanji* it still makes me think about the littleness of my life. When you stop to consider the lifetime of history and intrigue all hidden in a single scripted picture tinier than an ant how can you not feel like a waste of air? *Kanji* had a beautiful logic for me. I understood why the symbol for 'ear' pressed close up to the symbol for 'gate' would mean 'listen'. I understood why three women clustered together meant 'noisy' and why adding splashy lines to the left of any character would change its meaning to include water. A field with an added water symbol meant sea.

The dictionary was my constant companion. It was small and soft and white and familiar, bound in something that could have been calfskin, and it fitted inside my hand as if it was moulded there. The girl with the dreadlocks had stolen it from a library when she got out of hospital. She had mailed it to me as a present when it got round the patients that I was leaving at last. She'd put a card between the pages that said: '*I believe you. Stick it to them all. Go and PROVE IT, girl.*' Even all those years later I was still secretly thrilled by that card.

I opened the dictionary to the front page, the page with the library stamp on it. The characters for the Chinese name Shi Chongming meant something like 'He who sees clearly both

24

history and the future.' With a red felt-tip from the bottom of my
bag I began to sketch out the *kanji*, intertwining them, turning
them upside-down, sideways, until the page was covered with red.
Then in the gaps, using very tiny letters, I wrote Shi Chongming
in English, over and over again. When there was no more room I
turned to the back page and sketched out a map of the campus,
putting in a few hedges and trees from memory. The campus was
so beautiful. I'd only seen it for a few minutes, but it had seemed
like a wonderland in the middle of the city: shadowy gingko
crowded around white gravel paths, ornate roofs and the cool
sounds of a dark lake in the forest. I drew in the archery hall, then
added a few stone lanterns from my imagination. Lastly over Shi
Chongming's office I carefully drew a picture of me standing in
front of him. We were shaking hands. In his other hand he was
holding a film in a canister, ready to pass it over to me. In my
image I was trembling. After nine years, seven months and
eighteen days, I was at last going to get an answer.

At six thirty the sun was still hot, but the big oak doors to the
Institute of Social Sciences were locked, and when I pressed my
ear to them I couldn't hear anything inside. I turned and looked
around, wondering what to do next. I'd waited for Shi
Chongming in the Bambi café for six hours and although no one
had said anything I'd felt obliged to keep buying iced coffees. I'd
had four. And four more melon pastries, wetting my fingers and
dabbing up the stray grains of sugar on the plate; reaching a
sneaky hand under the table and digging surreptitiously in my bag
for some Rich Tea biscuits whenever the waitress wasn't looking.
I had to break bits off under the table and put my hand casually
to my mouth pretending I was yawning. The handful of yen notes
dwindled. Now I realized it had been a waste of time. Shi
Chongming must have gone a long time ago, leaving from a
different entrance. Maybe he'd guessed I'd be waiting.

I went back to the street and pulled several folded pages from
my bag. One of the last things I'd done in London was to photocopy a map of Tokyo. It was on a very big scale: it covered several
pages. I stood in the late sunshine with the crowd streaming

round me, and inspected the pages. I looked up and down the long thoroughfare I stood on. It seemed like a canyon because the buildings were so dense and precipitous, the crowds and the neon signs and the buildings bristling with shops and business and noise. What was I supposed to do now? I'd given up every-thing to come here to see Shi Chongming, and now there was nowhere for me to go, nothing more for me to do.

Eventually when I'd studied the pages for ten minutes and still couldn't decide what to do, I crumpled them back into the bag, put the strap across my chest, closed my eyes and turned round and round on the spot, counting out loud. When I reached twenty-five I opened my eyes and, ignoring the strange looks from other pedestrians, headed off in the direction I faced.

3

I walked round Tokyo for hours, amazed by the skyscrapers like glass precipices, the cigarette and drinks advertising boards, the tinselly, mechanical voices that floated down everywhere I went, making me picture asylums up there in the sky. Round and round I went, directionless as a worm, dodging commuters, cyclists, tiny lonely schoolchildren immaculate in sailor suits, their leather backpacks polished like beetles' wings. I have no idea how far I walked, or where I went. When the light had gone from the city, the sweat had soaked through my clothes, the strap of the holdall had dug a groove across my shoulder and there were blisters on my feet, I stopped. I was standing in the grounds of a temple, surrounded by maples and cypresses, fading camellias spotting the shade. It was cool in there, and silent, only the occasional shiver of hundreds of Buddhist prayer slips tied to the branches rustling as a breeze moved through. Then I saw, lined up in ghostly silence under the trees, rows and rows of stone child effigies. Hundreds of them, each wearing a hand-knitted red bonnet.

I sat down on a bench with a shocked bump and stared back at them. They stood in neat lines, some holding a windmill or a teddy, some wearing little bibs. Rows and rows of blank, sad faces turned to look at me. They could make you cry, those children and their expressions, so I stood and went to another bench where I didn't have to look at them. I pulled off my shoes and stripped off my tights. My bare feet felt lovely in the cool – I

27

pushed them out in front of me and wriggled my toes. At the entrance to the shrine there was a bowl of water. It was meant for worshippers to purify their hands, but I went to it and used the bamboo ladle to dribble water over my feet. It was cool and clear, and afterwards I scooped a handful into my mouth. When I had finished and turned back, the stone children seemed to have moved. They seemed to have taken a collective step backwards as if they were shocked by my behaviour in this sacred place. I stared at them for a while. Then I went back to the bench, got a packet of biscuits from my bag and started munching.

I didn't have anywhere to go. The night was warm and the park was quiet, the great red and white Tokyo Tower all lit up above me. As the sun went down a lamp came on in the trees, and before long the homeless joined me on the surrounding benches. The vagrants, no matter how down and out, all seemed to have little meals, complete with chopsticks, some in lacquered bento lunch-boxes. I sat on my bench eating my biscuits and watching them. They ate their rice and stared back at me.

One of the homeless men had brought with him a pile of card-board, which he placed near the tiled entrance gate and perched on, naked except for a pair of filthy, stained jogging bottoms, dirt on his round belly. He spent a long time looking at me and laugh-ing – a tiny manic Buddha who had been rolled in soot. I didn't laugh. I sat on my bench staring at him in silence. He made me think of a photograph in one of my textbooks showing a starving Tokyo man after the war. In that first year when MacArthur set up headquarters, the Japanese lived on sawdust and acorns, peanut shells and tea-leaves, pumpkin stalks and seeds. People starved to death in the streets. The man in my book had a cloth spread out in front of him, two crudely made spoons resting on it. As a teenager I had worried endlessly about those spoons. There was nothing special about them, they weren't silver or engraved, they were just common little everyday spoons. Probably all that he had left in the world and, because he needed to eat, he was trying to sell them to someone who lacked nothing in the world but two ordinary little spoons.

They called it the bamboo-shoot existence, the onion life, every layer you peeled away made you cry more, and even if you could find the food you couldn't get it home because dysentery was breeding in the street mud and you might trail it back to your family. Children appeared on the docksides, fresh from independent Manchuria, the ashes of their families in white wisteria boxes slung round their necks.

Maybe that was the price of ignorance, I thought, looking at the naked vagrant. Maybe Japan had to pay for the ignorant things it did in Nanking. Because ignorance, as I'd got tired of hearing, is no excuse for evil.

The homeless were gone when I woke the following morning. In their place, watching me from the bench opposite, his feet planted wide, his elbows on his knees, was a western man of about my age. He wore a salt-bleached T-shirt with the words *Big Daddy Blake/Killtime Mix*, and a leather thong round his neck, fastened with what looked like a shark's tooth. His ankles were bare and tanned, and he was smiling as if I was the funniest thing he'd ever seen. 'Hey,' he said, raising his hand. 'You looked so comfortable. The sleep of angels.'

I sat up hurriedly, my holdall falling to the ground. I grabbed up my cardigan and wrapped it round me, batting at my hair, licking my fingers and wiping them hurriedly round my mouth, my eyes. I knew he was smiling at me, giving me that look, the half-wondering look that people always give me.

'Hey, did you hear me?' He came to stand next to me, his shadow falling over my holdall. 'I said, did you hear me? Can you speak English?' He had an odd accent. He might have been from England or America or Australia. Or all three. It made him sound as if he came from a beach somewhere. 'Can – you – speak – English?'

I nodded.

'Oh, you can?'

I nodded again.

He sat down on the seat next to me and put out his hand – pushed straight under my eyes so I couldn't avoid seeing it. 'Well, hi, then. I'm Jason.'

I stared at the hand.

'Said hi. Said I'm Jason.'

I shook his hand hurriedly then leaned sideways so I wouldn't brush against him, and fumbled under the bench for my holdall. It was always like this at university, the boys all teasing me because I was so defensive, always making me feel like I should just fall into a hole. I found my shoes inside it and began to pull them on.

'Are those your shoes?' he said. 'Are you really going to wear those?'

I didn't answer. The shoes were quite old-fashioned. They were black, lace-ups, rather stern-looking, I supposed, and thick-soled. They were quite wrong for a hot day in Tokyo.

'Are you always this rude?'

I pulled on the shoes and began to tie them, pulling the laces tighter than I needed to, my fingers a little white with the pressure. On my ankles the blisters rubbed against the hard leather.

'Cool,' he said, amused. He pronounced it *kewl*. 'You really are weird.'

There was something in the way he spoke that made me stop tying the shoes and turn to look at him. The sun was coming through the trees from behind him and I got a brief impression of dark hair, cut quite short, with soft flicks at the back of his neck and round his ears. Sometimes, although no one would guess and I would never ever admit it, sometimes all I ever thought about was sex.

'Well, you are,' he said. 'Aren't you? Weird, I mean. In a nice way. A kind of English way. Is that where you're from?'

'I . . .' Beyond him the ghostly stone children stood in their lines, the beginnings of the sun touching the branches above them, catching the dew on their shoulders and bonnets. In the distance the calm skyscrapers sent back a reflection of Tokyo as clean and crisp as a cave lake. 'I didn't . . .' I said faintly. 'I didn't know where to sleep.'

'You haven't got a hotel?'

'No.'

'You just arrived?'

'Yes.'

He laughed. 'There's a room at my place. There's just about a *hundred* rooms at my place.'

'At your place?'

'Sure. My house. You can rent a room there.'

'I haven't got any money.'

'Well, hell-oh! We're in Tokyo. Don't listen to the economists, there's still truckloads of money to be had here. You just open your eyes. There are still hostess clubs on every corner.'

The girls at university used to fantasize about working in the Tokyo hostess clubs. They'd go on and on about how much they'd earn, the gifts they'd be showered with. I used to sit in the corner in silence, thinking it must be lovely to be that confident.

'I wait tables in one,' he said. 'I'll introduce you to the mama-san, if you want.'

The colour rushed to my face. He couldn't imagine how it made me feel to imagine working in a hostess club. I turned away and finished tying my shoes. I got to my feet and brushed my clothes down.

'Serious. It's awesome money. The recession hasn't hit the clubs yet. And she likes weirdos, Mama-san.'

I didn't answer. I zipped up my cardigan, heaved the holdall over my head so the strap lay diagonally across my chest. 'Sorry,' I said clumsily. 'Got to go.' I folded my arms and headed away from Jason, across the park. A breeze came through and rattled all the children's windmills. Above me the sun glinted on the skyscrapers.

He caught up with me at the park exit. 'Hey,' he said. I didn't stop so he walked sideways next to me, grinning. 'Hey, weirdo. Here's my address.' He shoved out his hand and I stopped to look at it. He was holding a scrap of a cigarette carton with an address and phone number scrawled on it in biro. 'Go on, take it. You'd be funny in our house.'

I gazed at it.

'Go on.'

I hesitated, then grabbed the piece of cardboard, crunched my hand back up into my armpit, put my head forward and went on my way. Behind me I heard him laugh and cheer. 'You're awesome, weirdo. I *like* you.'

*

That morning, when the Bambi café waitress brought my iced coffee and Danish, she also put down on the table a huge plate of rice, some balls of fried fish, two small dishes of pickled vegetables and a bowl of miso soup.

'No,' I said in Japanese. 'No. I didn't order this.'

She glanced over to where the manager was checking receipts at the cash desk, then turned to me, rolled her eyes to the ceiling and put her finger to her lips. Later, when she brought me the chit I saw she'd charged me only for the Danish. I sat for a while, not knowing what to say, staring at her as she went round the other tables, pulling her notepad out of her pie-crust apron pocket, scratching her head with a pink Maruko Chan pen. You just don't get that sort of generosity every day, at least not as far as I know. I suddenly wondered who her father was. Her grandfather. I wondered if he'd ever talked to her about what happened in Nanking. For long years the schools hadn't taught about the massacre. All mention of the war was whited out of textbooks. Most Japanese adults had only the vaguest idea of what had happened in China in 1937. I wondered if the waitress even knew the name Nanking.

You have to study something for a long time before you understand it. Nine years, seven months and nineteen days. And even that, it turns out, isn't long enough for some things. Even after everything I've read about the years when Japan invaded China, I still don't really know why the massacre happened. The experts – the sociologists and the psychologists and the historians – they all seem to understand. They say it was about fear. They say that the Japanese soldiers were afraid and tired and hungry, they'd fought tooth and nail for Shanghai, beaten off cholera and dysentery, marched across half of China, and were close to breaking-point when they got to the capital. Some of them say that the Japanese soldiers were just products of a power-hungry society, that they'd been brainwashed into seeing the Chinese as a lesser species. Some say that an army like that, walking into Nanking and finding hundreds of thousands of defenceless citizens hiding in the

32

bombed-out buildings ... Well, some people say, maybe what happened next was hardly surprising.

It didn't take the Imperial Japanese Army long. In only a few weeks they'd killed anything up to three hundred thousand civilians. When they had finished, so the stories go, you didn't need boats to get from one side of the Yangtze river to the other. You could walk across the corpses. They were so inventive in the new ways they found to kill. They buried young men up to their necks in sand and drove tanks at their heads. They raped old women, children and animals. They beheaded and dismembered and tortured; they used babies for bayonet practice. You wouldn't expect anyone who had lived through that holocaust to trust the Japanese again.

There had been a 16mm projector in Shi Chongming's office. I'd been wondering about it all night. Whenever I started to think I'd imagined the reference in the journal I'd whisper to myself: 'What does a professor of sociology need a film projector for?'

He arrived at the university just before ten o'clock. I saw him at a great distance, very tiny like a child, moving painfully along the pavement. His navy tunic was fastened in ties at one side in a very unJapanese way and he hobbled along on his cane, going at half the speed of the others, a black plastic fisherman's hat crammed down over his long white hair. By the time he reached the red lacquered gate I was waiting, watching him coming down the street towards me.

'Hello?' I took a step forward and Shi Chongming stopped in his tracks.

He looked at me angrily. 'Don't talk to me,' he muttered. 'I don't want to talk to you.' He limped away in the direction of the Institute. I followed, walking shoulder to shoulder with him. It must have looked rather polite in a way, a dour little academic hobbling along, pretending there wasn't a gangling foreign girl in strange clothes keeping pace with him. 'I don't like what you're bringing.'

'But you've got to talk to me. This is the most important thing in the world.'

'No. You've got the wrong man.'

'I haven't. It's you. Shi Chongming. What's on that film is what I've been looking for for nearly ten years. Nine years, seven months and—'

'And eighteen days. I know. I know. I know.' He came to a halt and looked at me. The anger had brought out little orange flecks in his irises. He gazed at me for a long, long time, and I remember thinking vaguely that I must remind him of something because his expression was so intent and thoughtful. At length he sighed and shook his head. 'Where are you staying?'

'Here, in Tokyo. And it's seven months and *nineteen* days now.'

'Tell me, then, where to contact you. Maybe, in a week or two when I'm not so busy, maybe I can give you an interview about my time in Nanking.'

'A *week*? Oh, no, I can't wait a week. I haven't got any—'

He made an impatient noise in his throat. 'Tell me something,' he said. 'Tell me, do you know what some rich Beijingers will do to teach their sons English?'

'I'm sorry?'

'Do you know the lengths they will go to?' He lifted his tongue and indicated the connective tissue there. 'They like to cut their sons' tongues, here, under here, when the boys are only three or four. Just so the child can say an English *r* sound.' He nodded. 'So. Tell me, what do you think of my English?'

'It's perfect.'

'Even without wealthy parents, without mutilation?'

'Yes.'

'Hard work brought me this. That is all. Twenty years of hard work. And do you know what? I didn't spend twenty years learning English so that I could waste my words. Now, I said one week. Or even two. And that's what I meant.'

He began to hobble away. I took off after him.

'Look, I'm sorry. A week. That's okay, it's okay.' I got in front, turned to him, holding up my hands to halt him in his tracks. 'Yes. A week. I'll – I'll – I'll call you. In a week I'll come and see you.'

'I won't be held to your timetable. I'll contact you when I'm ready.'

'I'll telephone you. One week.'

'I don't think so.' Shi Chongming made a move to the side to get past me.

'Wait.' My mind was racing. 'Look, okay.' I patted my clothes desperately, trying to think what to do. I hesitated, my hand over the pocket of my cardigan. There was something in it. The scrap of cigarette box that Jason had handed me. I took a deep breath. 'Okay,' I said, pulling it out. 'My address. This is it. Just give me a moment to write it out for you.'

4

Someone has appeared in my life. Out of the blue, it seems. She could not be more unwelcome. Twice I have been taken off guard by her, buzzing me, like an insistent hornet. Twice! She shouts and she proclaims, she throws her arms into the air and gives me baleful looks, as if I alone am responsible for all the ills of the world. She says she wants to discuss things that happened in Nanking.

'Wants'? No, indeed, 'wants' is scarcely the right word. It is far more than that, far more than 'want'. It is a sickness. She is crazed with desire to hear about Nanking. How I regret the few times in Jiangsu, those distant, pre-cultural revolution days when I was so comfortable in my position at the university that I loosened enough to talk! How I scourge myself now for the few vague allusions I made to the events of the winter of 1937. I believed they would go no further. I did. I trusted that no one would talk. How was I to know that my mumblings would some day make their way into a Western journal, to be picked up and fawned over obsessively by this stranger? I am in a state of some desperation because of this. I have told her twice to let me alone, but she refuses to hear me, and today I was ruthlessly backed into a corner by her until, only to make her desist, I found myself agreeing to a future meeting.

But (oh, and here is the crux) what really plagues me is something deeper than just her stubbornness. Because something about her insistence has set things askew for me. I feel a new, a dark unease, and I can't help wondering if she is a harbinger, if her appearance here, her sudden, bright determination to rake over the ashes of Nanking, means that the final chapter is even nearer than I thought.

This is a species of insanity! In all these years I have kept my vow never to revisit that winter, never to read the words I wrote that year. I have kept the vow rigidly, and yet today, for a reason that is entirely beyond my understanding, when I came back to my office after speaking with her, I instinctively reached into the desk drawer for the battered old diary and placed it on the desk where I can now see but not touch it. Why, I wonder, why after all these years, do I itch to open the first page? It is all I can do not to reach out and devour it. What fatal longing has she started? This is the answer – I will bury it. Yes. Somewhere – maybe here, under the piles of books and notes. Or maybe lock it in one of these cupboards, where I can forget it, where it will never distract me again.

Or (and here my voice must become hushed), or I will read it. I will open it and read. Only a sentence. Only a paragraph. After all, when you consider it properly, what is the purpose of carrying around these forty thousand words, forty thousand words for the massacre, if they were never intended to be read? What harm can words do me? Can they pierce my flesh? And who is to care if I break my vow and grow fat eating these words? Maybe vows are made to be broken . . .

I wonder, Will I recognize myself? I wonder, Will I care?

史 Nanking, 28 February 1937 (the eighteenth day of the first month by Shujin's calendar)

What has happened to the sun? Something in nature must have become unbalanced for the rising sun to look like that. I sit at this familiar window, the only window in the house that looks east over the city, and I am gripped with overwhelming unease. My hand is shaking as I write. The sun is red. And worse – through some trick, some conspiracy of the atmosphere and the landscape, its rays have been arranged symmetrically so that they shoot out-wards across the sky in solid red stripes. It looks exactly like . . . exactly like . . .

Heavens! What is the matter? I dare not even write the words. What manner of madness is this? Seeing signs in the sky! I must turn away and try not to let my thoughts wander like this. I am in danger of sounding like Shujin, of becoming like her – dealing remorselessly in superstitions. Really, I do wonder daily about Shujin. If she were awake now she would put her head on one side, look at the horizon thoughtfully, and immediately recall her old village wisdom: the folklore that ten suns take turns rising in the east, swimming in queues through the underworld to circle round and rise up in the east. She would look at this sun for a while then declare that something had gone wrong with it during its swim through the underworld, that it was the victim of an injury – an omen of something terrible to come. Because if there is anything she persists in it is this: the belief that time moves around us like a barrel – rolling up in front of our eyes, circling back round. She says, and she never tires of saying this, that she can see the future for the simple reason that the future is our past.

I don't argue with her village superstitions, I am helpless in the face of her vehemence. 'Don't ever try to change her,' my mother said, before she died. 'The tusks of an elephant will never grow out of a dog's mouth. You know that.'

But malleable though I have become, I am not an entire fool. While it is true that there is no need to change her, neither is there any call to encourage this hysterical nature of hers. No need, for example, to rouse her now from bed and bring her here to my study, where I sit on my day-bed looking fearfully out at the sun.

It is hovering there even now, like a giant eyeing the city, terrible and red. Shujin would call it an omen. She would do something ridiculous if she saw it, she would run screaming round the house maybe. And so I will keep it to myself. I will tell no one that today I have witnessed the Chinese sun rising in the shape and colour of the *Hi No Maru* – the red disc on the Imperial Japanese Army flag.

*

38

So! It is done! I should throw down the book and cover my face with shame. I have broken my vow. How odd, after all these years, to have given up quite suddenly and unexpectedly on an unremarkable summer morning much like any other, how odd to have succumbed. Now, as I run my fingers down the pages of the book, I wonder if I have learned anything. The paper is old, the ink faded, and my *kaishu* script looks rather quaint. But – and how funny this is, to discover that the important things remain the same – the dread is no different. The dread I felt on that morning more than fifty years ago is something I recognize well. It is the same feeling I have now, when I pull back the blinds and look out of the window at the sun beating down on Tokyo.

5

That day was so interminably hot that the pavements were gooey underfoot. Condensed sweat dripped out of the air-conditioners on to the pedestrians below and Tokyo seemed ready to slide off the continental plate and slip sizzling into the ocean. I found a kiosk selling magazines and bought a can of cold green tea and some Lotte coconut chocolate that melted on my tongue. I ate and drank as I limped along the road, and soon I was feeling a little better. I got on to the subway and travelled packed in with all the sparkling clean commuters, my dirty cardigan rubbing against their laundered shirts. I noticed that in Tokyo people didn't smell. It was funny. I couldn't smell them, and they didn't say very much: the trains were packed but it was quite silent, like being jammed into a carriage with a thousand shop-window mannequins.

Jason's house was in an area called Takadanobaba, 'the high-up horse field'. When the train stopped and I had to get out, I did it very cautiously, stepping on to the platform and staring curiously up and down at the machines and the energy-drink posters. Someone bumped into me, and there was a moment of confusion as the rest of the crowd hopped and skipped and tried not to fall over. *Remember – there are rules in society that you'll always have to consider.*

Outside the station the streets were crammed with students from Waseda University. At the top of the road, next to a

Citibank, I turned off the main road, and suddenly everything changed. I found myself in a scrap of old Tokyo. Away from the electronic roar of commerce there were silent, cool alleys: a warren of cranky little streets jammed into the crevices behind the skyscrapers, a dark, breathing patch like a jungle floor. I held my breath and looked around in wonder: it was just like the pictures in my books! Crooked wooden houses leaned wearily against each other, rotting and broken – exhausted survivors of decades of earthquakes, fires, bombing. In the cracks between the houses lush, carnivorous-looking plants crowded together.

Jason's house was the biggest, the oldest and the most decrepit I had seen in Tokyo so far. Forming the corner of two small streets, all its ground-floor windows were boarded up, nailed over, padlocked, and tropical creepers had broken through the pavement, coiling up round it like *Sleeping Beauty* thorns. Tacked to the side of the house, protected from the elements by a corrugated-plastic roof, a staircase led to the first floor, guarded by a little wooden door and a grimy old doorbell.

I remember exactly what Jason was wearing when he opened the door. He had on an olive green shirt, shorts and a pair of battered old desert boots, unlaced, his feet crammed into them so that the backs were squashed down. On his wrist was a woven bracelet and he was holding a silver can of beer, Asahi written on the side, condensation running down it. I had a brief chance to study him in the sunlight – he had a clean, unlined skin that looked as if he spent a lot of time outdoors. The words 'He is beautiful' flashed briefly in my mind.

'Hey,' he said, surprised to see me. 'Hi, weirdo. You changed your mind? About the room?'

I looked up at the house. 'Who else lives here?'

He shrugged. 'Me. Two of the girls from the nightclub. Some ghosts. Don't know how many of them, to be honest.'

'Ghosts?'

'That's what everyone says.'

I was silent for a while, looking up at the tiled roofs, the upturned eaves crested with chipped dragons and dolphins. The house did seem bigger and darker than its neighbours. 'Okay,' I said eventually, picking up my bag. 'I don't mind about the ghosts. I want to live here.'

He didn't offer to carry my bag and, anyway, I wouldn't have known what to say if he had. I followed him up the staircase, our footsteps echoing on the cast iron.

'The bottom floor's closed off,' he said, waving the beer can in the direction of the boarded windows. 'No way into it. We live upstairs and you've got to come and go this way.'

At the top of the stairs we stopped. We stood at the corner of the house in a gloomy, shuttered gallery, which led away at right angles to our right and left. I could see about fifteen feet in both directions, then the long dusty corridors seemed to dwindle, as if they ended in the distance, in cool, shaded parts of Tokyo that I could only guess at. It was gone midday, and the house was silent.

'Most of it's closed off. The land deals in Tokyo've gone toes up since the bubble burst, but the landlord's still trying to push through a deal with a developer. If it works they're going to knock the whole thing down and build another high-rise, so the rent's like nearly *nada*.' Jason kicked off his boots. 'Course, you've got to put up with the place falling down around your ears.' He gestured vaguely down the right-hand corridor. 'The girls sleep down there – down that wing. They spend the whole day in bed. They're Russian. You'll notice that here – now that someone left the kennel door open the Russians're running all over the planet. Message hasn't got to them that Japan's face down in a recession. Here—' He pushed a pair of battered hessian slippers at me and watched as I changed into them, taking off my hard little lace-up shoes and sliding the slippers over my stockinged feet. 'Don't they hurt?' He pointed to the shoes. 'They look painful.'

'Yes. I've got blisters.'

'Haven't you got anything else to wear?'

'No.'

'What's in your bag? It looks heavy.'

'Books,' I said.

'Books?'

'That's right.'

'What sort of books?'

'Books with pictures.'

Jason laughed. He lit a cigarette and watched in amusement as I got the slippers on. I pulled my cardigan straight, pressed my hands down on my hair and stood up in front of him, and that made him laugh again. 'So,' he said, 'what's your name?'

'Grey.'

'Grey? What sort of a name is that?'

I hesitated. It was so strange to be in a place where no one knew me. I took a breath and tried to sound casual. 'It's my surname. Everyone always calls me by my surname.'

Jason took me down the right-hand corridor, stopping to point things out as we went. The house was curiously soft and organic-feeling – the floors were covered in straw *tatami* matting and each movement released the secret smell of insect cocoons. Rooms led off from one side of the corridor; on the other, battered wooden screens concealed the facing walls, from waist height up.

'The bathroom's traditional so you squat. Think you can do that?' He looked me up and down. 'Squat? Wash out of a bucket? You know that's the point of living in Japan – to do things differently.' Before I could answer he turned away, to the other side of the corridor, and slid back a shutter. Sunlight flooded in through grimy glass. 'The air-conditioner's fucked so in the summer you gotta keep these closed all day.'

We stood at the window and looked down at an enclosed garden. It was deep and lush like a jungle, overgrown to above the height of the ground-floor windows, packed with dark persimmon and heavy leaves that cracked the walls and stole the sunlight. I put my hands on the pane, my nose up to the glass, and stared out. At the foot of the garden was the rear of a white skyscraper.

'The Salt Building,' Jason said. 'Don't know why it's called that, just got handed on, I s'pose, like the rooms, from one hostess to another.'

I was about to turn away when I noticed, almost a hundred feet away across the tops of the trees, a red-tiled roof basking in the heat.

'What's that?'

'That?' He pressed his nose against the window. 'That's the third wing. Closed off too.'

'Part of this house?'

'I know. We inhabit a zip code. The Forbidden Palace. There are maybe twenty rooms in this place that I know exist for sure, another twenty you only get to hear about in rumours.'

Now I could see how much ground the house took up. It covered most of a city block and was arranged round the garden, on three sides of a square. From above, it would look like a bridge with the Salt Building blocking the fourth side. The house was decaying; rot had started in the far wing and Jason said he didn't like to think what was in the closed-off rooms downstairs. 'That's where the ghosts hang out,' he said, rolling his eyes. 'According to the *baba yaga* twins.'

We passed countless sliding *shoji* doors, some locked, some open. I got glimpses of belongings in the gloom, piled-up furniture, dusty and forgotten – a teak butsudan, an ancestor's shrine, empty except for a stack of dusty glass jars. My slippers slapped in the silence. Out of the gloom ahead of us appeared the door to the closed wing, padlocked and braced with an iron bar. Jason stopped at the barricade. 'This is no go.' He put his nose to the door and sniffed. 'And, *Jesus*, in the hot weather the *stink*.' He wiped his face and turned back, tapping the last door on the corridor. 'Don't worry, you're cool here – this would be yours.'

He slid back the door. Sunshine poured through grimy sheets tacked over two windows at right angles. The walls had once been covered in pale brown silk and the remains of it hung down, disintegrating in long, vertical slashes, as if a huge clawed animal had been kept locked in here. The *tatami* mats were fraying, there were dead flies on the windowsill and spiders' webs in the light fitting.

'What do you think?'

I stepped inside and stood in the centre of the room, slowly turning round and round. On the near wall there was a *tokonoma* alcove, with a battered rattan rocking-chair pushed against the wall where the seasonal scroll should hang.

'You could do anything you wanted to it. The landlord doesn't give a shit. Even forgets to collect the rent most times.'

I closed my eyes and held out my hands, feeling the softness of the air, the dusty sunlight on my back. It was twice the size of my bedroom in London and it seemed to me so welcoming. There was a soft smell in there, of decaying silk and straw.

'Well?'

'It's . . .' I said, opening my eyes and fingering the silk on the walls '. . . it's beautiful.'

Jason pulled back the sheet covering the window and opened it, letting some of the hot air into the room. 'There,' he said, pointing out of the window. 'Godzilla's playpen.'

Coming here, dwarfed by all the skyscrapers, I hadn't realized how high Takadanobaba was. It was only now that I saw the land dropped away from this vantage-point. The tops of buildings stood level with my window and everywhere faces shouted from video screens hung up high. A vast advertising hoarding, only fifty feet away, filled most of the view. It was a huge sepia photograph of a movie star smiling a crooked smile, holding a glass up, as if he was toasting the whole of Takadanobaba. The glass had the words 'Suntory Reserve' etched on it.

'Mickey Rourke,' said Jason. 'Babe magnet, evidently.'

'Mickey Rourke,' I echoed. I'd never heard of him, but I liked his face. I liked the way he was smiling down at us. I held the window frame and leaned out a little. 'Which way is Hongo?'

'Hongo? I don't know – I think it's . . . that way, maybe.'

I stood on tiptoe, looking sideways, out over the distant roofs and the neon signs and the TV aerials painted gold by the sun. We must be miles away. I'd never be able to see Shi Chongming's office among all those other buildings. But it made me feel better to think that it was there, somewhere out there. I tipped back on to my heels.

'How much is it?'

'Two hundred dollars a month.'

'I only need it for a week.'

'Fifty dollars, then. It's a steal.'

'I can't afford it.'

'You can't afford fifty dollars? How much d'you think it costs to live in Tokyo? Fifty dollars is so outrageously *not* expensive.'

'I haven't got any money.'

Jason sighed. He finished his cigarette, chucked it out on to the street and pointed at the skyline. 'Look,' he said leaning out. 'Look there, to the south-east. Those tall buildings are Kabuki Cho. And see beyond them?'

In the distance, black against the sky, a behemoth of tinted glass supported by eight massive black columns, rocketed up above all the other skyscrapers. Four gigantic black marble gargoyles crouched on each corner of the roof, gas streams in their mouths blowing fire jets fifty feet out until the sky seemed to be on fire.

'The building is private. It's one of the Mori brothers' buildings. But see that, on the top floor?'

I squinted. Bolted by a mechanical arm to the crown of the skyscraper there was a vast cut-out of a woman sitting on a swing. 'I know who that is,' I said. 'I recognize her.'

'It's Marilyn Monroe.'

Marilyn Monroe. She must have been thirty feet from her white high heels to her peroxide hair, and she swung back and forward in fifty-foot arcs, molten neon flickering so that her white summer dress appeared to be blowing up above her waist.

'That's Some Like It Hot. The club where we work – me and the *baba yaga*s. I'll take you there tonight. You'll pay your week's rent in a few hours.'

'Oh,' I said, backing away from the window. 'Oh. No – you already said about it. It's a hostess club.'

'It's cool, laid back – Strawberry's really gonna go for you.'

'No,' I said, suddenly uncomfortable and clumsy again. 'No. Don't say that, because she won't.'

'Why not?'

'Because . . .' I trailed off. I couldn't explain to someone like Jason. 'No. She definitely wouldn't hire me.'

'I think you're wrong. And, anyways, from where I'm standing it seems like you don't have a choice.'

6

The hostesses who lived in the rooms on the north wing, the *baba yaga*s, were twins from Vladivostok. Svetlana and Irina. Jason took me in to see them when the sun was getting low and the heat had let up a little. They were in Irina's room, getting ready for work at the club, almost identical in their black leggings and Spandex bras: tall as stevedores, and well fed, with strong arms and muscular legs. They looked as if they spent a lot of time in the sun and both had lots of long, bobbly, permed hair. The only difference was that Irina's was yellow-blonde and Svetlana's was black. I'd seen the dye, Naples Black, in a faded pink box on the kitchen shelf.

They sat me on a stool in front of a small vanity table and started firing questions at me.

'You know Jason? Before you come here?'

'No. I met him this morning.'

'This *morning*?'

'In the park.'

The girls exchanged glances. 'He work fast, eh?' Svetlana made a clicking noise in her throat and winked at me. 'Fast work.'

They offered me a cigarette. I liked to smoke. In hospital the girl in the next bed had taught me how, and it made me feel very adult, but I hardly ever had the money to keep it up. I looked at the carton in Irina's red polished fingertips. 'I haven't got any to give you in return.'

Irina half dropped her eyelids and pursed her lips as if she was kissing the air. 'No problem.' She waggled the box at me again. 'No problem. You take.'

I took one and for a while we all smoked, looking back and forward at each other. If their hair hadn't been so different Svetlana and Irina would have been almost indistinguishable: they both had a sort of confident glitter in their eyes that I recognized from some of the girls at university. I must have looked very odd to them, all scrunched up like a bundle of dirty laundry on their stool.

'You going to work in club?'

'No,' I said. 'They won't want me.'

Svetlana clicked her tongue against her mouth. 'Don't be stupid. It easy easy easy. Easy like eating the candy.'

'Is it sex?'

'No!' They laughed. 'Not sex! You do sex, you do it outside. Mama don't wanna hear about it.'

'Then what do you do?'

'Do? You don't *do* nothing. You talk to customer. Light his cigarette. Tell him he's great. Put ice in his fuckink disgustink fuckink drink.'

'What do you talk about?'

They looked at each other and shrugged. 'Just make him happy, make him to like you. Make him laugh. He gonna like *you* no problem, because you are English girl.'

I looked down at the heavy black skirt I was wearing, second hand. Its original owner would have remembered the Korean war. My black buttoned-up blouse had cost me 50p in the Oxfam shop in the Harrow Road and my tights were thick and opaque.

'Here.'

I looked up. Svetlana was holding out a little gold makeup bag. 'What?'

'Do your face. We gotta go in twenny minutes.'

The twins knew the art of holding two conversations at once. Everything they did was achieved with the phone glued to their ears, cigarettes between their teeth. They were doing the nightly dial-round of customers: 'You going to be there tonight, eh? I'll be so *sabishi* without you.' As they talked, they painted in eyebrows, fixed on eyelashes, squeezed themselves into shiny white trousers and impossibly high silver sandals. I watched them silently. Svetlana, who spent a long time standing in front of the mirror in her bra, her arms above her head, studying her armpits for hairs, thought that I should wear something gold to brighten myself up.

'You gotta look sophisticated. You wanna wear my belt, eh? My belt is gold. Black and gold nice!'

'I'd look stupid.'

'Silver, then,' said Irina. I was trying not to stare at her. She'd stripped off her bra and was standing topless near the window picking with her long nails at a roll of Sellotape, tearing off strips with her teeth. 'You wear black, you look like widow.'

'I always wear black.'

'What? You mourning someone?'

'No,' I said, steadily. 'Don't be stupid. Who would I be mourning?'

She studied me for a moment. 'Okay,' she said. 'If it make you happy. But you go to club looking like that you probably gonna make the men to cry.' She put one end of the tape in her mouth, squashed her breasts together as tightly as she could, and passed the tape under them from left underarm to right and back again. When she released her breasts they remained where she'd lifted them, precarious on a shelf of Sellotape. She pulled on an off-the-shoulder blouse and stood in front of the mirror, smoothing it down and checking her shape under the flimsy fabric. I bit my fingers, wishing I had the courage to ask for another cigarette.

Svetlana had finished her makeup – her lips were outlined in dark pencil. She got on her knees, rummaged in one of the drawers and pulled out a stapler. 'Come here,' she said, beckoning to me. 'Come here.'

'No.'

'Yes. Come here.' She shuffled towards me on her knees, wielding the stapler. She caught the hem of my skirt, folded it up and under and clamped the stapler's jaws, fastening the hem to the lining.

'Don't,' I said, trying to push her hand away. 'Don't.'

'Wassamatter? You got sexy legs, better you show them. Now keep still.'

'*Please!*'

'Don't you wanna job, eh?'

I put my hands over my face, my eyes rolling under my fingers, and took deep breaths while Svetlana moved round me, clipping my hem up. I could feel from the air that she'd exposed my knees. I kept imagining the way my legs would look. I kept imagining the things people would think if they saw me. 'No . . .'

'Jjjzzzt!' Svetlana put her hands on my shoulders. 'Let us work.'

I closed my eyes and breathed in and out through my nose. Irina was trying to draw a line around the outside of my lips. I jumped up. 'Please, *no* . . .'

Irina took a step back in amazement. 'What? You don't wanna look sexy?'

I grabbed a tissue and wiped the lipstick off my face. I was trembling. 'I look weird. I just look weird.'

'It only old Japanese men. Old squinters. They not gonna touch you.'

'You wouldn't understand.'

Svetlana raised an eyebrow. 'We don't understand? Hey, Irina, baby, we don't understand.'

'No, really,' I said. 'You *really* don't understand.'

You don't have to understand sex to want to do it. So say the bees and the birds. I was the worst combination you could imagine – ignorant of the nuts and bolts and as fascinated as the day is long. Maybe it's no wonder I got into trouble.

At first the doctors tried to get me to say that it had been a rape. Why else would a girl of thirteen allow five teenage boys to do something like that to her, if it hadn't been rape? Unless she was crazy, of course. I listened to this with a sort of dreamy puzzlement. Why were they focusing on *that* part of what happened? Was that part wrong too? In the end I'd have saved myself a lot of problems if I'd agreed with them and said it had been rape. Maybe then they wouldn't have gone on and on about how my sexual behaviour alone was evidence that something was very wrong with me. But it would have been a lie. I'd *let* them do it to me. I'd wanted it maybe even more than the boys did. I'd welcomed them into that van, parked down the country lane.

It had been one of those misty summer evenings where the night sky stays an intense blue in the west, and you can imagine all sorts of astonishing pagan dances happening just over the horizon where the sun has gone. There was new grass and a breeze and the sound of traffic in the distance, and when they stopped the van I looked down into the valley and saw the ghostly white smudges of the Stonehenge monument.

In the back was an old tartan blanket that smelt of grass seed and engine oil. I took all my clothes off and lay down on it and opened my legs, which were very white, even though it was summer. One by one they got inside and took their turns, making the van creak on its rusty axle. It was the fourth boy – sandy-haired with a lovely face and the beginnings of stubble – who spoke to me. He pulled the van doors closed behind him so that there was no light, and the others sitting out on the verge smoking cigarettes couldn't see us.

'Hi,' he said.

I put my hands on my knees and opened my legs wider. He didn't move towards me. He knelt there in front of me, looking between my legs, with an odd, uncomfortable expression on his face.

'You know you don't have to do this, don't you? You know nobody's forcing you?'

I was silent for a while, looking at him with a puzzled frown. 'I know.'

'And you still want to do it?'

'Of course,' I said, holding out my arms. 'Why not?'

'Didn't anyone talk about protection?' The nurse who didn't like me said that this just went to show how diseases like herpes and gonorrhoea and syphilis were spreading round the world, through the lack of control of disgusting people like me. 'Don't tell me that out of all those five boys not one of them even suggested using a contraceptive.' I lay in my bed in silence, my eyes closed. I wasn't going to tell her the truth, that I didn't really know what a contraceptive was, that I hadn't known it was wrong, that my mother would have died rather than talk to me about these things. I wasn't going to let her go on and on about my stupid ignorance. 'And as for you! Not even trying to stop them.' She'd lick her lips then, a sound like legs slapping together in the dark. 'If you want my opinion, you're the sickest person I've ever met.'

The doctors said it was all about control. 'We all have impulses, everyone has urges. They are what make us human. The key to a happy and balanced life is learning to control them.'

But by that time, of course, there wasn't much I could do to put things right. You can't mend something without practising, and you only had to take one look at my hospital notes, or see me naked, to know that there wasn't going to be much of a sex life for me in the future.

7

In the end the Russians and I reached a compromise. I let them leave the staples in the skirt, they let me flatten down my hair and wipe off the iridescent eyeshadow. Instead I drew very careful black lines above my eyelashes, because when I sat and thought hard about makeup the only thing that came to my mind were the pictures I'd seen in a book of Audrey Hepburn. I thought I'd have liked Audrey Hepburn if I'd met her. She always looked kind. I rubbed off the blusher and painted my lips in a plain, matt red. The twins stood back to look at the result.

'Not bad,' Irina admitted, with a sour look. 'You still look like widow, but this time not-bad widow.'

Jason said nothing when he saw me. He looked thoughtfully at my legs and gave a short, dry laugh, as if he knew a rude joke about me. 'C'mon,' he said, lighting a cigarette. 'Let's go.'

We walked in a line, strung out across the pavement. The sun was low in the sky, lighting up the sides of the buildings. In the little streets they were preparing the lanterns for the O-Bon festival later that week – the stalls and the banners were going up in Toyama park, and a cemetery that we passed was dotted with vegetables, fruit and rice wine for the spirits. I looked at it all in silence, every now and then stopping to check my footing. Irina had given me black high heels to wear, they were too big so I'd stuffed paper into the toes and I had to concentrate hard on walking.

You wouldn't need a street map to get to the club: the building was visible for miles around, the gargoyles choking their red flames into the night. We reached the building as darkness came. I stood and stared up at it until the others got bored waiting, and took my arm and guided me into a glass lift that went up the outside of the skyscraper, all the way to the top where the Marilyn Monroe sign was swinging to and fro among the stars. The 'crystal lift', they told me it was called, because it was like a crystal catching and scattering all the lights of Tokyo. I stood with my nose pressed to the glass as it soared up outside the building, amazed by how quickly the greasy street dropped away beneath us.

'Wait here,' said Jason, when the lift stopped. We were in a marble-floored reception area, separated from the club by doors of industrial aluminium. A giant model of a red rose, five foot tall, stood in a huge vase in one corner. 'I'll send Mama-san out.' He indicated a plush velvet *chaise-longue*, and disappeared with the Russians through the doors. I caught a glimpse of a club as big as a skating rink – occupying the entire top of the building, skyscrapers reflected in the polished floor – a constellation of lights. Then the door swung closed and I was left, sitting on the *chaise-longue*, with only the top of the hat-check girl's head visible over the counter for company.

I crossed my legs, then uncrossed them. I looked at my vague reflection in the aluminium doors. Stencilled in black on the doors were the words Some Like It Hot.

The club's Mama-san, Strawberry Nakatani, was an old hand, according to Jason. She had been a call girl in the seventies, famous for turning up to clubs naked under her white fur coat, and when her husband, a show-business impresario and minor hoodlum, died, he had given her the club. 'Don't look surprised when you see her,' Jason warned. Her life was devoted to Marilyn Monroe, he said. She'd had her nose reconstructed, and had got unethical surgeons in Waikiki to put western lines into her eyelids. 'Just act like you think she looks fabulous.'

I put my hands on my skirt, pressing it down against my thighs. You have to be very brave or desperate to stick things out, and I was about to give up, stand and turn for the lift when the aluminium doors opened and out she stalked: a small, bleached woman dressed in a gold lamé Marilyn Monroe dress, carrying an ornate cigarette-holder and a fur stole. She was boxy and muscular, like a Chinese war-horse, and her Asian hair had been peroxided, ferociously backcombed into a Marilyn bob. She clipped across to me on her stilettos, flinging back her fur stole, licking her fingers and smoothing her haircut into shape. She stopped a few inches in front of me, saying nothing, letting her eyes flick over my face. That is it, I thought, she's going to throw me out.

'Stand up.'

I stood.

'Where you from? Hmmm?' She prowled in a circle, looking at the wrinkled black tights, Irina's stilettos crammed with paper. 'Where you come from?'

'England.'

'England?' She stood back and plugged a cigarette into the holder, narrowing her eyes. 'Yes. You look like English girl. What you want to work here for? Eh?'

'The same reason everyone wants to work here.'

'What that, then, hmm? You like Japanese man?'

'No. I need the money.'

Her mouth curled then, as if she was amused. She lit the cigarette. 'Okay,' she said. '*Peachy*.' She tilted her head and blew the smoke in a stream over her shoulder. 'You try tonight. You nice to customer I give you three thousand yen an hour. Three thousand. Okay?'

'Does that mean you want me to work?'

'Why you surprised? You want something else? Three thousand. Take it or fly away, lady. I can't give you no more.'

'I just thought . . .'

Mama Strawberry held up her hand to silence me. 'And if it goes peachy tonight, then tomorrow you come back and you wear nice dress. Okay? You no wear nice dress and you pay ten thousand yen penalty. *Penalty*. You get it, lady? This very high-class club.'

*

The club seemed to me the most magical place I'd ever seen – the floor like a starlit pool floating fifty storeys above the world, surrounded on all sides by panoramic views of the Tokyo skyline, the video screens on neighbouring buildings showing newsreels and music videos. I moved through it in a kind of nervous awe, looking at the *ikebana* flower arrangements, the muted downlighting. One or two customers were already there, small men in business suits, at tables dotted around, some in banquettes, some in deep leather armchairs, pools of smoke hanging above the tables. On a raised platform a thin-faced piano-player in his bow-tie warmed up with tinkling arpeggios. The only place the view of the city was interrupted was where Marilyn – the blank reverse of her, girdered, engineered and supported with metal struts – creaked and rattled back and forth through the night, blocking our view completely every ten seconds or so.

Mama Strawberry was sitting at a reproduction Louis Quatorze gilded desk just in front of the Marilyn swing, smoking from her elaborate cigarette-holder and punching numbers into a calculator. Not far from her was a table where the hostesses sat, waiting to be assigned to a customer, smoking and chattering – twenty of us, all Japanese with the exception of me and the twins. Irina had given me a handful of Sobranie 'Pinks' cigarettes and I sat in silence, smoking intently, looking warily across the club at the aluminium doors where the customers would arrive.

Eventually the lift bell pinged and a large party of suited men came through the aluminium doors. 'She's going to put you with them,' Irina whispered, sliding up to me, her hand held to the side of her mouth. 'These ones, they always leave the *tip*. For their favourite girls. Mama gonna watch and see if you get tip. This is your test, bay-beee!'

I was summoned, discreetly, along with the Russians and three Japanese hostesses, and sent to a table next to the panoramic window, where we stood formally with our hands resting lightly on the chair backs waiting for the men to cross the polished parquet floor. I copied the others, stepping agitatedly from foot to foot, wishing I could tug my skirt down. A string of waiters appeared from nowhere, hurriedly setting the table with piles of snowy white linen, a silver candlestick, gleaming glasses, finishing just as the men arrived and seated themselves, pulling back chairs and unbuttoning jackets.

'*Irasshaimase*,' said the Japanese girls, bowing, and sliding into the chairs, taking hot towels from the bamboo dish that appeared on the table.

'Welcome,' I mumbled, taking my cue from the others.

A bottle of champagne and some Scotch appeared. I shuffled my chair forward and sat, glancing at everyone, waiting to see what to do next. The girls were slitting the hot towels from their wrappers, unfolding them into the men's waiting hands, so I quickly copied, dropping one into the hands of the man on my left. He didn't acknowledge me. He took the towel, wiped his hands, dropped it carelessly on the table in front of me, and turned away to speak to the hostess on his other side. The rules were clear: my job was to light cigarettes, pour whisky, feed the men finger food and entertain them. No sex. Just conversation and flattery. It was all printed out for the new girls to read on a laminated card. 'Better you say something funny,' Mama Strawberry had whispered to me. 'Strawberry's customers want to relax.'

'Hallo,' Svetlana said boldly, settling her bottom into one of the seats, dwarfing the men, moving from side to side like a broody hen so that everyone had to make room. She picked up a glass from the centre of the table and chimed it against the bottle. 'Shampansky, darlink. So nice!' She unloaded the entire bottle into four glasses then waggled the empty bottle above her head to summon the waiter for more.

The men seemed to like the twins, they kept singing tunes to them that must have been from TV or radio because I didn't recognize them: '"Double the pleasure, double the fun . . . Give me that little LIFT. Come and get you SOME!"' Everyone would laugh and applaud and the conversation, in a mixture of Japanese and broken English, would take off again. The twins got drunk very quickly. Svetlana's eye makeup was smudged and Irina kept jumping up to light the men's cigarettes with a disposable Thai Air lighter, leaning across the table, knocking over the little bowls of seaweed and dried cuttlefish. 'Don't make me laugh,' she squealed, when someone told a joke. She was flushed and slurring. 'Make me laugh some more and I *explode*!'

I sat quietly, not drawing attention to myself, pretending that this was all normal, that I'd done this a thousand times and really didn't care that nobody was talking to me, that I didn't get the jokes, didn't recognize the songs. At about nine o'clock, just when I thought I could keep quiet all night long, and maybe they'd forget I was there, someone suddenly said, 'And what about you?'

Silence fell at the table. I looked up and found everyone halted in mid-conversation, staring at me curiously. 'What about you?' someone repeated. 'What do you think?'

What did I think? I had no idea. I'd been drifting off somewhere, wondering if these men's fathers, their uncles, their grandfathers had been in China. I wondered if they had any sense of what their lives were built on. I tried to picture their faces in the tall collars of the IJA uniform, in the snowy streets of Nanking, one of them raising a glinting *katana* sword . . .

'What about you?'

'What *about* me?'

They exchanged glances, unaccustomed to this rudeness. Someone kicked me under the table. I looked up and found Irina making a face at me, nodding at my chest, using both hands to push her breasts up, her shoulders pinned back. 'Sit up,' she mouthed. 'Put your busts out.'

I turned to the man sitting next to me, took a deep breath and said the first thing that came into my head: 'Did your father fight in China?'

His face changed. Someone sucked in a sharp breath. The hostesses frowned and Irina put down her drink with a shocked *clink*. The man next to me was thinking about what I'd said. At length he took a breath and said, 'What an odd question. Why do you ask?'

'Because,' I said, in a tiny voice, my heart sinking, 'because it's what I've been studying for nine years. Nine years and seven months and nineteen days.'

He was silent for a moment, looking at my face, trying to read me. Nobody at the table seemed to breathe: they were all sitting forward, poised on their chair edges, waiting to hear what his response would be. After a long time he lit a cigarette, took a few puffs, and rested it carefully, deliberately, in the ashtray.

'My father was in China,' he said seriously, sitting back and folding his arms. 'In Manchuria. And as long as he lived he wouldn't talk about what happened.' His cigarette smoke moved up to the ceiling in a long, unbroken stream, like a white finger. 'My schoolbooks had all mention of it removed. I remember sitting in class, all of us holding the paper up to the light, making sure we couldn't read what was written under the white-out. Maybe,' he said, not looking at anyone, but directing the words into the air, 'maybe you'll tell me about it.'

I'd been sitting with my mouth open stupidly, terrified of what he might say. Slowly it dawned on me that he wasn't angry and the colour came back to my face. I sat forward, excited. 'Yes,' I said eagerly. 'Of course. I can tell you anything you want to know. Anything—' Suddenly the words were backing up in my throat, wanting to spill out. I pushed my hair behind my ears and put my hands on the table. 'Now, I think that the most interesting part was what happened in Nanking. No. Actually, not what happened in Nanking itself, but – let me . . . let me put it a different way. The most interesting thing was what happened while the troops were marching from Shanghai to Nanking. No one ever has really understood what happened, you see, why they changed . . .'

And that was how I started talking. I talked and talked into the night. I talked about Manchuria and Shanghai and Unit 731. Most of all, of course, I talked about Nanking. The hostesses sat in boredom, inspecting their nails, or leaning together and whispering to each other, shooting me glances. But the men all sat forward in eerie silence, staring at me, their faces taut with concentration. They didn't say much more that evening. They left in silence and, at the end of the night, when Mama Strawberry clipped over to us with the tips, a sour look on her face, it was me she singled out. The men had left me the biggest tip. More than three times what they'd left anyone else.

8

史 Nanking, 1 March 1937

The time I spend fretting about my wife! Thinking about our differences! For many of my colleagues this quaint, arranged marriage is anathema to all their ideals and, indeed, I had always expected to make a sensible alliance, maybe with someone from the university, one of those forward thinkers who take time, like our president Chiang Kai-shek, to truly consider China and her future. But, then, I hadn't bargained for my mother's hand in the matter.

How infuriating! To be thinking even today of my mother. I tremble with embarrassment when I consider her, when I consider all my superstitious and backward family. The family that enjoyed wealth, but was never inclined or able to escape the provincial village, to break free of the Poyang summer floods. Maybe I'll never truly escape either, and maybe this is the worst of the enduring truths about me: the proud young linguist from Jinling University, who is underneath just a boy from a China that doesn't look forward and doesn't change – that only stands still and waits for death. I think about that green and yellow countryside, punctuated by white goats and juniper trees, the plains where a man grows only sufficient to feed his family, where the ducks wander wild and pigs snout through the bean groves, and I wonder, can I hope to escape my past?

With the clear eyes of hindsight, I see that my mother always had plans for Shujin. They had been together to the village

61

fortune-teller, an old man whom I recall with no fondness, a blind man with a long white beard, persistently led round the villages like a trained bear by a child in straw sandals. The fortune-teller carefully noted down Shujin's date, time and place of birth, and with a few scribbled characters and a juggling of his mysterious ivory tablets, soon, to my mother's delight, judged Shujin to have the perfect proportion of the five elements, the correct balance of metal, wood, water, fire and earth, to produce myriad sons for me.

Naturally I resisted. And would have resisted to this day, had my mother not become ill. To my fury, my desperation, even as she drew close to death she refused to forsake her country beliefs, her distrust of new technology. Instead of travelling, at my fevered insistence, to the good modern hospitals in Nanking, she put her trust in the local quacks, who spent long hours examining her tongue, emerging from her sick room with declarations of 'An impossible surfeit of *yin*. It is a mystery, a scandal, that Doctor Yuan did not comment on this earlier.' In spite of their potions, their brews and prognostications, she grew sicker and sicker.

'So much for your superstitions,' I told her, as she lay in her sickbed. 'You understand, do you, that you are destroying me by refusing to come to Nanking?'

'Listen.' She rested her hand on my arm. Her brown hand, weathered by years in the provinces, lying across the crisp sleeve of the western suit I wore. I remember looking at it and thinking, Is this really the flesh that gave me life? Is it really? 'You can still make me happy.'

'Happy?'

'Yes.' Her eyes were bright and feverish. 'Make me happy. Marry the Wangs' daughter.'

And eventually, out of nothing more than weary guilt, I capitulated. Really, the outrageous power our mothers have! Even the great Chiang Kai-shek was similarly swayed by his mother, even he submitted to an arranged marriage to please her. My qualms were terrible – what a disastrous match: the village girl with her *ri shu* almanacs, her lunar calendars, and me, the clear-eyed calculator, rapt in his logic and his foreign dictionaries. I worried intensely about what my colleagues would think, for I am, like most of them, a devout Republican, an admirer of the clear, forward-looking ideology of the Kuomintang, a cheerful supporter of Chiang Kai-shek, deeply sceptical about superstition, and everything that has held back China for so long. When the marriage took place, in my home town, I told no one. There were no colleagues to witness the rambling ceremony, no one to see me undergo the humiliating rituals – the token argument with the bridesmaids on the doorstep, caps of cypress, the tortuous procession avoiding wells or the houses of widows – every moment firecrackers making the entire ensemble jump like startled rabbits.

But my family were satisfied and I was regarded as heroic. My mother, maybe feeling she had been released from her earthly obligation, died shortly afterwards. 'With a smile on her face that was marvellous to see', if my dear sisters are to be believed. Shujin became a proper mourner, getting down on her knees herself to dust the floor of my parents' house with talcum powder: 'We'll marvel at her footprints when her spirit comes back to us.'

'Please don't talk like that,' I said impatiently. 'It was these very peasant beliefs that killed her. If she had listened to the teachings of our president—'

'Hmmph,' said Shujin, getting up and dusting off her hands. 'I've heard enough about your precious president, thank you. All this rubbish about New Life. Tell me, what is this marvellous New Life he preaches, if not exactly this, our old life, re-created?'

Now, still in mourning for my mother, with my business cards still printed on white paper, I find in her place, as if from the same bud, that a replacement has appeared, this troublesome, infinitely frustrating, fascinating wife. Fascinating, I say, because what is odd, what is wholly unexpected and improbable, is – and I quake to write this – that in spite of my impatience with Shujin, in spite of her backwardness, in spite of everything, she stirs something in me.

This embarrasses me intensely. I would not admit it to a soul – certainly not to my colleagues, who would challenge her ridiculous beliefs on every intellectual level! She can't even be called beautiful, at least not beautiful as is commonly regarded. But, from time to time I find myself lost, for several minutes, in the habit of watching her eyes. They are so much paler than other women's, and I notice this particularly when she studies something, because then they seem to open abnormally wide and soak up the light, igniting tigerish stripes in them. Even an ugly toad dreams of eating a beautiful swan, they say, and this ugly toad, this skinny, truncated, pedantic toad, dreams daily of Shujin. She is my weakness.

 Nanking, 5 March 1937 (the twenty-third day of the first month by Shujin's lunar calendar)

Our house is small but it is modern. It is one of the two-storey lime-plaster whitewashed houses that have sprung up just north of the intersections of Zhongshan and Zhongyang Roads. The front door opens into a small, walled piece of land and from there into a tar-paved alley; at the back, past the kitchen, is a small plot of scrubland with pomegranate and teak trees and a disused well that becomes stagnant in the summer. We don't need the well, we have running water: astonishing for this part of Nanking where you can still see shanty-like shacks constructed from only tyres and wooden crates. And we have not only water but electricity, too, a lightbulb in each room, and imported flowered wallpaper in the bedroom! This house should make Shujin the envy of the neighbourhood, yet she prowls the place like a hunter, seeking out all the crevices and gaps that bad spirits could creep through. Now in every room there are altars to the household gods, separate cloths and brushes set aside to clean them; a spirit wall at the front door and blue *ba-gua* mirrors facing the interior doors. A carving of a *qilin* has appeared over our bed to help us conceive a son, and there are small yellow mantras tied to all the doors and windows, even to the trees outside.

'Really,' I say. 'Can you not see how this sort of behaviour has held our nation back?'

But she has no concept of nation-building, or moving forward.

She is afraid of the new and the unfamiliar. She still wears trousers under her *qipao* and thinks the girls in Shanghai, with their silk stockings and short skirts, are scandalous. She worries that I won't love her because her feet aren't bound and has somehow contrived to be the owner of an old pair of clogs with embroidered tops that are rather Manchu in style and give her feet a pointed appearance as if they had been in bindings since she was a child. Sometimes she sits in bed looking at her feet, pressing them and wiggling the toes as if natural, unrestrained feet are something she feels a mild disgust for.

'Are you sure, Chongming, that these feet are pretty?'

'Don't speak nonsense. Of course I'm sure.'

Only last night when I was preparing for bed, oiling my hair and pulling on my pyjamas, she started again with her petitioning. 'Are you? Quite sure?'

I sighed and sat on the small stool, taking a pair of ivory-handled scissors from the chest. 'There was nothing,' I clipped my thumbnail, 'absolutely nothing, lovely about tortured feet.'

'Oh,' Shujin gasped behind me. 'Oh, no!'

I dropped my hand, and turned. 'What is it now?'

She was sitting upright, utterly distraught, a little band of red breaking out over her cheeks. 'What is it? It's *you*! What in heaven's name are you doing?'

I looked down at my hands. 'I'm cutting my nails.'

'But –' she put her hands to her face, horrified '– Chongming, it's dark outside. Haven't you noticed? Didn't your mother teach you anything?'

And then I recalled a superstition from my childhood: to cut your nails after dark will certainly bring demons to the house. 'Well, really, Shujin,' I said, in a teacherly voice, 'I do think you're taking this a little too far—'

'No!' she insisted, white in the face. 'No. Do you want to bring death and destruction on our house?'

I looked at her for a long time, not knowing whether to laugh. At length, when I could see no good reason to antagonize her, I abandoned my nails and returned the scissors to the box. 'Really,'

I muttered, under my breath. 'Really, a man has no liberty in his own home.'

It wasn't until later that night, when she was asleep and I was left alone to stare at the ceiling and wonder, that her words came back to me. Death and destruction. Death and destruction, the last things that should be on our minds. And yet sometimes I wonder about this peace, these long days when Shujin and I lie in our cheerful disagreement under the sullen Nanking skies. Are these days too quiet? Too dream-filled? And then I wonder, Why does last week's terrible sunrise return to my thoughts hour after hour after hour?

9

All through my teens, in the hospital and at university, whenever I thought about my future it didn't have wealth attached to it, so I really didn't know what to do with money. That night, when I put together the tip and my evening's wages, and worked out that it was the equivalent of a little over a hundred and fifty pounds, I stuffed it into the bottom of my holdall, zipped it up, hurriedly pushed it into the wardrobe and stood back, my heart pounding. *A hundred and fifty pounds!* I stared at the bag on the floor. *A hundred and fifty pounds!*

I had made the money I needed for rent and there was no need for me to go back to the club, but something odd had happened. Those customers listening to me had made a tiny part of me open like a flower. 'I can always tell when a woman's enjoyed herself,' Jason said wryly, at the end of the night when we all stood in the lift together. 'It's all about blood.' He held the back of his hand to my face, making me shrink against the glass wall. 'The way the blood flows to the skin. Fascinating.' He dropped his hand and gave me a sly wink. 'You'll be back tomorrow.'

And he was right. The next day my instinct was to go to Shi Chongming, but how could I approach him after yesterday's angry scene? I knew I'd have to be patient and wait out the week. But instead of waiting at the house among my books and notes, I went to Omotesando and got the first dress that wasn't above my knee and didn't show my cleavage. A tunic in a kind of stiff black bombazine, with three-quarter sleeves. It was smart and didn't say anything much except 'I am a dress'. That night Mama Strawberry gave it one cursory look, and nodded. She wetted her finger and pasted aside a strand of my hair, then tapped my arm, pointed to a table of customers and sent me straight out into service, into a whirl of lighted cigarettes, drinks poured and countless ice cubes tonged into glasses.

I can still picture myself that first week, sitting in the club and staring out over the city, wondering which of the lights was Shi Chongming's. Tokyo was in the grip of a heatwave and the air-conditioner was kept on high, so the hostesses all sat in cool pools of light, their shoulders in their evening dresses bare and silvery like moonlight. In my memory I see myself from outside the building and it's as if I'm suspended in nothingness, my silhouette bright and blurred behind the plate-glass window, my expressionless white face obscured every few moments by Marilyn swinging past, no one suspecting the thoughts that flit crazily across my mind.

Strawberry seemed to like me, and that was a surprise because her standards were legendary. She spent thousands and thousands of dollars a month on flowers: crab-orange protea flown in refrigerated cartons from South Africa, amaryllis, great ginger lilies and orchids from mountain peaks in Thailand. Sometimes I'd stare at her openly because she held herself up so straight and seemed to love being sexy. She was sexy and she knew it. And that was that. I envied her confidence. She loved her outfits so much: every night it was something different: pink satin, white crêpe-de-Chine, a dress in magenta, roped with sequined straps 'From *How to Marry a Millionaire*,' she said, dropping her arm, pushing out her hip and turning to pout over her square shoulder at the customers. 'It's "charmeuse", you know,' as if it was a name everyone should recognize. 'Strawberry can't walk nice if she not dressed like Marilyn.' And she'd waggle her mother-of-pearl cigarette-holder at anyone who'd listen. 'Marilyn and Strawberry same build. Only Strawberry more petite.' She was short-tempered, always snapping at people, but I didn't see her really upset until the fifth night I was there. Then something happened that revealed an entirely different side of Mama Strawberry.

It was a hot night, so hot that steam seemed to be coming off the city, a kind of condensation that rose above the top of the buildings and blurred the red sunset. Everyone moved languidly, even Strawberry, drifting round the dance floor, gleaming in her full-length, sequined 'Happy birthday, Mr President' gown. She would stop occasionally to murmur something to the pianist, or to place her hand on the back of a chair and throw back her head at a customer's joke. It was about ten p.m., and she had retreated to the bar where she was sipping champagne, when something made her put down her glass with a terrible clatter. She sat up straight on her stool, and stared stonily at the entrance lobby, her face white.

Six enormous heavies in sharp suits and punch perms had come through the aluminium doors and were looking round the club, snapping cuffs over the wrists, running fingers between collars and thick necks. In the centre of the gang was a slim man in a black polo-neck, his hair tied in a ponytail. He was pushing a wheelchair, in which sat a diminutive insectile man, fragile as an ageing iguana. His head was small, his skin as dry and crenulated as a walnut, and his nose was just a tiny isosceles, nothing more than two shady dabs for nostrils – like a skull's. The wizened hands that poked out from his suit cuffs were long and brown and dry as dead leaves.

'*Dame! Konaide yo!*' Mama Strawberry slipped off the stool, pushed herself up to full height, raising the champagne to her mouth and swallowing it in one, her eyes locked on the group. She put the glass down, snapped a cigarette into her holder, smoothed her dress over her hips, swivelled on her heels and clicked away across the club, her elbow locked against her ribs, the cigarette out at an angle. The piano-player, leaning back on his bench to see what the fuss was, faltered on the keys.

A few feet from the head table, next to the east-facing window with all the best views of Tokyo, Strawberry stopped. Her chin was up, her solid little shoulders pushed back. She put her feet very smartly together and turned boldly to face the group. You could tell she was struggling to control her feelings. She put one hand on a chair, and raised the other stiffly, beckoning to them, using that peculiarly Japanese downward hand movement.

As other customers became aware of the new arrivals, the roar of conversation slowly diminished and every eye swivelled to watch the group make its slow progress across the club. But something else had caught my eye. A small alcove was cut into the wall behind the reception desk, a rectangular area with a table and chairs. Although there was no door, it was at such an angle that anyone inside could be seated out of sight of the other customers and sometimes Mama Strawberry had private meetings in there, or chauffeurs would use it to drink their tea and wait for their clients. As the group moved from the reception area, one figure detached itself, made its way to the alcove and slipped silently inside. The movement was so swift, the shadows on that side of the club so patchy, that I got little more than a glimpse, but what I saw made me sit forward a little, fascinated, uneasy.

The figure was dressed as a woman, in a neat black wool jacket and pencil skirt, but if she was a woman, she was incredibly tall. I had an impression of wide, masculine shoulders, long arms, sinewy legs crammed into large, highly polished black stilettos. But what really struck me was her hair: cut in a long, fringed bob, and so glossy it must have been a wig, worn hanging down in such a way that her face was almost totally obscured. Although the wig was extremely long, its ends only reached her shoulders, as if her head and neck were strangely attenuated.

As I watched her, my mouth hanging open a little, the group had reached the table. The waiters were setting it in a flurry of activity, and the invalid was wheeled to the head position, where he sat, crabbed and black as a scarab beetle, while the ponytailed man fussed around, getting him comfortable, directing the waiters where to place the glasses, the carafes of water. From the dark corners of the club twenty hostesses turned nervous eyes to Strawberry, who was moving among the tables, whispering names, calling them up to sit with the group. In her face there was a strange, bloodless look of something like anger. For a moment

I couldn't place that expression, but when she threw back her head and clipped across the floor to me, I saw it. All the small muscles in her face were twitching. Strawberry was nervous.

'Grey san,' she said, leaning over to me and speaking in a low voice. 'Mr Fuyuki. You go now and sit with him.'

I reached for my bag, but she stalled me with a finger to her lip.

'Be careful,' she whispered. 'Be very careful. Don't say nothing about *nothing*. There are good reason people afraid of him. And . . .' She hesitated and looked at me very carefully. Her eyes had narrowed and the tiniest rim of brown iris showed behind the blue contact lenses. 'Most important of all is her.' She raised her chin to indicate the alcove. 'Ogawa. His Nurse. You must never try to speak to her, or look her in the eye. Do you understand?'

'Yes,' I said faintly, my eyes drifting to the huge shadow. 'Yes I think so.'

Anywhere in Tokyo you could be aware of the presence of the *yakuza*: the underground gangs who claimed to be descendants of the *samurai* tradition. They were some of the most feared and violent men in Asia. Sometimes it was just the sounds of the *bosozoku* motorcycle gangs that reminded you of their existence, like a chrome wave rolling down Meiji Dori at dead of night, sweeping everything in front of them, the characters for kamikaze painted on their helmets. But at other times you'd be aware of gang members in less tangible ways: odd visual segments – the flash of a Rolex in a café, a boxy man with a punch perm rising from a restaurant table and tucking his polo shirt into black Crimplene trousers, a pair of shiny snakeskin shoes on a hot day on the subway. Or a tattoo on the hand that bought a ticket in the queue in front of you. I didn't give them much thought, not until I walked across the club that night and, in the hushed silence that had fallen, heard someone sitting near the dance floor whisper, '*Yakuza.*'

At the table there was absolute silence. All the hostesses seemed sunk inside themselves, nervously avoiding meeting anyone else's gaze. Everyone seemed determined not to sit with their back to the Nurse, who was still seated in the alcove, motionless as a snake. I was given a place near Fuyuki in his wheelchair and I was close enough to study him. His nose was so small it looked as if it had been eaten away in a fire, making every breath rattle noisily. But his face, if not exactly kindly, was peaceful, or watchful, like a very old tree frog's. He didn't attempt to speak to anyone.

His men sat quietly, their hands placed respectfully on the table while they waited for the man in the ponytail to prepare Fuyuki's drink. He produced a heavy shot glass wrapped in a white linen napkin, which he filled to the brim with the malt whisky, swirled it twice, dumped the whisky in the ice bucket, wiped the glass carefully with the napkin, then refilled it. He held up his hand to stall the other men from drinking and there was a brief hiatus while he passed the glass to Fuyuki, who lifted it with a trembling hand and sipped. He lowered the glass, pressed one hand to his stomach, the other to his mouth to hide a belch, and, satisfied, nodded.

'*Omaetachi mo yare.*' The ponytailed man jerked his chin towards the ceiling to indicate that the men could now drink. '*Nonde.*'

The henchmen relaxed. They lifted their glasses and drank. Someone stood and removed his jacket, someone else pulled out a cigar and snipped it. Slowly the mood softened. The girls refilled the glasses, tonged in ice and mixed the drink with the Some Like It Hot swizzle sticks, using the little plastic silhouettes of Marilyn to push the ice around in the glass and it wasn't long before everyone was talking at once and the conversation was louder than at any other table in the club. Within an hour all the men were drunk. The table was littered with bottles and half-finished dishes of pickled radish, dainty purple yam and lobster crackers.

Irina and Svetlana asked for Fuyuki's *meishi*. It wasn't an odd thing to do – out of habit most customers presented us with their business cards within a few minutes of being seated, but Fuyuki didn't give out his cards lightly. He frowned and coughed and looked the Russians up and down suspiciously. It took a long time and a lot of cajoling to get him to fish into his suit – his name, I noticed, when he moved, was embroidered in gold thread above the inside pocket – slide out some *meishi* and distribute them around the table, scissoring them between his brown fingers, his palm facing down. He leaned over to the ponytailed man and whispered in a dry, scratched voice, 'Tell them not to treat me like a trained monkey. I don't want anyone calling me and asking me to the club. I'll come when I want to come.'

I stared down at the card in my hands. I'd never seen one so beautiful before. It was on rough, unbleached handmade paper, the edges ragged. Unlike most cards it had no address and no English translation on the back. It bore only a telephone number and Fuyuki's *kanji*, only his second name, hand-calligraphed in pine-soot ink.

'What is it?' Fuyuki whispered. 'Is something wrong?'

I shook my head and gazed at it. The little *kanji* were beautiful. I was thinking how wonderful this old alphabet was – how morose and thin the English language seemed in comparison.

'What is it?'

'Winter Tree,' I murmured. 'Winter Tree.'

One of the men at the end of the table began to laugh before I'd finished. When no one else joined in, he changed the laugh to a cough, covering his mouth with a napkin and fumbling to take a swallow of his drink. A baffled silence fell, and Irina scowled, shaking her head regretfully. But Fuyuki sat forward and said, in his whispery Japanese, 'My name. How did you know what my name means? Do you speak Japanese?'

I looked up at him, my face white. 'Yes,' I replied, a little unsteadily. 'Just a little.'

'You can read it too?'

'Only five hundred *kanji*.'

'Five hundred? *Sugoi*. That's a lot.' People were looking at me as if they had only just realized I was a human being, and not a piece of the furniture. 'And where did you say you were from?'

'England?' It came out as a tentative question.

'England?' He leaned over and seemed to be peering at me. 'Tell me, are they all so pretty in England?'

*

Being told I was pretty by anyone . . . well, it was just lucky that it didn't happen very often, because that was when I got itchy and uncomfortable, remembering all the things that were probably never going to happen to me. Even if I was 'pretty'. Old Fuyuki's comment made me blush and retreat into myself. I didn't speak from that moment on. I sat in silence smoking cigarette after cigarette and made every excuse to get away from the table. If there was a fresh glass to be brought from the bar, or a new plate of snacks, I'd leap up and get it, taking my time.

The Nurse barely moved all night. I couldn't help sneaking glimpses at her – her shadow almost motionless on the alcove wall. I could tell the waiters were uneasy about her presence: usually one of them would slip into the room and find out what the occupant wanted to drink, but tonight it seemed only Jason had the courage to speak to her. When I came to the bar for a fresh hot towel, I saw him in there. He had taken the whisky menu to her, moving confidently, unafraid, and was sitting casually against the table, his arms crossed, looking down at her. I had a few moments to study her.

She sat side on to me and she was amazing to look at – every inch of her skin was covered in a crumbly white powdered makeup, caking the cracks on her neck, the lines on her wrists. The only breaks in the white were her odd tiny eyes, small and dark as finger-holes in dough, single-lidded, set a long way from her nose, so deep inside her head that the sockets seemed empty. Mama Strawberry had been worried about me looking at the Nurse, but you couldn't have met her eyes if you tried, and their odd positioning must have meant she had poor eyesight, because she was holding the menu very close to her face, passing it back and forward in front of her face almost as if she was smelling it. I didn't turn and go straight back to the table, but lingered for a few moments at the bar, pretending to be preoccupied with inspecting the hot towel, as if it might be flawed.

'She's kinda sexy,' I heard Jason tell the bar staff when he came out with her order. He leaned his elbows casually on the bar and spoke to no one in particular. 'Sexy in a freako S and M way.' He looked over his shoulder at her, a small, amused smile twitching at his mouth. 'Reckon I'd do the bad thang with her if I had to.' He turned back then, and saw me standing at the bar, staring at him in silence. He winked and raised his eyebrows, as if sharing a tremendous joke with me. 'Nice legs,' he explained, nodding at the Nurse. 'Or maybe it's the heels that are doing it for me.'

I didn't answer. I snatched up the *oshibori* and turned away, a stupid blush spreading all over my face and my shoulders. The thing about Jason was that he always made me feel a little like crying.

It's funny how people can plant ideas in your head. Much, much later that night, I looked down at my legs, crossed neatly under the table. I was quite drunk, and I remember seeing them, crossed primly at the ankles, and thinking, What do nice legs look like? I smoothed down my tights and moved my knees apart a little, so that I could see my thighs a little more clearly. I turned them so I could see the calf and the little tautness when I flexed my feet. I wondered if 'nice legs' looked anything like my legs.

10

史 Nanking, 4 April 1937, the Festival of the Clear and
Bright

My mother must be laughing now – she must be looking at me
and laughing at all my reservations and my cold impatience over
this marriage. Because, it seems, Shujin and I are going to have a
child! A child! Imagine that. Shi Chongming, the ugly little toad,
a father! Here, at last, is something to celebrate. A child to bring
order to the laws of physics and love, a child to reveal reason
behind the subtle codes of society. A child to help me embrace the
future wholeheartedly.

Shujin, naturally, has been thrown into a frenzy of superstition.
There are so many important things to consider. I watch her in
bemusement, trying to take it all in, trying to treat it all with the
deepest seriousness. First, this morning, came a long list of forbidden food – she will no longer allow squid and octopus and
pineapple into the house, and I am to make a daily trip to the
market to buy black boned chicken, liver, plum, lotus seed and
balls of congealed duck blood. And from today it is my responsibility to kill the chickens that come squawking home from
market, for if Shujin kills any animal, even an animal for food, it
appears that our baby will take on the beast's shape and she will
give birth to a chicken or a duck!

But, and this is the most important of all, we must not refer to
our son (she is sure we will have a son) as 'baby' or 'child',
because the bad spirits might hear us and try to steal him at birth.

Instead she has given him a name to confuse the spirits, a 'milk-name', she calls it. From herein 'moon' is how we must refer to our child whenever we speak. 'You cannot imagine the manner of evil beings who would snatch away a newborn. Our moon soul would be the most precious prize a demon could ever hope for. And,' here she held up her hand to stave off my interruption, 'never forget – our little moon is very fragile. Please don't shout or be argumentative around me. We must not disturb his soul.'

'I see,' I said, a small smile playing on my mouth, because I found the level of her ingenuity quite marvellous. 'Well, in that case, moon soul it is. And from this moment on let only peace exist between these four walls.'

11

The Russians said it was no surprise that Jason was making jokes about the Nurse. They said they'd always known he was a strange one. They said that his walls were covered with horrible photographs, that he often received wrapped specialist magazines from mailing addresses in Thailand, and that sometimes odd things with no great value went missing around the house: Irina's statuette of a fighting bear in real animal skin, a single wolf-fur glove, a photograph of the girls' grandparents. Maybe, they speculated, he was a devil worshipper. 'He watch sick stuff, sick till it make you to puke. His videos, always the videos with *death*.'

You could see the videos they were talking about displayed in the rental shops on Waseda Street. They all had titles like *Faces of Death* and *Mortuary Madness* and all the lettering seemed to be in lurid blood drips. *Genuine autopsy footage!* the covers boasted, and you'd have thought they were all about sex if you saw the crowds of adolescent boys that always seemed to be hanging around that corner of the shop. I'd never actually seen one of the videos in the house so I didn't know if the Russians were telling the truth. But I had seen Jason's photographs.

'I've been in Asia for four years,' he'd told me. 'You can take your Taj Mahals and your Angkor Wats. I'm looking for something . . .' he'd paused then and rubbed his fingers together, as if he was trying to mould the words from the air, '. . . I'm looking for something more – something different.' Once I'd happened to

78

pass his room when the door was open and the room was empty. I couldn't help it, I had to step inside.

I saw what the Russians meant. There were photographs pinned to every inch of the wall and the images were as horrible as they'd said: here was a pitifully crippled man, naked except for a garland of marigolds, sitting dejectedly on the banks of what I decided must be the Ganges, there were young Filipino men nailed to crucifixes, vultures gathering for human flesh on the incredible Towers of Silence at a Parsi funeral. I even recognized the prayer flags and smouldering juniper of a sky-burial charnel ground outside Lhasa because I'd done Tibet in a module at university. But, I thought, looking at a photo of a wide plume of smoke shooting from an indistinct shape on a platform, the words '*Varanasi funeral pyre*' scrawled below it, there was something oddly beautiful about all this, a sense in this room, like a scent, of a vivid curiosity. When at last, unnoticed, I stepped quietly out into the corridor, I had decided that the Russians were wrong. Jason wasn't odd or morbid, he was fascinating.

He was supposed to be a waiter at the club, but all week I'd barely seen him lift a tray. Sometimes he'd stop at tables and chat amiably for some time with the customers, just as if he, not Strawberry, was the owner. 'He's waiter but he don't do nuh-think,' murmured Irina. 'He don't need to do no work because Mama Strawberry lurve him.' She seemed to like the cachet that a *gaijin* waiter gave her. And then there were his looks. The Japanese hostesses all giggled and blushed when he walked by. Often he would sit at Strawberry's desk, sipping champagne, with his waiter's tuxedo all open and showing off his body, while she simpered and adjusted her dress straps, sometimes leaning back in her chair and running her hands down her body.

He didn't spend much time in the house – and finding his room open like that was unusual. Ordinarily the door was shut, we all had locks on our bedroom doors, and often he'd lock up and leave early, before any of us woke, or he'd take a taxi from the club and not come home until the following night. Maybe he was out in the parks, looking for women asleep on benches. But there were impressions of him everywhere – a pair of moccasins lying on the staircase, lime-scented shaving cream drying in rings on the bathroom shelf, business cards in pale pink propped up against the kettle, with names like Yuko and Moe in feminine script.

I pretended not to be fazed by all this, but I was. Secretly I was completely dazzled by Jason.

I bought a diary from Kiddyland, a schoolgirl's shop in Omotesando. It was pink, with a clear plastic cover containing a sparkling gel that moved round and round. I would hold it up to the window and marvel at the way the light caught the little specks of glitter. I had scratch'n'sniff cream-cake stickers, and every day that passed I placed a sticker over the space in my diary. Some days I took a train over to Hongo and sat in the Bambi restaurant, watching the sun playing on the big *Akamon* gate as the students came and went. But I didn't see Shi Chongming. There were five days to go, four days, three days, two. He had said a week. That meant Sunday. But Sunday came, and he didn't call.

I couldn't believe it. He had broken his promise. I waited the whole day, sitting on the sofa in the living room, the shades all drawn against the heat, a pile of my books scattered around me. I stared and stared at the phone. But the only times it rang it was for Jason. I'd snatch it up and it would be a Japanese girl sighing plaintively down the line, refusing to believe it when I told her he was out.

That Sunday I took five messages for him, all from different girls. Most of them were sweet and sad, some were rude. One took a shocked breath when she heard my voice, and screamed at me in shrill Japanese, '*Who the fuck are you? What the fuck are you doing answering the phone? Put Jason on the fucking phone. NOW.*'

I spent some time listing all the names. I doodled faces next to them, trying to imagine what they looked like. Then, when that got boring, I sat with my chin in my hands, staring glumly at the phone that didn't ring for me all day and night.

12

史 **Nanking, 1 September 1937**

Trouble is coming out of the east. It is just as I thought. The Japanese are in Shanghai and fighting for it street by street. Could it really be the Japanese, and not the Communists, who are the greatest threat to our stability? Could it even be that the Communists were correct to force this military unison on Chiang? Pu Yi, the Japanese puppet, has been on his borrowed throne in Manchuria for six years, no fault of our president, and five years ago the Japanese bombed Shanghai. But nobody has spoken about our safety in Nanking. Until now. Now, and only now, citizens are starting to take precautions. I spent this morning painting our blue-tiled roof black, to hide it from the Japanese bombers that we are warned will rise up one day from behind Purple Mountain, coming with the morning sun.

At about ten, when I'd finished half of the roof, something made me pause. I don't know if it was a noise or a premonition, but as I stood on my ladder something made me turn to look out to the east. Dotted on the city skyline there were maybe twenty other men like me, high up on their ladders, spidery against the sky, their half-painted roofs glistening beneath them. And further, further beyond them, the spreading horizon. Purple Mountain. The red east.

Shujin has always said there is something bad in Nanking's future. In her doomy prophetic way, she has always talked about it. She says she has known from the moment she stepped from the train a year ago that she was trapped here. She says that the weight of the sky dropped straight down on her and the air infected her lungs and the city's future pressed against her so hard she had to fight to remain standing. Even the slick dark train she had just alighted from, boring its way out through the milky light, wasn't an escape. At that moment, standing on the Nanking platform, she looked up at the ring of mountains, dark, like an opened ribcage set in the land, and knew they were a great danger. They would hold her like a claw, those poisonous mountains, and the trains would stop running while she was here. Then Nanking would have her and use its weak, acid air to dissolve her slowly into its heart.

I know something vital happened to her that day, when I escorted her back to Nanking from Poyang lake, because I remember one vivid grain of colour in the train journey. A cherry pink parasol. A girl in the rice fields had paused to wait for the goat she was leading to catch up. When the animal stopped stubbornly the girl tugged on the rope, half-heartedly, more concerned with the idleness of watching than with the animal coming towards her. We had come to a halt somewhere just south of Wuhu and everyone in the train stopped what they were doing and turned to the windows to watch the girl waiting for the goat. At last the animal relented and the girl continued, and soon there was nothing left but the emerald paddy-field. The other passengers turned away from the window and went back to their games, to their conversations, but Shujin remained motionless, still watching the patch of land where the girl had been.

I leaned over to her and whispered, 'What are you looking at?'

'What am I looking at?' The question seemed to puzzle her. 'What am I looking at?' She repeated it several times – her hand on the window, still staring at the empty space left by the girl. 'What am I looking at?'

It is only now, so many months later, that I understand exactly what Shujin was looking at. Gazing at the girl under the cherry pink parasol she was looking at herself. She was saying goodbye. The country girl in her was going. When we got to Nanking she lingered on for a while in some places – the tender lines on the backs of her knees, the dusting of colour on her arms and the steady non-lilting Jiangxi dialect so amusing to the Nanking citizens – but everywhere else the woman was coming through, unwillingly, emerging blinking and baffled in the huge city. The city that she believes will never let her leave.

13

I watched Shi Chongming arrive at Todai University at eight o'clock the following morning. I'd been there since six thirty, waiting first on the street corner, then in the Bambi café when it opened. I ordered a large breakfast – miso soup, tuna flakes on rice, green tea. Before the waitress placed my order in the kitchen she whispered the price to me. I looked up at her, not understanding. Then I realized: she didn't want me to think I'd get it for free again. I took the chit to the counter and paid it. Then, when she brought the food, I gave her three thousand yen notes. She stared at the money in silence, then blushed and tucked it into her pie-crust frill apron.

It was a hot day, but Shi Chongming wore a blue cotton Mao-style shirt, odd little black rubber plimsolls, the elasticated sort that English schoolchildren used to wear for PE, and his strange fisherman's hat. He walked very slowly and carefully, his eyes on the pavement. He didn't notice me loitering at the gate until I had stepped out of the shaded trees and was standing right in front of him. He saw my feet and came to a halt, his cane outstretched, his head down.

'You said you were going to phone.'

Slowly, very slowly, Shi Chongming raised his face. His eyes were dim, like cloudy marbles. 'You're here again,' he said. 'You said you weren't going to come here again.'

'You were supposed to call me. Yesterday.'

He narrowed his eyes at me. 'You look different,' he said. 'Why do you look different?'

'You didn't call me.'

He looked at me for an instant more, taking this in, then made a noise in his throat, and began to walk away. 'You're very rude,' he muttered. 'Very rude.'

'But I've *waited a week*,' I said, catching up and walking alongside. 'I didn't call you, I didn't come here, I did what I was supposed to do, but you, you forgot.'

'I didn't promise to call you—'

'Yes, you—'

'No. No.' He stopped and held up his walking-stick, pointing at me. 'I made no promises. I have a very good memory and I know I didn't promise you anything.'

'I can't wait for ever.'

He gave a short laugh. 'Do you like wise old Chinese sayings? Would you like to hear a profound truth about a mulberry leaf? Would you? We say that patience turns a mulberry leaf into silk. Silk! Imagine that, from nothing but a dried-out old leaf. All it takes is patience.'

'Well, that's stupid,' I said. 'Worms turn it into silk.'

He closed his mouth and sighed. 'Yes,' he said. 'Yes. I don't see a very long life for this friendship, do you?'

'Not if you don't call me when you promise. You've *got* to keep your promises.'

'I haven't *got* to do anything.'

'But . . .' my voice was rising and one or two of the passing students gave us curious looks '. . . I'm at work in the evenings. How do I know you won't call me in the evenings? There's no answerphone. How do I know you won't call me one evening and then never again? If I miss your call it'll all go wrong and then . . .'

'Leave me now,' he said. 'You have said enough. Now please let me alone.' And he hobbled away across the campus, leaving me standing in the shadows under a gingko tree.

'Professor Shi,' I called, after his retreating back. 'Please. I didn't mean to be rude. I didn't mean it.'

But he kept walking, disappearing eventually beyond the dusty rotary hedge, into the shaded forest. At my feet the shadows of the gingko trees shifted. I turned and kicked the low fence at the edge of the path, then put my face in my hands and began to shiver.

I went home in a kind of trance, going straight to my room, not stopping to speak to the Russians, who were watching TV in the living room and who made a sarcastic *ooooh*ing noise to my retreating back. I slid the bedroom door closed with a bang and stood with my back to it, my eyes shut, listening to my heart beating.

When you know you're right about something, the important thing is to keep going.

After a long time I opened my eyes and went to where I kept my paints stacked, against the wall in the alcove. I mixed some paint, set the brushes and the water in a jar near the wall and opened the window wide. It was already getting dark, a burnt-food smell was coming up from the streets, and Tokyo was lighting up for the night. The city stretched away into the distance like a small galaxy. I imagined it from outer space – buildings like mountains, streets glittering like Emperor Qin Shi Huangdi's rivers of mercury.

How could this be? When the air raids ended, when the last American bomber retreated over the blue Pacific, there were over a hundred square miles of flattened streets in Tokyo. The city was unrecognizable. Cars couldn't drive through it because no one knew where the streets ended and the buildings began. In the shanty-towns along the river, the *tadon* they burned, a foul-smelling, smoky combination of coal dust and tar, hung over the city like a cloud.

The silk walls of my room had been ripped down to waist height. Below that they were intact. I loaded the paintbrush with cobalt and began to paint. I painted broken rooftops and the spindly rafters of burned-away houses. I painted fires raging out of control and streets strewn in rubble. As I painted my mind drifted free. I was in such a daze that at seven o'clock the Russians had to come and knock on the door and ask me if I was thinking of going to work that evening.

'Or you just gonna stay in there? Like a crab, hmm?'

I pulled back the door and looked out at them, brush in my hand, face smeared with paint.

'My God! You coming like that?'

I blinked at them. I didn't know it then, but I was lucky they had knocked on the door: if they hadn't I might have missed one of the most important nights of my time in Tokyo.

14

史 Nanking, 12 November 1937 (the tenth day of the tenth month)

Shanghai fell last week. The enormity of this news is still sinking in. Our president's best troops were defending the city: we outnumbered the Japanese marines ten to one, and yet somehow the city fell. The streets are said to be deserted, only the empty vomit and blister-gas canisters of the Japanese scattered in the gutters, dead zoo animals rotting on the floors of their cages. News comes that the Imperial Japanese Army is fanning out across the delta and now it seems that an assault on Nanking is inevitable. Ten divisions are pushing inland towards us: walking, riding motorbikes and armoured cars. I can imagine them, their army-issue puttees soaked to the brims with yellow river mud, certain that if they can only take Nanking, our nation's great capital, they will have the giant's heart in their fists.

But naturally it won't happen. Our president will not allow harm to come to his city. And yet something has changed in the citizens, a wavering of faith. As I was walking home today after my morning class (only four students attended, what am I to make of that?), the fog that has been hanging over the city lifted and it became sunny, as if the sky had taken pity on Nanking. Yet I noticed that no laundry appeared on poles as it usually does at the first hint of sun. Then I noticed that the street sprinklers, the poor ragged coolies who clean our thoroughfares, hadn't come through, and that people were scurrying from doorway to doorway, carrying more belongings than seemed necessary. It took me some time to realize what was happening and when I did my heart sank. People are fleeing. The city is closing down. I am ashamed to say that even some lecturers at the university were talking today about heading inland. Imagine that! Imagine such a lack of faith in our president. Imagine what he will think to see us fleeing his great city.

Shujin seems almost gleeful that Shanghai has been taken. It seems to prove everything she has always claimed about the Nationalists. She, too, has been caught up in the frenzy to desert the capital. When I returned home today I found her packing belongings into a chest. 'There you are,' she said. 'I've been waiting. Now, please bring the cart from the courtyard.'

'The cart?'

'Yes! We're leaving. We're going back to Poyang.' She folded a white swaddling cloth from her grandmother's *cui sheng* parcel, and packed it into the chest. I noticed she had reserved the largest space for a tortoiseshell money case of my mother's – a case I remembered to contain several I Ching passages, written in blood, and wrapped in cloth. My mother had put all her faith in those words, yet they had been unable to save her. 'Oh, don't look so anxious,' said Shujin. 'My almanac marks today as a perfectly auspicious day for travel.'

'Now, look here, there's no need to be hasty—' I began.

'Is there not?' She rocked back on her heels and looked at me thoughtfully. 'I think there is. Come with me.' She got up and beckoned me to the window, opened it and pointed up to the Purple Mountain where Sun Yat-sen's mausoleum sits. 'There,' she said. It was getting late and behind the mountain the moon was already showing, low and orange. 'Zijin.'

'What about it?'

'Chongming, listen, please, my husband.' Her voice became low and serious. 'Last night I had a dream. I dreamed that Zijin was burning—'

'Shujin,' I began, 'this is nonsense—'

'No,' she said fiercely. 'It is not nonsense. It is real. In my dream Purple Mountain was burning. And when I saw it I knew. I knew instantly that disaster was going to strike Nanking—'

'Shujin, please—'

'A disaster the like of which no one has seen before, not even during the Christian rebellion.'

'Really! Tell me, are you as wise as the blind men at festivals, boasting they've smeared their eyelids with – with – I don't know, the fluid from a dog's eye or such nonsense? A soothsayer? Let's put an end to this rubbish now. You cannot, *cannot* predict the future.'

But she wasn't to be shaken. She stood stiffly next to me, her eyes locked on Purple Mountain. 'Yes, you can,' she whispered. 'You *can* predict the future. The future is an open window.' She put her hand lightly on the shutters. 'Just like this one. It is easy to look ahead because the future is the past. Everything in life revolves, and I have already seen exactly what will happen.' She turned and looked at me with her yellow eyes, and for a moment it seemed she was staring steadily into my heart. 'If we stay in Nanking we will die. You know it too. I can see it in your eyes – you know it very well. You know your precious president is too weak to save us. Nanking doesn't stand a chance in his hands.'

'I will not listen to another word,' I said firmly. 'I will not have the generalissimo spoken about like this. I forbid it. Absolutely forbid it. Chiang Kai-shek will save this city.'

'That foreigner's lapdog.' She sniffed contemptuously. 'First his own generals have to force him to fight and now he can't even defeat the Japanese – the very same army that trained him!'

'Enough!' I was shaking with anger. 'I have heard enough. Chiang Kai-shek will defend Nanking and we, yes, you and I, we will be here to see it.' I took her by the wrist and led her back to the chest. 'I'm your husband and you need to trust my judgement. Unpack this now. We're going nowhere – certainly not back to Poyang. Poyang killed my mother and for once I am instructing you clearly, as befits a husband: you will put your faith in Chiang Kai-shek, the supreme arbiter, a man far greater, far stronger than all of your superstitions put together.'

Nanking, 16 November 1937

How I regret those words now. Now that I am here, alone in my study, the door locked, my ear pressed furtively to the radio, how I regret my proud stand. I am afraid to let Shujin hear the news the radio is delivering because she would crow with delight to hear today's terrible report, so terrible that even I quake to write it down here. I will write it in small characters to make it easier to bear: Chiang Kai-shek and the Kuomintang government have fled the city, leaving it in the hands of General Tang Shengzhi.

Now I have written the appalling sentence what is there to do but stare at it, the blood rushing in my head. What shall I do? I can neither sit still, nor stand, nor think about anything else. Commander Chiang gone? General Tang in his place? Can we trust him? Am I to crawl to Shujin and tell her that I was wrong? Allow her to see me weakened in my resolve? I cannot. I cannot retreat. I am caught in a wretched web of my own making, but I must stand my ground, no matter how queasy it makes me. I will barricade the house and we shall wait out the arrival of the Imperial forces. Even if the unthinkable does happen, and our troops are defeated, I know the Japanese will treat us well. I visited Kyoto as a student and I speak the language well. They behave with infinite care and sophistication – one only has to study their deportment in the Russian war to know them as a civilized people. Shujin will be surprised to find that they even have things to teach us. We will prepare a sign in Japanese saying, 'Welcome', and we'll be safe. Today I saw two families in an alley off the Hanzhong Road working on such a sign.

But as I write, as night falls on Nanking outside the walls of the house, as the city descends into perfect silence, with only the occasional distant shudder of a Nationalist tank prowling Zhongshan Road, my heart is like ice. It is all I can do not to go downstairs and confess my fears to Shujin.

She has hardened to me since I refused to return to Poyang. Daily I repeat my list of reasons for not fleeing, pretending not to know how hollow they sound: in the countryside there will be no medical care, no sophisticated methods for our child's birth. I have tried to paint a picture of the disasters that would follow if we were stranded in the countryside, with only an old peasant woman to help Shujin in her confinement, but every time I say this she flies at me with fire in her eyes: 'An old peasant woman? An old peasant woman? She would know better than your foreign doctors! Christians!'

And maybe I have worn her down, because she has lapsed into silence. She has spent most of today sitting limply in her chair, her hands folded on her stomach. I can't help thinking about those hands, so small, so white. All day I was unable to stop staring at them. They must have drifted unconsciously to her stomach because she would never knowingly stroke her abdomen – she is certain that to do so would make the baby spoiled and demanding, the very words my mother used with me: 'Really, I must have rubbed my stomach too often to produce such a proud and obstinate child.'

When I consider the possibility that our child could be obstinate, or arrogant, or selfish, or any other undesirable characteristic, I could weep. Proud and inflexible or spoiled and demanding – all these things depend on one thing: on our child having life in the first place. It all depends on Shujin surviving the inevitable attack on Nanking.

15

Maybe the worst thing that can happen to you is to lose someone and not know where to look for them. The Japanese believe that on O-Bon night the dead come back to their loved ones. They swoop out of the ether, sucked out of their eternal doze by the call of their living descendants. I'd always imagined O-Bon night as dreadfully chaotic, with spirits zipping around the air, knocking people over because they were going so fast. Now that I was in Japan I wondered what happened to those who didn't know where their dead lay. What happened if they had died in a different country? I wondered if spirits could cross continents. If they couldn't, then how would they find their way back to their families?

It was spirits I was thinking about that night, sitting in the gloom with my endless cigarettes, trying to decide how I was going to convince Shi Chongming to talk to me, when Junzo Fuyuki and his men came to the club for the second time.

I was summoned by Strawberry to join them. They were seated at the usual long table – all except the Nurse, who was already sequestered in the dark alcove, the light malforming her shadow on the wall, horse-like, a chess-set knight, so tall that she almost appeared not to grow upwards from the floor but to be suspended by her shoulders from the ceiling. Fuyuki seemed to be in a good mood, and there was a new guest in the seat next to me, a huge man in a silver suit, with a congested face and hair so short that

93

the fat ridges at the back of his skull were visible. He was already drunk – telling jokes, slamming his chair on the floor every time he got to the punchline, lifting his eyebrows comically and muttering something that made the men hoot with laughter. He spoke Japanese with an Osaka accent, the way I used to imagine all the *yakuza* did, but he wasn't one of the gang. He was a friend of Fuyuki's and the Japanese girls said he was famous – they were giggling at him, hands up to their mouths, sighing to each other over him.

'My name is Baisho,' he told the Russians, in stilted English, waving at them with his thick, gold-ringed fingers. 'My friends call me Bai, because I have twice their money and I am twice' – he waggled his eyebrows suggestively – 'twice the man!' I sat silently, painting the kanji for *Bai* in my head. Bai san was using it to mean double, but it had other meanings too – it could mean 'plum' if written with a tree combined with the symbol for 'every', or it could mean shellfish, or it could mean cultivation. But what Bai san really made me think of was the way his name sounded in English: *Bison*.

'My job is singer. Me number-one Japanese singing boy.' He waved his hand around the table at anyone who cared to listen to him. 'And my new friend,' he said, jabbing the cigar in the direction of the black spectre in the wheelchair, 'Mr Fuyuki. He number-one man in Tokyo!' He flexed his fist, curling it to make the muscles bulk out. 'The oldest in Tokyo, but healthy and strong like his age is thirty years. Strong, very strong.' He turned drunkenly to him and said in loud Japanese, as if the old man was deaf, 'Fuyuki-san, You Are Very Strong. You are the greatest, the oldest man I know.'

Fuyuki nodded. 'I am. I am,' he whispered. 'I am stronger today than I was at twenty.'

Bison raised his glass. 'To the strongest man in Tokyo.'

'The strongest man in Tokyo!' everyone chorused.

Sometimes it's a mistake to show off – you can never know for sure when things are about to change, and you're going to end up looking foolish. Less than half an hour after he'd been boasting about his health, Fuyuki began to look unwell. No one drew attention to it, but I could see – he was breathing hard, muttering something and groping for the arm of the ponytailed man, who leaned forward and listened carefully, his eyes expressionless. After a few moments he nodded, then stood, pulling himself up straight and smoothing down his sweater, pushing his chair sharply under the table. He went discreetly across the club to the alcove, hesitated then stepped inside.

One of the other men sat a little closer to Fuyuki, watching him discreetly, but otherwise there seemed to be an effort at the table to pretend that nothing had happened, as if it might be disrespectful to draw attention to the old man's discomfort. I was the only one following the ponytailed man with my eyes. I saw him sit where Jason had sat, the shadows deep on his face as he spoke to the Nurse. There was a moment's pause, then the Nurse reached inside her jacket and fished out a pouch from which she retrieved what looked like a small phial. With her long white fingers held out delicately at an angle, she tapped something from the phial into a glass, filled it with water from a jug on the table, and handed it to the man, who covered it with a white napkin and came back silently to the table, handing the glass to Fuyuki. The old man took a trembling sip, then another. I noticed a residue of something coarse, something like nutmeg, clinging to the glass. In the alcove the Nurse returned the pouch to her jacket, pushing it deep inside the pocket. She smoothed down the wig with her big hands.

At my side Bison made a small, fascinated noise in his throat, sitting forward with one elbow on the table, the cigar in his fingers heavy with ash. He watched, entranced, as Fuyuki downed the rest of the drink, dropped the glass on the table and sank back, both hands on the arms of the wheelchair, his head tipped back, breathing noisily through his tiny nose.

Bison began to laugh. He shook his head and laughed until his whole body was shaking and his face was getting red. He leaned across me and spoke to Fuyuki in a loud, slurry voice. 'Hey, *oniisan*,' he said, indicating the drink with his cigar. 'Haven't you got some medicine for me too? Something to make me stand up proud, like I did when I was twenty?' Fuyuki didn't answer. He continued breathing laboriously. 'You know what I mean, you old goat. A cure to keep you as strong as when you were twenty.' Around the table one or two conversations stopped and people turned to look. Bison smacked his lips and waved a hand in the air. 'Something to keep the ladies happy? Eh?' He nudged me roughly. 'You'd like that, wouldn't you? Wouldn't you? You'd like a twenty-year-old man, someone who could STAND UP.' He leaped to his feet, stumbling against the table, sending a plate crashing to the floor. 'This is what I want. I want to stand up like Mr Fuyuki! Like my *onii-san*, I want to live for ever!'

His neighbour reached out to touch his sleeve; one of the other men rested a finger on his mouth. 'I want to stand up stiff like I used to,' Bison sang, in his crooner's voice, his hands on his chest. 'As stiff as I was at eighteen. Oh, tell me, *kami sama*, is that too much to ask?'

When no one laughed he stopped in his tracks, the words drying in his mouth. Everyone had stopped talking, and the ponytailed man, in a small, barely perceptible gesture, not even raising his eyes, had pinched his lips together discreetly with his thumb and forefinger. Bison's smile dissolved. He opened his hands in a mute gesture: *What? What have I said?* But the ponytailed man had already removed his fingers and was pretending to be interested in inspecting his nails, just as if nothing had happened. Someone else coughed, an embarrassed noise. Then, almost as if at a signal, all the conversations restarted at once. Bison looked round the table. 'What?' he said into the noise. '*What?*' But no one paid him any attention. They had all turned in opposite directions, finding more interesting things to look at, more important things to talk about, swirling their drinks, clearing their throats, lighting cigars.

After a long, puzzled hesitation, he sat down very, very slowly. He picked up a hot towel, held it to his face and breathed in and out. 'My God,' he muttered, lowering the towel, and looking anxiously to where the Nurse's shadow flickered on the wall. 'It can't be true . . .'

'What he say?' hissed Irina, leaning towards me. 'What he say?'

'I don't know,' I murmured, not looking at her. 'I didn't understand.'

For some time after that the conversation at the table was conducted on a high, slightly forced note. Fuyuki gradually recovered. Eventually he wiped his mouth and folded the glass into the napkin, placed it inside his pocket, then tilted his head back and stared at the ceiling for a while. The men went on talking, the girls refilled their drinks and no one referred to the incident. Only Bison didn't join in – he sat in a stunned silence, one moment staring glumly at the bulge in Fuyuki's jacket where the glass was hidden, the next glancing across at the ominous shadow of the Nurse. His cheeks were damp, his eyes watered, and for the rest of the night his Adam's apple worked painfully as if he might be sick.

16

史 Nanking, 9 December 1937 (by Shujin's calendar the seventh day of the eleventh month)

There is wholescale panic in the city. Last week Japanese forces took Suzhou, the Venice of China, and began to move north of the Tai Wu lake. They must have travelled quickly, going in an arc along the Yangtze and coming in from the north, because four days ago Zhejiang fell. General Tang has vowed to do his utmost to defend us, but nothing about him inspires confidence in the citizens, and now almost anyone who can afford to is leaving. 'It will be like the Taiping invasion again,' they whisper. The trucks are piled high, the poor and the desperate clinging to the sides, the vehicles swaying wide-bellied out into the tiny distance. I pray that the specks you can occasionally observe dropping from the sides of the trucks as they disappear towards the rail ferry at Xiaguan, the dark objects that once or twice fall away and drop in slow motion against the misty background, I pray they are belongings: baskets or chickens coming untethered. I pray they are not the children of the poor.

Today the Red Cross issued a warning. They have defined a refugee zone centred on the university, not far from our house, just south of the railway line, and they are urging all non-combatants to gather there for safety. Most of the teaching rooms and offices have been converted into dormitories. I wondered if I had found a solution to my anxieties: in a safe zone there would be no talk of leaving Nanking, of not trusting the Kuomintang. And yet there I'd be able to protect Shujin.

With this in mind today I went in secret to the zone, where I saw crowds and crowds of people piling up at the entrance with their bedding and belongings, the air-raid warnings howling overhead. Some of the refugees had livestock in tow, chickens, ducks, a water-buffalo, even, and I saw a family arguing with officials about whether they could bring in a pig. Eventually they were persuaded to abandon the animal and it wandered away, disoriented, into the crowd. I lingered for a while, watching the pig, until another refugee further back in the crowd spotted it, claimed it, and slowly led it back through the crowds to the gate, where the argument with the official started all over again.

For a long time I stared at that throng of the poor and the itinerant, some coughing, some squatting casually in the gutter to defecate as must still be the practice in some rural communities. Eventually I turned away, pulling up my collar, and walked back to the house with my head bowed. I cannot take Shujin there. It would be no better than dragging her across the Yangtze and back to Poyang.

We are some of the last people left in the alley – there are only us and a few labourers who work in the brocade factory on Guofu Road. They live in the dormitory building at the head of the alley and are very poor – I doubt they have family or places to flee. Sometimes, secretively, I stand in the road and look at our alley, trying to see it through the eyes of an invading army. I am convinced that we will be safe – the alley leads nowhere and few people have call to pass our house. With the shutters locked you wouldn't believe anyone was living here. In the tiny courtyard at the front, where Shujin dries vegetables in shallow pans, I have stockpiled several *jin* of firewood, wax-sealed jars of peanut oil, several sacks of sorghum grain and supplies of dried meat. There is even a pannier of dried hairy crabs, a luxury! I pray that I am adequately prepared. I even have several old-fashioned caskets of water stored because the city supply is unreliable and the ancient well on our land is beyond question.

As I sit writing at the window, the lattice shutters open, I am looking directly down into the street, and what can I see? A woman wheeling a handcart in the direction of the Shangyuan gate. It is piled with mattresses and furniture and soybean sacks. On top of the bundle is strapped a dead man, quite naked. Her husband maybe, or a relative who has been waiting for the money for a funeral. Look at that sight! Have we become insane? Are we so eager to abandon our city that we can't even bury our dead here?

 Nanking, 10 December 1937

At my elbow lie two small cards. Refugee certificates. One for Shujin, one for me. If the day comes when the Japanese arrive we will wear them pinned to our clothing. I collected them this morning at the Red Swastika Society. When the sun came out as I was walking home, I took off my cap. One of the lecturers had told me to do this. He has decided not to stay in Nanking: he's going to head for the river, hoping to break through somewhere upstream of Xiaguan and make for Chongqing. As we said goodbye he looked at me carefully and said, 'If you are outside in the sun today take off your cap. Get a tan on your forehead. I heard they'll tear off a civilian's cap and if he's pale on the forehead they take him for military.'

'But we're civilians,' I said.

'Yes,' he said, looking at me with something like pity in his eyes. 'Yes.'

'We're civilians,' I repeated, as he walked away. I had to raise my voice. 'And if it comes to it the Japanese will know us as such and leave us in peace.'

I stood for a while, my heart beating angrily as he disappeared down the corridor. It was a long time before I made my way out on to the street. I walked for a short way, then glanced over my shoulder. I was out of sight of the campus, so I snatched off the cap quickly, shovelled it into my pocket and walked the rest of the way home with my head back, my face turned up to the sun, the words my mother said on her deathbed running through my head: 'Turn your face to the sun, my boy. Remember that life is short. Always turn your face to the sun when you have the chance.'

Snow came in the night. All night long I listened to the muffled silence, Shujin completely quiet next to me. She has to lie on her side now because she is getting big, and I can feel her feet, the tips of her fingers cold on the occasions they brush my skin. She is so quiet, these days, that she seems almost transparent, as if one day she might just dissolve away leaving a baby in her place. So contained. Maybe she thinks that these are the crucial days, when our baby is exposed to primal human forces – love, truth, compassion and justice – and maybe she needs to keep quiet and concentrate so that these elements will come in their purest form. She rarely mentions leaving any more. From time to time she asks me, 'Chongming, what's happening? What's happening in the east?' And each time I have no words for her, only lies: 'Nothing. Nothing. All is as it should be. General Tang is in control.'

When we drew back the bed-curtains this morning condensation had gathered on the glass in the windows, and outside the snow was deep on the ground. Usually by midday it has been turned to slush by the carts, but today Nanking is eerily silent. Only the army vehicles move through the streets and when I went to a market near the Ming Palace ruins to buy locks for the doors, nails to barricade the house, I was surprised to see that only a handful of traders was setting up stall, the snowflakes hissing on their red charcoal-burners. I bought padlocks from a vendor who charged ten times the normal amount. They are almost certainly stolen, but he seemed to have no difficulty selling them.

'Mr Shi!'

I turned from the stall and was surprised to see, of all people, a professor of literature from Shanghai University, Liu Runde. I have met him only once before and I couldn't immediately fathom what he was doing in a Nanking market.

I cupped my gloved hands, lifted them above my face and bowed to him. 'How odd to see you,' I said, lowering my hands, 'here in Nanking.'

'How odd to see you, Mr Shi.' He was wearing a traditional

man's gown, his hands folded around a hand brazier inside his copious sleeves, and, incongruously, a western hat with a wide grey band. He removed his brazier from inside the folds of his gown, stooping to place it on the ground, so he could return the bow. 'How odd to see anyone. I imagined the entire staff of Jinling University had fled the city.'

'Oh no. No, no. Not me.' I tightened my jacket at the throat and tried to sound casual, just as if staying here had always been my intention. 'My wife is expecting a baby, you know. She needs to be near the hospitals, the city health centre. A fine institute, some of the very latest technology.' I stamped my feet a few times, as if I was not nervous but merely trying to keep out the cold. When he didn't say anything else I looked around the deserted street then leaned nearer to him, saying in a low whisper, 'Why? Do you think I'm unwise?'

'Unwise?' He looked ruminatively along the street, over my shoulder, out across the galvanized roofs, in the direction of the east, a thoughtful, pinched expression on his face. After a while his expression cleared, a little colour came to his cheeks, and he looked back down at me with a warm smile. 'No. Not unwise at all. Quite the contrary.'

I blinked at him, my heart rising. 'The contrary?'

'Yes. Oh, let's not doubt there are those who have no faith in our president – sometimes it seems as if the whole of China has lost trust in him and is fleeing to the interior. But as for me? I have made up my mind. I fled Shanghai, I admit that, but my days of flight are over.'

'There are those who say Tang is weak, not committed. What do you think of those opinions? Some people say the Japanese will walk all over him. Some people say they'll come into the city and kill us in our homes.'

'Pah! Some people are too afraid of change, if you ask me. It takes men like us, like you and me, Master Shi, to stand firm. To forget the cowardly, backward nation we have left behind us – to show faith in our city, in our president's choice of general. Otherwise what do we amount to? A gaggle of whey-faced cowards, that's what. Besides, the Nationalist forces have every trick up their sleeves. Just look out there, beyond the eastern walls. Can you see the smoke?'

'Yes.'

'Buildings burning outside the eastern walls. Burned by our men. To those who say Chiang Kai-shek has no military policy, give them this: scorched earth. The policy of scorched earth. Let the Japanese find nothing, nothing to subsist on as they march. That'll finish them in no time.'

The relief I felt was indescribable. Suddenly, after all this anxiety, I am vindicated, reassured that I am not alone. Standing there, all at once it seemed as if I was with a very dear old friend. We talked and talked, the snow falling on our shoulders, and when, in the course of our conversation, we discovered that he and his family are living, coincidentally, less than half a *li* away from Shujin and myself, we decided to continue the conversation at his house. We walked amicably, arm in arm, back to his house, a one-storey adobe shack with a *kaoling* thatch, no courtyard and no electricity, in which live old Liu, his wife and their teenage son, a dark little thing who appears to my eyes to have been rubbed in dirt.

Liu has brought many things from Shanghai, foreign luxuries: cans of condensed milk and French cigarettes, which we smoked while we talked, like a pair of fashionable Parisian intellectuals. Earlier this summer, it transpires, old Liu locked up his house near Shanghai's Bund and sent his wife and son ahead of him, here, to Nanking, while he stayed on at the university, sleeping in a lecture hall and holding out in his job for as long as was possible. When eventually the city was overrun he evaded capture by hiding in a waste barrel in the university kitchen, and had reached Nanking with a great tide of peasants, just ahead of the Japanese Army, everywhere seeing flatboats and sampans crammed with evacuees cowering under the reeds.

'When I got to Suzhou I saw the Japanese soldiers first hand. I saw them jumping across the canals. Leaping across the water like demons, *arisakas* jangling on their backs. They are so nimble nothing can stop them. The *riben guizi*.'

Hearing this I felt a vague unease. Here, in the privacy of his house, Liu Runde seemed less brave and zealous than he had out

103

on the street – from time to time he would rub his nose or glance nervously in the direction of the windows. It crossed my mind then that in spite of his big words he might be as anxious as I was.

'Do you know,' he said, raising his eyebrows and leaning in to me, giving me a dry smile, 'I even saw Shanghai, the whole city of Shanghai, floating inland across the plains?'

'Shanghai? How can that be?'

'Yes. You think I'm crazy. Or dreaming. But it's true. I stood on an escarpment and saw Shanghai drifting inland.'

I frowned. 'I don't understand.'

He laughed. 'Yes! That look! That is exactly the same look I had on my face when I saw it. It took some time for me to believe I wasn't going mad. Do you know what I was really seeing?'

'No.'

'I was seeing the panic of the Shanghai residents. They've dismantled whole buildings. Whole factories. Can you imagine it? They're moving them inland on junks and steamers, south-west to Chongqing. I saw turbines floating down the Yangtze, an entire plant, a textile mill . . .' He held out his hand and mimicked the gay bobbing motion of a boat on a horizon. 'All of Shanghai sailing upstream to Chongqing.'

He smiled at me, encouraging a response, but I was silent. Something here was wrong. Earlier Liu's wife had placed a pie of grated chestnut on the table. It was decorated with the character for good luck in egg white, and now my eye was drawn to that familiar character. I raised my eyes to the corridor, to where she had retired, then dropped them back to the pie. I considered her earlier demeanour – oddly withdrawn – and suddenly the picture became clear.

Of course. Of course. I saw it now. I looked up at Old Liu, with his pinched face and greying hair, and understood. He was fighting the same battle with his wife as I was with Shujin. There is no doubt he fears the Japanese, but he fears years of superstition and backward beliefs more. We are in the same bed, Liu and I, and, unlike the old saying, we are dreaming exactly the same dream.

'Old Liu.' I leaned a little closer, and spoke in a low whisper: 'Forgive me.' I swallowed and tapped my fingers on the table.

This was an awkward thing to say. 'Forgive me if I haven't understood you. I believe that earlier you said there was nothing to fear from the Japanese.'

At that Liu's face changed. He became very red and he rubbed his nose compulsively, as if he was trying not to sneeze. He straightened in his chair and cast a glance in the direction his wife had retreated. 'Yes, yes,' he said bluffly. 'Yes, that is exactly what I said.' He held up a reproving finger. 'We must be at pains to remember this: those who doubt the Kuomintang will always look to us, searching for faith in our eyes. Keep the faith, Master Shi, keep the faith. We *are* doing the right thing.'

As I walked home through the snow, I tried to keep my head high. *Keep the faith. We are doing the right thing.* But I was remembering something else about our meeting that had made me uneasy. As we were talking in the market I had noticed that the women of Nanking were hiding. I was watching them during the conversation, glancing over the professor's shoulder, and I had quite forgotten about it until now. They had come to the market as usual, but they all wore shawls over their heads and their faces were blackened with charcoal. They walked almost bent double like old crones, although I knew many of them were young.

I felt suddenly angry. I knew what they are afraid of at the hands of the Japanese. I knew they were hiding, turning inwards like hibernating animals, disappearing inside themselves. But must this happen? Must the colour in our country change? We, the Chinese, a whole people, a whole cowardly, backward nation, we are disappearing into our landscape. Running and hiding. Chameleonizing ourselves into a million outlines scratched into the dry rock and stone of the Gobi desert. We'd rather disappear and sink into our land than stand up straight and look the Japanese in the eye.

17

Jason said the house had belonged to the landlord's mother, that she had become very ill, maybe crazy, and the lower levels had fallen into such disrepair that they had become uninhabitable. Clouds of mosquitoes always hung around the closed-up windows and Svetlana said there were ghosts down there. She told us that the Japanese believed in a strange creature: a winged goblin, a feathered mountain man – Tengu, they called him – an abductor of human beings, who could flit as easily as a moth. Svetlana swore she'd heard a rustling in the garden and seen something heavy picking its way through the persimmon trees. 'Sssh!' she'd say, breaking off dramatically in the middle of a story, her finger to her lips. 'Did you hear that? From downstairs?'

Jason laughed at her, Irina was condescending. I said nothing. On the subject of ghosts I wasn't going to commit. I loved the house and its quirks – I soon got used to the peeling walls, the musty, closed-off rooms, the rows of disused *kotatsu* electric heaters in the store rooms – but there were times in my room, so close to the barricaded wing, that I felt like the last line of defence. Defence against what, I didn't know. The rats? The emptiness? I wasn't sure. I'd lived alone for so long now that I should have been accustomed to great empty spaces pressing against my bedroom walls at night, but there were times in Takadanobaba that I'd wake in the night, rigid with fear, convinced that someone had just walked past the bedroom door.

'Something's waiting here,' Shi Chongming said, when he first saw the house. The day after Fuyuki's gang had come into the club he called. He wanted to see me. That's what I liked – his choice of words: *he* wanted to see *me*. I hurried around agitatedly, buying tea and cakes and cleaning my room, while he made his way across Tokyo to Takadanobaba. Now he stood in the corridor, in that rigid way of his with his hands next to his sides, his eyes focusing far away in the gloom of the corridor. 'Something's waiting to be uncovered.'

'It's very old.' I was making tea in the kitchen, green tea, and I'd bought some chestnut *mochi* – little bean-paste cakes wrapped in demure semi-opaque paper. I hoped he couldn't see how nervous I was. 'I wish I could have seen it when it was first built. It survived the *Kanto* earthquake, it even survived the bombing. Lots has happened here. Lots.'

I arranged the pastel pale *mochi* on a small, lacquered tray, loosening the paper on each so the wrappers drooped open, like flower petals revealing secret fat stamens. I'd never prepared Japanese food, and I had no reason to think that Shi Chongming would have any appreciation of it, but I wanted to get it right, not make a mess of it, and I spent a long time choosing the angle at which to place the teapot on the tray. A man eats first, the Japanese say, with his eyes. Every object must be looked at carefully, its impact on its neighbours considered in detail. Next to the pot I placed the small Japanese cups – more like earthenware bowls than cups – picked up the tray, turned into the passage, and saw that Shi Chongming had moved to the shutters and was standing with his hands up, as if he was feeling the warmth of the sun penetrating them. There was a look of peculiar concentration on his face.

'Mr Shi?'

He turned to me. In the piebald shadows of the corridor he seemed suddenly pale. 'What is beyond this?'

'The garden. Open it.'

He hesitated a moment, then pulled back the screen and stared out through the grimy window. In the glaring white sunlight the garden was breathless and still, not a thing moving in that ticking, throbbing heat. The trees and creepers seemed dusty and almost unreal. Shi Chongming stood for a long time until I wasn't sure if he was breathing or not. 'I'd like to go into the garden, if I may. Let us take our tea in the garden.'

I'd never been down there. I wasn't even sure there was access to it. The Russians had both gone out so I had to wake up Jason and ask. He came to the door crumpled and yawning, pulling on a T-shirt – a cigarette between his teeth. He looked Shi Chongming up and down wordlessly, then shrugged. 'Yeah, sure. There's a way.' He led us down to where, only two rooms along from mine, an unlocked door opened on to a tiny wooden staircase.

I was astonished. I hadn't realized there were staircases going down – I had imagined the ground floor to be completely sealed. But there, at the bottom of the dark stairwell, was one room, empty of furniture, only drifts of dead leaves on the stone floor. Facing us was a ripped paper *shoji* screen, coloured green by the underwater light of the garden beyond. Shi Chongming and I stood for a moment, looking at it.

'I'm sure there'll be nowhere to sit,' I said.

Shi Chongming rested his hand on the screen. Something mechanical, a nuclear buzz like a small generator, maybe one of the air-conditioners on the Salt Building, echoed from beyond. He paused for a moment, then pulled. The screen was rusty: it resisted briefly, then gave suddenly, rolling back, and the bitter, coiled underbelly of a jungle filled the doorway with green. We stood in silence, staring out at it. A wisteria, as thick and muscled as the woody wrists of a fighter, had been so long ignored that it no longer flowered but had become a living cage stretching outwards from the doorway. Hair moss and tropical creepers coiled round it, mosquitoes hovered in its dark spaces, untidy persimmon and maple battled for space, festooned with moss and ivy.

Shi Chongming walked out into the thicket, moving quickly on his cane, the green and yellow light dappling the back of his strange head. I followed, treading carefully, balancing the tray. The air was thick with heat, insects and stinging, bitter tree saps.

A huge winged beetle sprang from under my feet, hinged like a man-made bird, and whirred out of the undergrowth towards my face. I took a step back to avoid it, spilling a little tea on the lacquer tray, and watched it spiral past my face and up, crystalline and mechanical, clack-clack-clack, into the branches. It sat above me, as big as a wren, stretching its polished chestnut wings and began to make the electrical buzz I'd taken for a generator. I stared up at it, thrilled. The poet Basho's *semi-no-koe*, I thought. The voice of the cicada. The oldest sound in Japan.

Ahead of me Shi Chongming had emerged into a clearing. I followed, stepping out into the glare, shrugging at the cobwebs on my arms and squinting in the sun at the glittering white Salt Building, flat against the blue sky. The garden was even bigger than I'd imagined: on my left lay a boggy area, a lotus pond, congested with rotting leaves, clouds of gnats hovering in the shadows of a giant *acer* that trailed into it.

Next to this, in the mossed and derelict remains of a Japanese rock garden, Shi Chongming had stopped. He was looking back across the garden, his head moving from side to side, as if he was straining for a fleeting glimpse of something, like a man who has let a dog run off into a forest and is trying to catch sight of it from the outskirts. He was so intent that I turned to look in the same direction. Tucked behind swathes of bamboo I could see glimpses of the red-ochre security grilles on the ground-floor windows, I could see a crumbling ornamental bridge spanning the lotus pond, but I couldn't see what had so captured Shi Chongming's attention. I looked again at his eyes, followed their trajectory and eventually settled in the region of a stone bench and stone lantern, the latter standing next to the lotus pond.

'Mr Shi?'

He frowned and shook his head. Then he seemed to recover himself, noticing for the first time that I was carrying a tray. 'Please.' He took it from me. 'Please, let's sit down. Let's drink.'

I found some mildewed steamer chairs and we sat at the edge of the rock garden in the shade, out of reach of the white flashes of sunlight. It was so hot that I had to do everything very slowly – pouring the tea, passing Shi Chongming a *mochi* on an individual lacquer tray. He took the tray and inspected it, then took the fork and carefully drew a line down the centre of the cake, cutting it so it fell open in two halves. A *mochi* is a floury, pale colour until it is opened, when it reveals a startling purple-red paste, like raw meat against a sliver of pastel skin. Shi Chongming's face changed minutely when he saw it: I saw him hesitate, then politely lift a very small section to his mouth. He chewed it cautiously, swallowing painfully. Just as if he's afraid of eating, I thought.

'Tell me,' he said at last, sipping his tea and patting his mouth with a handkerchief, 'you seem much happier than when I first met you. Are you? Are you happy here in Tokyo?'

'*Happy?* I don't know. I haven't thought about it.'

'You have somewhere to live.' He raised his hand to the house, to the upper floor gallery where a few puffy clouds were reflected in the dirty windows. 'A safe place to live. And you have enough money.'

'Yes.'

'And you like your job?'

I looked down at the plate. 'Sort of.'

'You work in a club? You said you work in the evenings.'

'I'm a hostess. It's not exciting.'

'I'm sure it's not. I know a little about these clubs, I'm not the ignorant old man I appear. Where do you work? There are two chief areas – Roppongi and Akasaka.'

'Yotsuya.' I waved my hand in the vague direction. 'The big building in Yotsuya. The black one.'

'Ah, yes,' he said thoughtfully. 'Yes, I *do* know.'

Something in his voice made me look up. But wasn't looking at me, instead his milky eyes were focused in mid-air, as if he was thinking about something very puzzling.

'Professor Shi? Have you come to tell me about the film?'

He inclined his head, his eyes still distant. It wasn't a yes, and it wasn't a no. I waited for him to continue but he didn't, he seemed for a while to have forgotten that I was there. Then he said suddenly, in a quiet voice, 'Do you know? To conceal the past is not such a rare trick.'

'What?'

He regarded me thoughtfully, as if he was thinking not about Nanking but, rather, about me. I stared back at him, my face getting redder and redder.

'*What?*'

'It's not such an unusual thing. It's a trick that relies only on silence.'

'I don't know what you're talking about.'

He reached inside his pocket and produced what looked like a small origami crane about the size of a matchbox, made from vivid red and purple *washi* paper. Its head was held back, its wings were extended dramatically. 'Look at this – this perfect bird.' He put the crane on my palm. I stared down at it. It was heavier than it looked; it seemed to be bound round the base with a complex structure of rubber bands. I looked up at him questioningly. He was nodding, his eyes on the little bird. 'Imagine that this, this calm little bird, is the past. Imagine.'

I looked down at the crane, not understanding. Then I saw something was happening. It was quivering. I could feel the tremor in my wrist, my arms, all over my skin. The purple wings were shivering. I opened my mouth to say something, but the bird seemed to explode. From its centre leaped something red and terrifying, like a jack-in-the-box: the hideous face of a Chinese dragon shooting up at me, making me drop it and jump to my feet. My chair toppled over and I stood trembling, my hands out, staring down to where the odd, paper-accordion dragon twitched and twisted on the ground, the rubber bands unwinding.

Shi Chongming hooked it up on his cane, catching it and crumpling it into his pocket. 'Don't worry. I'm not a magician.'

I glanced up at him, my face red, my heart pounding.

'It's only a children's trick. Don't look so bewildered. Please, sit down.'

After a while, when I was sure the dragon wasn't going to leap from his pocket, I picked up my chair and sat, looking at him warily.

'I mean you to understand that when you talk about the past it is like putting a ball of phosphorous out under a cloudy sky. The past has transforming energy. The energy of wind or fire. We need to have respect for something so destructive. And *you* are asking to walk straight into it without a thought? It is a dangerous land. You have to be sure that you want to go ahead.'

'Of course I am,' I said, still watching him guardedly. 'Of course I want to.'

'There was a professor who wanted to do his best for his university in China.' Shi Chongming sat holding his teacup primly, his feet close together. As he spoke he didn't let his eyes meet mine, but addressed his words to the air. 'I hope you understand my meaning. This professor heard that there was a company in Hong Kong, a manufacturer of Chinese medicine, that wanted to join with a university to cast a scientific eye over traditional cures. He knew how important it was that his university win this partnership, but he also knew that his research team would have to find something special to interest the company.' Shi Chongming sat forward and lowered his voice: 'Then one day he heard rumours, through strange and unnamable networks, whispers of a tonic that had remarkable effects. It was rumoured, among other things, to cure chronic diabetes, arthritis, even malaria.' He raised his eyebrows at me. 'Can you imagine how astounding it would be if it were true?'

I didn't answer. I was still uncomfortable, still wary of Shi Chongming and the paper dragon in his jacket. I didn't know what I had expected from this meeting – his acquiescence, maybe, or simply more obstinacy. What I hadn't expected was the focused, determined look on his face now as he spoke.

'The professor knew that if only his university could find the ingredients in this tonic they would have a chance of winning the partnership deal. It took him much hard work and many secretive enquiries, but at last he tracked down someone who was said to be in possession of the tonic. There was only one problem. That person lived in Japan.'

He put down his cup and sat up a little straighter in his chair, placing both hands stiffly on his thighs as if he were a small child in a confessional. 'I have not been completely honest with Todai

University. They are under the impression that I am interested in what Chinese traditions the Japanese Army brought home. And, largely speaking, that is true. But there is a little more to it than that. I secured my post at Todai for one reason: to get to Japan and track down the ingredients.'

'You lied, you mean. You lied to them to get your fellowship.'

He smiled wryly. 'If you want to put it like that. Yes, I lied. The truth is that I am in Tokyo to secure the future of my university. If I could find what this mysterious substance is, things would change – not only for me but for hundreds of others.' He rubbed his eyes wearily. 'Unfortunately my arrival in Tokyo was not the end of the hunt. Rather, it was the beginning. The man I want to talk to is very elderly, more than eighty years old, and he is one of the most powerful men in Japan. He is surrounded by people who are absolutely forbidden to talk and most information that comes out is rumours and superstition.' Shi Chongming smiled. 'To put things in brief, I have come up against a wall.'

'I don't know why you're telling me this. It's got nothing to do with me.'

He nodded, as if for once I was right. 'Except that when he is feeling well he sometimes visits the hostess clubs in Tokyo. Yes. And one of the places he is sometimes seen is the very club that you work in. Maybe now you can understand the way my mind is working.'

I paused, the cup up to my lips, my eyes on his. Things were becoming clearer. Shi Chongming was talking about Junzo Fuyuki.

'Yes?' he said, rather archly, taking in my surprised look. 'What is it? Have I upset you?'

'I know who you mean. I think I've met him. Junzo Fuyuki.'

Shi Chongming's eyes gleamed, intelligent and acute. 'You've met him,' he said, sitting forward a little. 'My instincts were correct.'

'He's in a wheelchair?'

'Yes.'

'Professor Shi.' I lowered the cup slowly. 'Junzo Fuyuki is a gangster. Did you know that?'

'Of course. That is what I have been telling you. He is the *oyabun*, the godfather of the Fuyuki *gumi*.' He picked up his cup, took a few delicate sips of tea and returned it to the table. He seemed to draw himself up to his full height, to his formal, military-parade bearing. 'Now, this is what I am going to ask you. Fuyuki is sometimes friendly with the hostesses in the clubs. He entertains sometimes, at his apartment, where I am sure he keeps the ingredient we are discussing. He likes to drink too, and I am certain that sometimes he lets down his guard. I think maybe he would talk to you. I think you will be able to discover the true nature of the ingredient.'

'I've already seen it. I mean I've seen him taking *something*. Something – a . . .' I held my thumb and forefinger an inch apart to indicate the size of the Nurse's phial. 'A fluid. With a brownish powder in it.'

Shi Chongming looked at me for a long time. He rubbed his lips as if they were chapped. Eventually he said, in a controlled voice, 'Brownish?'

'Isn't that what you expected?'

'No, no, indeed,' he said, fumbling a handkerchief from his pocket and mopping his forehead. 'It is exactly what I was expecting. A powder. A decoction.' He finished patting his brow and returned the handkerchief to the pocket. 'Now then . . .' he said, and I could tell it was an effort to keep his voice steady. 'Now, this is where you can help me. I need to know what that powder is.'

I didn't reply at first. I leaned forward, placed the cup carefully on the tray and sat, my hands flat between my knees, hunched over, looking at the cup, thinking about what he was saying. When a long time had passed I cleared my throat and looked up at him. 'You're telling me that in return for me finding out what that powder is you'll let me see the film?'

'Don't take this lightly. You cannot understand how dangerous it is. If anyone ever knew, or suspected, that I was asking questions . . .' He held up his finger, his face intense. '*He must never know I am asking questions.* You cannot approach him directly. You must work with the utmost discretion. Even if it takes weeks, months.'

'I didn't ask you that. I said, if I do it will you let me see the film?'

'Will you do it?'

'Will you let me see the film?'

He didn't blink. His face didn't change. He looked back at me stonily.

'Well? Will you show me th—'

'Yes,' he said abruptly. 'Yes. I will.'

I hesitated, my mouth open. 'You will?'

'Yes.'

'So it exists,' I said. 'It does exist. I didn't invent it?'

He sighed, lowered his eyes and put a hand wearily to his temple. 'It exists,' he muttered. 'You didn't invent it.'

I dropped my head then because a smile was spreading across my face and I didn't want him to see. My shoulders were quivering and I had to put my thumb and forefinger on either side of my nose and shake my head, relief popping like laughter bubbles in my ears.

'Now, will you or won't you?' he said. 'Will you help me?'

At last, when I had stopped smiling, I dropped my hand and looked at him.

He seemed somehow even smaller, more crumpled and frail with his threadbare jacket pulled up round his shoulders. His eyes had focused to pinpoints and there was a light sweat on the bridge of his nose. 'Will you?'

What an amazing thing. To enter into a deal with an ageing professor, who could, for all I knew, be just as insane as everyone said *I* was. Isn't it a constant surprise the things people will do for peace of mind? We sat for ages looking at each other, the sound of the insects pounding in my head, while above us the planes heading for Narita made vapour trails across the hot blue sky. Then at last I nodded. 'Yes,' I said quietly. 'Yes. I'll do it.'

There were gates to the street set in the ground floor, creating a tunnel under the upper storey of the house. It came as a surprise to find, when Shi Chongming left in the early afternoon, that the rusting key in the lock still worked and that the old gates could still, with a struggle, be opened, allowing him to step straight out into the street. 'In China,' he told me, as he stood in the doorway, his hat pulled down, 'we don't think of time the way you do in the West. We believe that our future . . . that our future can be seen in our past.' His eyes drifted to the garden again, as if someone had whispered his name. He put up his hand, as if he was feeling the air, or a breath on his palms.

I turned and looked hard at the stone lantern. 'What can you see, Shi Chongming?' I said. 'What do you see?'

He was calm and soft-spoken when he answered. 'I see . . . A garden. I see a garden. And I see its future. Waiting to be uncovered.'

When he'd gone I locked the gates behind him and stood, for a moment, in the shade of the tunnel, where the plaster was falling from the underside of the top floor to reveal cobwebby grey lathes. I looked out at the garden. I had an image of the landlord's mother and father here – her clogs tapping on the *tobi-ishi* stepping-stones, a scarlet parasol, maybe a bleached bone comb fashioned like a butterfly, accidentally dropped and forgotten, kicked under the leaf cover, where it remained hidden and, over the years, changed and grew slowly into the stone. Shintoism puts spirits in trees, plants, birds and insects, but in Tokyo there were few green areas and the only flowers were the strings of plastic cherry blossom hanging outside the shops at festival times. You never heard birdsong. Maybe, I thought, all the spirits in the city had to cram into forgotten places like this.

At that moment, standing in the shade, knowing Shi Chongming had the film that would make sense of what had happened to me, of what I believed I'd read in a little orange book all those years ago, I knew that the answer I wanted was somewhere very near by – that it wouldn't be long before I would reach out into the air and find, when I drew my hand back, that it had crept up to me and was lodged firmly in my palm.

18

史 Nanking, 12 December 1937 (the tenth day of the eleventh month) late afternoon

I am writing this by the light of a single candle. We cannot risk kerosene or electric lamps. We must make our buildings look as if they are uninhabited.

All day yesterday we could hear explosions from the direction of the Rain Flower Terrace. I told Shujin it must be our military blowing trenches outside the city wall, or destroying the bridges over the canal, but in the streets I heard people whispering, 'It's the Japanese. The Japanese.' Then, earlier this afternoon, after a long period of silence, there came an almighty explosion, shaking the city, making Shujin and me stop what we were doing and turn to each other with deadly pale faces.

'The gate,' shouted a boy from the street. 'Zhonghua gate! The Japanese!'

I went to the window and watched him as he stood, his arms stretched wide, expecting shutters to fly open, voices to answer his, as would ordinarily be the way. Usually our lives are lived in the streets, but on this occasion all that could be heard up and down the neighbourhood was the furtive barricading of doors and shutters. It wasn't long before the boy noticed the silence. He dropped his arms and scuttled away.

I turned. Shujin was sitting like a column of stone, her hands folded neatly, her long face as still as marble. She was dressed in a house *qipao* and trousers in a bronze colour that made her

117

skin seem almost bloodless. I watched her for a while, my back to the open shutters, the cold street silent behind me. The light in the city, these days, is very odd, very white and clear: it flooded into the room, illuminating her skin in great detail – as if I was sitting very close to her. I stared. Her face, her neck and her hands were all covered in tiny bumps like goose-skin and her eyelids seemed almost translucent as if I could see her secret fears moving under them.

At that moment, as I looked at her, something elemental seemed to rise up in me, something that tasted of saffron and the thick smoke of cooking pots in Poyang, something that made me choke, brought tears to my eyes. I hovered, moving anxiously from foot to foot, vacillating over the choice of words: *Shujin, I am wrong, and you are right. I cannot tell you how afraid I am. Let's leave the city. Quickly now, go and make some* guoba, *let's pack, let's go. We'll be at Meitan harbour by midnight.* Or more dignified, *Shujin, there has been a small change of plan . . .*

'Shujin,' I began. 'Shujin maybe . . . we should—'

'Yes?' She raised her eyes hopefully to mine. 'Maybe we should . . . ?'

I was about to answer, when a frenzied screeching came from behind me and something shot through the window, slamming into the back of my head, sending me stumbling forwards. Instantly the room was filled with a terrible sound. I cried out where I lay on the floor, my hands over my head. In the commotion a bowl shattered, water flooded across the table and Shujin jumped up, knocking her chair over in her panic. Overhead something large and shadowed ricocheted furiously from wall to wall. Cautiously, my hands protecting my face, I raised my eyes.

It was a bird, a huge, clumsy bird, flapping desperately, catapulting into the walls, bouncing off the floor. Feathers flew everywhere. Shujin was on her feet, staring at it in astonishment, as it squawked and clattered, sending things crashing down. At length it exhausted itself. It dropped to the floor, where it hopped around dejectedly for a while, bumping into walls.

Shujin and I took a step forward and peered at it in disbelief. It was a golden pheasant. The bird that some say stands for China.

Unbelievable. Until today I had only ever seen a golden pheasant in paintings, I couldn't have been more surprised had the *feng huang* itself flown through the window. Its orange feathers were as bright as if a fire had been lit in the centre of our house. Every time I took a step forward, it hopped away, trying to flee, colliding with the furniture. I couldn't understand why it had burst in here. It was only when the bird took a desperate leap in the air and passed quite close to me that I saw its eyes and understood.

'Move away,' I told Shujin, snatching up my brocaded *chang-pao* from the chair, gathering it and casting it like a net over the bird. It panicked, jumping and beating its wings and lifting a foot or so into the air, and for a moment the gown seemed to move around the room independently – a brightly patchworked spirit slithering across the floor. Then I crouched next to it, quickly trapping the bird with both hands. I straightened, carefully peeled out the bird, exposing first its little head, its sightless eyes, then its wings so that Shujin could see.

'It's blind,' I murmured.

'Blind?'

'Yes. Maybe the explosions at Zhonghua—'

'No!' Shujin's hands flew to her face. 'No. This is the worst of luck, the worst! A golden pheasant! China's bird. And blinded at the hands of the Japanese.' She dug her fingers in her scalp like a crazed thing, looking frantically around the room as if searching for some miraculous means of escape. 'It's true – now it's really going to happen. The earth, our soil. The Japanese are going to harm the earth – they're going to destroy the dragon lines in the ground and—'

'Hush, now. There is no such thing as a dragon line—'

'They will destroy the dragon lines and then there will be nothing but drought and famine in China. All the pheasants will be blinded, not only this one. All of them. And all the humans too. We'll be killed in our beds and—'

'Shujin, please. Please keep calm. It is only a bird.'

'No! Not only a bird – a golden pheasant! We're all going to die.' She was moving round the room in circles, erratic and fevered, throwing her hands up and down despairingly. 'The president, your precious president, your supreme arbiter, has run away like a hunted dog, all the way to Chongqing, and all that's left in Nanking are the poor and the sick and—'

'*Enough!*'

'Oh!' she cried, dropping her hands and staring at me with the most intense anguish. 'Oh – you'll see! You'll see! I am *right*.' And with that she ran from the room, her feet thundering on the stairs.

I stood for a long time, staring after her, the blood pounding in my temples, astonished that everything had changed so rapidly. I had been ready to concede to her, prepared to flee the city. But her taunts had me leaping in defence of a position that I am quite unsure of.

I might have stood there for ever, staring at the empty staircase, had the pheasant not begun to struggle. Wearily I took its feet in one hand and whipped it through the air in the swift, curling movement my mother had taught me as a child, windmilling it down at my side as if I was shaking water from a cloth, once, twice, until the bird's neck was broken and I was left holding only a limp clot of feathers. I locked the shutters and carried the dead bird, wings lifting feebly once in a death spasm, into the kitchen.

I rarely go into Shujin's kitchen, but now it was the only place I wanted to be. It comforted me. When I was a boy I would sit on the floor of the kitchen and watch my mother drop chickens into boiling water to soften the feathers. Now I filled a pot with water, lit the fire and waited until the bubbles rose to the surface. Moving in a daze, I scalded the bird, holding it by the feet, then sat at the table, plucking it, scraping at the pinfeathers on the breast, letting my mind rest on the familiar picture of my mother's kitchen. I recalled her face in the days before my father's business began to thrive and we could afford an *amah*, when she would spend all day in the kitchen, patiently packing cooked ducks in salt, wrapping them in cloth for storage, winding the birds' intestines on to a skewer to be dried out in the pantry. Chiang Kai-shek, I thought dully, wants China to look forward. But is it so simple for a nation to rip the history from inside its heart?

I finished plucking the bird and carefully tucked its head under its wing, tying it with string the way my mother used to, the way

Chinese women have done for generations. Then I put it into the pot and sat, the brilliant wet feathers sticking to my arms, and watched the bloody foam rise to the surface.

史 **Nanking, 13 December, afternoon**

Last night I boarded up the house, nailing wood across every window and door. (Shujin would not help because her superstitions tell her that hammering in a nail will cause a deformity in our baby.) All evening we heard strange noises coming from the east, and before we went to bed I rested an iron bar against the spirit screen. Who knows if I will be able to use it, should the need arise? This morning we were woken by a distant rumble, like thunder, and half an hour ago Shujin filled up a pan to boil noodles for lunch. When she went to rinse her fingers the tap bucked and shuddered and only a thin brown liquid came out of it. What does this mean? Does it mean that the Japanese—

It's happening even as I write! The single lightbulb overhead has just died. Now we are . . . We are in semi-darkness and I can hardly see my words on the paper. Outside the house the dying whine of failing machinery is terrible. The city is shutting down around our ears. Shujin is rummaging in the kitchen, trying to find our oil lamps, and from the end of the alley I can hear someone shouting hysterically.

I can't sit here any longer. I can't sit here and listen. I am going to investigate.

19

When I went upstairs, the house seemed very dark and cool after the hot garden. I had a bath in the echoey old bathroom, with its green mould between the tiles and the pipes all showing. I washed carefully, staring at my reflection thoughtfully, at the way the running water magnified my white skin, the silvery hairs and pores. Shi Chongming wanted me to get Fuyuki to talk. What he was saying, I was sure, was that I had to flirt with him. He meant I had to be sexy.

In the hospital they had never got tired of lecturing me about my sexual behaviour, so I decided fairly early on that it wouldn't be very bright to tell them how I'd really felt about the boys in the van. I could guess what they'd say: 'Ah! See? An entirely inappropriate response!' So I didn't admit the truth: that after the boys had all taken their turns, and we'd got dressed and were heading back along the A303 the way we'd come, I was happier than I'd ever been. I didn't tell them how bright everything looked, with the stars shining and the white line in the road slipping under the van. The four in the back kept yelling out not to go over the bumps too quickly, and I sat in the front humming and listening to a battered tape called XTC that kept *wah*ing and cracking up through the van's broken speakers. I felt light inside, as if something dark and secret had been washed out of me by the boys.

We got to the place on the country road where they'd picked

me up and the driver pulled the van over to the verge. With the engine still running he leaned across me and opened the door. I stared at him, not understanding.

'Well,' he said, 'see you around.'

'What?'

'See you around.'

'Am I supposed to get out now?'

'Yes.'

I was silent for a while, looking at the side of his face. There were some pimples on his neck just above his collar. 'Aren't I going to the pub with you? You said we were going to the pub. I've never been inside a pub.'

He pinched out his cigarette and threw it out of the window. There was a little line of turquoise still on the horizon over his left shoulder, and the clouds were rolling across it as if they were boiling. 'Don't be stupid,' he said. 'You're too young for the pub. You'll get us chucked out.'

I twisted round and looked into the back of the van. Four heads turned away from me, pretending to stare out of the windows. The sandy-haired boy was at the very back, meeting my eyes with a serious expression, as if he'd caught me stealing. I looked at the driver, but he was staring intently out of his window, tapping his fingers impatiently on the steering-wheel. I opened my mouth to say something, then changed my mind. I swung my legs out of the van and dropped out on to the road.

The driver reached over and slammed the door. I put my hands on the window and started to speak, but he'd already taken the handbrake off. The gears squealed, the indicator came on, the van rolled away. I was left on the roadside, watching its lights dwindle, then disappear. Overhead the clouds rolled and rolled until they'd entirely obscured the moon, and the little part of England that I stood in was completely dark.

And so I had to agree with the doctors – the immediate result of sex hadn't been what I'd expected. And with the way my body was now, there probably wasn't ever going to be a chance to find out if it could be different in the future. I didn't dare tell the doctors this, I didn't dare say how much I wished I could have a boyfriend, someone to go to bed with: I knew if I said anything they'd tell me my outrageous impulses were the root of a greater evil, that I was walking around with a wolf living inside me. I listened to the lessons about personal dignity and about self-respect, all the complex stuff about consent and self-control, and it didn't take long to decide that sex was dangerous and un-predictable, like Shi Chongming's magic crane of the past, phosphorous on a cloudy day. I came to the conclusion that I'd be better off just pretending it didn't exist.

In the end it was the girl in the bed next to me, the one who taught me how to smoke, who gave me a kind of solution. She used to masturbate every night. 'Jigging', she called it. 'I'll stay in here for ever, me. Don't care. Long as I've got me fags and a good jigging I'm sound.' She'd do it under the covers when the lights went out. She wasn't ashamed. I'd lie in the next bed with my sheets up to my chin, staring with wide eyes at the covers going up and down. She made it seem so gleeful, as if there was nothing wrong at all.

As soon as I got out of hospital, and wasn't being watched every five minutes, I began my own guilty experiments. I soon knew how to make myself come, and although I never actually squatted over a mirror (the jigging girl promised me there were people who did) I was sure no other girl on earth had got to know the dark tract between her legs the way I knew mine. Sometimes I'd wonder about the wolf. I was afraid that one day I'd reach down there and my fingers would brush over its wet nose.

Now in the bathroom in Takadanobaba, I rinsed out the flan-nel and looked thoughtfully at my reflection, a thin-limbed spectre squatting on the little rubber stool. The girl who might go to the grave with only five boys in the back of a Ford Transit to reckon as her life's loves. I filled up the little plastic bowl, swirling the hot and the cold water together, and tipped it down my body, letting the water lift and furl in the hollows of my collar-bone, fil-ter down into the scars on my stomach. I put down the bowl and slowly, dreamily, spanned my hands across my abdomen, linking my thumbs and fanning my fingers into a frame, staring vacantly at the way the water gathered in the hatched gouges, silvery, reflecting the light like mercury.

No one, only the doctors and a man who came from the police to take photographs of them, had ever seen my scars. In my daydreams I imagined there was someone who would understand – someone who would look at them and not recoil, who would hear the story and instead of burying their face, averting their eyes, would say something sweet and sad and sympathetic. But of course I knew it would never happen, because I'd never ever get that far. Never. If I imagined taking off my clothes, if I pictured myself revealing the truth to someone, I'd get a sickening, rushing sensation in my inner ear that would weaken my knees and have me tugging frantically at whatever I happened to be wearing, wrapping it tightly round my stomach as if I could hide what was there.

I suppose there are some things you just have to be grown-up about. Sometimes you have to take a deep breath and say: 'This is not something I can expect in my life.' And if you say it enough times, it's surprising – after a while it doesn't even feel that horrible any more.

While I was in the bathroom, thinking about Fuyuki, the Russians had got dressed and now they were going down to the garden. They must have seen me out there and decided that if I could venture out so could they. Svetlana was dressed in only a tiny lime green bikini and a straw sun-hat, which she held on to her head with her free hand. When I was dried and dressed I stood in the upstairs gallery and watched her make her way through the undergrowth, her tanned limbs flashing through the leaves. Irina came behind in a bikini top, pink shorts, sweetheart sunglasses and a bright pink baseball hat, worn backwards so her neck was shaded. She'd shoved a packet of cigarettes into the strap of her bikini top. They both picked their way out through the undergrowth, squealing and bickering, and lifting their feet in their high heels like odd wading birds, coming blinking out into the sunshine. 'Sun, sun!' they chorused, adjusting their glasses and staring up at the sky.

I put my nose silently to the window and watched them rubbing on sun lotion, undoing packets of cherry KissMint chewing-gum and drinking beer out of frozen cans they'd bought from the machines on the street. Svetlana had fire-engine-red polish on her toes. I stared down at my white feet, wondering whether I had the courage to paint my nails. All of a sudden I had a hot, overwhelming feeling that made me shiver and rub my arms – it was something about wasted time and how lucky they were to be so comfortable in their skin. To move and stretch and be at home in the sun, nobody accusing them of madness.

And right there and then I made up my mind. As long as I was dressed, as long as my stomach was covered, there was nothing, no physical mark, that gave it away. If you didn't know, and no one here in Tokyo did, you'd look at me and say I was normal. I could be as 'sexy' as anyone else.

20

I couldn't stop thinking about Fuyuki. Every time the lift bell rang and the hostesses swivelled round to yell in unison across the club, '*Irasshaimase!* Welcome!' I'd sit forward on the edge of my seat, my pulse leaping, thinking I might see his wheelchair gliding across the floor. But he didn't come into the club that night, or the next.

Over the days that followed, I would take out his card and look at it several times a day. Sometimes I went into a kind of trance holding it, turning it over and over in my fingers. His name meant Winter Tree and something in the combination of the calligraphy and the nature of the characters was so powerful that I only had to glance at the black on white to visualize, in astonishing clarity, a forest deep in snow. I would retrace the *kanji* with my calligraphy brushes, picturing a mountainside, a pine forest, snowdrifts and icicles in the trees.

Now that I knew what would make Shi Chongming relent and give me the film, now that I was going to make the leap, I had become a serious student of the erotic. I started to watch the Japanese girls on the streets in their Victorian petticoats and lacy pumps, their 'loose socks' and short kilts. In traditional Japan, eroticism was something slender and pale like a flower stalk – the erotic was the tiny patch of bare skin on the back of a geisha's neck. It's something different the world over. I stared for hours at the Russians in their big high heels and orange suntans.

127

I had a lot of wage packets backed up, just sitting in a bag in the wardrobe doing nothing except making me jittery. Eventually I got up my courage and started shopping. I went to astonishing places in Ginza and Omotesando, caves crammed with sequined slippers, pink négligés, hats trimmed in purple marabou and rose pink velvet. There were cherry pink platform boots, and turquoise bags covered in hundreds of stick-on Elvis Presleys. The salesgirls with their bunches and ballerina skirts had no idea how to deal with me. They chewed their nails and watched me with their heads on one side as I trailed up and down the aisles in amazement, getting to know how people made themselves look sexy.

I began to buy things – I bought taffeta and velvet dresses, little shrug-on skirts in silk. And shoes, so many shoes: kitten heels, stilettos, court shoes, black-ribboned sandals. In a place called the Sweet Girls Emporium and Relax Centre, I bought a box of Stoppy hold-up stockings. I'd never worn stockings in my life. I dragged home piles of bags, weighed down like an ant.

But, of course, I didn't have the courage to wear any of it. Everything stayed packed away in the wardrobe, day after day, all the dresses with red tissue paper taped round them. I thought about them, though, I thought about them a lot. Some nights I had a little ceremony that I kept absolutely secret. When the others were in bed, I would open the wardrobe and take out all the things I'd bought. I'd pour a glass of chilled plum liquor and drag the little dressing-table to a place under the light so that the mirror was properly illuminated. Then I'd go to the wardrobe and take a dress from its hanger.

It was horrible and exciting. Every time I saw myself in the mirror and reached automatically for the zip, ready to rip off the dress, I would think about Fuyuki sitting in his wheelchair, saying, 'Are they all so pretty in England?' Then I would stop, take a deep breath, slowly rezip the dress, and force myself to turn back and look, to study the white tops of my breasts, my legs in silk, dark, like inky water. I put on very high heels and painted my lips in a deep red, pure like heart-blood. I crayoned in eyebrows, and for a long time I practised lighting and smoking a cigarette. I tried to imagine myself, sitting formally in Fuyuki's home, leaning towards him, cigarette smoke trailing across my painted lips. In my mind's eye one of my hands was resting on a locked chest, the other was extended elegantly, palm up, to receive a large key that Fuyuki was passing to me.

After a long time I would open my eyes, go to the wardrobe and take everything out of its tissue paper, then arrange it in a ring round me. There were velvet strappy sandals, négligés in tangerine and cream, a crimson Ravage bra in the shape of a butterfly, still in its Cellophane. Things and things and more things, stretching out across the shadows. I'd lie down then, stretching out my bare arms, and roll over, mingling with my belongings, smelling the newness, letting them brush my skin. Sometimes I'd group them according to different rules: according to material, for example, black piqué crushing peach silk noil, or according to colour, saffron with copper, silver with teal, lilac and electric pink and grey. I held them up to my face and breathed in their expensive smells. And, because I must be a bit funny like that, the ritual always seemed to lead to one thing: my hands in my knickers.

The Takadanobaba house was big, but sound spread like water along the timbers and through the flimsy rice-paper screens. I had to be quiet. I thought I'd been careful until very late one night, when it was over, I slid back the door to go to the bathroom and found Jason a few feet away in the moonlit corridor, leaning out of the window, a cigarette between his fingers.

When he heard the door open he turned to me. He didn't say anything. He looked lazily down at my bare feet, then up to the short *yukata*, to the flushed skin on my chest. He let the smoke curl up out of his mouth and smiled, raising an eyebrow, as if I was a huge and pleasant surprise to him.

'Hello,' he said.

I didn't answer. I slid the door closed with a bang and locked it, sinking down with my back against it. Dressing like a sexy person – that was one thing. But Jason – well, Jason made me think things about sex that were much, much more frightening.

21

 Nanking, 13 December 1937, nightfall

They are here. They are here. It is real.

I left the house at midday, and the streets seemed silent. I didn't see another soul, only shuttered houses, the shops boarded – some with notices pasted on the doors giving details of the rural district where the owners could be found. I turned right on to Zhongyang Road and followed it past the railway where I took a short-cut through an alley to meet up with Zhongshan Road. There I saw three men running towards me as fast as they could. They were dressed as peasants and were blackened all over, as if from an explosion. When I looked up, in the distance over the houses in the area of the Shuixi gate, a pall of smoke was rising grey against the sky. The men continued away from me in the direction I'd come, running in silence, only the sound of their straw shoes slapping on the pavement. I stood on the street, staring after them, listening to the city around me. Now that I wasn't moving I could hear the distant sound of car horns, mingling horribly with faint human cries. My heart sank. I continued south, expecting the worst as I crept through the streets, keeping close to the houses, ready to dash inside at any moment or prostrate myself and cry, '*Dongyang Xiansheng!* Eastern Masters!'

On the streets nearer the refugee centre one or two businesses had found the courage to open, the owners standing anxiously in the doorway, staring off down the street in the direction of the eastern gates.

I skipped between buildings, running low to the ground, switching and doubling back through the familiar streets, my heart racing. I could hear the low murmur of a crowd somewhere ahead, and at last I came to a side-street that led up to Zhongshan Road and there, at its head, a huge tide of people crushed against each other, straining in the direction of the Yijiang gate – the great 'water' gate that opens out of the city and on to the Yangtze – grim expressions on their faces. They all pulled handcarts loaded down with possessions. One or two glanced at me, curious to see someone making no attempt to flee, others ignored me, putting their heads down and leaning their weight into the handcart. Children watched me silently from their perches on top of the carts, bundled up against the cold in quilted jackets, their hands blunt in wool mittens. A wild dog ran among them, hoping to steal food.

'Are they in the city?' I asked a woman who had broken free of the crowd and was racing away down the alley I stood in. I stepped in front of her and stopped her in her tracks, my hands on her shoulders. 'Have the Japanese taken the walls?'

'Run!' Her face was wild. The charcoal she'd used to cover her face was smeared with tears. 'Run!'

She struggled out of my grasp and headed away, screaming something at the top of her voice. I watched her disappear as, behind me, the shouts of the crowd grew to a crescendo, running footsteps scattering into the alleys around me. Then slowly, slowly the footsteps died away, the crush on the road dwindled. At length I crept forward and peered out on to the main road. To my right, in the west, I could see the tail end of the crowd shuffling on towards the river, one or two stragglers, the elderly and sick, hurrying to catch up. The road to my left was empty, the ground churned into mud by hundreds of pairs of feet.

I stepped out cautiously and, my heart in my throat, turned in the direction they'd come. I walked in near silence. Outside the ruined Ming Palace, where yesterday I had chatted to the history professor, a few Nationalist tanks rumbled past, kicking up sprays of dirt, the soldiers shouting and waving at me to get off the streets. Then, slowly, silence came back to the city and I was alone, walking very quietly in the centre of the empty Zhongshan Road.

At last I came to a halt. Around me nothing was moving. Even the birds seemed to have been silenced on their perches. The pollarded trees on either side led the eye into the distance, straight down the churned-up road, absolutely still and empty and clear as far as the eye could see to where, about half a mile away, the winter sun shone down on the triple arches of the Zhongshan gate. I stood in the centre of the road, took a deep breath and slowly opened my hands, holding them up to the sky. My heart was thumping so loudly it seemed to be almost inside my head.

Was the ground beneath me shuddering, the way it would in a distant earthquake? I looked down at my feet and as I did, from the direction of the gate, there came an explosion that ripped through the silence, making the sycamores bend as if in a strong wind, the birds taking to the air with panicked speed. Flames shot into the sky and a cloud of smoke and dust erupted above the gate. I fell to a crouch, my hands over my head, as another explosion rocketed across the sky. Then came a sound like distant rain that grew and grew until it was a roar, and suddenly the sky was dark, and dust and masonry were falling on top of me and I could see, coming out of the dim horizon, ten or more tanks, their blank, fierce faces bearing down on Zhongshan Road, the terrible *hi no maru* flag fluttering behind them.

I jumped up and ran in the direction of my house, the sound of my breathing and my footsteps drowned by the rumble of tanks and the shrill peal of whistles coming from behind me. I ran and ran, my lungs screaming, my pulse thundering, on and on up Zhongshan Road, right on to Zhongyang Road, ducking into a side-street, then slipping behind the Liu house, and into the alley where at last the steady rain of dust and masonry dwindled. The house was silent. I battered on the door until the locks opened and Shujin was standing there, looking at me as if she was seeing a ghost.

'They're here,' she said, when she saw my face, when she saw how out of breath I was. 'Aren't they?'

I didn't answer. I came inside and locked the door carefully behind me, securing all the bolts and braces. Then, when my breathing had returned to normal, I went upstairs and sat on my day-bed, finding a place among the Japanese language books, and pulling a quilted throw over my feet.

And so – what can I write? Only that it has happened. And that it was straightforward. On this crisp afternoon, which should have been beautiful, they have taken Nanking as casually as a child reaches into the air and squashes a dragonfly. I am afraid to look out of the window – the Japanese flag must be flying all over the city.

史　Nanking, 14 December 1937, morning (by the lunar calendar the twelfth day of the eleventh month)

In the night it snowed, and now, looming up beyond the city walls, Purple Mountain, Great Zijin, is not white, but red with fire. The flames bathe everything around it in the colour of blood, casting a terrible halo in the sky. Shujin spends a long time staring at it, standing at the opened door, silhouetted against the sky, the cold air coming in until the house is freezing and I can see my own breath.

'See?' she says, turning stiffly to look at me. Her hair is loose and straight down the back of her gown, and her triumphant eyes are filled with red light. 'Zijin is burning. Isn't it exactly as I said?'

'Shujin,' I say, 'come away from the door. It's not safe.'

She obeys, but it takes time. She closes the door and comes to sit in silence in the corner, clutching against her stomach the two ancestor scrolls she brought from Poyang, her cheeks red from the cold.

Most of this morning I have been sitting at the table with a pot of tea, the bolts shot on the door, the tea in the cup getting cold. Last night we got a few minutes of fitful sleep, both dressed and still wearing shoes in case we had to flee. From time to time one of us would sit up and stare at the closed shutters, but neither of us spoke much, and now, although it is a bright day, in here

133

the rooms are dark, shuttered and silent. Every half an hour or so we switch on the radio. The reports are confused – an impossible mixture of propaganda and misinformation. Who knows what is true? We can only guess at what is happening. From time to time I recognize the rumble of tanks on Zhongshan Road, and occasional gunfire, but everything seems distant and punctuated by such long silences that sometimes my mind wanders, and I forget briefly that we are being invaded.

At about eleven o'clock we heard something that might have been a mortar attack, and for a moment our eyes met. Then came distant explosions, one–two–three–four in a sudden continuous string, and silence again. Ten minutes later a demon clattering rose in the alley. I went to the back, peeped through a shutter and saw that someone's goat had slipped its tether, and was now in panic – racing aimlessly through the back plots, bucking and charging into trees and corrugated-iron buildings. Under its hoofs it crushed the summer's rotten pomegranates until the snow appeared filthy with blood. No one came to catch the goat, the owners must have already fled the city, and it was twenty minutes before it found its way into the street and silence once again descended on our alley.

22

After that night Jason started watching me. He developed a habit of staring right at me, when we were walking home from the club, when I was cooking, or just when we were all sitting in the living room in front of the television. Sometimes I'd turn round to light a customer's cigarette and Jason would be standing a few feet away, looking at me as if he was secretly entertained by everything I did. It was horrible and scary and exciting all at the same time – I'd never had anyone look at me like that before and I couldn't imagine what I'd do if he ever came near me. I found excuses to keep out of his way.

Autumn came. The winey heat, the hot metal, frying and drains smell of Tokyo gave way to a cooler, starker Japan that must have been waiting near the surface all along. The skies were cleared of their haze, the maples drenched the city with russet, and the smell of woodsmoke came out of nowhere, as if we were back in post-war Japan among the cooking fires of old Tokyo. From the gallery I could reach out and pick ripening persimmon straight from the branch. The mosquitoes left the garden and that made Svetlana sad – she said that now they had left we were all doomed.

Still Fuyuki hadn't come to the club. Shi Chongming remained as obstinate, as tight-lipped as ever, and sometimes I thought my chances of ever seeing the film were slipping away. One day, when I couldn't bear it any longer, I took a train to Akasaka and in a public booth called the number on Fuyuki's card. The Nurse, I was sure it was the Nurse, answered, with a feminine, '*Moshi moshi*,' and I froze, the receiver to my ear, all my courage disappearing in a second. '*Moshi moshi?*' she repeated, but I had already changed my mind. I slammed down the phone and walked away from the booth as quickly as I could, not looking back. Maybe Shi Chongming had been right when he said that I'd never make silk out of a mulberry leaf.

From Kinokuniya, the big bookshop in Shinjuku, I got every publication I could find on alternative medicine. I also bought some Chinese–Japanese dictionaries, and collections of essays about the *yakuza*. Over the next few days, while I waited for Fuyuki to come back to the club, I'd lock myself in my room for long, long hours, reading about Chinese medicine until I knew all about Bian Que's moxibustion and acupuncture with stone needles, about Hua Tuo's early operations and experiments with anaesthetics. Soon I understood the *Qi Gong*, 'frolics of the five animals' exercises back to front, and could recite the taxonomy of herbs from Shen Nong's Materia Medica. I read about tiger bones and turtle jelly and the gall bladders of bears. I went to *kampo* shops and got free samples of eel oil and bear bile from Karuizawa. I was looking for something that could reverse all the principles of regeneration and degeneration. A key to immortality. It was a search that had been going on in one form or another since time began. Even humble tofu, they said, was created by a Chinese emperor in his quest for life without end.

But Shi Chongming was talking about something that no one had ever encountered before. Something surrounded in secrecy.

One day I took all my paints and carefully etched out a picture of a man among the buildings on my wartime Tokyo walls. His face came out crunched, like a *kabuki* man, so I drew in a Hawaiian shirt, and behind him an American car, the sort of car a gangster might drive. Scattered at his feet, I drew in medicine bottles, an alembic, a still. Something so precious – illegal? – that no one dared talk about it.

*

'It's beautiful,' said Shi Chongming. 'Isn't it?'

I stared out of his window at the campus, at the trees turning gold and red. The moss on the gymnasium had deepened to a dark purply green, like an underripe plum, and from time to time a ghostly figure in *kendo* mask and robes passed the opened doors. The shouts of the *dojo* echoed across the campus, sending the crows up into the trees in great rustling clouds. It *was* beautiful. I didn't understand why I couldn't separate it from its context. I couldn't help thinking of it trapped by the strapping modern city, by power-hungry Japan. When I didn't turn from the window, Shi Chongming laughed.

'So you, too, are one of the number who cannot forgive.'

I turned and looked at him directly. 'Forgive?'

'Japan. For what she did in China.'

The words of a Chinese-American historian I'd studied at university went through my head: *'The Japanese were brutal beyond imagination. They elevated cruelty to an art form. If an official apology did come would it be sufficient for us to forgive?'*

'Why?' I asked. 'Are you saying you have?'

He nodded.

'How could you?'

Shi Chongming closed his eyes, a little smile on his face. He was silent for a long time, thinking about this, and I might have thought he had fallen asleep if it wasn't for the way his hands moved and twitched, like dying birds. 'How?' he said eventually, looking up. 'How, indeed? It would seem impossible, wouldn't it? But I have had many, many years to think about it – years when I couldn't move outside my own country, years when I couldn't move outside my own house. Until you have been pelted in the street, paraded through your own town bearing propaganda . . .' He spread his thumb and forefinger across his chest and I thought immediately of Cultural Revolution photographs, men huddled pitifully together, hounded by the Red Guard, slogans like *Intellectual Renegade* and *Anti-Party Element* screaming from placards around their necks. '. . . until you have experienced this you don't have the tools to understand human nature. It took a long time, but I came to understand one simple thing. I understood *ignorance*. The more I studied it, the more it became clear that their behaviour was all about ignorance. Oh, there were soldiers in Nanking, a handful, who were truly evil. I don't dispute that. But the others? Their biggest sin was their ignorance. It is that simple.'

Ignorance. That was something I thought I knew a lot about. 'What they did on your film. Is that what you mean? Was *that* ignorance?'

Shi Chongming didn't reply. His face closed and he pretended to be busying himself with some papers. The mention of the film always turned him a little quiet with me.

'Is that what you meant? Professor Shi?'

He pushed aside his papers, clearing his desk, ready to get to business. 'Come,' he said, gesturing to me. 'Let's not talk of that now. Come and sit down and tell me why you're here.'

'I want to know what you mean. Did you mean that what they did to the—'

'Please! Please – you haven't come here today for nothing. You've come to me with ideas – I can see them in your face. Sit down.'

Reluctantly, I came to the desk. I sat opposite him, my hands in my lap.

'Well?' he said. 'What is it?'

I sighed. 'I've been reading,' I said. 'About Chinese medicine.'

'Good.'

'There was a myth. A story about a god, the divine farmer who divided the plants into orders. I'm right, aren't I?'

'Taste, temperature and quality. Yes. You're talking about Shen Nong.'

'So what I ought to do is decide where Fuyuki's cure falls in that order. I've got to put it in a category?'

Shi Chongming held my eyes.

'What?' I said. 'What have I said?'

He sighed and sat back with his hands on the table, lightly tapping his fingertips together. 'It's time I told you a little more about myself.'

'Yes?'

'I don't want you to waste your time. You should know that I have some very, very good suspicions about what we are looking for.'

'Then you don't need me to—'

'Ah.' He smiled. 'Yes, I do.'

'Why?'

'Because I don't want to hear what I want to hear. I don't want a parrot to come back to me, cheeky and obsequious, telling me, "Yes, sir, yes, sir, you were correct all along, O wise one." No. I want the truth.' He pulled a battered portfolio out of the pile of books on the desk. 'I have been working on this for too long to make a mistake at this point. I will tell you everything you need to know. But I will not tell you *exactly* what I suspect.'

From the portfolio he pulled a handful of yellowing paper tied with a scruffy black ribbon. Out it came, dragging with it pencil shavings, paper-clips, balled tissues.

'It took me a long time to find Fuyuki, more years than I care to consider. I discovered many, many things about him. Here.' He pushed the bundle of papers across the table to me. I looked at them, a big untidy pile that threatened to slip off on to the ground. They were in Chinese and Japanese, official letters, photocopied newspapers; one seemed to be a memo on notepaper from a government office. I recognized the *kanji* for the Land-based Defence Agency.

'What am I looking at?'

'Years and years of work. Most of it done a long time before I was permitted to travel to Japan. Letters, newspaper articles and – maybe the riskiest thing I did – reports from special investigators. I don't expect you to understand them, but you do need to know how dangerous Fuyuki is.'

'You've said that already.'

He smiled thoughtfully. 'Yes. I understand your scepticism. He seems like a very old man. Maybe even kind. Benevolent?'

'You can't say what someone's like until you've talked to them for a bit.'

'Interesting, isn't it? The most powerful *sarakin* loan shark in Tokyo, one of the biggest manufacturers and illegal importers of methamphetamine – interesting how innocuous he appears. And yet don't be fooled.' Shi Chongming sat forward, looking at me intently. 'He is ruthless. You cannot imagine how many died in his determination to establish his amphetamine routes between here and any number of poor Korean ports. And maybe the most intriguing thing is the care with which he chooses the people who surround him. He has a unique technique – it's all in there in those papers, if you know how to look. What a skilled manipulator he is! He scours the newspapers for arrests, carefully selects certain offenders and finances their defence cases. If they escape conviction they are sworn to Fuyuki for life.'

'Do you know about . . .' I leaned closer, my voice lowering instinctively '. . . about his Nurse?'

Shi Chongming nodded seriously. 'Yes, I do. His Nurse, his bodyguard. Ogawa. Those who are afraid of her are quite right to be cautious.' He lowered his voice to match mine, as if we might be overheard. 'You must appreciate that Mr Fuyuki favours sadists. Those with no concept of good or bad. His Nurse is there for her criminal brilliance, her absolute inability to emphathize with her victims.' He indicated the pile of papers. 'If you spend time looking through these you will find her referred to by the popular press as the Beast of Saitama. For her methods she is a living myth in Japan, a subject of intense speculation.'

'Her methods?'

He nodded, and squeezed his nose lightly, as if trying to suppress a sneeze or a memory. 'Naturally,' he said, dropping his hand and breathing out, 'violence is a necessary part of life in the *yakuza*. Maybe it is not surprising, no, considering her sexual confusion, maybe it's not altogether surprising the way she seems compelled to . . .' his eyes wandered briefly to a point just above my head '. . . to embellish her crimes.'

'Embellish?'

He didn't answer. Instead he pursed his mouth and said, conversationally, 'I haven't seen her but I understand she is unusually tall?'

'Some of the people in the club think she's a man.'

'Nevertheless she is a woman. A woman with a – I don't know

the word in English – a disorder of the skeleton, maybe. But, enough of that. Let us not speculate our morning away.' He looked at me very carefully. 'I need to know. Are you quite sure you want to continue?'

I moved my shoulders, a little shudder going down my back. 'Well,' I said eventually, rubbing my arms, 'well, actually, yes. That's the thing, you see – this is the most important thing in my life. I've been doing it for nine years and eight months and twenty-nine days, and I've never even once thought about giving it up. Sometimes I think it annoys people.' I thought about this for a moment, then looked up at him. 'Yes. It does. It annoys people.'

He laughed and gathered up the papers. While he was returning them to the portfolio he noticed a photograph that had been hiding at the bottom of the pile. 'Ah,' he said casually, pulling it free from the stack. 'Ah, yes. I wonder if you'd be interested in this.' He slid it across the table, his long brown hand half covering the image. I could see an official stamp in the top right corner, the *kanji* for 'Police Department', and under his hand a grainy black-and-white image. I saw what I thought looked like police tape, a car with its boot open. There was something in the boot, something I couldn't recognize, until Shi Chongming lifted his hand and I understood.

'Oh,' I said faintly, instinctively covering my mouth with my hand. It felt like having all the blood drained from my head in one sweep. The picture showed an arm – a human arm with an expensive watch on it, hanging lifelessly out of the boot. I'd seen similar pictures of mob victims in the university library, but it was what lay under the exhaust pipe of the car that I couldn't tear my eyes from. Arranged almost ritualistically, coiled like a boa constrictor, was a pile of . . . 'Are they . . .' I said faintly '. . . are they what I think they are? Are they human? Are they his?'

'Yes.'

'Is that what you meant by . . . embellish?'

'Yes. It's one of Ogawa's crime scenes.' Calmly he put his finger on the photo and pulled it across the table. 'One of the crimes attributed to the Beast of Saitama. The rumour is that on first glance at the body, the police could see no clear way that the – the *internals* had been removed. It is a source of amazement to me, really it is, the level of ingenuity that mankind, or womankind, can reach when dealing in cruelty.' He pushed the photo back and began tying the portfolio with the battered black ribbon. 'Oh, and by the way,' he said, 'I shouldn't waste time looking at Shen Nong's classifications if I were you.'

I looked up, blinking at him, my face numb. 'I'm – I'm sorry?'

'I said don't waste time with Shen Nong's classifications. It's not a plant you're looking for.'

23

I had stopped sleeping. The photograph in Shi Chongming's port-folio kept waking me, infecting my thoughts, making me wonder how far I was prepared to go to please him. And when it wasn't the Nurse's 'embellishments', it was Jason who agonized me and kept my skin electric and uncomfortable against the sheets at night. Sometimes, on the occasions when he appeared where I least expected him, in the corridor outside my room, or at the bar when I got up to find a clean glass, watching me in silence with his calm eyes, I told myself he was teasing me – performing an elaborate *pas de deux* for his own amusement, dancing round me in shadowy places in the house, a harlequin slithering down the corridor in the night. But sometimes, particularly when he watched me as we all walked home from the club at night, I had the sense he was trying to look deeper – trying to see under my clothes. Then I'd get the usual horrible sensation in my stomach, and I'd have to belt my coat tighter, turn up the collar, cross my arms and walk faster, so that he fell away behind me, and all I had to think about were the caustic comments coming from the twins.

The house seemed to get lonelier and lonelier. One morning, a few days after I'd visited Shi Chongming, I woke early and lay on my futon listening to the silence, acutely conscious of the rooms stretching away from me in every direction, the clicking floor-boards and unswept corners, full of secrets and maybe unexpected deaths. Locked-off rooms that no one alive had ever been inside. The others were still asleep, and suddenly I couldn't bear the silence any longer. I got up, had breakfast of Chinese duck-pears and strong coffee, then put on a linen dress, gathered up my notepads, my *kanji* books, and carried everything down into the garden.

It was an unusually warm, motionless day – almost like summer. One of those mid-autumn mornings when the sky was so clear you almost feared to let go of belongings for the chance that they could be whisked straight up into the blue, disappearing for ever. I'd never imagined Japanese skies to be so clear. The steamer chairs were still there, surrounded by soggy mounds of cigarette ends where the Russians had sat gossiping in the summer. I put all my stuff down on one and turned to look round. Next to the old pond I could see the remains of a path – ornamental stepping-stones winding away into the undergrowth towards the closed-off rooms. I took a few steps along it, my arms out as if I was balancing. I followed it round the pond, past the lantern and the stone bench, into the area that Shi Chongming had found so fascinating. I got to the edge of the undergrowth and stopped, looking down at my feet.

The path continued into the trees, but in the centre of the stepping-stone I'd stopped at was a single white stone, fist-sized and tied like a gift in rotting bamboo. In a Japanese garden everything is coded and arcane – a stone placed on a stepping-stone was a clear signal to guests: *Do not go any further. This is private.* I stood for a while staring at it, wondering what it was hiding. The sun went behind a cloud and I rubbed my arms, suddenly cold. What happens when you break the rules in a place where you don't belong? I took a breath and stepped over the stone.

I paused, expecting something to happen. A small bird with long trailing wings lifted off the ground and settled in one of the trees above, but otherwise the garden was silent. The bird sat there, seeming to watch me, and for a while I stared back at it. Then, conscious of its gaze on me, I turned and continued through the roots and shadows to the closed-off wing until I found myself at the wall where I could look along the length of the house at all the firmly barricaded windows twined with creepers. I stepped over a fallen branch and stood close to one of the security grilles, the baked metal making my skin warm. I put my nose up to it and I could smell the dust and mould of the closed-off rooms. The basement was supposed to be flooded and dangerous. Jason had been in there once, months ago, he had told us. There were piles of rubbish and things that he didn't want to look at too closely. Pipes had cracked in earthquakes and some of the rooms were like underground lakes.

I turned back to the garden, thinking of Shi Chongming's words: *Its future is waiting to be uncovered. Its future is waiting to be uncovered.* I had the oddest feeling. The feeling that the future of this garden was focused specifically on the area I was standing in: the area around the stone lantern.

24

 Nanking, 14 December 1937, midday

The truth is emerging on the radio. It is not good. Yesterday, after the explosion of Zhongshan gate, it seems the IJA poured through two openings in the city wall. I was lucky to escape in time. During the afternoon they moved into the city, bringing their tanks, their flame-throwers, their howitzers. By nightfall the Japanese had captured every government building in Nanking.

When we heard this Shujin and I hung our heads. We didn't speak for a long time. Eventually I got to my feet, switched off the radio and put my hands on her shoulders.

'Don't worry. It will all be over before our b—' I hesitated, looking down at her head, at the thick dark hair, the vulnerable stripe of white skin along the parting. 'It will be over before little moon arrives. We've enough food and water for more than two weeks. And besides,' I took a breath and tried to sound reassuring and calm, 'the Japanese are civilized. It won't be very long before we are told it is safe to return to the streets.'

'Our future is our past and our past is our future,' she whispered. 'We already know what will happen . . .'

We already know what will happen?

Maybe she is right. Maybe all truths are in us at birth. Maybe for years all we do is swim away from what we already know, and maybe only old age and death allow us to swim back, back to something that is pure, something unchanged by the act of surviving. What if she is right? What if everything is there already

– our fate, and our loves, and our children to be? What if they are all in us from the day we are born? If that is so then I already know what is going to happen in Nanking. I just need to reach for that answer . . .

史 ## Nanking, 15 December 1937, midnight (the thirteenth day of the eleventh month)

Ha! Look at us now. Just one short day later and all my confidence is exhausted. Shujin, my clairvoyant, did not foresee this! The food is gone. At about one o'clock this morning we heard a sound in the front courtyard. When I crept to the shutters to look I saw two boys in shabby clothes dragging the sorghum sack and the strings of meat over the wall. They had thrown down a rope and were clambering up it. I shouted and ran down the stairs, grabbing up the iron bar and bellowing at them in rage, but by the time I had unbolted the door and raced out into the street, clattering among livestock braces and overturning old water barrels, they had disappeared.

'What is it?' Shujin appeared in the doorway, wearing a long nightgown. Her hair was loose around her shoulders and she was holding an oil lamp. 'Chongming? What's happened?'

'Ssssh. Hand me my coat, then go back inside and lock the doors. Don't open them until I return.'

I slipped between the abandoned houses and scrubland until I reached the Lius' street. His was the only inhabited house in his alley, and as I turned the corner I saw the three of them outside the house, milling around in the watery moonlight. Liu's wife was crying, and his son was standing at the head of the alley, facing out into the street, iron legged, trembling with fury. He was holding a wooden cart shaft straight in front of him as if ready to strike someone. I knew even before I approached that the family had suffered the same fate as us.

They took me into the house. Liu and I lit a pipe and sat near the coal-burning stove to keep warm, with the door to the alley standing open because his son insisted on staying a few feet from it, in the street-squat position the young find so natural, with his knees near his shoulders like bony wings. The shaft lay at his feet, ready to be snatched up. His eyes were intent, as fierce as a tiger's, fixed on the street at the top of the alley.

'We should have left the city a long time ago,' Liu's wife said bitterly, turning away from us. 'We're all going to die here.'

We watched her retreat, and soon we could hear muffled weeping from a room at the back. I shot an embarrassed look at Liu, but he sat, expressionless, looking through the doorway over the roofs to where, in the distance, a grey pall of smoke blotted out the stars. It was only the flickering pulse in his neck that gave away his feelings.

'What do you think?' he said eventually, not turning to look at me. 'We have food for two days, then we'll starve. Do you think we should go out to look?'

I shook my head. 'No,' I said quietly, watching the flicker of red illuminate the underside of the billowing smoke. 'The city has fallen. It won't be long before it's safe to leave our houses. Maybe two days, maybe less. Soon they'll tell us that it's safe to go out again.'

'We should wait until then?'

'Yes. I believe we should wait. It won't be long.'

史 Nanking, 17 December 1937

We haven't eaten for two days. I worry about how long Shujin can go on like this. It can't be much longer before peace is restored. There are radio reports of attempts to set up a Self-governing Committee for the city – they say it won't be long before we can walk around openly and the Red Cross will be giving out free rice rations on the Shanghai road. But as yet there has been no announcement. We swept up the rice that had been spilled during the theft and mixed it with the remainder of the pickled vegetables that Shujin happened to have stored in the kitchen, and that lasted us for two meals; and because Liu's wife is concerned about Shujin they distributed what little they had left. But now there is nothing. This is life laid bare to the bone. Shujin doesn't complain, but I wonder about the baby. Sometimes, in the dead of night, I have an odd sensation that something in Shujin, something intangible, like an essence or a spirit, is stretching, and I can't help imagining it's our moon soul reaching out in hunger.

I leave the chores until after dark – taking out our soil pot and bringing in wood for the fire. I guard jealously the little oil I have for my lamp. It is bitterly cold and even in the daytime we wrap ourselves in quilts and coats. I am beginning to forget that there are good things in this world – books and beliefs, and mist above the Yangtze. This morning I found six boiled eggs that had been wrapped in a *qipao* and tucked into a chest at the foot of the bed. They were dyed red.

'What are these?' I asked, taking them downstairs to Shujin.

She didn't look up. 'Put them back where you found them.'

'What are they for?'

'You know the answer to that.'

'For our moon soul's *man yue*? Is that it?'

She didn't answer.

I looked down at the eggs in my hands. It is surprising how changed only two days without food can make a person. My head became very light when I considered cracking the eggs and eating them. I set them hurriedly on the table in front of her and took a step back. 'Eat,' I said, pointing at them. 'Quickly. Eat them now.'

She sat and stared at them, her coat wrapped tightly around her, a distant, blank look on her face.

'I said *eat*. Eat them now.'

'It would be bad luck for our moon soul.'

'Bad luck? Don't talk to me about bad luck. Do you think I don't know the meaning of bad luck?' I was beginning to shake. 'EAT!'

But she sat silent and obstinate, her face closed in on itself, while I paced round the room, my frustration wanting to burst out of me. How can she be so foolish – to put our baby's health in jeopardy? Eventually, with a supreme struggle of will, I turned my back on the eggs, slammed the door and went into my study, where I have been sitting ever since, unable to concentrate on anything.

 Nanking, 17 December 1937, afternoon

As I was writing the last entry something happened. I had to stop and put my pen down and raise my head in wonder. A smell drifted through the shuttered windows. A smell both terrible and wonderful. The smell of meat cooking! Someone nearby is cooking meat. The smell shot me from my desk and sent me to the shutters, where I stood, trembling, my nose to the gaps, hungrily sucking in the air. I imagined a family – maybe only in the next alley – sitting round the table, looking at fluffy piles of rice, corn cakes, succulent pork. Could it be the thieves, cooking what they stole from us? If it is they've forgotten the legend of the beggar's chicken, they've forgotten what every thief in Jiangsu should know – to cook stolen food underground and not in the open air, where the smell advertises itself to everyone.

I have to stop myself rising from the table, seduced by that aroma. It is so sweet, so pungent. It has decided me. If people feel safe enough to cook lunch so openly – to allow the smell to drift wantonly through the streets, then peace can only be hours away. It must be safe to go outside. I am going out now. I'm going to find food for Shujin.

25

Not a plant. That was what Shi Chongming had said. *Not a plant.*

That morning I thought about this, poring over my textbooks sitting hunched on the steamer chair. I had been reading for almost an hour when something distracted me. Less than a foot away from my feet, a cicada nymph was dragging itself out of the ground, first a feeler, then a tiny face like a newborn dragon. I put down my book and watched it. It crept a short way up a piece of rotten wood and, after a few minutes of resting, began the laborious process of pulling its wings out of its shell, one at a time, painfully slowly, the casing flaking off in iridescent slivers. I'd read in one of the books that the wings of cicadas could be used in a traditional cure for earache. I thought of the dried powder clinging to the sides of Fuyuki's glass. *It's not a plant you're looking for.* If not a plant then . . . ?

The beetle straightened, new and confused, its wings white-webbed with birth, looking around itself. Why was it coming out now? All the cicadas had come and gone weeks ago.

'What're you dreaming about?'

I jumped. Jason had come through the wisteria tunnel and was standing a few feet away from me, holding a mug of coffee. He was dressed in jeans and a T-shirt; his face was clear and tanned. He was staring at my exposed legs and arms, a look on his face as if they reminded him of something.

Instinctively I folded my arms round my knees and bent

151

forward a little, hunching over the book I'd been reading. 'A cicada,' I said. 'See?'

He squatted down and looked, shielding his eyes with his hand. His arms were the colour of burnt butter and he must have had his hair cut that morning, because I could see the round shape of his head, and the nice slope of his neck where it met his shoulders. The hair-cut had revealed a small mole just below his ear.

'I thought they should all be dead,' I said. 'I thought it was too cold.'

'But it's hot today,' he said. 'And, anyway, all manner of weird shit goes on in this garden, you know. Ask Svetlana. The rules are suspended.'

He came and settled down on the steamer chair next to me, the coffee cup resting on his thigh, his feet crossed. 'The *baba yagas*'ve gone to Yoyogi Park to watch the rockabilly boys,' he said. 'We're all alone.'

I didn't answer. I bit my lip and stared at the gallery windows.

'Well?' he said.

'Well what?'

'What were you thinking about?'

'I wasn't. I was thinking about . . . about nothing.'

He raised his eyebrows.

'Nothing,' I repeated.

'Yes. I heard.' He finished his coffee, up-ended the cup so a few mud-brown drops fell on to the dry earth. Then he looked sideways at me and said, 'Tell me something.'

'Tell you what?'

'Tell me – why do I keep staring at you?'

I dropped my eyes and fiddled with the book cover, pretending he hadn't spoken.

'I said, why do I want to stare at you? Why do I keep looking at you and thinking that you're hiding something that I'd find really interesting?'

All of a sudden, in spite of the sun, my skin seemed cold. I blinked at him. 'I'm sorry,' I said, in a voice that sounded small and distant. 'What did you say?'

'You're hiding something.' He raised his arms and used the sleeves of his T-shirt to wipe his forehead. 'It's easy. I just look at you and I can see it. I don't know what it is exactly, but I've got the – the *instinct* it's something I'm going to like. See I'm a . . .' he raised two fingers and lightly tapped his forehead '. . . I'm a visionary when it comes to women. I can feel it in the air. My God, my skin.' He shivered and ran his hands down his arms. 'My skin just about changes colour.'

'You're wrong.' I wrapped my hands round my stomach. 'I'm not hiding anything.'

'Yes, you are.'

'I'm not.'

He looked at me in amusement. For a moment I thought he was going to laugh. Instead he sighed. He got to his feet and stood, stretching languidly, running his hands up and down his arms, ruffling his T-shirt, giving me glimpses of his flat abdomen. 'No,' he said, squinting thoughtfully up at the sky. 'No.' He dropped his hands and turned in the direction of the wisteria tunnel. 'Of course you're not.'

26

I once read a story about a Japanese girl trapped in a garden when the cicadas came out of the ground. They all came at once. She looked up at one moment and there they were, everywhere, colonizing the air and the trees, so many that the branches were loaded and drooping. All around her the soil was pockmarked, a million maiden flights going up into the branches, the noise getting louder, echoing around the walls until it was almost deafening. Terrified, she ran for shelter, crushing cicadas, hopelessly fracturing their wings, cracking them out of their protective cases so they squealed and spun on the ground like broken catherine wheels, round and round, a blur of brown and black wings. When at last she found a way out of the garden she ran straight into the arms of a boy, who caught her up and carried her to safety. She didn't know it then but the cicadas had been a blessing. This was the boy she was destined to love. One day she'd become his wife.

I jumped. Something had hit my foot. I sat up quickly, looking around blearily. The garden was different – dark. The sun had gone. I'd been lost in a daydream. In my dream it was Jason who caught up the girl and carried her away. His shirt was open at the neck and as he carried her he was whispering something rude and seductive into her ear, making her blush and cover her face. Something hit my arm and I stumbled off the chair in shock, dropping my books. Everywhere little dimples were appearing in the earth, dust flying up as if from bullet hits. Rain. It was only rain, but I was still in the story, with the Japanese girl, a million beetles jumping from the dust and catching in her hair. The drops on my bare skin were like acid. Quickly I gathered up as many books as I could, and raced across the garden to the wisteria tunnel.

I slid closed the screen door. The stairwell was cool; there were dead leaves in the crevices of the stairs. Behind me the rain beat against the rice-paper screen and I imagined the garden getting darker and darker, beetles shaking the branches and coalescing above it, like a huge dust-devil funnelling upwards above the roofs. In the gloom I kicked off my shoes and hurried up the stairs.

Jason was at the top, standing in the corridor, just as if he'd expected me. He was dressed to go out, but his feet were bare. I came to a halt in front of him and dropped my books on the floor. 'What is it?'

'It's cut me,' I said, running my hands over my arms, imagining beetle wings fraying my skin. 'I think the wisteria's cut me.'

He bent over and pressed my ankles between thumb and forefinger. I flinched, jerking my leg back instinctively. 'What're you—'

He put his fingers to his lips. 'What'm I—' he mimicked, looking up and raising his eyebrows at me. 'What'm I what?'

I stood paralysed, my legs slightly apart, staring at him in silence, as he calmly ran his hands up and down my calves, like a stablehand feeling a horse for flaws. He let his hands rest on my knees, a few inches inside the hem of my skirt, half closing his eyes as if his fingers were a stethoscope and he was listening for damage. Sweat broke across my shoulders, on the back of my neck. He straightened and lifted my right hand and ran his palms up my arm, cupping the elbows, running his thumb over the thin skin of my wrists. The roar of the rain echoed through the house, rattling down the fragile corridors like hail. Jason put his right hand on my right shoulder and pulled my hair up and round behind my neck, gathering it all on the left side of my head in a bundle and raking his fingers through it. I could feel my pulse pounding against his palm.

'Please—'

He smiled out of the side of his mouth, showing the edge of a chipped tooth. 'You're clean,' he said. 'Very clean.'

I wanted to put my fingers to my eyes because there were little bubbles of light popping against my retina. I could see the mole on the side of his neck, and under it the faint flutter of his pulse.

'You know what time it is now?' he said.

'No. What time is it?'

'It's time for us to do it.' He took my hand lightly, holding it at the palm between his thumb and forefinger. 'Come on. We're going to find out what you're hiding.'

I tightened my knees, digging my heels into the spot. My skin was unbearably taut, as if every hair was standing straight up in its bed, struggling to stop a phantom me that wanted to slide out and slip straight into Jason. Two distinct rivulets of sweat ran down between my shoulder-blades.

'Hey,' he said, smiling slyly, 'don't worry – I'll take my hoofs off before we start.'

'Let go,' I said, pulling my hand away from him and stepping back, almost stumbling. 'Please, leave me alone.'

I gathered up my books clumsily and ran back to my room, bent forward a little, the books crushed against my stomach. I slammed the door and leaned against it, in the semi-dark, for a long time my heart beating so loudly I couldn't hear anything else.

At six p.m. it was already dark and the light from Mickey Rourke was filtering into the room through the curtains. I could just see my silhouette in the mirror outlined in gold, sitting in trembly silence, a wavery line of cigarette smoke rising into the air. I had been sitting there for almost five hours, doing nothing but smoking one cigarette after another, and still the feeling hadn't gone. It was a fizzing, euphoric sensation, like bubbles bursting all over my skin. Whenever it faded, I'd only have to think of Jason saying, *'We're going to find out what you're hiding,'* and the feeling would rush back at me.

After a while I pushed a strand of hair from my forehead and stubbed out the cigarette. It was time to get ready for the club. I was shaking as I stood up, took off my clothes, opened the wardrobe and pulled out the bags. Sometimes you get to a point in your life when you just have to hold your breath and jump.

I found a pair of French knickers, crushed iridescent silk, with wide grosgrain ribbons hanging low, a single central pane in devoré velvet, hundreds and hundreds of purple medieval flowers twining through the panel and bursting out on to the silk like a psalter illumination. I stepped into them, pulling them up high so that the waistband was sitting across my navel. Then I turned and looked at my reflection. All of my stomach was covered, from the navel to the tops of my thighs. You couldn't see anything.

At the other end of the house, the Russians were shouting at each other, squabbling as they usually did when they were getting ready for work. Vague howls of outrage echoed along the corridor, but I hardly heard them. I put a finger inside the crotch of the knickers and pulled aside the lace. You could get inside there and the top of the knickers wouldn't move. You really wouldn't know there was anything wrong. Maybe life could change I thought. Maybe I'd been wrong, maybe I could make it change, after all.

I dressed in a trance, pulling on a slim black velvet dress. I sat on the stool, my feet planted slightly apart, and dropped my head between my knees the way I'd seen the Russians do it, spraying my hair so that when I sat up it was heavy and glossy, very black against my white skin. The velvet dress held me closely where I'd gained weight, touching me, making me want to push back at it in some places.

Outside, the Russians were still yelling, the argument raging up and down the corridor. Very carefully I blotted my lipstick, took a little patent-leather clutch bag, pushed it tight up under my arm, put on stiletto shoes and left the room, walking down the corridor a little unsteady on the heels, my shoulders back, my head held high.

There was a light on in the kitchen. Jason was in there with his back to the door, singing to himself to try to drown the racket, moving around, looking in cupboards, in the fridge, mixing a last-minute martini. 'Dumb-ass Ruskies,' he was singing to him-self. 'Dumb-ass, katsap, glimmer girls.' His voice trailed off when he heard me passing the door.

I kept walking. I was some way down the corridor when, from behind me, he said, in a loud voice, 'Grey.'

I stopped dead, my hands in tight balls, my eyes closed. I waited until my breathing had calmed, then I turned. He was standing in the corridor staring at me as if he'd seen a ghost.

'Yes?' I said.

He stared at my makeup, my hair, the shiny black stilettos.

'Yes?' I repeated, knowing my face was colouring.

'That's new,' he said eventually. 'The dress. Isn't it?'

I didn't answer. I fixed my eyes on the ceiling, my head pounding.

'I knew it,' he said, and there was a kind of fascinated smugness in his voice. 'I always knew that underneath it all you were just pure, pure sex.'

27

Jason rarely spoke to any of us, but that night, during the walk to the club, he wouldn't stop talking. 'You put that on for me, didn't you?' he kept saying, walking along next to me, his hands linked into the holdall strap that he wore across his chest, a cigarette in his mouth. 'It's for me, isn't it? Go on – admit it.'

The Russians found this the funniest thing that had happened for a long time, but I couldn't find the words to answer. I was sure my skin was reddening on the side that was exposed to him, and the French knickers seemed to slither around under the dress, as if they had a life of their own and wanted to communicate their presence to Jason: *Yes, she did – she put it on for you.*

Eventually he gave up, and spent the rest of the walk in silence, an amused, thoughtful expression on his face. When we all got into the crystal lift he turned his back to us, hands in his pockets, staring out at Tokyo, pushing up on to his toes then dropping down to his heels. I stared at the back of his head thinking: *Do you mean it? You're not teasing me. Please don't let this be you teasing me. It would be too much . . .*

The club was busy – a party from Hitachi had taken over four tables and Mama was in a good mood. In my velvet dress everyone was aware of me, as if I was incandescent, like a geisha's lantern glowing in a Kyoto alley. It's amazing how seductive flattery and sex can be – it was only when the Fuyuki gang came into the club that I realized I hadn't thought about Shi

Chongming's medicine all evening. When I saw them in the doorway I sat straight in my chair, preternaturally alive.

The table was set. Strawberry sent the waiters off round the club, pinching dead blooms from the flower arrangements, putting out hand-towels in the gents', making sure that Fuyuki's personalized Scotch bottles were polished and catching the light, and I was summoned, along with six other hostesses. The group had been gambling at the Gamagori speedboat stadium in Aichi and they were in a good mood. The Nurse had hung back, not coming into the alcove but waiting instead in the lobby, sitting on the *chaise-longue*, her legs crossed. I'd get glimpses of her foot in its stiletto every time the aluminium doors opened, and each time I would forget what I was saying and trail off, thinking of the crime photograph. The Beast of Saitama. I remembered the pinched look on Shi Chongming's face when he pronounced the word *embellishments*. How strong would you have to be to murder a man? How much would you have to know about anatomy to remove what was inside him, and not leave a mark on the outside? Or had Shi Chongming made up that bit to scare me?

Fuyuki was talkative. He'd had a big win and later that night he'd be hosting a party at his apartment. The message soon got round the table that he'd stopped here to trawl for hostesses to take home. Just as Shi Chongming said he might. His house, I thought, running my fingers across my hair, up my calves to smooth out my stockings, maybe the place his secret was kept. I adjusted my dress so that it ran in an exact straight line across my shoulders. *Are they all so pretty in England?*

Amazingly, Bison was there. Still confident, blue-chinned like a henchman, his elbows resting on the table, jacket sleeves rolled up to show his massive forearms and still entertaining the group with stories – the club circuit in Akasaka, a scam he'd become embroiled in, shares that had been sold in a non-existent golf club. On and on went the stories, but something in his face was missing. He was subdued, the ready entertainer's smile had gone, and I got the impression that he was there under duress – the court dwarf. I pretended to listen politely, smoking and nodding thoughtfully, but actually I was staring at Fuyuki, trying to work out how to pin my existence into his head.

'They'd sold nearly all the shares when they were rumbled,' Bison said, shaking his head. 'Imagine that. When Bob Hope heard a Japanese golf club had been set up in his name, he nearly killed someone.'

'Excuse me,' I said, stubbing out my cigarette and pushing back my chair. 'Excuse me for a few moments.'

The toilets were in the corner block abutting the entrance hall. I'd have to pass Fuyuki's wheelchair to get to them. I smoothed my dress, straightened my shoulders, let my arms drop loosely at my sides and began to walk. I was trembling, but I willed myself to keep going, slowly, in a fake sexy way that made my face burn and my legs feel weak. Even above the music and conversation I could hear the *shoosh-shoosh* of nylon as my thighs brushed against each other. Fuyuki's small head was only a few feet from me, and as I drew nearer I dipped my hip, just enough to catch the back of his wheelchair and startle him.

'I beg your pardon.' I placed my hands on the chair to steady it. 'I'm sorry.' He raised his arms slightly, trying to twist his stiff old neck round to look at me. I calmed him, pressing my fingers reassuringly on his shoulders, deliberately moving my right leg against him again, letting the beguiling crackle of nylon static and warm flesh rise up to him. 'I'm so sorry,' I repeated, and pushed the chair back to where it had belonged. 'It won't happen again.'

The henchmen were staring at me. And then I saw Jason at the bar, frozen with a glass of champagne to his mouth, his eyes fixed on me. I didn't wait. I straightened my dress and went on my way. I got to the bathroom and locked myself in, shaking uncontrollably, staring at my hectic face in the mirror. This was incredible. I was turning into a vampire. You would look at me now and not think me the same person who had arrived in Tokyo two months ago.

'My advice is, don't go,' Strawberry said. 'Fuyuki ask you to his apartment, but Strawberry think it bad idea.' When the gang had first arrived she'd got the table arranged, then retreated moodily behind her desk where she'd stayed all night, drinking champagne as fast as possible and scrutinizing us all with her narrow, suspicious eyes. By the time the club was empty, all the chairs were on the tables and a man with an industrial polisher was moving silently between them, she was furiously drunk. Under the floury Marilyn makeup her skin showed a deep pink round her nostrils, her hairline, on her neck. 'You don't understand.' She pointed her cigarette-holder at me, stabbing it in the air. 'You not like Japanese girls. Japanese girls understand people like Mr Fuyuki.'

'What about the Russians? They're going.'

'The Russians!' She sniffed indignantly, pushing a tiny straggle of white-blonde hair off her forehead. 'The Russians!'

'They don't understand any better than I do.'

'Okay.' She held up her hand to stop me. She drained her glass, sat up straight and patted her mouth, her hair, trying to regain her composure. 'Okay,' she said, sitting forward and pointing the cigarette-holder at me. Sometimes when she was drunk like this she'd show her teeth and gums. The funny thing was that with all the surgery she'd never had her teeth fixed – they remained discoloured, one or two were even black. 'You go to Fuyuki apartment you *be careful*. Okay? If it me, I don't going to eat nothing in his house.'

'Don't what?'

'I don't going to eat any meat.'

The hairs on the back of my neck rose. 'What do you mean?' I said faintly.

'Too many stories.'

'What stories?'

Strawberry shrugged. She let her eyes wander out to the club. Fuyuki's cars were waiting fifty floors down and most of the girls were already in the cloakroom getting their bags and coats. Outside a sour wind had started to blow, and from the panorama windows we could see that it had taken down power lines. Parts of the city were in darkness.

'What do you mean?' I repeated. 'What stories? What meat?'

'Nothing!' She shook her hand dismissively, still not meeting my eyes. 'Just jokes.' She laughed then, a high, artificial laugh, and noticed her cigarette had gone out. She plugged a new one into the holder and waved it at me. 'Better we finish this. This discussion finish now. Finish.'

I stared at her, my mind cantering forward. *Don't eat the meat?* I was thinking how to pursue it, how to stalk her, sure she was dropping a vital clue, when quite suddenly Jason appeared, sitting next to me, leaning forward and gripping my chair, turning it round to face him.

'You're going to Fuyuki's?' he whispered.

He had already changed out of his waiter's tuxedo into a grey T-shirt with a faded *Goa Trance* slogan. His holdall was strapped across his chest, ready to walk home.

'The twins told me,' he said. 'You're going.'

'Yes.'

'Then I'll have to go too.'

'What?'

'Because we're spending the night together. You and me. We'd already agreed that.'

I opened my mouth to speak, but I couldn't make anything come out. I must have looked odd, my pupils wide, my mouth open, a light haze of sweat on my neck.

'The Nurse,' Jason said, as if I'd asked a question. 'That's why I'll be welcome.' He licked his lips and glanced at Strawberry, who was smoking another cigarette, her eyebrows raised knowingly at this exchange. 'Let me put it this way,' he whispered. 'She's kind of itchy for me. If you know what I mean.'

28

Fuyuki and his entourage had gone ahead, leaving a string of black cars, with 'Lincoln Continental' written in curlicue script on their boots, in the street to pick up the guests. I was one of the last to leave the club, and by the time I got to street level almost all of the hostesses, and Jason, had followed him, leaving just one car. I slid into the back seat with three Japanese hostesses whose names I didn't know. As we drove they chattered about their customers, but I was quiet, smoking a cigarette and staring out of the window at the moats of the Imperial Palace flashing past the car. As we came through Nishi Shinbashi we passed the garden where I had first met Jason. I didn't recognize it at first: it was almost behind us when I realized that the odd rows gleaming in the moonlight were the silent stone children lined up under the trees. I swivelled in my seat to stare at them through the back window.

'What's that place?' I asked the driver in Japanese. 'The temple?'

'That's Zojoji temple.'

'Zojoji? What are all the children for?'

The driver looked at me hard in the rear-view mirror, as if I was a surprise to him. 'Those are the Jizo. The angels for the dead children. The children who are stillborn.' When I didn't answer he said, 'Do you understand my Japanese?'

I turned back to gaze at the ghostly lines under the trees. A little shudder crossed my heart. You can never be sure what's going on in your subconscious. Maybe I'd always known what the statues were. Maybe that was why I had chosen the park to sleep in.

'Yes,' I said distantly, my mouth dry. 'Yes, I do. I understand.'

Fuyuki lived near the Tokyo Tower, in an imposing apartment building set in private gardens behind security gates. As the Continental swept down the driveway, the wind coming off the bay made the big palm trees rustle. The guard roused himself from behind a low-lit reception desk, crouched to unlock the bottom of the glass doors, and escorted our party through a quiet marble lobby to a private lift, which he opened with a key. We crammed in, the Japanese girls giggling and whispering behind their hands.

When the doors opened at the penthouse the man in the ponytail was waiting for us. He didn't speak or meet anyone's eye as we filed out into the small hallway, but turned smartly and led us into a long passage. The apartment was arranged round a square. A long walnut-panelled corridor linked all the rooms and seemed to go on for ever; concealed lighting dropped round pools of light in front of us, like a runway, inviting us into the distance. I walked cautiously, shooting looks around me, wondering if the Nurse lived here too, if she had a lair behind one of these doors.

We passed a ripped and stained Japanese flag hung in a lighted frame, a ceremonial ashes box carved from wisteria, painted white and displayed in a glass cabinet. No locks, I noticed. I allowed myself to drop to the back of the group. We passed a military uniform, battle-worn and mounted so that it appeared to have flesh and substance. I bent a little as I passed the glass cabinet, keeping my eyes on the group ahead, and trailed my hand up inside the open base of the case, brushing the hem of the uniform.

'What're you up to?' asked one of the hostesses, as I caught up with the group.

'Nothing,' I murmured, but my heart was picking up speed. No alarms. I hadn't dared hope that there would be no alarms.

We passed a flight of stairs that led down into darkness. I hesitated, staring down into the gloom, resisting the urge to break from the group and slip down the steps. The apartment was arranged over two floors. What sort of rooms would be down there? I wondered, suddenly and inexplicably picturing cages. *It is not a plant that you're looking for . . .*

Just then the group stopped up ahead and were depositing their bags and jackets in a small cloakroom. I had to leave the staircase and catch up with them, pausing to leave my coat too. Soon we could hear low music, the gentle clink of ice in glasses, and presently came into a smoky, low-ceilinged room, full of carefully lit alcoves and display cabinets. I stood for a moment, my eyes getting used to the light. The hostesses from the earlier cars were already seated in large oxblood chesterfields, balancing glasses and talking in low murmurs. Jason was in an armchair, comfortably reclined, one bare ankle resting lightly on the other knee, a cigarette burning in his fingers – just as if he was relaxing at home after a long day's work. Fuyuki was at the far end of the room in a wheelchair. He was dressed in a loose *yukata*, his legs bare, and he was backing and shunting the wheelchair along the edges of the room, leading Bison around. They were looking at erotic woodcut prints on the walls, long-bodied courtesans with skeletal white legs, embroidered kimonos swirling apart to reveal oversized genitals.

I couldn't help it. I was immediately mesmerized by those prints. I could sense Jason a few feet away, watching my reaction with amusement, but I couldn't tear my eyes away. This one showed a woman so aroused that something was dripping from between her legs. At last, when I couldn't stop myself, I turned. Jason raised his eyebrows and smiled, that long, slow smile that showed just the corner of his chipped tooth, the smile he'd given me in the corridor in Takadanobaba. The blood rushed to my face. I put my fingers on my cheeks and turned away.

'This one,' Bison said in Japanese, tilting his cigar at a print. 'The one with the red kimono?'

'By Shuncho,' Fuyuki said, in his cracked whisper. He planted the cane on the floor and rested his chin on it, looking ruminatively up at the print. 'Eighteenth century. Insured for four million yen. Beautiful, isn't it? Had a little *chimpira* from Saitama liberate it for me from a house in Waikiki.'

The ponytailed man coughed discreetly and Bison turned. Fuyuki rotated the motorized wheelchair to look at us.

'Come with me,' he whispered, to the assembled girls. 'This way.'

We went through an archway to a room where, under two *samurai* swords suspended from the ceiling on invisible wires, a group of men in Aloha shirts sat drinking Scotch from crystal tumblers. They half stood, bowing as Fuyuki glided past them in his chair. Sliding glass doors stood open to reveal a central court-yard lined entirely with gleaming black marble, the night sky reflected in it like a mirror. In the centre, black as jet, as if hollowed from the same block, was a spotlighted swimming-pool, a faint chlorine steam hanging above its surface. Several gas-powered heaters, tall, like lamp-posts, were dotted around, and six large dining-tables were arranged beside the pool, each set with black enamel place mats, silver chopsticks and heavy glass goblets, napkins stirring in the breeze.

Several of the places had already been taken. Large men with cropped hair sat smoking cigars and talking to young women in backless evening dresses. There were so many girls. Fuyuki must know a lot of hostess clubs, I thought.

'Mr Fuyuki,' I said, coming up behind him as we crossed to the tables. He brought the wheelchair to a stop and turned to look at me in surprise. None of the girls had dared to speak to him yet. My legs were wobbly and the heat from the burners made the side of my face red. 'I – I want to sit next to you.'

He narrowed his eyes at me. Maybe he was intrigued by my rudeness. I stepped closer, standing in front of him, near enough for him to be aware of my breasts and my hips, taut inside the dress. On an impulse, the vampire in me stirring, I took his hands and placed them on my hips. 'I want to sit next to you.'

Fuyuki looked at his hands, pressed into the folds of my dress. Maybe he could feel the French knickers beneath it, the slither of silk on silk, the elastic stretch under his fingers. Maybe he just thought I was crazy and clumsy, because after a moment or two he laughed hoarsely. 'Come, then,' he whispered. 'Sit next to me, if you want.'

He propelled his wheelchair into a place under the table and I sat down shakily, pulling my chair up next to him. Bison was already settled a few seats away, picking up a napkin, flicking it out and tucking it into his collar. A waiter in black jeans and T-shirt hovered around us with chilled vodka cocktails in cloudy white glasses, vaporous trails coming from them like dry ice. I sipped, surreptitiously surveying the courtyard. Somewhere, I thought, looking at the windows, some lit, others in darkness, somewhere in this apartment is the thing that keeps Shi Chongming awake at night. *Not a plant. If not a plant, then what?* There was a red light set high up on the wall. I wondered if it was an alarm.

Food arrived at the table: slabs of tuna piled like dominoes on beds of nettle; bowls of walnut tofu sprinkled with seaweed; grated radish, crunchy as salt. Bison sat immobilized, staring down at a plate of *yakitori* chicken, as if it posed a huge problem, his face pale and sweaty, as if he might be sick. I watched him in silence, thinking of how he'd been last time at the club, his expression of amazement, the way he'd been transfixed by the residue on the sides of Fuyuki's glass. Just like Strawberry, I thought. He doesn't want to eat the meat. He's heard the same stories she has . . .

I licked my dry lips and leaned over to Fuyuki. 'We've met before tonight,' I murmured in Japanese. 'Do you remember?'

'Have we?' He didn't look at me.

'Yes. In the summer. I was hoping to see you again.'

He paused for a moment, then said, 'Is that so? Is that so?' When he spoke, his eyes and his odd little nose didn't move, but the skin on his upper lip adhered to his teeth and lifted to reveal strange pointed canines in the top corners of his mouth, just like a cat's. I stared at those teeth. 'I'd like to see your apartment,' I said quietly.

'You can see it from here.' He felt in his pocket and pulled out a cigar, which he unwrapped, clipped with a discreet silver tool taken from his breast pocket, and inspected, turning it this way and that, picking flakes of tobacco off it.

'I'd like to look around. I'd like to . . .' I hesitated. I gestured to the room where the prints were hung and said, in a low voice, 'To see the prints. I've read about *shunga*. The ones you've got are very rare.'

He lit the cigar and yawned. 'They were bringed to Japan by me,' he said, switching to clumsy English. 'Back to homeland. My hobby is to – *Eigo deha nanto iu no desuka? Kaimodosu kotowa – Nihon no bijutsuhinwo Kaimodosu no desuyo.*'

'Repatriate,' I said. 'Repatriate Japanese art.'

'*So, so.* Yes. Re-pa-tri-ate Japan art.'

'Would you like to show them to me?'

'No.' He let his eyes close slowly, like a very old reptile at leisure, vaguely resting his hand across them, as if that was enough conversation for now. 'Thank you, not now.'

'Are you sure?'

He opened one eye and regarded me suspiciously. I started to speak, but something in his look made me think better of it. I dropped my hands into my lap. *He must never know*, Shi Chongming had said. *Never suspect.*

'Yes.' I cleared my throat and fiddled with the napkin. 'Of course. Now is the wrong time. Quite the wrong time.' I lit a cigarette and smoked, turning the lighter over and over in my hands, as if it was utterly fascinating. Fuyuki watched me for a few more seconds. Then, seeming satisfied, he closed his eyes again.

After that I didn't speak to him much. He dozed for a few minutes, and when he woke up the Japanese girl on his right took over from me, telling him a long story about an American girl who went out jogging braless, which made him laugh and shake his head enthusiastically. I sat in silence, smoking cigarette after cigarette, thinking, *What next, what next, what next?* I had the distinct idea I was getting near, that I was circling something closely. I drank two glasses of champagne very quickly, stubbed out my cigarette, and took a deep breath, leaning towards him. 'Fuyuki-san?' I murmured. 'I need the bathroom.'

'*Hi hi,*' he said distractedly. The hostess on his right was demonstrating a trick with a book of matches. He waved a hand vaguely behind him to a double glass door. 'Through there.'

I stared at him. I'd expected more. Some resistance. I pushed back my chair and stood, looking down at his small brown skull, expecting him to move. But he didn't. No one at the table even glanced up, they were all too absorbed in their conversations. I crossed the patio, got through the glass doors, and closed them quickly, standing for a moment, my hands flat on the glass, looking back. No one had noticed me leave. At a table near the far end of the pool I could see the back of Jason's head between two hostesses and nearer me was Fuyuki, exactly as I'd left him, the back of his thin shoulders moving as he laughed. The hostess had set light to the match book and was standing, holding it above the table like a beacon, waving it to a round of applause from the other guests.

I turned away from the door. I was standing in a panelled corridor, the mirror image of the one we'd entered earlier, full of more lighted glass cabinets – I could see a Noh actor's costume, *samurai* armour glinting in the low lights. Countless doors stretched into the distance. I took a deep breath and started to walk.

The carpet muffled my footfalls; the noise of the air-conditioning made me think of the enclosed, capsular atmosphere of an aeroplane. I sniffed – what was I expecting to smell? *Don't eat the meat* . . . There should be more stairs on this side of the apartment. I passed doorway after doorway, but no staircase. At the end of the corridor I turned smartly at right angles into another corridor, and my pulse quickened. There it was, up on the right: the staircase, heavy double doors standing open, hooked back to the wall.

I was about ten yards away from it when a long way up ahead, at the next corner, a shadow appeared at the foot of the wall.

I froze. The Nurse. It could only be her, approaching from the next corridor. She must have been walking quickly because the shadow was getting bigger, climbing rapidly up the wall until it almost met the ceiling. I stood, paralysed, my heart thumping furiously. Any minute now she'd reach the corner and see me.

Now I could hear her shoe leather squeaking efficiently. I groped blindly at the nearest door. It opened. Inside a light came on automatically and, just as the shadow dropped to the floor and shot sideways along the wall towards me, I stepped in, closing the door behind me with a discreet click.

It was a bathroom, a windowless room all in a fabulous blood red marble, veined like fat in beef with a hot tub surrounded by mirrors and a stack of immaculate starched towels on a ledge. I stood for a few moments, shaking uncontrollably, my ear pressed against the door, listening to the corridor. If she had seen me I would say what I'd said to Fuyuki: I was looking for the bathroom. I breathed cautiously, trying to pick up a sound from outside. But minutes passed and I could hear nothing. Maybe she had gone into a different room. I clicked the lock, and then, because my legs were weak, sank on to the toilet lid. This was impossible, impossible. How did Shi Chongming expect me to deal with this? What did he think I was?

After several minutes, when nothing had happened, no sound, no breath, I pulled a cigarette from my bag and lit it. I smoked silently, biting my nails and staring at the door. I checked my watch, wondering how long I'd been in there, whether she'd still be out there. Slowly, slowly, the trembling subsided. I finished the cigarette, dropped it into the toilet and lit another, smoking it slowly. Then I stood and ran my fingers up and down the edge of the mirrors, wondering if there was room behind them to hide a surveillance camera. I opened drawers and rummaged through stacks of soap and little complimentary toiletry sets embossed with JAL and Singapore Airlines logos. When an age seemed to have passed, I flushed the toilet, took a deep breath, clicked the door open and put my head out. The corridor was empty. The Nurse was gone and the double doors to the staircase had been closed. When I crept across the passage and tried the handle, I found they'd been locked.

Outside the sky was clear, just a shred of cloud lit pink from beneath by city lights moved silently over the stars, like a giant's breath on a cold day. While I'd been in the corridor the guests had left their places and were perched on striped recliners, starting mah-jongg games on foldaway tables. The waiters cleared away the plates. Nobody noticed me come back and sit, still jittery, on a seat near the pool.

Fuyuki had been moved to a far corner of the courtyard and the Nurse was with him, bent over, busily tucking a fur throw over his legs. She was dressed in a very tight skirt, a high-collared jacket and her usual high heels. Her hair was tucked behind her ears, revealing her white, oddly pitted cheek. She'd painted her lips in a deep red – on her tight mouth it looked almost bluish. The men nearby sat with their backs turned pointedly to her, concentrating on their conversations, pretending not to be aware of her presence.

She didn't look up at me. She had probably intended to lock those doors anyway, I thought. There was no reason to think she'd known I was there. Fuyuki muttered something to her, his frail hand groping for her sleeve. She lowered her head to his mouth, and I held my breath, staring at her nails, each oval painted a careful matt red. The nail on her smallest finger had been grown long and curved, the way Chinese merchants traditionally grew them to show they didn't do manual labour. I wondered if Fuyuki was telling her about my insistence that he show me the apartment, but after a few moments she straightened and, instead of looking at me, slipped silently away past the pool, through the opposite doors.

I sat forward, tense, my hands grasping the chair, my attention going with her, following her every inch of the way along the corridors, maybe down the stairs. I knew what she was going to do. I knew it instinctively. The noise of the party faded into the background and all I could hear was the pulse of the night, the lapping of water against the pool filter. My ears expanded with my heart, until all the small sounds seemed amplified a thousand times and I thought I could hear the apartment shifting and murmuring around me. I could hear someone washing dishes in the kitchen. I could hear the Nurse's soft footfalls moving down the stairs. I was sure I could hear padlocks rattling, iron doors creaking open. She was going to get Fuyuki's medicine.

And then something happened. In the pool, at a depth of about eight feet, there were two underwater windows covered by slatted blinds. I hadn't noticed them before because they had been in darkness. But a light had just come on in the room, sending vertical yellow stripes into the water. Quickly I fished inside my handbag, lit a cigarette and got up, moving past the crowd and going casually to the pool edge. I stood, one hand in the small of my back, taking a few draws on the cigarette to calm myself. Then, when I was sure no one was watching me, I peered down into the water. A guest nearby began to sing a loud *enka* song, and one of the hostesses was giggling loudly, but I was barely aware of it. I closed off my mind until all there was in the world were me and those stripes of light in the water.

I was sure, without knowing how, that just beyond those blinds was the room where Fuyuki's medicine was kept. The slats were open far enough to show part of the floor and I could see the Nurse's shadow moving around in there. From time to time she came sufficiently close to the window for me to see her feet in their hard, shiny stilettos. My attention narrowed. There was something else in the room with the Nurse. Something made of glass. Something square, like a case or a—

'What are you doing?'

I jumped. Jason was standing next to me, holding his drink and looking down into the water. Suddenly all the noise started again and the colour came back into the world. The singing guest was grinding out the last few bars of his song, and the waiters were opening bottles of brandy, distributing glasses among the guests.

'What're you staring at?'

'Nothing.' I shot a look back down into the pool. The light had gone out. The pool was dark again. 'I mean, I was looking at the water. It's so – so clear.'

'Be careful,' Jason murmured. 'Be very careful.'

'Yes,' I said, stepping away from the pool. 'Of course.'

'You're here for something, aren't you?'

I met his eyes. 'What?'

'You're looking for something.'

'No. I mean – no, of course I'm . . . What a funny thing to say.'

He gave a short, dry laugh. 'You forget, I can tell when you're lying.' He looked at my face, then at my hair and my neck, as if they had just asked him a complex question. He touched my shoulder lightly and a bolt of static made my hair leap up at him, wrapping itself round his fingers. He looked down at it with a long, slow smile. 'I'm going to get all the way inside you,' he said quietly. 'All the way. But don't be scared, I'm going to do it very, very slowly.'

29

史 Nanking, 18 December 1937, eight o'clock (the sixteenth day of the eleventh month)

At last I can write. At last I have some peace. I have been gone from home for more than a day. When, in the late afternoon, I made up my mind to leave the house, nothing could have stopped me. I pinned my refugee certificate to my jacket and slipped out into the alleyway, dragged onwards by the smell. It was the first time I had been outside in daylight since the thirteenth. The air seemed heavy and cold, the snow stale. I went quietly, using alleys and climbing over gates to get to Liu's house. His front door was open and he was sitting just inside, almost as if he hadn't moved since I left him. He was smoking a pipe, a desultory look on his face.

'Liu Runde,' I said, stepping into the receiving room, 'can you smell it? Can you smell the meat cooking?'

He bent forward and put his nose out into the cold air, tilting his head and looking up thoughtfully at the sky.

'It could be the food they stole from us,' I said. 'Maybe they've got the gall to cook it.'

'Maybe.'

'I'm going to search. Out on the streets. Shujin needs food.'

'Are you sure? What about the Japanese?'

I didn't answer. I was recalling with some embarrassment his insistence that we would be safe, I thought of the example we were to be setting. After a long silence I gathered myself and patted my refugee certificate. 'Haven't you – haven't you got one of these, old man?'

He shrugged and got to his feet, putting down the pipe. 'Wait there,' he said. 'I'm going to get it.'

He had a hurried, whispered conversation with his wife. I could see them in the dimly lit room at the back of the house, facing each other, just her faded blue silk sleeve visible in the doorway, moving every now and then as she raised her hand to make an earnest point. Shortly he came outside to meet me, closing the door carefully behind him and glancing up and down the alley. He had his certificate pinned to his jacket and an anxious, drawn look on his face. 'I never expected it would come to this,' he whispered, turning up his collar against the cold. 'I never would have imagined. Sometimes I wonder who is the foolish one in my marriage . . .'

We crept to the head of the alley and peered along the deserted street. There wasn't a sound or a movement anywhere. Not even a dog. Only rows and rows of shuttered houses, blackened with soot, an abandoned handcart up-ended against the front of a house. Small fires burned on the roadside, and in the direction of the river the sky was red with flames. I sniffed the air. That incredible tantalizing smell seemed stronger. Almost as if we could expect at any moment to hear the sizzle and pop of frying coming from one of the houses.

We crept up the road like a pair of starving cats, hovering in the shadows, scurrying from doorway to doorway, all the time working towards the Zhongyang gate in the north, the direction the thieves had run. From time to time we happened on bundles of possessions, the owner nowhere to be seen, and we would drag them into the nearest doorway, rummaging desperately through them, hoping for food. Every rickety house we saw we pushed our noses against the doors, whispering through the knotholes, 'Who's cooking? Who's cooking?' A fist of hunger was working its way through my body, so intense I found it difficult to stand up straight. I could see from the look on Liu's face that he felt the same. 'Come out,' we hissed into the houses. 'Show us – show us what you are cooking.'

In winter, darkness comes early to us in the east of China, and before long the sun had gone and we were picking our way through the streets using just the light from the fires to guide us. We were exhausted. We seemed to have walked several *li* – I felt as if I had walked all the way to Pagoda Bridge Road – yet we still hadn't passed through the city wall. The only other living creature we had seen was a lean and hungry-looking dog, wild and covered with such terrible sores that part of its backbone was exposed. It followed us for a while, and although it was horribly diseased we tried half-heartedly to entice it to us: it was big enough to feed both our families. But it was nervous and barked loudly when we got near it, the sound echoing dangerously through the silent streets. Eventually we abandoned the pursuit.

'It's late,' I said, stopping somewhere near the gate. The smell of cooking had been replaced by something else, the stench of polluted drains. Our spirits were failing. I looked at the rickety buildings lining the street. 'I'm not so hungry any more, old man. I'm not.'

'You're tired. Only tired.'

I was about to answer when something over Liu's shoulder caught my eye. 'Be quite still,' I hissed, gripping his arm. 'Don't speak.'

He whipped round. At the end of the road, in the distance, his face lit from underneath by a small lantern placed on a water barrel, a Japanese soldier had appeared, his rifle hooked on his shoulder. Only five minutes ago we had been standing exactly where he stood now.

We darted quickly into the nearest doorway, breathing hard, pressing ourselves back and shooting looks at each other.

'He wasn't there a minute ago,' Liu hissed. 'Did you see him?'

'No.'

'How in heaven's name are we going to get home now?'

We stood there for a long time, our eyes locked, our hearts thudding in our chests, both hoping the other would decide what to do. I knew this road ran in a straight line with no gaps in the houses for a long way – we would have to cover a lot of ground in full view of the soldier before we found a side road to disappear into. I took a deep breath, pulled my cap down low on my brow, and risked putting my head out into the street, just for a second, just long enough to see the soldier. I shot back, flat against the wall, breathing hard.

'What?' hissed Liu. 'What can you see?'

'He's waiting for something.'

'Waiting? Waiting for—'

But before he could complete the question the answer came to us: a familiar sound rolling menacingly out of the distance, a low, dreadful rumbling that made the houses around us shudder. We both knew what that sound was. Tanks.

Instinctively we pushed away from the street, inwards, throwing our weight at the wooden door, trusting that the noise of the tanks would drown our efforts. We were ready to climb the side of the house barehanded if necessary, but the door crumpled with an appalling splintering, just as the noise of the tanks grew louder behind us – they must have turned a corner into the street. The door fell inwards with a sudden rush of stale air, and we tumbled inside, a mess of sweat and fear and heavy clothing, tripping and stumbling into the darkness.

It was pitch black, only a faint wash of moonlight creeping in from a hole in the roof.

'Liu?' My voice sounded hushed and small. 'Old man, are you there?'

'Yes. Yes. Here I am.'

Together we pushed the remains of the door closed as best we could, then shrank to the walls, inching our way round the room, heading for the hole in the ceiling. It is astonishing the rural habits that people import to a city: livestock had been living in this house, maybe to keep the residents warm at night, and Liu and I were wading through warmish animal bedding and manure. The roar of the tanks was getting louder in the street, rattling the little house, threatening to make it collapse.

'This way,' Liu whispered. He had stopped, and now I saw he was holding the rungs of a ladder that led up through the hole in the roof. I followed him to the foot and looked up. Above us the night sky was bright, the distant stars cold and polished. 'Let's go.'

He scampered up the ladder more agilely than I could have imagined for a man of his age and stopped at the top, turning to hold out a hand to me. I took it and climbed hurriedly, letting him haul me through the gap. At the top of the ladder I straightened and looked around. We stood in the open air: the building was a ruin, the roof had long since been destroyed, leaving only a scattering of rotting millet stalks and lime mortar.

I beckoned to Liu and we crept to the edge, peering cautiously over the broken wall. We had made it just in time. Below us a barrage of tanks proceeded slowly down the street. The noise was deafening. It funnelled along the street and rose, like a heatwave, powerful enough, it seemed, to reach up and shake the moon. Lamps swayed on the tank turrets, sending strange shadows shooting up the outsides of the houses. Soldiers carrying swords and glittering carbines walked erectly on either side of the tanks, their faces expressionless. It must have been a mass movement to different quarters because behind the tanks came other vehicles: scout cars, a water-purifying truck, two pontoon bridges towed by a truck.

As we watched I noticed a dog, maybe the same one we'd been pursuing earlier, appear as if from nowhere and get itself hopelessly tangled among the soldiers' legs. Yelping and whimpering it allowed itself to be kicked so ferociously by the men that within a very short time it was edged into the path of the tank tracks, where it rapidly disappeared from view. Two soldiers in the tank turret noticed this and bent over the side to watch, laughing and curious, as the wretched beast reappeared, mangled in the tread, one hind leg, the only part not crushed, protruding sideways from the track, still twitching convulsively. I am no lover of dogs, yet the pleasure in the soldiers' laughter turned my heart to stone.

'Look,' I murmured. 'Look at this, old Liu.' It was dawning on me how foolish I had been to imagine the Japanese to be somehow a little like us, to imagine we might even be safe with them. These men were not like us. I sank down behind the small parapet and put my head in my hands. 'What a mistake we've made. What a terrible mistake.'

179

Liu moved to sit next to me, his big hand gently on my back. I am glad he didn't speak to me. I am glad, because if I had opened my mouth to reply I might have said these words: *Maybe not now, maybe not tonight, but soon the end will come. Trust me, old Liu, our wives have been right all along. Soon we are going to die.*

30

In the taxi on the way home Jason and I sat in silence, not speaking. Irina and Svetlana giggled and smoked and lapsed in and out of Russian, but I didn't hear a word. I was conscious of every inch of my skin, itchy like an animal whose fur has been stroked against the grain. I kept shuffling and moving my bottom around on the seat until Irina got irritated and nudged me. 'Stop it. Stop fuckink wiggling like a worm. You gone crazy?' On the other side of her, next to the window, sitting in profile, Jason shook his head in secret amusement. He lowered his face and put a finger to the tip of his nose and nodded, as if someone invisible had just whispered a question in his ear.

Back at the house the Russians went straight to bed and I pulled off my coat, hung it next to Jason's holdall on the peg at the top of the stairs and walked, without a word, down the corridor to my room. He followed me. When he stepped inside he could see I was jittery. 'I know you're scared.'

'No.' I rubbed my arms. 'No. I'm not scared.'

He must have been wondering what was making me so flustered – maybe he had thoughts about assault, child abuse, rape. I was trembling so hard I had to take deep breaths every time he touched me. I tried to keep calm and visualize something serene, something dark and weighty sitting just under my ribs, so I didn't collapse. But Jason didn't seem to notice anything until he'd got me backed up to the dressing-table, and was standing between my open legs, my dress pushed up above my waist. He stared down at the flushed tops of my thighs, hypnotized by the place where we were going to be locked together. Where the thin skin on my inner thighs touched his, I could feel his heart beating in the big vessels going to his groin. 'These,' he said, putting his fingers inside the elastic of my knickers. 'Take them off.'

'No.' I grabbed at them. 'Please.'

'Ah,' he said, in a low, fascinated voice, looking curiously into my face. 'Is this it? Have I found it?' He hooked his fingers into the waistband again. 'Is this what you're hiding—'

'No!' I shot backwards, scattering things on the dressing-table, making them smash on the floor. 'Please don't. Please!'

'Christ,' he said, taking a sudden breath, almost as if I'd hurt him. 'Easy, easy.' He took a few surprised steps sideways, putting his hands on the dressing-table to get his balance. 'Fuck, weirdo. Easy.'

I sank back, dropping my legs, my hands over my eyes. 'I'm sorry,' I muttered. 'I'm sorry. Please. Don't take them off.'

He didn't answer at first, and for a long time there was nothing, only the shocked silence and the sound of my heartbeat. I wished I could tell him. I wished I could. I wished that everything was different. Eventually he brought his lips near my neck and breathed lightly on it. I froze, afraid of what he was going to say.

'Know something, weirdo? You just cannot imagine how alike we are, you and me. I know exactly what's going on in your head.'

'Please don't take them off.'

'I'm not going to. Not now. But let me tell you what's going to happen. One day, one day soon, you'll tell me what it is. And you know what?'

I dropped my hands and looked at him. 'What?'

'It won't even be a big deal. Because . . .' He looked up at the walls, at the mural of Tokyo, at the paintings of Nanking pinned on the walls. His eyes gleamed in the half-light. '. . . because you and me are – we're the same. Did you know that?'

I shook my head, wiped my face with my hands and pushed the

hair out of my eyes. 'I'm sorry,' I said, in a tight voice. 'I'm really sorry.'

'You don't need to be.' He kissed my neck, licking me with the flat of his tongue, just below my ear, waiting a moment for me to soften and absorb him. 'You don't need to be. The only problem is . . .'

'Mmmm?'

'If you keep those panties on, how'm I going to fuck you?'

I took a deep breath. I pushed him away and bunched my skirt up round my waist. Then I put my index finger into the crotch and pulled it aside. It only took him a moment to see how the magic knickers worked.

And after that the whole thing was so perfect – it was just as if the loose atoms and membranes in me all stretched up at once and leaped free of me, whirling among the stars and the planets. Afterwards I could hardly speak. Jason pulled on his jeans, took one of my cigarettes, put it in his mouth and lit it, tilting his chin back so the cigarette looked as if it was doing a handstand. He folded his arms across his chest, his hands tucked into his armpits, and looked sideways through the smoke at the flowers on my knickers, as if he suspected I was playing some sort of joke on him.

'What?' I said nervously, smoothing my knickers across my stomach, checking nothing was showing. 'What?'

He took the cigarette out of his mouth and laughed. 'Nothing.' He flicked the ash into the air with a flourish, like a conjuror. Then he went to the door and stepped outside without a word. I heard him at the end of the corridor, getting his keys, putting on his shoes, and clattering down the steps. Then the house was silent. And I was sitting on my own, on the dressing-table, naked except for my magic knickers.

I slid off the table with a thump and went to the window. The alley was empty – Jason was nowhere to be seen. He really had gone. I turned my face baldly up to Mickey Rourke, meeting his eyes. He was smiling as if nothing had happened. There was the smallest, sweetest breeze coming in from the Tokyo bay, making the bamboo move, and on the breeze I thought I could smell south-sea islands and shrimp frying on distant lighted junks. The only sounds were the rustling of the wind in the bamboo, the far-away rumble of traffic.

What did this mean? Had he left me, just like the boys in the van? Had I got it all wrong? I sat down on the floor, rubbing my stomach over and over again. My heart was hammering in my chest. I should never have let it go this far – I should have left everything just as it was. I looked at the condom he'd left in the bin, and the same blank feeling I'd had watching the van's lights disappear came over me again, like nausea. *Didn't you learn your lesson, then?*

Eventually I picked up my dress and pulled it on. I went to the bin, lifted the condom on my fingernail and carried it down the corridor in the dark. I dropped it into the scooped-out Japanese-style toilet bowl, stared at it for a few moments then flushed. The water rushed in, silvery in the moonlight, making the condom spin a few times. Then it was sucked away and I was looking at nothing.

At the far end of the house the front door slammed and I heard footsteps on the stairs.

'Grey?'

He was back. I pushed myself away from the wall, stepped into the corridor and there he was, his arms full of bags from the all-night convenience store. It sounds silly now, but at the time, knowing he'd come back, he really looked to me like an angel. I could see *sake* bottles and a huge bag of dried cuttlefish sticking out of the tops of the bags.

'We need fuel.' He pulled out a packet of *sembei* to show me. 'We need energy so we can do it again.'

I closed my eyes, and let my hands drop.

'What is it?'

'Nothing,' I said, a stupid, involuntary smile spreading across my face. 'Nothing.'

31

Nanking, 18 December 1937

After the vehicles, after the shattering roar and flash of lights, came the soldiers. They ran through the streets like the devils Liu had described in Suzhou. Every time the road had been silent for a while, and we began to hope it was safe to venture out, we'd hear the sinister jangle of a bayonet frog, the slap-slap of pigskin boots, and three or four more IJA soldiers, *arisaka* rifles at the ready, would come. The patrolman at the head of the street had found a packing crate and was sitting on it, smoking cigarettes, waving his comrades through. Eventually, exhausted and freezing, Liu and I curled up next to each other for warmth, our backs to the wall, his arm round my shoulders, like an older brother.

When we'd been there for more than two hours the moon, which was a solid silver disc, so breathlessly clear that we could see the cups and crenations in its surface, slid another degree down the western sky and suddenly illuminated a deformed black anomaly in the horizon, gently sloped and blocking the sky. For a while we looked at it in silence.

'What's that?' Liu murmured.

'Tiger Mountain?'

They say that only in some parts of Nanking can the tiger's head in Tiger Mountain be seen properly. It has to be viewed from the correct direction. From this angle it was unrecognizable as the mountain I knew – an altogether different shape, and oddly small, as if dreadfully diminished by the invasion. 'It can only be Tiger Mountain.'

'I had no idea we were so close.'

'I know,' I whispered. 'It means we're nearer the walls than I thought.'

A cloud crossed the moon, a silver and red scrap of lace, and the shadows on our roof seemed to shift and flutter. I closed my eyes and huddled closer to Liu. Behind us in the street we could still hear the Japanese troops. Suddenly all the tiredness in the world came to me: I knew we were going to have to sleep there on the roof. Liu pulled his jacket tight round him and began to talk very quietly. He told me about the day his son was born, in Shanghai, in a house not far from the fabulous Bund, about how all the family had come to the *man yue* when the boy was a month old, bringing him coins in envelopes, playing with him, making him kick and laugh and squirm so that the little gold bells on his ankles and wrists jingled. Liu could hardly believe that now he was living in a one-storey hut in an alley, scurrying through the streets hunting sick dogs for food.

While he talked I tucked my sleeves into my gloves and arranged my tunic so that it covered as much of me as possible. Liu's words flowed over me, and my mind drifted out, past Tiger Mountain and along up the Yangtze, stretching away from Nanking: across the salty alluvial plains stretching eastwards to Shanghai over miles of countryside, wayside shrines littered with incense ash, graves dug on the slivers of ground next to the railways, the clatter of ducks being driven to market, dwellings carved into the yellow stone – unbearably hot in the summer, insulated and safe in the winter. I thought of all the families across China, waiting patiently under teak trees in villages, of all the smallholdings where people are honest and nothing is wasted – straw and grass are burned for fuel, and children's balloons are made from nothing more than pig bladders. I tried – I tried hard not to imagine Japanese tanks rumbling through it all. I tried hard not to picture them crushing the countryside under their treads, the rising-sun flags fluttering as the entire continent quaked.

Eventually my eyes grew heavy, and before long old Liu's

words became quieter. They faded with my thoughts into the night, and I fell into a light sleep.

史 Nanking, 19 December 1937 (the seventeenth day of the eleventh month)

'Wake up.'

I opened my eyes and the first thing I saw, very close to me, was Liu Runde's face, wet and pink, his eyelashes covered in snow. 'Wake up and look.'

It was early morning and he was pointing out over the roof, an uneasy expression on his face. I jerked up, startled. I had forgotten where I was. The roof was covered with snow and the dawn was sidelighting everything a weak, supernatural pink.

'Look,' he urged. 'Look.'

Hurriedly I brushed at the layer of snow that had fallen on me in the night and tried to push myself up. I was so cold that my body creaked and seized up, and Liu had to grab me by the shoulders and lift me to a sitting position, setting my body in a westerly direction, forcing me to look in the direction of the mountain.

'Tiger Mountain. See?' There was a kind of ghastly awe in his voice, something that made him sound very young and unsure. He stood at my side, brushing the snow from his gloves. 'Tell me, Shi Chongming, is that the Tiger Mountain you know?'

I blinked, sleepy and confused. The skyline was red with fire, as if we were in hell, its oblique blood-tinted light falling on the terrible mountain. And then I saw what he meant. No. It wasn't Tiger Mountain at all. I was looking at something completely different. As if the earth had coughed up something poisonous. Something too fearsome to keep in its bowels.

'It can't be,' I whispered, pushing myself to my feet in a daze. 'Old Father Heaven, am I imagining this?'

It was a hundred, no, a thousand, corpses. They had been carelessly piled, one on top of the other, countless levels of twisted bodies, their heads pointing in unnatural directions, shoes hanging from limp feet. Liu and I had fallen asleep gazing at a corpse mountain in the moonlight. I can't chronicle here everything I saw – if I put down the truth it might burn through the paper – the fathers, the sons, the brothers, the infinite variations of sorrow. There was a noise, too, a low murmur that seemed to come from the direction of the mountain. Now that I thought about it, I realized that it had been there for a long time, since before I had woken. It had been in my dreams.

Liu got to his feet and picked his way across the roof, his gloved hands held out in front of him. My frozen body numb, I stumbled clumsily after him. The view yawned wider and wider in front of me – the whole of western Nanking spread out: to our right the intermittent grey glitter of the Yangtze, the slim, dun beak of Baguazhou Island, to our left the brown factory chimneys of Xiaguan. And in the centre, about half a *li* away, dominating everything around it, the dreadful corpse mountain, rising up from the earth.

We put our hands on the crumbling wall and, very slowly, hardly breathing, dared to put our noses over the top. The ground between the house and the mountain, which was open scrubland with neither streets nor buildings, was swarming with people. Thick on the ground they moved in a single tide, some carrying possessions, bedrolls, cooking pots, small sacks of rice as if they anticipated only a few days' absence from home, some supporting others, jostling and tripping. Dotted among them were the distinctive mustard-brown caps of Japanese officers, their heads switching back and forward like oiled machinery. These were prisoners being rounded up. The backs of their heads were lit by the rising sun, and although we couldn't see their faces, we knew what was happening from the low murmur that rose from them as they recognized the true nature of the mountain ahead. It was the sound of a thousand voices whispering their fear.

They were all men, but they weren't all soldiers. This soon became clear. I could see grey heads among them. 'They're civilians,' I hissed to Liu. 'Can you see?'

He put his hand on my arm. 'Dear Shi Chongming,' he

whispered sorrowfully, 'I have no words for this. There was nothing in Shanghai to compare with this.'

As we watched, those at the head of the crowd must have grasped that they were being led to their death because panic broke out. Shouts went up and a wave of bodies bucked, backing away from their fate, trying desperately to reverse. Instead they collided with the prisoners behind, creating a pleat of mayhem, all fighting to run in different directions. Seeing the chaos, the Japanese officers, working with mystic, silent communication, formed themselves into a horseshoe round the prisoners, limiting and confining the crowd, raising their rifles. As the prisoners on the outskirts spotted the rifles and terrified skirmishes broke out, belongings were held up in defence: anything – a cap, a tin cup, or a shoe – would do. The sounds of the first shot rang across the heads of the crowd.

The effect was astonishing. It was as if we were watching a single living entity, water maybe, or something more viscid, moving as a single organism. A wave started. The force of bodies held the injured and dying erect, while in the centre of the crowd a pucker appeared, a protrusion where the bodies pressing forward were causing some in the crowd to clamber on to each other. More shots rang out. Even above the shouts I could hear the metallic shunt of the rifles being reloaded, and the small raised bud in the centre began to grow and grow, people climbing over each other to escape, until in front of my eyes it evolved into a terrible human column, slowly, slowly stretching skywards like a tremulous finger.

The screams came to us and, next to me, Liu dropped his face into his hands, beginning to shudder. I didn't put out a hand to him, I was so horribly riveted by that wavering finger. The human spirit is so strong, I thought distantly, maybe it can climb all the way to the sky without anything to hold on to. Maybe it can climb on air. But after a few minutes, when the column seemed impossibly high – maybe twenty feet – something in its structure collapsed, and it dissolved, tumbling outwards, crushing everyone beneath it. Within seconds the tower was re-forming in a different part of the crowd, the little liquid beginnings of a finger pointing inquisitively out of a lake, then rising and rising until, before long, it was pointing rigidly at the sky, screaming out with accusation, 'Will *you* allow this to happen?'

Just then a flurry of activity erupted close to the house where we were sheltering – someone had broken loose from the crowd and was racing towards us, pursued by another figure. I grabbed Liu's arm. 'Look.'

He dropped his hands and raised fearful eyes to the gap. As the men drew near we saw a young Japanese soldier, bareheaded, his face grim and determined, chased by three older men, senior officers, I guessed, from their uniforms. Swords bounced at their sides, hampering their progress, but they were strong and tall and they closed quickly on the fleeing man, one lunging forward and catching his sleeve, sending him whirling round, his free arm flying out.

Liu and I pressed ourselves even lower into the crumbling roof. The men were only a few yards away. We could have leaned over and spat on them.

The fugitive stumbled on for a few steps, moving in a circle, windmilling his arm, only just managing to regain his balance. He came to a halt, his hands on his knees, breathing hard. The officer released him and took a step back. 'Stand up,' he barked. 'Stand up, you pig.'

Reluctantly the man straightened. He pulled back his shoulders and faced the men, his chest rising and falling. His uniform was torn and pulled out of shape, and I was so close that I could see white ringworm circles on his cropped scalp.

'What do you think you're doing?' one of the officers demanded. 'You broke ranks.'

The soldier started to say something, but he was trembling so hard that he couldn't speak. He turned mutely and looked back at the scene from hell, at the human column, men being dropped like crows from the sky. When he turned back to the officers he wore an expression of such pain that I felt a moment of pity for him. There were tears on his cheeks and this seemed to infuriate the officers. They gathered round him, their faces rigid. One was moving his jaw, as if grinding his teeth. Without a word he unbuckled his sword. The young soldier took a step back.

'Change your mind,' ordered the officer, advancing on him. 'Go back.'

The soldier took another step backwards.

'Change your mind and go back.'

'*What are they saying?*' hissed Liu at my side.

'*He doesn't want to shoot the prisoners.*'

'Go back now!'

The soldier shook his head. This angered the officer even more. He grabbed the soldier by both ears and swung him round, twisting him bodily, dropping him on to the ground. 'Change your mind.' He pressed the sole of his hobnailed marching boot against the soft side of the soldier's face and put some weight behind it. The other officers gathered even closer. 'Pig.' He put more pressure on the boot and the skin on the junior's face pulled forward until a big soft part of his cheek was hanging across his mouth and he couldn't stop his own saliva spilling out. His flesh would tear soon, I thought. 'One more chance – CHANGE YOUR MIND.'

'No,' he stammered. 'No.'

The officer took a step back, raised the sword above his head. The soldier half raised his hand and tried to say something, but the officer had his momentum now and stepped forward. The sword slammed down, the shadow whipping across the ground, the blade glinting and whistling in the morning sun. It made contact and the soldier jolted once, then rolled forward, his hands over his face, his eyes closed.

'No. Heavens, no,' Liu whispered, covering his eyes. 'Tell me, what do you see? He's dead?'

'No.'

The soldier was rolling and squirming on the ground. The officer had only slapped him with the side of the blade, but it had almost destroyed him. As he tried to get to his feet he lost his footing, his legs treadmilling in the snow. He collapsed to his knees and one of the other officers took the opportunity to swipe at him with his gloved fist, sending him backwards, blood spurting from his mouth. I clenched my teeth. I would have liked to leap over the wall and grab that officer.

At last the soldier made a concerted effort and got himself upright. He was in a pitiful state, twitching and staggering, blood covering his chin. He muttered something under his breath, held up a hand to the captain, and stumbled back in the direction of the massacre. He stopped to pick up his rifle, lifted it to his shoulder and continued on in zigzags as if he were drunk, aiming haphazardly into the crowd, letting loose a volley of shots. One or two of the junior soldiers at the edge of the crowd looked at him, but on seeing the three officers standing silent and stony-faced, they hurriedly turned their eyes back to the panicking prisoners.

The officers watched this retreat, absolutely motionless, only their shadows diminishing as the sun crested the top of the house. None of them moved a muscle, not one spoke or even looked at his colleagues. It was only when the soldier showed no signs of running again that they moved. One swiped a hand across his brow, one wiped his sword and returned it to the sheath, and the third spat in the snow, pulling violently at his mouth as if he couldn't bear the taste a moment longer. Then, one after another, they straightened their caps, and walked back to the massacre, large spaces between them, their arms loose and drooping, their swords and shadows dragging wearily along the ground next to them.

32

'You seem very different.' Shi Chongming was studying me from where he sat on the steamer chair. His coat was wrapped tightly round him, his white hair had been brushed and maybe oiled so that it lay long and straight over his ears, and the pink skin was showing through, like the skin of an albino rat. 'You're shivering.'

I looked down at my hands. He was right. They were shaking. That was from a lack of food. Yesterday morning, as the sun was coming up, Jason and I had made breakfast from the convenience-store snacks. And that was the last thing I could remember eating in almost thirty hours.

'I think you've changed.'

'Yes,' I said. I had allowed a day and a half to go by, and it was only when he'd called me that I mentioned I'd been at Fuyuki's. Shi Chongming had wanted to come over straight away – he was 'astonished', 'disappointed' that I hadn't called earlier. I couldn't explain it. I couldn't describe what he couldn't see – that in just one day something hard and sweet and old had spread out under my ribs, like a kiss, and that somehow things that had once seemed urgent didn't sting any more. 'Yes,' I said quietly. 'I suppose I have.'

He waited as if he expected me to say something else. Then, when he saw I wasn't going to, he sighed. He opened his hands and looked round the garden. 'It's beautiful here,' he said. '*Niwa*, they call the garden, the pure place. Not like your corruptible

193

Edens in the West. To the Japanese a garden is the place where harmony reigns. A perfect beauty.'

I looked at the garden. It had changed since I was last out here. The subtle varnish of autumn was on it: the maple was a deep butterscotch colour and the ginkgo had dropped some of its leaves. The tangled undergrowth was bare, like a collection of dried bird bones. But I could see what he meant. There was something beautiful about it. Maybe, I thought, you have to work to experience beauty. 'I suppose it is rather.'

'You suppose it is rather what? Rather beautiful?'

I looked carefully at the long line of white Hansel-and-Gretel stones leading past the do-not-go-here stone and into the undergrowth. 'Yes. That is what I mean. It's very beautiful.'

He tapped his fingers on the chair arm and smiled thoughtfully at me. 'You can see a beauty in this country that you're living in? At last?'

'Isn't that what you're supposed to do?' I said. 'Aren't you supposed to adjust?'

Shi Chongming made a small sound of amusement in his throat. 'Ah, yes. I see you are suddenly very, very wise.'

I adjusted the coat across my legs, moving subtly on the chair. I hadn't bathed, and the smallest movement released the trapped smell of Jason. Under my coat I wore a black camisole I'd bought weeks ago in Omotesando. Tight-fitting and ribbed with tiny silk flowers stitched on the neckline, it stretched all the way down over my stomach, clinging tightly to my hips. I still hadn't had the courage to show Jason my wounds, and he hadn't pushed me. He was so confident that one day I'd reveal everything. He said I should realize that for every person on the planet there was another who would understand them perfectly. It was like being two pieces in a huge metaphysical jigsaw puzzle.

'Why didn't you call me?' Shi Chongming said.

'What?'

'Why didn't you call me?'

I fumbled out a cigarette and lit it, blowing the smoke up into the cloudless sky. 'I – I don't know. I'm not sure.'

'When you were at Fuyuki's did you see anything?'

'Maybe. Maybe not.'

He sat forward and lowered his voice. 'You did? You saw something?'

'Only a glimpse.'

'A glimpse of what?'

'I'm not certain – a sort of glass box.'

'A tank, you mean?'

'I don't know. I've never seen anything like it.' I blew a lungful of smoke into the thin air. The clouds, I noticed, were reflected in the windows of the gallery. Jason was asleep in my room, lying on his back on the futon. I could see the layout of his body in my head, I could hold all the details of it – the way his arm would be curled across his chest, the sound his breath would make coming in and out of his nose.

'What about at a zoo?'

I looked sideways at him. 'A zoo?'

'Yes,' Shi Chongming said. 'Have you seen anything like it at a zoo? I mean, the sort of tank that could be climate-controlled, maybe.'

'I don't know.'

'Were there gauges? The sort that would monitor the air inside? Or thermometers, humidity monitors?'

'I don't know. It was . . .'

'Yes?' Shi Chongming was sitting forward in his seat, looking at me intently. 'It was what? You said you saw something in the tank.'

I blinked at him. He was wrong. I hadn't said that.

'Maybe something . . .' he held out his hands to represent something the size of a small cat '. . . about this big.'

'No. I didn't see anything.'

Shi Chongming closed his mouth tightly and looked at me for a long time, his face perfectly still. I could see sweat breaking out on his forehead. Then he pulled a handkerchief from his coat and quickly mopped his face. 'Yes,' he said, returning the handkerchief and sitting back in his seat with a long exhalation. 'I see you've changed your mind. Haven't you?'

I tapped the ash from my cigarette and frowned at him.

'I have invested an enormous amount of time in you and now you've changed your mind.'

He left by the big gates, and when he'd gone I went upstairs. The Russians were wandering around the house, cooking and squabbling, and while I'd been in the garden Jason had been to the One Stop Best Friend Bento Bar and brought back rice, fish and pickled *daikon*. He'd put it all on the dresser with a bottle of plum liquor and two beautiful pale-violet glasses, and was lying on the futon when I came in. I locked the door behind me and walked straight past the food to the futon, pulling off my coat as I went.

'So? Who was the old guy?'

I knelt astride Jason, facing him. I wasn't wearing knickers, just the camisole. He pushed my knees further apart and ran his hands up my legs. We both looked down at the long expanse of cool flesh he was unpeeling. It seemed to me dense, very un-modern flesh. I still found it amazing that Jason liked it so much.

'Who was the guy in the garden?'

'Something to do with my university.'

'He was looking at you like you were saying the most incredible thing in the world.'

'Not really,' I murmured. 'We were talking about his research. You wouldn't call it incredible at all.'

'Good. I don't like you saying incredible things to anyone else. You spend too much time with him.'

'Too much time?'

'Yes.' He flipped out his palm, holding it up to me. 'See?'

'See what?'

The dim light glinted on his broken nails as he dabbled his fingertips in his palm, slowly at first: tiny, tiny movements. I stared at his fingers, transfixed. They lifted from his palm, flew up swiftly into the air, coming to rest at eye-level, flapping slowly like a bird's wings, yawing and dipping on an air current. It was Shi Chongming's magic crane. The crane of the past.

'You were watching us,' I said, my eyes fixed on his hand. 'Last time.'

He smiled and made the bird do a slow, graceful dive. It twisted elegantly, swooped back up again, dived. He dipped and rolled his hand, humming under his breath. Suddenly it turned and came at me, his fingers flying forward, the bird-hand flapping crazily at my face. I flinched away, half up to my feet, breathing fast.

'Don't do that!' I said. 'Don't.'

He was laughing. He sat up and grabbed my wrists, pulling me back towards him. 'Did you like that?'

'You're teasing me.'

'Teasing you? No. Not teasing you. I wouldn't tease you. I know what it's like to be searching.'

'No.' I resisted his pull. 'I don't understand you.'

He laughed. 'You won't get anywhere.' He pulled me gently backwards, dropping his head back on to the futon, putting my hands to his mouth: licking my palm, chewing gently at my flesh. 'You won't get anywhere pretending to me.'

I watched his teeth, clean and white, fascinated by the healthy glint of dentine and red membrane. 'I'm not pretending,' I murmured vaguely.

'You almost forgot, didn't you?' He slid his hands between my thighs, tangling his fingers in my pubic hair, his eyes on my face. I let my fingers stay on his lips as he spoke. 'You almost forgot that I only have to look at you and I know everything, *everything* that goes on inside your head.'

33

 Nanking, 19 December 1937, night (the seventeenth day of the eleventh month)

Many centuries ago, when the great bronze azimuth was moved from Linfen to the Purple Mountain, it suddenly, inexplicably, became crucially misaligned. No matter what engineers did, it had made up its mind not to function. A few moments ago I peeped out of the shutters at that great chronicler of the heavens and wondered whether maybe, when it settled on the cold mountainside, it had looked up into the cold stars and seen what Shujin had seen. The future of Nanking. It had seen the city's future and had given up caring.

Enough. I must stop thinking like this – of spirits and soothsayers and clairvoyants. I know it is a kind of insanity and yet even here, safe in my study, I cannot help a shiver when I think how Shujin foresaw all of this in her dream. The radio says that last night, while Liu and I were on the roof, several buildings near the refugee centre caught fire. The Nanking city health centre was one of those burned, so where will the injured and the sick go? Our baby would have been born at the health centre. Now there is nowhere for us.

Liu and I still haven't discussed these doubts, even after what we saw this morning. We still haven't said the words, 'Maybe we were wrong.' When we got out of the house in the late afternoon, when the troops had gone and the streets had been quiet for some time, we didn't speak. We ran, crouched, bolting from door to door, terrified. I ran faster than I have ever run before, and all the time I was thinking, *Civilians, civilians, civilians. They are killing civilians.* Everything I have imagined, everything I have promised myself, all that I have forced Shujin to believe, it has all been wrong. The Japanese are not civilized. They are slaughtering civilians. There were no women in that crowd, true, but even that is a poor relief. *No women.* I repeated the words over and again as we flew back to our houses: *No women.*

When I burst through the door, panting and wild-eyed, my clothes covered in sweat, Shujin jumped up in shock, spilling her cup of tea on the table. 'Oh!' She had been crying. Her cheeks were stained. 'I thought you were dead,' she said, taking a few steps towards me. Then she saw my expression and stopped in her tracks. She put her hand up to my face. 'Chongming? What is it?'

'Nothing.' I closed the door and stood for a while, leaning against it for support, catching my breath.

'I did. I thought you were dead.'

I shook my head. She looked very pale, very fragile. Her stomach was big but her limbs were thin and breakable. How vulnerable instincts make us, I thought vaguely, looking down openly at the place our son lies. Soon she will be two and there will be twice the fear and twice the danger and twice the pain. Twice the amount to protect.

'Chongming? What happened?'

I looked up at her, licking my lips.

'What? For heaven's sake, tell me, Chongming.'

'There's no food,' I said. 'I couldn't find any food.'

'You ran back here like the wind to give me the news that there's no food?'

'I am sorry. I am so sorry.'

'No,' she said, coming nearer, her eyes on my face. 'No, it's more than that. You've seen it. You've seen all my premonitions, haven't you?'

I sat down in my chair with a long exhalation of breath. I am the tiredest man in the world. 'Please eat the *man yue* eggs,' I said wearily. 'Please. Do it for me. Do it for our moon soul.'

And to my astonishment she listened. As if she sensed my despair. It wasn't the eggs she ate, nevertheless she did something that came some way towards me. Instead of flying into a superstitious rage, she ate the beans from the pillow that she'd made especially for the baby. She brought it from upstairs, slit it open, emptied the beans into the wok, and cooked them. She offered some to me but I refused, and instead sat and watched her putting the food into her mouth, not a hint of expression on her face.

My stomach aches unbearably: it is like having a living sore, the size of a gourd, under my ribs. This is what it is like to starve, and yet it is only three days that I have been without food. But, and this is surely the worst thing, later, when we were preparing for bed, through the closed shutters the smell came back. That delicious, maddening smell of meat cooking. It drove me to insanity. It sent me on to my feet, ready to rush out into the street, careless of the dangers that lie out there. It was only when I remembered the Japanese officers – when I remembered tanks rumbling down the street, the sound of rifles reloading – that I sank back on to the bed, knowing that I had to find a better way.

 ### Nanking, 20 December 1937

We slept fitfully, in our shoes just as before. A little before dawn we were woken by a series of tremendous screams. It seemed to be coming from only a few streets away and it was distinctly a woman's voice. I looked across at Shujin. She lay absolutely rigid, her eyes fixed on the ceiling, her head resting on the wooden pillow. The screaming continued for about five minutes, getting more desperate and more horrible, until at last it faded to indistinct sobs, and finally silence. Then the noise of a motorcycle on the main street thundered down the alley, shaking the shutters and making the bowl of tea on the bed-stand rock.

Neither Shujin nor I moved as we watched red shadows flicker on the ceiling. There had been a report earlier that the Japanese were burning houses near the Xuanwu lakes – surely those weren't the flames I could see moving on the ceiling. After a long time Shujin got up from the bed and went to where the kitchen range had died down to ashes. I followed her and watched as, without a word, she crouched, took up a handful of the soot and rubbed it into her face until I couldn't recognize her. She rubbed it all over her arms and into her hair, even into her ears. Then she went into the other room and came back with a pair of scissors. She sat in the corner of the room, her face expressionless, took a lock of her hair and began to hack at it.

For a long time after the screaming stopped, even when the city was silent again, I couldn't settle. Here I am at my desk, the window open a chink, not knowing what to do. We could try to escape now, but I am sure it is too late – the city is completely cut off. It is dawn and outside the sun filters through a yellow miasma that hovers above Nanking. Where has that fog come from? It is not smoke from the Xiaguan chimneys mingling with river mist because all the plants there have come to a halt. Shujin would say it is something else: a pall that contains all the deeds of this war. She would say that it is unburied souls and guilt, rising and mingling in the heat above this cursed place, the sky teeming with wandering spirits. She would say that the clouds must have become poisonous, that it is an unspeakable, fatal blow dealt to nature, having so many troubled souls crushed into one earthly location. And who would I be to contradict her? History has shown me that, in spite of what I have long suspected, I am neither brave nor wise.

34

Suddenly, almost overnight, I wasn't afraid of Tokyo. There were even things I liked about it. I liked the view from my window, for example, because I could tell hours in advance when there was a typhoon in the east, just from the bruised colour of the sky. The gargoyles on the roof of the club seemed to crouch a little lower and the gas streams, red against the blackening sky, sputtered in the gathering wind, spitting and guttering until someone in the building thought to switch them off.

That year venture capitalists were throwing themselves off the top of the skyscrapers they'd built, but I was oblivious to the depression that was creeping through the country. I was happy there. I liked the way no one on the trains stared at me. I liked the girls sashaying down the street in oversized sunglasses and embroidered bell-bottom jeans, wearing the glittery red eyelashes they got in the shops in Omotesando. I liked the way everyone here was a little bit odd. *The nail that sticks up will be hammered down.* That was how I'd expected the Japanese to be. One nation, one philosophy. It's funny how sometimes things turn out so differently from the way you picture them.

I worked on my room. I cleared everything out, all the furniture, the dust and the sheets tacked on the walls. I bought new *tatami* mats, washed every inch and replaced the dangling lightbulb with a flush, almost invisible fitting. I mixed up pigments and painted a picture of Jason and me on the silk in the far corner of the room. In the picture he was sitting in the garden next to the stone lantern. He was smoking a cigarette and watching someone just out of the frame. Someone moving, maybe, or dancing in the sun. I was standing behind him, gazing up into the trees. I drew myself very tall, with my hair full of reflections and a smile on my face. I was wearing a black satin Suzie Wong dress and I had one knee slightly forward and bent a little.

I bought a sewing kit and pounds and pounds of silver and gold beads from a shop called La Droguerie. One Saturday I tied a scarf over my hair, put on black linen Chinese worker's pants, and stood for hours sewing constellations into the ruined silk sky, above the dark painted buildings of Tokyo. When I had finished, the tears in the sky were healed and it lay flat against the walls, criss-crossed with glittering rivers of gold and silver. The effect was mesmerizing – it was like living inside an exploding star.

The funny thing was that I was happy in spite of the way things had become between me and Shi Chongming. Something had shifted – it was as if the dry, frantic neediness I'd brought with me to Tokyo had somehow edged out of me and infected him instead.

On the Monday following Fuyuki's party, I'd tried to get Strawberry to tell me more about the stories she'd heard. I'd sat down in front of her and said, 'I ate some meat when I was at the party. Something about it tasted odd.' When she didn't answer I leaned towards her and spoke in a low voice, 'And then I remembered – you'd told me not to eat anything.'

She fixed me with an intense look. For a short time it seemed as if she was going to say something, but instead she jumped up and nodded at her reflection in the plate-glass window. 'Look,' she said conversationally, as if I'd said nothing. 'Look. This dress nice dress from movie *Bus Stop*.' It was a mothy green coat-dress she was wearing, with attached black net and a fur collar, worn unbuttoned to show her daringly engineered bosom. She smoothed it over her hips. 'Dress suit Strawberry figure, *ne*? Suit Strawberry more good than suit Marilyn.'

'I said, I think I've eaten something bad.'

She turned to me, her face serious, her head unsteady from the champagne. I could see her jaw working in tiny movements under the skin. She put her hands on the desk and leaned forward so that her face was close to mine. 'You must forget this,' she whispered. 'Japanese Mafia very complicated. You cannot easily understand it.'

'It didn't taste like anything I recognized. And I'm not the only one who noticed. Mr Bai. He thought there was something strange, too.'

'Mr Bai?' She made a contemptuous clicking sound in her throat. 'You listen to Mr Bai? Mr Bai like Fuyuki's pet. Like dog with collar. He famous singer once, but maybe now not so famous. All fine now, until . . .' She held up her hand warningly. '*Until he make mistake!*' She drew her hand across her throat. 'Nobody too important to make a mistake. Understand?'

I swallowed and said, very slowly, 'Why did you tell me not to eat anything?'

'All rumours. All gossip.' She grabbed the champagne bottle, filled her glass and drained it in one, using the glass to point at me. 'And, Grey-san, you never repeat what I have told you. Understand?' She shook the glass, and I could see how serious she was. 'You want happy life? You want happy life working in high-class club? In Some Like It Hot?'

'What does that mean?'

'It mean your mouth. Keep shut your mouth. Okay?'

Which meant, of course, that when Shi Chongming telephoned, unusually early the following day, I had nothing more to tell him. He didn't take it well: 'I find this attitude most odd, yes, most odd. I understood you were "desperate" to see my film.'

'I am.'

'Then explain to me, an old man with a poor grasp of the vicissitudes of youth, please do me the honour of explaining this sudden unwillingness to talk.'

'I'm not unwilling. I just don't know what you want me to say. I can't make things up. I've got nothing new to tell you.'

'Yes.' His voice was tremulous with anger. 'It is as I suspected. You've changed your mind. Am I wrong?'

'Yes, you're—'

'I find this quite unacceptable. You have happily allowed me to make a monumental effort,' I could tell he was trying not to shout, 'and now such casualness! Such casualness when you tell me that you are no longer involved.'

'I haven't said that—'

'I think you have.' He coughed and made an odd sound, as if exhaling through his nostrils in little staccato bursts. 'Yes, yes, I believe that, where you are concerned, I will trust my instincts. I will say goodbye.' And he put the phone down.

I sat in the chilly living room staring at the dead receiver in my hand, my face blazing with colour. No, I thought. No. Shi Chongming, you're wrong. I pictured the Nurse's shadow, climbing up the corridor wall, I remembered standing inside the bathroom door, my heart leaping out of my chest, memories of the crime-scene photo playing in my head. I put my fingers over my closed eyes, pushing gently at them. I'd done so much, gone so far, and it wasn't that I'd changed my mind – it was just that the picture had got hazy, like seeing something familiar through a steamed window. Wasn't it? I dropped my hands and looked up at the door, at the long corridor, stretching away, a few rays of sunshine illuminating the dusty floor. Jason was asleep in my room. We'd been up together until five o'clock that morning, drinking beer he'd got from the machine in the street. Something odd was dawning on me. Something I could never have predicted. What if, I thought, shivering in the cold morning air, what if there was more than one route to peace of mind? Now, wouldn't that be something?

35

In the end it didn't matter what Shi Chongming said because Fuyuki didn't come to the club for days. And then it was weeks. And then, suddenly, I realized that I'd stopped jumping every time the lift bell rang. Something was sliding away from me, and for a long time I did nothing, only watched apathetically, lighting a cigarette and shrugging and thinking instead about Jason, about the muscles in his arms, for example, and how they trembled slightly with the effort of supporting his body above mine.

I couldn't concentrate on my work at the club. Quite often I'd hear my name and come out of a trance to find a customer staring at me oddly, or Mama Strawberry frowning at me, and I'd know a whole conversation had passed and all anyone had got from me was a blank because I was off somewhere else with Jason. Sometimes he would watch me when I was working. If I caught him looking he'd run his tongue across his teeth. It amused him to see the way goosebumps jumped out on my arms. The Russians kept reminding me about his strange pictures, putting their fingers warningly to their lips and whispering the titles of the autopsy videos. 'A woman cut in half by a truck – imagine that!' But I'd stopped listening to them. At night, if I happened to wake and hear the sound of another human being breathing near me, the sound of Jason rubbing his face in his sleep, or muttering and turning over, I'd get a lovely tight feeling in my chest, and I'd wonder if this was how it was supposed to feel. I'd wonder if maybe I was in love, and the thought made me feel panicky and short of breath. Was that possible? Could people like me fall in love? I wasn't sure. Sometimes I'd lie awake for hours worrying about it, taking deep breaths, trying to keep calm.

The way it was going you'd think I would never, ever get round to showing him the scars. I kept finding excuses. I had ten camisoles now, all lined up in the wardrobe, and I wore them all the time, even when I was asleep, my back to him, crunched over my stomach like a foetus. I didn't know where to start. What would the right words be? *Jason, some people, a long time ago, thought I was crazy. I made a mistake . . .* What if he was horrified? He kept saying that he wouldn't be, but how do you explain that understanding, or even the illusion of it, would be the most wonderful feeling imaginable, almost as wonderful as knowing for sure that you hadn't imagined the orange book, and that if you were to take the chance and tell someone, and if it were to go wrong . . . well, it would be like – like dying. Like falling into a dark hole, over and over again.

I started dreaming about my skin a lot. In the dreams it would be loosening and lifting up from me, unsticking from my body, unpopping along seams down my spine and under my arms. Then it would drift upwards in one piece, like a ghost on an air current, ready to sail off. But there'd always be a jolt. Something would shudder and I'd look down and see that the beautiful shimmery parachute was tethered and bloodied, tacked in a puckered criss-cross to my stomach. Then I'd start to cry and rub frantically at the skin to loosen it. I'd tug and scratch at myself until I was bloodied and shaking and—

'Grey?'

One night I woke with a start, sweat streaming from me, the images from my nightmare scuttling away like shadows. It was dark, except for the light from Mickey Rourke, and I was lying on my side, clinging to Jason, my heart pounding. My legs were clamped as tightly as possible round his thighs, and he was looking down at me in surprise.

'What?' I said. 'What was I doing?'

'Rubbing against me.'

I groped under the covers. My camisole was crumpled and damp with sweat. I yanked it all the way down over my hips and put my face into my hands, trying to steady my breathing.

'Hey.' He pushed away the hair that was sticking to my forehead. 'Sssh. Sssh. Don't worry.' He put his hands under my armpits and gently encouraged me higher up the futon, so I was level with him. 'Here.' He kissed my face, stroked my hair, smoothed my skin calmingly. We lay there for a while, until my heart had stopped thumping. 'You okay?' he whispered, putting his mouth to my ear.

I nodded, pressing my knuckles into my eyes. It was so dark and cold. I felt as if I was floating. Jason kissed me again. 'Listen, weirdo,' he said softly, resting his hand on my neck, 'I've had an idea.'

'An idea?'

'A good idea. I know what you need. I'm going to tell you something that you're going to like.'

'Are you?'

He pushed me on to my back and gently nudged my left shoulder up so that I rolled away, my back to him. I could feel his breath on my neck. 'Listen,' he whispered, 'do you want me to make you happy?'

'Yes.'

'Good. Now concentrate hard.' I lay there, staring blankly at the chink of light coming from under the door, at all the hairs and balls of dust collecting there on the *tatami* mat, and concentrated on Jason's voice. 'Listen carefully.' He shuffled himself up behind me, his arms round me, his lips on my neck. 'This is how the story goes. Years and years ago, long before I came here, I used to fuck a girl in South America. She was a little crazy, I can't remember her name, but what I can remember was how she liked to be fucked.'

He reached down between my thighs and parted them, running the flat of his palm along the inside of my left thigh, carefully raising my knee, cupping it in his hand and bending it up to my chest. I felt the hard, cold node of my knee brush my nipple as he moved behind me.

'What she really liked was for me to put her on her side like this,' he whispered into my neck, 'like I'm doing now. And lift up her knee like this, so that I could get my cock in her. Like this.'

I took a sharp breath and Jason smiled against my neck.

'Do you see? Do you see why she liked it so much?'

Winter was creeping into spaces in the house. The few trees were bare, only the occasional papery leaf clinging to a branch, and the cold seeped up through the pavement. In public places they planted ornamental cabbage in Christmas colours of red and green. The heating in the house wasn't working and Jason was too preoccupied with me to fix it. The air vents in the rooms rattled and whined and stirred the dust, but they gave off no heat.

I was never sure if it was normal, the way all Jason's ex-girlfriends came into bed with us. I didn't like it, but for ages I didn't say anything. *Listen*, he'd murmur in the dark, *listen. I'm going to tell you something that you're going to like. Years ago I used to fuck this Dutch girl. I can't remember her name but I do remember what she really liked* ... And he'd manoeuvre my limbs, choreographing a private dance between him and my body. He liked the way I was always ready for him. 'You're so dirty,' he told me once, and there was admiration in his voice. 'You are the dirtiest woman I've ever met.'

'Listen,' I blurted one night. 'This is important. You keep telling me about those women. And I know it's true because every woman you meet wants to do it with you.'

He was lying between my legs with his head on my thigh, his hands resting lightly on my calves. 'I know.'

'Mama Strawberry. All the other hostesses.'

'Yes.'

'Fuyuki's Nurse. She wants to.'

'She? Is it a she? I can't help wondering.' Distractedly he pushed his nails into the flesh of my leg. I noticed he was pressing fractionally too hard. 'I'd like to find out. I'd like to know what she looks like naked. Yeah, I think that's mostly it, I'd like to see her naked and—'

'Jason.'

He swivelled his head. 'Mmmm?'

I propped myself up on my elbows and stared at him. 'Why are you sleeping with me?'

'What?'

'Why are you sleeping with me? There are so many other people out there.'

He seemed about to answer, but instead paused and I could feel his muscles tighten minutely. At length he sat up and groped for the bottom of my camisole. 'Take this off—'

'No. No, not now, I—'

'Oh, for Chrissake.' He pushed himself away, jumping to his feet. 'This is—' He got a cigarette from his jeans, which were lying on the floor, and lit it. 'Look,' he said, drawing in a lungful of smoke and turning to me. 'Look—' He shook his head and blew out the smoke. 'This is turning into a long story.'

I stared at him, my mouth slightly open. 'A long story?'

'Yes – a long, long pain-in-the-ass story.' He sighed. 'I've been patient but you're . . . It's going on for ever. It's not funny any more.'

A strange feeling came up through me, a horrible feeling, as if I was being swung round and round in a vacuum. Nothing looked right. The galaxies on the wall behind him seemed to be moving – drifting slowly across the sky over Tokyo like necklaces of light. Jason's face looked dark and insubstantial. 'But I . . .' I pressed fingers to my throat, trying to stop my voice wobbling '. . . I wanted to – to – I wanted to show you. I really wanted to. It's just I . . .'

I got to my feet and fumbled on the dresser for my cigarettes, knocking things over. I found the packet and shakily pulled one out, lit it and stood facing the wall, smoking in tight, feverish bursts, pushing the tears out of my eyes. *This is stupid. Just do it. It's like jumping off a cliff, like jumping off a cliff . . . There's only one way to find out if you'll survive.*

I stubbed out the cigarette in the ashtray on the dresser, and turned to him, breathing fast. There was a lump in my throat, as if my heart was trying to squeeze out of my mouth.

'Well,' he said, 'what is it?'

I pulled the camisole up over my head, dropped it on to the floor, and stood, facing him, my hands covering my stomach, my eyes locked on a point above his head. I took deep, deep breaths, imagining my body through his eyes – pale and thin, laced with veins.

'Please understand,' I whispered, mantra-like, under my breath. 'Please understand.'

And then I dropped my hands.

I don't know if it was me who gasped, or Jason, but there was a distinct intake of breath in the room. I stood, my hands in fists clenched at my sides, my eyes on the ceiling, feeling as if my head was going to burst. Jason was silent, and when at last I dared to look down at him I found his face was very still, very controlled, nothing in his expression as he studied the scars on my stomach.

'My God,' he breathed, after a long time. 'What happened to you?' He got up and took a step towards me, his hands lifting up, reaching curiously to my stomach, as if the scars were emanating a glow. His eyes were calm and clear. He stopped a pace away from me, to the side, his right hand flat against the scars.

I shuddered and closed my eyes.

'What on earth happened here?'

'A baby,' I said unsteadily. 'That's where my baby was.'

36

They taught me about condoms in the hospital, when it was far, far too late anyway. In the few months before I was discharged, when everyone was talking about AIDs, we had HIV-awareness groups, and one of the nurses, a girl called Emma with a nose-ring and sturdy calves, would sit in front of us, blushing a bright red as she showed us how to roll a condom on to a banana. A *sheath*, she called it, because in those days that was what the newspapers called them – and when she talked about anal sex, she called it 'rectal sex'. She said it with her face turned to the window as if she was addressing the trees. The others would be laughing and joking, but I'd be sitting at the back of the group, as red-faced as Emma, staring at the condom. A condom. I'd never heard of a condom. Honestly, how could anyone so ignorant have managed to live for so long?

For example, the significance of nine months. Over the years I'd caught jokes and muttered asides: 'Oh, yeah, cat's got the cream *now*, but wait till you see his face in nine months' time.' That sort of thing. But I didn't understand. The really stupid thing was that if they'd asked me the gestational period of an elephant I'd have prob-ably known. But truths about humans I was lost with. My parents had done a good job of filtering the information that got through to me. Except for the orange book, of course, they weren't that vigilant.

The jigging girl in the next bed stared at me really hard when I admitted how ignorant I was.

'You're not serious?'

I shrugged.

'Well, bollocks,' she said, a faint note of awe in her voice. 'You really are serious.'

In their exasperation the nurses found me a book about the facts of life. It was called *Mummy, What's That In Your Tummy?* and it had a pale pink cover with a cartoon of a girl in bunches looking up at a big pregnant stomach in a flowery dress. One of the reviews on the back said: 'Tender and informative: everything you need to know to answer your children's little questions.' I'd read it from cover to cover and I kept it in a brown bag pushed right to the back of my locker. I wished I'd had it earlier. Then I'd have understood what was happening to me.

I didn't tell a soul in hospital what those weeks after the van were like. How it took me weeks and months to piece it all together from whispers and odd allusions in the ravaged paperbacks on the shelves at home. How when I realized there was going to be a baby I knew, beyond any doubt, that my mother would kill either me or the baby or both. This, I suppose, is the true price of ignorance.

In the alley outside a car door slammed. Someone jingled keys, and a woman giggled in a high thin voice, 'I'm not going to drink a thing, I swear.' Their laughter dwindled as they continued down the alley to Waseda Street. I didn't move, or breathe – I was staring at Jason, waiting to hear what he would say.

'You're a good girl.' Eventually he took a step back and gave me a slow, sly smile. 'You're a good girl, you know that? And now things are going to be fine.'

'*Fine?*'

'Yes.' He put his tongue between his teeth and ran his finger carefully along the biggest of the scars, the central one that ran from two inches right of my navel diagonally to my hipbone. He clicked his nail over the knotty place in the centre of it, and navigated his way round the little holes where the surgeon had tried to stitch me up. There was a note of curious wonder in his voice when he spoke: 'There are so many of them. What made them?'

'A—' I tried to speak but my jaw was locked. I had to shake my head to make it move. 'A knife. A kitchen knife.'

'Aah,' he said, wryly. 'A knife.' He closed his eyes and slowly licked his lips, letting his fingers linger on the gristly whirl of scar tissue in the middle. The first place the knife had gone in. I flinched and he opened his eyes, looking at me intently. 'Did it go deep here? Hmmm? Here?' He pressed his finger into it. 'That's what it feels like. Feels like it went in deep.'

'*Deep?*' I echoed. There was something in his voice, something rich and horrible, as if he was taking immense pleasure in this. The air in the room seemed staler than it had a few minutes ago. 'I—' Why did he want to know how deep it went? Why was he asking me this?

'Did it? Did it go in deep?'

'Yes,' I said faintly, and he gave a delighted shiver, as if something was walking across his shoulders.

'Look at this.' He ran his palm down the skin on his arm. 'Look, my hair's standing up on end. I get such a stiff for this kind of thing. The girl I told you about? In South America?' He circled his fingers around his bicep, half closing his eyes in pleasure at the memory. 'She'd lost her arm. And the place where they took it off . . . it was like a . . .' He held his fingers bunched up, as if he was balancing the most delicate, the softest fruit on his fingertips. 'It was beautiful, like a plum. Whoah—' He grinned at me. 'But you've always known about me, haven't you?'

'Always known? No – I—'

'Yes.' He dropped to his knees in front of me, his hands on my hips, breathing hotly on to my stomach. 'You did. You knew what gets me.' His tongue, dry and corrugated, stretched out to meet my skin. 'You knew I just *love* to fuck freaks.'

My paralysis broke. I pushed him away and stumbled backwards. He rocked back on his heels, looking mildly surprised, as I grabbed up my camisole, fumbling it on. I wanted to run out of the room before I started to cry, but he was between me and the doorway, so I turned and crouched in the corner, facing the wall. Everything was coming back to me – the photographs in his room, the videos the Russians swore he watched, the way he'd

214

talked about the Nurse. I was one of them – a freak. Something mangled to turn him on, just like in the videos he watched.

'What is it?'

'Um . . .' I said, in a tiny voice, using my palms to wipe my eyes. 'Um . . . I think, I think maybe I'd—' The tears were running into my mouth. I cupped my hands to catch them so he wouldn't see them dropping on to the floor. 'Nothing.'

He put a hand on my shoulder. 'See? I told you it would be okay. I told you I'd understand.'

I didn't answer. I was trying not to sob.

'This is what we've been moving towards all along, isn't it? It's what pulled us together. I knew the moment I saw all this – your paintings, all the freaky photos in your books – I knew you and me were . . . I knew we were the same.' I heard him fumble out another cigarette and I imagined his face, smirking, confident, finding sex in this, sex in the scars I'd been hiding for so long. I imagined what I looked like to him, crouched in the corner, my thin, cold arms wrapped round me. 'It just took you a little longer,' he said. 'A little longer to recognize that we're a pair. A pair of perverts. We're made for each other.'

I leaped up and grabbed my clothes from the chair, dressing quickly, not looking at him, my legs shaking helplessly. I pulled on my coat and fumbled for my keys in my handbag, all the time taking short, desperate gulps of air, trying to hold back the tears. He didn't say anything or attempt to stop me. He watched me in silence, smoking thoughtfully, a half-smile on his face.

'I'm going out,' I said, throwing open the door.

'It's okay,' I heard him say behind me. 'It's okay. You'll be okay soon.'

Even as recently as 1980, it was possible in England for a stillborn baby not to be buried. For her not to be buried in a grave, but instead to be taken in a yellow waste-bag and incinerated with other clinical waste. It was even possible for her mother, a teenage girl with no experience, to let the baby go and never dare ask where she went. It was all possible, because of a simple accident of the calendar: my baby had failed to live inside me for a crucial twenty-eight weeks. Just one day short, and the state said that my baby should not be buried, that she was a day too small to be a human being, a day too small to get a funeral or a proper girl's name, and so would for ever carry the name *foetus*. A name that is full of sickness and nothing like my little girl when she was born.

It was a late December night when the trees were heavy with snow and the moon was full. The nurses in the emergency room thought I shouldn't be crying like I was. 'Try to relax.' The doctor couldn't meet my eyes when I came to, stretched out on the operating table, and found him dressing the wounds in my stomach. He worked in chilly silence, and when eventually he told me the outcome, he did it standing in profile, speaking to the wall and not to me.

I tried to sit up, not understanding what he'd said. '*What?*'

'We're very sorry.'

'No. She's not dead. She's—'

'Well, of course she is. Of course she's dead.'

'*But she's not supposed to be dead. She's supposed to be—*'

'Please.' He put his hand on my shoulder, edging me back down on to the table. 'You didn't really expect anything else, did you? Now, lie down. Relax.'

They tried to hold me down, they tried to stop me looking. But I cheated. I looked. And I discovered something I'll never forget: I discovered that it is also possible, along with all the other in-credible possibilities in life, to see, in one brief moment, everything a child might have been – to see through that almost transparent, inadequate skin, and see her soul, her voice, her real and complex self, to see the long story of her life stretching away ahead of her. All of these things are possible.

There was an agency nurse who didn't know or care how I'd ended up like this. She was the only one who saw what it meant to me. She was the one who pressed a tissue into the corners of my eyes and stroked my hand. 'You poor little thing, poor little thing.' She looked across the room to the humped shape in the kidney bowl, to the small curve of shoulder, the dab of dark hair.

'You'll have to stop worrying about her now, lovey. You'll have to stop worrying. Wherever her soul is, God will find it.'

The moon was still out when I left the house, hurrying down the alley clasping my coat at the neck, but by the time I reached Shiba-Koen dawn was coming – you could see it between the buildings. The sky was a pretty washed-out pink, and an artificially warm wind blew through the streets, as if a nuclear wind was coming from the west. It made the bare branches in the Zojoji temple spin and whip. At the purifying bowl in front of the rows of child statues, silent and sightless in their red bonnets, I stopped and ladled freezing water first into my left hand, the way you were supposed to, then into the right. I dropped a few yen into the offertory box, tugged off my shoes and went into the freezing grass, wandering up and down the rows of stone children.

The shadows of the white prayer slips tied in the branches over my head moved and shifted. I found a place in the corner of the gardens, a place between two rows of statues where I couldn't be seen from the road, and sat down on the ground, my coat pulled tightly round me. You were supposed to clap your hands when you prayed. There was a sequence, but I couldn't remember it, so in the end I did what I was used to seeing people do in my own, Christian country. I put my hands together, dropped my forehead on to the tips of my fingers and closed my eyes.

Maybe the nurse had been right. Maybe 'God', or the gods, or something greater than any of us, knew where my baby's soul was. But I didn't. I didn't know where she was buried, so I had nowhere to start. Without a grave to visit I had learned to imagine her as nowhere and everywhere, flying somewhere above me. Sometimes when I squeezed my eyes closed I would picture her in the black, pitted night sky, so high up that her head was brushing the roof of the world. In my dreams she'd be able to fly anywhere she wanted. Maybe even from England to Tokyo. She would have to set her course straight for the east, then off she'd go, fast, looking down from time to time and seeing the travelling lights beneath her: Europe, with all its bridges lit up and decorated like wedding cakes. She'd know when she was over the sea from the dark stretches, or the ridged reflection of the moon, or the little pearl drops of tankers. After Europe she'd fly fast into the rising sun. Over the Russian steppes and bottomless Baikal lake with its strange seals and landlocked fish. And further, past rice fields and industrial chimneys and oleander-fringed roads, over the stretching, hardening crust of the whole of Shi Chongming's homeland. Then Tokyo, and on and on until she was over Takadanobaba, and she would see the curled eaves of the old house. Then she would be above my window and at last . . .

But, of course, she hadn't come. Even at O-Bon, when the dead were supposed to visit the living, when I'd sat in my window watching lighted candles floating down the Kanda river as the Japanese guided their dead back, all the time I thought stupidly that maybe she'd find me. But she didn't. I told myself that I shouldn't have expected it, that she'd probably tried hard. It was such a long way from England for only a small spirit, maybe she'd got lost, or just very, very tired.

I lifted my head from my pseudo-prayer. Around me the children's windmills were spinning in the warm wind, the wooden memorial slats clicking and clattering. Every hand-made bonnet, every bib, every toy ornamenting the statues had been placed there by a mother who had prayed, like I had just prayed. It was getting light and the first commuters were walking fast along the street next to the temple.

Jason, I thought, getting to my feet and brushing down my coat, Jason, believe me, you are stranger, stranger and more insane than I have ever been. What I did was ignorant and wrong, but I was never as wrong as you are. I took a few deep breaths of clean air and looked up into the sky. He had brought me back to something. I had almost forgotten, but he'd reminded me. There was only one way I could go. There had only ever been one way.

37

 Nanking, 20 December 1937 (the eighteenth day of the eleventh month)

This is how you learn.

As the sun came up I listened to the radio for a while. Still no official announcement that it was safe to go into the streets. When full daylight was at last with us I drank some tea, dressed quietly, tied my quilted jacket and slipped out into the alley, barricading the door behind me and stopping once to check for any movement. Outside, a light snow was falling: thin white flakes covering the old dirty snow. I slipped silently between the houses, reached the Liu house within minutes, went to the back door and gave a coded series of knocks. After a while the door was opened by Liu's wife, who stood back wordlessly and allowed me to pass. Her eyes were red, and she was wearing a tattered man's winter robe over several layers of her own clothes.

It was bitterly cold in the house, and immediately I could feel the strained atmosphere. When Liu came to the hallway to greet me I knew that something had happened.

'What is it?'

He didn't answer. He beckoned me out of the hall and into a small cluttered room where his son sat in abject misery, his head hanging low. He wore a Sun Yat-sen military-style jacket, torn and ripped and hanging on his frail shoulders, making him look more dishevelled and pitifully stained than ever. On the table in front of him lay a filthy sack, what appeared to be buckwheat spilling out of it.

'He's been out all night,' said Liu. 'Brought back food.'

I stared hungrily at it. 'Master Liu, I commend your bravery. This is indeed news. Good, good news.'

Liu's wife brought buckwheat dumplings – some wrapped in muslin and crammed into a bamboo steaming basket for me to take to Shujin, and another dish for me to eat now. She put them down in front of me without a word or a look, and left the room. I ate as fast as I could, standing up, cramming them into my mouth and looking blankly at the ceiling as I chewed. Liu and his son averted their eyes out of decency. But, in spite of the food, I couldn't avoid noticing the atmosphere between them.

'What?' I said, through a mouthful. 'What is it?'

Liu touched the boy's foot with his toes. 'Tell him what's happened.'

The boy looked up at me. His face was white and serious. It was as if overnight he had lost his childhood. 'I've been out,' he whispered.

'Yes?'

He lifted his chin in the direction of the street. 'Out there. All night I've been walking in the city. I've spoken to people.'

I swallowed the last of the dumpling, feeling it stick in my throat. 'And you've come back safely. The streets are safe?'

'No.' A sudden tear ran down his face. My heart sank. 'No. The streets are not safe. The Japanese are devils. The *riben guizi.*' He gave his father an anguished look. 'You told me they would only kill soldiers. Why did you say that?'

'I believed it. I thought they'd leave us be. I thought we'd be considered refugees.'

'Refugees.' He batted the tears away with his sleeve. 'There's a place for people they call refugees.'

'At the university,' I said. 'Have you been there?'

'Not only me. I am not the only one who has been there. The Japanese have been too. They took the "refugees" away. I saw it. They were strung together.' He jabbed a finger into the soft flesh behind his collarbone. 'They put a wire through here and strung them together, like – like a necklace. A necklace of people.'

'You actually saw all of this? At the refugee zone?'

He pushed roughly at his eyes, the tears leaving streaks in the dirt. 'I've seen everything. Everything. And I've heard everything.'

'Tell me,' I said, sitting down on one of the rickety chairs and looking at him seriously, 'did you hear screaming? An hour ago. A woman screaming. Did you hear that?'

'I heard.'

'Do you know what it was?'

'Yes.' He looked at his father, then back at me, anxiously biting his lip. He felt in his pocket and pulled out something to show us. Liu and I both leaned forward. On his palm was a Japanese condom. I took it from him and turned it over in my hand. It bore a picture of a soldier racing forward, bayonet at the ready, the word *'Totsugeki'* written underneath. *Charge!* Liu and I exchanged looks. His face had become very grey, tension creeping into the skin round his mouth.

'Rape,' the boy said. 'They are raping women.'

Liu glanced at the doorway. His wife was in the back of the house and she couldn't have heard; nevertheless he put out his foot and kicked closed the door. My heart was thudding dully. When I was thirteen I had no idea what rape was, but this boy used the word matter-of-factly, as if it was an everyday event.

'Girl hunts,' he said. 'It's the Japanese's favourite pastime. They take coal trucks from Xiaguan and trawl the villages for women.' He raised his dirt-smeared face to me. 'And do you know what else?'

'No,' I said faintly. 'What else?'

'I've seen where the *yanwangye* lives.'

'*Yanwangye?*' A little ghost of fear crossed my heart. I glanced instinctively at Liu, who was contemplating his son with a mixture of fear and confusion. *Yanwangye.* The devil. The greatest of the death lords. The ruler of Buddhist hell. Ordinarily the likes of old Liu and I would roll our eyes at such folk-religion, but something in us has changed over the last few days. Hearing the name whispered in this cold house made us both shiver.

'What are you talking about,' said Liu, leaning closer to his son. '*Yanwangye*? I didn't teach you such nonsense. Who have you been speaking to?'

'He's here,' whispered the boy, his eyes meeting his father's. I could see goosebumps on his skin. I glanced up at the windows, locked tight. It was very quiet outside; the falling snow made the light flicker pink and white. 'The *yanwangye* has come to Nanking.' Not taking his eyes from his father's, he got slowly to his feet. 'If you don't believe it then come with me out there.' He gestured to the door and we both turned and looked at it in silence. 'I'll show you where he lives.'

38

Shi Chongming was surprised to see me. He opened his door with chilly civility and let me into his office. He clicked on a three-bar heater, pulling it nearer to the low, battered sofa that sat under the window, and filled a teapot from the Thermos on his desk. I watched distantly, thinking how odd – the last time we spoke he had put the phone down on me.

'Well, now,' he said, when I was seated. He was looking at me curiously because I had come straight from the temple and my skirt was still wet from the grass. 'Does this imply we are on speaking terms again?'

I didn't answer. I pulled off my coat, my gloves and my hat and bunched them all up on my knees.

'Have you some news? Are you here to tell me that you've seen Fuyuki?'

'No.'

'Then you've remembered something? Something about the glass box you saw?'

'No.'

'Is it possible that Fuyuki is preserving something in the box? Because that's how it sounded when you described it.'

'Did it?'

'Yes. Whatever it is that Mr Fuyuki is drinking, he believes it's saving him from death.' Shi Chongming swirled the teapot. 'He'd have to be careful how much he took. Especially if it was dangerous or difficult to replace his supply. From what I suspect, I am sure the tank is how he preserves it.' He poured the tea, his eyes not leaving my face, studying me for a reaction. 'Tell me more about the impression you had.'

I shook my head. I was too numb to pretend. I took the cup he gave me and held it tightly, in both hands, looking down through the steaming water at the greyish streak of sediment in the bottom. A long, awkward silence filled the room, until eventually I put down the cup.

'In China,' I said, although I knew it wasn't what he wanted to hear, 'what happens if someone isn't buried properly? What happens to their spirit?'

He had been about to sit down with his own cup, but my words stopped him. He checked himself, bent, half in, half out of the chair, digesting my question. When at last he spoke his voice had changed: 'What an odd thing to ask. What made you think of that?'

'What happens to their spirit?'

'What happens to their spirit?' He sat, taking some time to settle, straightening his tunic, moving his cup back and forward. At length he rubbed his mouth and looked up at me. There was a blush of red round his nostrils. 'The unburied? In China? Let me see. The simple answer is that we believe a ghost is produced. A mischievous spirit is released to come back and cause trouble. And so we bury our dead carefully. We give them money to pass into the next world. It was . . .' He cleared his throat, tapping his fingers distractedly. 'It was what always worried me about Nanking. I was always afraid of the thousands of mischievous spirits left in Nanking.'

I put down the cup and looked at him, my head on one side. He'd never talked about Nanking like this.

'Yes,' he said, running his fingers round the rim of his cup. 'It used to worry me. There wasn't enough land in Nanking for marked graves. Most people waited months to be buried. Some had already disappeared into the earth or into . . . into one another, before there was a chance to . . .' He hesitated, looking into his tea, and suddenly he seemed very old. I could see the blue veins under his loose skin. I could sense his bones, waiting under the surface. 'I saw a small child once,' he said, in a quiet voice. 'She'd had some – some flesh removed by the Japanese, here, under her ribs. Everyone thought she was dead, but no one had buried her. She lay there for days, in full view of the houses, but no one came out to bury her. I still don't understand why they didn't. In Nanking it was the lucky ones who were left with a body to bury . . .' He trailed off into silence, watching his fingers moving round the cup.

When it seemed that he wasn't going to speak again, I sat forward and lowered my voice to a whisper: 'Shi Chongming. Tell me what happens on the film.'

He shook his head.

'Please.'

'No.'

'I need to know, I need to know so much.'

'I'm sorry. If you need to know so much you'll help me with my research.' He looked up at me. 'That is why you're here, isn't it?'

I sighed and sat back in the chair. 'Yes,' I said. 'Yes, it is.'

He smiled sadly. 'I thought I had lost you. For a long time I thought you had drifted.' He gave me a look then that was sad and sweet and quite unlike any look he had ever given me before. For the first time since we'd met I had the feeling he liked me. I supposed I'll never know what journey he'd been on during those few weeks when we didn't speak. 'What made you come back?'

When I got up to go I should have just opened the door and left. But I couldn't help myself. I stopped at the door and turned back to where he sat at the desk. 'Shi Chongming?' I said.

'Hmmm?' He looked up, as if I'd interrupted his thoughts. 'Yes.'

'You told me that ignorance and evil are not the same thing. Do you remember?'

'Yes. I remember.'

'Is it true? Do you think it's true? That ignorance isn't evil?'

'Of course,' he said. 'Of course it's true.'

'You really mean it?'

'Of course I mean it. Ignorance you can forgive. Ignorance is never the same as evil. Why do you ask?'

'Because . . . because . . .' A feeling was racing through me, coming from nowhere, making me feel strangely powerful and lightheaded. 'Because it's one of the most important questions in the world.'

39

As the day went on it was getting colder. There was a threat of rain in the air and in the lines of traffic waiting at the lights car windows were closed tight, steamed up. The wind skulked round corners, out of sight, then leaped, picking things up and racing off into subway entrances with its prize. I got off the train a few blocks away from Fuyuki's apartment complex, tightened my coat and walked quickly, using the red and white Tokyo Tower as a guide, going through streets I didn't recognize, full of small restaurants and noodle-makers. I passed a wholesaler's called Meat Rush, and slowed, staring rudely at the customers in the basement car park loading up their huge cars with twenty-pound joints. Meat. Japan and China had shared years when the only protein people could get was silkworm cocoons, grasshoppers, snakes, frogs, rats. Now they had places called Meat Rush.

Meat, I thought, stopping at the iron railings outside Fuyuki's apartment. Meat. One of the garages was open and a man in overalls was waxing one of Fuyuki's big black cars. The windows were open, the keys were in the ignition, and the radio was playing a song that sounded to my ears like the Beatles. A gardener was using a hose to clean the path. I laced my hands round the railings and looked up the outside of the building to the penthouse. The windows were mirrored, black. They showed nothing, only the reflection of the cold sky. Shi Chongming thought that whatever Fuyuki had in his apartment needed to be preserved.

Especially if it was dangerous or difficult to replace his supply . . .

There was a phone box just opposite the apartment building so I went to it and got inside, where all the photos of Japanese girls in their knickers were wedged into the creases behind the coin box. I fumbled in my wallet, took out Fuyuki's *meishi* and stared at it. Winter Tree. Winter Tree. I pushed my hair off my face and dialled the number. I waited, biting my nails. Then there was a click and a mechanical woman's voice said in Japanese: 'Sorry, but this number is unobtainable. Please check and redial.'

Over in the apartment buildings the gardener was coiling up the hose. The water ran off into the flower-beds, where the ornamental cabbages had been wrapped with string to keep their shape over the winter. I hung up the receiver, pushed the *meishi* into the bag and turned for home. Tonight was the night Mama Strawberry got her drinks delivered. She was usually in a good mood. Tonight I was going to ask her again what she had meant when she told me not to eat at Fuyuki's.

When I saw Jason again, at the club that evening, it was almost as if nothing had happened. I was checking my makeup at the mirror in the little cloakroom when he stopped on his way to the bar and said, 'I know what you need. I know how to make you feel better.' He pointed at my stomach and winked slyly. 'You just need to work off a little frustration, that's all. We'll figure it out when we get home.' When he'd gone, and I was sitting on my own again, looking at my face in the mirror, I was surprised to find that I felt nothing. Nothing at all. There's something scary about how quickly I can draw back into myself. It's practice, I suppose.

It was an odd night. I didn't say much to the customers, and some of the other hostesses asked me if I was feeling well. From time to time, in a lull in the conversation, I'd find Jason staring confidently at me from where he stood in front of the bar. Once he raised his eyebrows and mouthed something I couldn't understand. I didn't respond.

Mama Strawberry had been drinking tequila for a long time. I'd been watching her out of the corner of my eye, seeing her light cigarettes then forget and leave them smouldering in ashtrays. She kept sitting on customers' knees, and swayed when she walked. When there was a break between customers I went to the desk and sat down opposite her. 'Strawberry,' I said. 'I still need to know. I need to know what stories you heard about Fuyuki.'

'Scccht!' she hissed, flashing a dangerous look at me, her blue contacts catching light from the skyscrapers outside and refracting it back like diamonds. 'You forget everything Strawberry say. Okay. *Everything*.'

'I can't forget. Why did you tell me not to eat anything?'

She swallowed more tequila and clumsily fitted a cigarette into her holder, making three or four stabs at it before she succeeded. She lit it, and searched my face with her watery eyes. 'Listen,' she said, after a while, in a different, softer voice. 'I'm gonna tell you something. I'm gonna tell you about Strawberry mother.'

'I don't want to hear about your—'

'Strawberry *mother*,' she said steadily. 'Very interesting woman. When she a girl, little girl like this big, everyone in Tokyo got no food.' I opened my mouth to interrupt but Mama Strawberry's hand lifted to stall me. Her voice was intense, focused, her eyes pinned on a point above my head. 'You know that, Grey? Everyone hungry.'

'I do know. They were starving.'

'Yes. Yes. *Starving*. Terrible. But then something happen. Something amazing for my mother. Suddenly the *yakuza* markets start.'

'The black-markets.'

'No one in Tokyo call them *black*. They call them blue. The Blue Sky markets.' She smiled up into the air, opening her hands as if describing the sun coming up. 'Blue Sky because it the only place in Tokyo there no clouds. The only place in Tokyo there food.' She looked out of the window, past the Marilyn swing. It was a rainy evening: the neon of Yotsuya Sanchome was spitting and fizzing, throwing little spurts of light down into the wet street hundreds of feet below. The skyline was shimmery, indistinct in the rain, as if it was a fairytale illustration. 'Biggest market was over there.' She pointed out into the night. 'In Shinjuku. *Brightness over Shinjuku*.'

I'd read about the Mafia-run market in Shinjuku. I'd always imagined it to be an incredible sight in bombed-out Tokyo – the sign was supposed to have been made from hundreds of light-bulbs: it would have been visible from miles around, blazing above the charcoaled city roofs, like a moon over a petrified forest. The stalls sold tinned whale, seal sausages, sugar, and there must have been the atmosphere of a street festival, with lanterns hanging from the trees and charcoal-burners hissing and men propped against stalls, drinking *kasutori* and spitting on the ground. In those days *kasutori* was the only substitute for *sake* you could find in Tokyo – the third glass, they said, made you blind, but who cared? What did a little blindness matter when everyone was dying?

'Strawberry mother love Blue Sky market. She always go with other children to see the car of *yakuza* boss. It the only car you ever see in Tokyo in those days and Blue Sky a place like heaven to her. She buy clothes and bread and *zanpan* stew.' Strawberry paused and looked at me sideways. 'Grey-san know what *zanpan* stew is?'

'No.'

'Leftover stew. Made from what the GI Joe don't eat. From GI Joe kitchen. There not many meat in *zanpan*. If *yakuza* put extra meat into *zanpan* they can ask more money. It all about ca-ching ca-ching.' She mimed cash going into a till. 'Ca-ching ca-ching! So the *yakuza* go inland, to Gumma and Kanagawa, and steal meat from farmers . . .' She raised her eyes to me. Suddenly she looked very small and young, sitting there with her hands folded penitently on the table.

'What?' I said. 'What is it?'

'*Zanpan*.' Her voice lowered to a whisper. Her car-enamel-red lipstick winked and glistened. 'That's what I want to tell Grey-san. Strawberry mother find something strange in *zanpan* from Brightness over Shinjuku market.'

'Strange?' The word came out in a whisper.

'Grey-san know who running Brightness over Shinjuku? The Fuyuki gang.'

'And what did your mother find in the stew?'

230

'Fat that taste bad. Not normal. And bones.' Her voice was almost inaudible now. She was sitting forward, her eyes gleaming at me. 'Long bones. Too long for pig, too thin for cow.' I thought I saw something like sadness in her eyes, as if she was seeing images she was ashamed of. Behind her, out of the window, Marilyn swung to and fro, flitting in front of the video screen that glowed on the opposite building.

'What sort of animal would have bones like that?' I said.

She narrowed her eyes and gave me a tight, sarcastic smile. 'In Blue Sky market you can buy anything. You can buy *oshaka*.'

Oshaka. I knew the word from somewhere. *Oshaka* . . .

Strawberry was about to speak when the crystal lift chimed its arrival and, just as if we'd been demon-conjuring, we turned to see one of the aluminium doors standing open, and hovering in the lobby, in her awkward, hunched way, her head averted slightly so that the glossy hair covered it, the unmistakable figure of the Nurse. She was dressed in a fawn-coloured raincoat and matching leather gloves, and she was clearly waiting for someone to come to her.

Moved by an almost physical force, Strawberry shot to her feet, colouring shockingly under her makeup. '*Dame!*' she hissed. 'Did you know she was coming?'

'No.' I didn't take my eyes off the Nurse, but leaned across the desk to Strawberry, whispering urgently. 'What did you mean *oshaka*? What's *oshaka*?'

'Ssh.' She gave a shudder and shifted around inside her coat as if ice had been poured down her back. 'Don't talk so loudly. Shut up now. It's not safe.'

Fuyuki had sent the Nurse to choose girls for another party at his apartment. The news got round the club in no time. I sat at the gilded desk, my head pounding, watching the Nurse speaking softly to Mama Strawberry, who stood with her head bowed, her face dark and bitter as she jotted down the names. At one point the Nurse pointed into the club and muttered something. Strawberry's little gold pen halted, poised in mid-air above the notepad. Her eyes drifted towards me and, for a moment, it seemed she would say something. Then she must have changed her mind, because she bit her lip and wrote another name on the list.

'You're chosen,' Jason said, sliding up to the desk. It wasn't closing time, but he had undone his bow-tie and there was a cigarette between his fingers. He was looking thoughtfully at the Nurse. 'Another party. And it couldn't be better for us.' When I didn't respond he murmured, 'Look at the heels she's wearing. Do you know what I'm saying?' His eyes were on her feet and legs, taking in her tight skirt. 'She's giving me serious ideas, weirdo. Something you're really going to love.'

He slipped away from the table and caught up with the Nurse at the crystal lift as she was waiting to leave. He stood close to her, his face near hers. She was unusually still while she listened to him. I stared at her long gloved hands.

'You think he going to put his hand in Ogawa's skirt?' Mama Strawberry said, sidling up to me, her eyes on Jason, her mouth close to my ear. I could smell the tequila on her breath. 'You make a bet with me, Grey. You bet when he put his hand in Miss Ogawa's skirt what he gonna find. Eh?' She clutched drunkenly at my arm for balance. 'Eh? You ask Strawberry, Jason gonna find a *chin chin* in her panties. You ask Strawberry – Ogawa look like a man.'

'Strawberry. What was the meat in the *zanpan*?'

She tightened her hold on my arm. 'Don't forget,' she hissed. 'It's all rumours. You don't repeat.'

40

 Nanking, 20 December 1937

First we delivered the dumplings to Shujin, then the three of us left the alley. We went through the early-morning streets, keeping a vigilant eye on all the barricaded doors. Nanking, I thought, you are a ghost town. Where are your citizens? Cowering in silence, tucked away inside the shuttered houses? Hiding in animal pens and under floors? The snow fell silently on us, settling on our caps and jackets, floating softly down to flake and lie yellow over the old goat dung in the gutters. We didn't see another soul.

'Look at this.' Within ten minutes we had reached a side road that led to Zhongyang Road. The boy held out his hand and indicated a row of blackened houses. They must have been burned recently because smoke still rose from them. 'This is him. The *yanwangye*. This is what he does when he's searching.'

Liu and I exchanged a look. 'Searching?'

'For women. That's his habit.'

We opened our mouths to speak, but he silenced us with a finger to his lips. 'Not now.'

He crept off then, leading us further down the street, eventually stopping outside a factory's industrial double doors, its galvanized tin roof higher than two houses. I've walked past that building a hundred times and never troubled before to wonder what it was. We gathered around, stamping our feet and slapping our hands together to bring the blood back, casting wary glances up the street.

233

The boy held his finger to his lips again. 'This is where he lives,' he whispered. 'This is his home.' He pushed the door open a crack. In the cold building beyond I could make out a few shadowy things, the edge of a piece of machinery, damp concrete walls, a conveyor-belt. A pile of old-fashioned reed baskets was stacked against the facing wall.

'What is this?' Liu whispered, and I could tell from his voice that, like me, he did not want to step through the door. The texture of the air coming from the factory reminded me of one of the slaughter-houses on the outskirts of the city. 'What have you brought us here for?'

'You wanted to know why the woman was screaming.'

We hesitated, looking at the door.

'Don't worry.' The boy saw our expressions and bent his head towards ours. 'It's safe. He's not here now.'

He pushed the door open a little further. A frightful screeching noise echoed through the cavernous building, then the boy slipped through the crack and was gone. Liu and I looked at each other. My eyes were watering with fear: irrational, I told myself, because there is no such thing as the devil. Nevertheless it took me a long time to work up the courage to push open the door and step inside. Liu followed and we stood for a moment, our eyes getting used to the light.

The building must have been a silk factory: I could see a vat for boiling cocoons, four or five industrial-sized looms and dozens of hexagonal silk bobbins. The boy was standing in the corner, next to a small door, beckoning us. We went to him, our footsteps hollow and lonely-sounding in this high-ceilinged industrial cathedral. He pushed open the door and stood, fingers resting on the doorhandle, showing us into what must have been the manager's office. We came to stand behind him. When I saw what was in there I put my hand over my mouth and groped for the wall, trying to stop my knees buckling.

'Old Father Heaven,' Liu whispered, 'what happens in here? What happens in here?'

41

Some things are more terrible, more awful than you can imagine. It was in the car on the way to Fuyuki's party that I remembered what *oshaka* meant. Where I'd read it. I sat up straight, breathing deeply to stop myself shaking. I should have stopped the driver. I should have opened the door and stepped right out of the moving car, but I was paralysed, the awful idea crawling through me. When I arrived at the apartment complex there was a faint glaze of sweat on the nape of my neck and in the hollows at the back of my knees.

My car had been the last in the convoy, and by the time I got upstairs people had already been seated to dine. It was chilly outside – the pool was freezing, crammed with reflected stars – so we were shown into a low-ceilinged dining room overlooking the pool. Tokyo Tower, on the other side, was so close that its red and white candy-cane light bathed the large round dining-tables.

I stood for a moment, surveying the scene. It all seemed so unthreatening. Fuyuki, tiny and skeletal and dressed in a red racing-driver's jacket emblazoned with the word 'BUD', was in his wheelchair at the head of the top table, smoking a cigar and nodding genially at his guests. There were only a few spaces left at the table near the window. I slipped into a seat, nodding tightly to my neighbours, two elderly men, grabbed a napkin and pretended to be absorbed in unfolding it.

In the corner, behind the display cabinet, was a small galley

235

kitchen where the waiters were busy with trays and glasses. Standing in the middle of the food-preparation area, cool and unflustered by all the activity, was the Nurse. Dressed in her trademark black skirt suit and turned a little away from the room, so that the glossy wig obscured part of her face, she was chopping meat on a large wooden board, her white-powdered hands moving deftly, almost a blur. Jason was watching her from the doorway, one hand raised casually to lean against the frame. A cigarette burned between his fingers, and he moved only to allow a waiter to pass with a plate or a bottle. I tucked the napkin over my lap, my movements wooden, automatic, unable to tear my eyes from the Nurse's hands. What strange meat, I wondered, were they accustomed to preparing? And how had she removed the insides of a man, a man whose watch hadn't even been disturbed in the process? The hostesses seated near the kitchen kept shooting her uncomfortable looks. With her holding the knife as she was, her hands moving so rapidly, you couldn't expect people to act naturally.

A waiter reached into a circular recess at the centre of the table where I sat. He twisted his hand a few times and a sudden blue flame leaped into the air, making some of the hostesses jump and giggle. I watched the waiter as he adjusted the flame, then placed a large stainless steel flask of water over it. Dark pulpy strands of kelp moved at the bottom and, as the first bright bubbles collected like silver stones, ready to rise to the surface, he scraped from a silver platter into the water a pile of chopped carrots, mushroom and cabbage, a handful of tofu squares, creamy as flesh. He stirred the soup once, covered it with a lid and moved to the next table.

I looked down at my place mat. A large linen bib was folded in front of me, next to it miniature bamboo tongs and a small bowl of sauce, gleaming with fat.

'What's this? What are we going to eat?' I asked the man on my right.

He grinned and fastened his bib round his neck. 'It's *shabu shabu*. Do you know *shabu shabu*?'

'*Shabu shabu*?' The skin round my mouth tingled minutely. 'Yes. Of course. I know *shabu shabu*.'

Sliced beef. Plain meat, brought raw to the table. Mama Strawberry wouldn't eat *shabu shabu* here. She wouldn't eat anything in this apartment because of those stories – the stories of strange meat, served up side by side with the stalls that sold *oshaka*. *Oshaka*. It was an odd word that meant something like second-hand, or discarded belongings, which would have been rare things in a city like post-war Tokyo where nothing that could have been eaten, burned or traded for food would have been discarded. But in the car I'd recalled there had been a more sinister meaning still: the *yakuza* had used a play on the words *osaka* and *shaka*, a reference to the Buddha, to describe very specific 'discarded' belongings. When Strawberry said *oshaka* she meant the possessions of the dead.

The waiter took the lid off the flask on the table and the sweet steam rose up in a column. In the boiling water the cubes of tofu bounced and lifted and somersaulted.

The sliced beef came round, cut as fine as a carpaccio, the plate visible through the flesh. I allowed the waiter to place the platter on my left, but I didn't immediately start rolling the meat on to my tongs as my neighbours were doing. Instead I sat and stared at it, my throat knotted. Everyone was eating, lifting the raw slices of beef, holding them up to the light so the meat was illuminated in its red and white marbling, then plunging it into the boiling water, swishing it back and forward – *swish swish*, *shabu shabu*. Dunk it in the sauce now, and throw back your head. The diners dropped the meat almost whole into their mouths. Pearls of grease collected on their chins.

People would soon notice I wasn't eating, I thought. I snapped up some meat, dipped it in the sizzling soup and lifted it to my mouth, taking a tiny nibble from the edge. I swallowed hard, not tasting it, thinking suddenly of Shi Chongming and how painful it was for him to eat. I rested the remainder of the meat in the sauce bowl and took a hasty swallow of red wine. Bison, over on Fuyuki's table, wasn't eating either. There was a faint look of unease on his face as he studied the Russians, who sat on either side of him, both shovelling the beef enthusiastically into their

237

mouths. *That's because you know, Bison,* I thought. *You know all about* oshaka *and* zanpan *stew and what Fuyuki thinks makes him immortal. Don't you? You know the truth.*

The waiters had stopped moving in and out of the little galley kitchen, and Jason had slipped inside. He stood quite close to the Nurse for some time, talking to her in a low murmur. Every time I looked up he was there, speaking urgently, trying to convince her of something. She didn't break off from her work – it was almost as if he wasn't there. Once he happened to turn and look into the dining room and caught me watching him. I must have looked very white and shocked, sitting so upright at my table. He opened his mouth, seemed about to say something, then swung his eyes to indicate the Nurse, and sent me a private smile, a smile I was supposed to share. He put the tip of his tongue on his bottom lip, pushing against it so that the inside of his mouth was momentarily revealed.

I dropped my eyes to the cooling meat on my chopsticks. A growing skin of congealing fat was whitening on it. My stomach cramped, discomfort raced through me.

At the other table Bison and Fuyuki were discussing a skinny young man with pockmarked skin and dyed-blond, feathered hair. A new recruit, he looked anxious to have been summoned to the table. 'Step forward, *chimpira*,' said Fuyuki. 'Come here, *chimpira*. Come here.' *Chimpira* was a word I hadn't encountered. It was only months later that I discovered it was a term for a Mafia junior soldier. It meant, literally, 'little dick'. The *chimpira* came to stand in front of Fuyuki, who turned his wheelchair away from the table and, using his cane, lifted one side of the *chimpira*'s baggy lavender suit to reveal not a shirt but a black T-shirt. 'Look at this,' he said to Bison. 'This is the way they dress today!' Bison smiled weakly. Fuyuki sucked in his cheeks and shook his head regretfully, dropping the cane. 'These young ones. What a disgrace.'

He made a gesture to the waiter, who went into the kitchen. Someone brought a chair and the neighbouring guests shuffled away so that the *chimpira* could edge in next to Fuyuki. He sat, nervously wrapping his jacket round the offending T-shirt, his face pale, glancing at the other guests. It was only when the waiter returned hotfoot with a tray from which he unloaded two small, unglazed cups, a jug of *sake*, a sheaf of heavy white paper and three small bowls, containing rice and salt, that the *chimpira* relaxed. A whole fish lay on a platter, its sunken eye on the ceiling. The *chimpira* was looking at all the equipment of the *sakazuki* ritual. It was good news. Fuyuki was welcoming him into the gang. As the ritual began – fish scales scraped into the *sake*, salt pinched into pyramids, oaths pronounced by Fuyuki and the *chimpira* – I realized that every guest in the room had turned their attention to it. Nobody was watching the kitchen, where the Nurse had laid down the kitchen knife and was rinsing her hands at the sink.

I lowered my glass and watched in silence as she wiped her hands on a towel, smoothed her wig – her big hands moving flat down the back of the crown – then removed from a drawer a large fliptop canister. She opened it, plunged her hands inside, moving them round and round. When she removed them they were covered in a fine white powder that might have been talc or flour. She shook them, allowing the excess to fall back into the tin, looked up and spoke one sentence to Jason. I edged forward on my chair, trying to read her lips, but she turned away and, whitened hands extended in front of her in the manner of a doctor entering an operating theatre, put her back to the door at the far end of the kitchen, pushed through it and was gone. No one noticed her leave, nor when Jason put out his cigarette and looked at me, his eyebrows raised, a smile working its way across his face. I held his gaze, my face colouring. He tipped his head in the direction the Nurse had gone and showed me his tongue again, moist above his chipped tooth. He held up his hand and mouthed the word 'five', then he was gone through the same door, leaving me sitting in silence, in a cold pool of thought.

Jason was like nothing I'd ever dreamed of. All this time I'd been dealing with something completely outside my understanding. I was meant to follow him. I was meant to wait five minutes then follow, to find him and the Nurse undressing each other. I was probably meant to watch them – the indescribable vignette he had fantasized about, the malformed and the lover. And then I was supposed to join in. I had a sudden, macabre picture of a Japanese dance I'd once heard described performed by the prostitutes in a hot spring: the dance in the stream, it was called. With every step she takes into the river she must raise her kimono a little higher to keep it dry. She is revealed inch by inch. A white calf. Pale, bruised skin. Everyone holding their breath at the promise of more to come. The hem rises a little more – a little more. What would the Nurse look like naked? What would he be thinking when he touched her? And what would she be thinking when she touched him? When she touched living human flesh, how did she separate it from the dead human flesh that she ground up for Fuyuki? Would he whisper to her what he'd whispered to me: *I just love to fuck freaks . . .*

I lit a cigarette, pushed back my chair with a sharp squeal and went to the glass doors that led to the swimming-pool. They were ajar, and the poolside was still and eerily silent – apart from the *bluk-bluk-bluk* of the pool filter and the muffled traffic coming from the Number One Expressway. Only my pupils narrowed. The rest of me was quite still. Noiseless. Slowly, moving like a snake, my focus stretched out into the corridors around me, slowly, slowly, moving sinuously across the courtyard. Small lamps were placed at intervals around the pool. I put my fingers on the glass pane. The lamps reminded me of the small Buddhist lamps that were burned next to a corpse.

Where had Jason and the Nurse gone? Wherever they were, it left the rest of the apartment empty, unguarded. This was the irony: Jason couldn't know how he had helped me. I imagined the rooms below me, as if a floorplan was drawn on the window in front of me. I saw myself, or my ghost, walking down the plush corridors, turning into the room under the pool. I saw myself bending over a glass tank, lifting something in both hands . . .

I glanced over my shoulder. Fuyuki and the *chimpira* were eating *shabu shabu*, Bison was on his feet, bent over a chair, talking to a hostess in a strapless dress. No one was looking at me. I pushed the glass doors open a fraction more and took a step into the damp night. The room under the pool where I'd seen the glass tank was in darkness. I took a breath and stepped forward, my heels metallic on the cold marble. I was about to push away from the doors when, in the room behind me, someone began to cough loudly.

I turned. The *chimpira* was patting Fuyuki on the back, his head bent in concern, muttering to him in a low voice. The wheelchair had been pushed back from the table, and Fuyuki was positioned with his head and shoulders pushed forward, his feet in the expensive designer shoes sticking out starkly in front of him, his body describing a hairpin. All the conversations in the room faltered, all eyes were on him as he clawed at his throat. The *chimpira* scraped his chair back and stood up, waving his hands uselessly, looking quickly from one door to the other as if expecting someone to come and help. Fuyuki's mouth opened, almost in slow motion, his head curled back, then – in a sudden spring – his arms shot out and his chest bent backwards as taut as a bow.

Everyone in the room moved at once. They leaped from their chairs, rushed to him. Someone was shouting orders, someone else knocked over a vase of flowers, glasses were dropped, the waiter slammed his hand on an emergency button. Above me the red light on the wall flashed silently on and off. Fuyuki was trying to stand now, rocking violently from side to side in his wheelchair, his hands flailing in panic. Next to him stood a hostess, making odd little sounds of distress, shadowing his moves, bobbing up and down, trying to hit him on the back.

'Out. Out.' The *chimpira* ushered the girls in the direction of the corridor. Other hostesses followed, corralled so swiftly that they all dominoed into each other, shuffling forward with surprised looks, squealing, pelvises forward in surprise as if they'd been goosed. The *chimpira* looked over his shoulder to where Fuyuki had dropped to the floor, on his knees, jerking and scrabbling at his throat. 'Out,' the *chimpira* shouted to the girls. '*Now! Out!*'

I was trembling. Instead of following the crowd I stepped away from the glass door and walked quickly towards the pool, heading for the far corridor. It was quiet in the courtyard, the red light flashing up off the water. Behind me in the lighted room the phone was ringing, someone was barking orders.

'Ogawa. Ogawa!' It was the first time I'd heard anyone address the Nurse by name. 'Ogawa! Where the fuck are you?'

I kept walking towards the far doors, out into the silence, my head held erect and sombre, the light and the sounds fading behind me. Just as I passed the pool and was almost home free, the doors ahead opened and out came the Nurse. She walked dazedly in my direction, pressing her wig into place, straightening her dishevelled clothes.

Maybe the enormity of the situation was only just dawning on her because she was trancelike as she headed for the commotion behind me. At first I thought she hadn't seen me, but as we drew close she automatically extended her hand to sweep me along, forcing me towards the room. I took a few steps backwards, keeping her pace, edging out sideways, wide, so I could slip out of her orbit and disappear back into the night. I glanced around – at the various doors and windows – for somewhere to slide into. Then, before I knew what was happening, the *chimpira* had appeared from nowhere, grabbing my hand as if I was a child.

'Let go,' I said, staring down at his hand. But he was pulling me back into the room, following the Nurse. '*Let me go.*'

'Get out of here. Go with the others. Now!'

He manoeuvred me through the doors, pushing me back into the noise and confusion. The room was in chaos. Men I didn't recognize had appeared in doorways, people were running down the corridors. I stood where I'd been ushered, the other girls in an uncertain cluster round me, bumping and shuffling, not knowing what to do. The Nurse pushed through the guests, elbowing people out of her way. At the far end of the room a lamp fell to the floor with a terrifying crash.

'My bag!' wailed Irina, sensing we were all about to be thrown out of the apartment. 'I'fe left my bag in there. What about my bag?'

The Nurse bent and lifted Fuyuki in one movement, catching him easily as a toddler round the waist, sweeping him immediately to a sofa under the window, shuffling his feet forward, bending him over. She put both arms round his ribcage, laid her face against his back and squeezed. In front of her legs his little feet lifted and dangled momentarily, marionette-like, then dropped to the floor. She repeated the movement. His feet made their little puppet dance again, then a third time, and this time something must have shot out because someone pointed to the floor, a waiter discreetly swiped it up with a napkin and someone else sank into a chair, hands on their temples.

'*Arigate-e!*' sighed one of the henchmen, clutching his chest in relief. '*Yokatta!*'

Fuyuki was breathing. The Nurse carried him to his wheelchair and dropped him into it. I got one clear view of him, slumped exhaustedly, his hands dangling limp, his head to one side. The waiter was trying to force a glass of water on him and the Nurse was kneeling at his side, holding his wrist between thumb and forefinger and timing his pulse. I didn't have a chance to stay and watch – a fat man in winklepickers had appeared in the door and was guiding all the girls back along the corridor towards the lift.

42

Over two thousand years ago, so the legend goes, lived the beautiful Miao-shan, youngest daughter of the king Miao-chuang. She refused to get married, in spite of her father's wishes, and in his anger he sent her into exile where she lived on a mountain called Xiangshan, the Fragrant Mountain, eating from the trees, drinking from the perfumed streams. But back at the palace her father was growing ill. His skin was diseased and he couldn't move from his bed. On Fragrant Mountain Miao-shan heard about his illness, and knowing, like every Chinese girl, the importance of filial piety, she didn't hesitate to pluck out her own eyes, or to instruct her servants to cut off her hands. Her hands and her eyes were sent back to the palace where they were made into medicine and fed to her father who, according to the myth, made a remarkable recovery.

Miao-shan was one of the beautiful links – she was one of the most perfect stitches in the tapestry I was about to unpick.

The Russians thought I was drunk or ill. In the confusion the three of us had got into the first taxi that pulled up outside the apartment block – I'd thrown myself into the corner and I sat all the way home with my head down, my hand clamped to my face. 'Don't throw up,' Irina said. 'I hate when people throw up.'

The house was freezing. I took off my shoes and went down the corridor to my room. One by one I pulled out the portfolios and stood in the middle of the room, emptying them so that all the notes and sketches floated down like snow and spread out across the floor. Some of them fell right side up, old faces looking at me. I took down all my books and built them into walls round the papers, making a little enclosure in the centre of the room. I put on the electric fire and sat down in the middle, my coat wrapped round me. Here was a sketch of Purple Mountain on fire. A long account of the bridge of corpses over the Jiangdongmen canal. Tomorrow I was going to go back to Fuyuki's. You can always tell when you're getting close to the truth – it's as if the air starts to tingle. I had made up my mind. I was going to be prepared.

The front door opened noisily and someone clattered up the stairs. We'd left Jason at the apartment building. I'd seen him briefly in the smoked-glass lobby, standing silently among the other hostesses, his holdall strapped across his chest. The door-man was struggling to deal with taxis for everyone, four paramedics were pushing in the opposite direction through the crowd, using their bags to get to the lift, but in the confusion Jason seemed very still: his face was an odd, shocked grey colour, and when he raised his eyes and caught mine, for a brief instant he didn't seem to recognize me. Then he raised his hand woodenly and began to make his way over. I turned, giving him the back of my head, and got into a taxi after the Russians. 'Hey!' I heard him call, but before he could reach the front of the crowd the taxi had pulled away.

Now I could hear him in the hallway, coming down the corridor, his footsteps heavy. I got off the futon and went to the door, but before I could touch it, he threw it open and stood in the half-light, swaying. He hadn't stopped to kick off his shoes or hang up his holdall, he had come straight down to my room. There was sweat on his face and stains on his sleeve.

'It's me.' He put a hand drunkenly on his chest. 'It's me.'

'I know.'

He gave a short laugh. 'You know something? I had no idea how perfect you are! No idea until tonight. You are *perfect*!' He wiped his face clumsily, and licked his lips, looking down at my blouse, at the tight velvet skirt I was wearing. There was a faint dampness to him. I could smell alcohol and his sweat and something else. Something like the saliva of an animal. 'Weirdo, I take my hat off to you. We're as bad as each other. As sick as each other. Jigsaw pieces – we've both got exactly what the other needs. And I,' he lifted his hand in the air, 'I am going to tell you something you're really going to love.' He grabbed the hem of my blouse. 'Take this off and show me your—'

'Don't.' I pushed his hands away. 'Don't touch me.'

'Come on—'

'*No!*'

He hesitated, caught off-guard.

'Listen,' I said, my throat tightening. The blood was coming fast to my face. 'Listen to me now. I've got something important to tell you. You're wrong when you say we're the same. We're not. Absolutely not.'

He started to laugh, shaking his head. 'Oh, come on.' He wagged a finger at me. 'Don't try and tell me you're not a bit of a pervert—'

'*We are not the same*,' I hissed, 'because ignorance, Jason, ignorance is *not* the *same* as insanity. And it never has been.'

He stared at me. Angry pink patches appeared on his face. 'Are you trying to be clever?'

'*Ignorance*,' I repeated, my pulse thumping loudly in my temples, 'is not the same as insanity. It's not the same as perversion, or evil, or any of the other things you could accuse me of. Some people are crazy and others are sick, and there are others still who are evil or freaky or whatever you call it. But this is very important.' I took a deep breath. '*They are not the same as the ignorant.*'

'I get it,' he said, breathing hard. His face was flushed and I glimpsed a much older, fleshier Jason waiting in his future – overweight and slack. He leaned back a little, unsteadily, then forward, trying to bring his head to the right distance to focus on the point where the pulse beat in my neck. 'I get it. You've suddenly, out of the blue, started being a bitch.' He put his foot in the door and leaned into the room, his face close to mine. 'I've been so fucking *patient* with you. Haven't I? Even though part of me's like, "Jason, you fucking asshole, why're you wasting your time with that little nutjob?" And all I've done is be *patient*. And what do I get in return? You. Being way, *way* weird with me.'

'Well, that,' I said rigidly, 'must be a direct result . . . of me . . . being a weirdo.'

He opened his mouth, then closed it. 'What's that? A joke?'

'No. Not a joke.' I reached out to slide the door closed. 'Goodnight.'

'You bitch,' he said, in quiet awe. 'You fucking little—'

I opened the door a few inches and hurtled it back along the rails towards his foot, making him jump back.

'*Fuck!*' he shouted. I closed the door and locked it. 'That does it, you asshole.' He kicked the door. 'Shitty little retard.' I could hear him faltering in the corridor, not certain what to do with his frustration. I expected him to boot the door down. Or to run at it with both fists out. I lit a cigarette and sat among my books, my fingers pressed to my head, and waited until I heard him give up.

He kicked the door once more, a parting shot: 'You've just made a big mistake, shithead. The biggest mistake of your life. You'll regret this till the day you die.'

Then I heard him stumbling back to his room, muttering to himself, thumping the shutters on the landing as he went.

When he'd gone, and the house was quiet, I sat still for some time. I smoked one cigarette after another, drawing the smoke deep into my lungs, calming myself. At last, when almost half an hour had gone by and I'd calmed down, I got up.

I flattened a piece of paper on the floor and got out my jar of paintbrushes. I sat for a while, surrounded by my books and paints, my hands resting on my ankles, staring up at Mickey Rourke's light. I was trying to imagine, really imagine, what it would be like to eat another human being. At university I'd been expected to read so much, about so many unimportant things: years of rubbish were lying around in my head. I had to concentrate very, very hard to remember the things I needed now.

After a while I put out my cigarette and mixed together a little yellow ochre, some rose madder and zinc white. I went quickly, letting the paint ridge and pool where it wanted. There was one reason you might eat another human, I thought, one good reason. A face flowed out of the end of my paintbrush, gaunt cheeks, neck like a stalk; below it, the shadowed rack of ribs, a tapering bone of a hand resting on the frozen ground. A starving man.

I understood about starvation. It is one of those cold shadows, like disease, that trail round the globe in the footsteps of war. There had been two great famines in Stalin's years: hundreds of Russians had had to survive by eating human flesh. At university I'd been to the inaugural lecture of a professor who'd got into the St Petersburg city archives and found evidence that Leningraders in the great Second World War siege had eaten their dead. I dripped on to the paper a long, dry shinbone, the foot growing on the end like an awkward fruit. You'd have to be so hungry, so desperate, to eat another human being. Other uneasy names were coming into my head: the Donner pass, the John Franklin expedition, the *Nottingham Galley*, the *Medusa*, the Old Christians' rugby team in the Andes. And what did the Chinese mean when they said *Yi zi er shi*: 'We are hungry enough to eat each other's children?'

I painted the *kanji* for it.

Hunger.

I lit another cigarette and scratched my head. You can't imagine what you might do if you were starving. But there was more: human beings cannibalize for other reasons. I switched to a calligraphy brush and wetted the pine soot tablet. I loaded the brush with ink and slowly, slowly drew out a single *kanji*: a little like the character for number nine, but with a backward flick to its tail.

Power.

There had been a research student at university who had been crazy about warlike sects in Africa – I remembered him fly-postering the university for a lecture on the Human Leopard Societies of Sierra Leone, and the Liberian Poro child soldiers. I didn't go to the lecture, but I'd overheard people talking about it afterwards: '*Believe me, what he was saying was as freaky* as '*parently they cut up their enemies and eat them. If it's someone they've defeated it's supposed to make them stronger.*' Some of the

Nanking testimonies recalled corpses on the street with hearts and livers missing. The whispers were that they'd been taken by the Japanese soldiers. To make them more potent in combat.

I looked at the symbol for 'power', then refilled my brush and under it drew out two more characters: 'Chinese' and 'method'. *Kampo*. Chinese medicine.

Healing.

What did I remember from the reading I'd done? I pulled out all the books from Kinokuniya and sat, some of them cracked open over my knee, some resting on top of the paintings. I kept one finger holding a place in one book while I leafed through another, the paintbrush between my teeth. Mickey Rourke's gold light shone in squares on the *tatami*.

It was amazing. It was all there. I'd been reading it for weeks, over and over again, and I still hadn't seen it. But now, with my new eyes, I was seeing it all. First I found Miao-chuang, eating his daughter's eyes and hands. Why? To cure himself. Then I found, in the translation of a sixteenth-century medical compendium, the *Ben Cao Gang Mu*, treatments made from thirty-five different human body parts. Bread soaked in human blood for pneumonia and impotence, human bile dripped into alcohol and used to treat rheumatism. The flesh of executed criminals to treat eating disorders. There were Lu Xun's outrageous tales of human meat eaten in Wolf Cub Village, and his genuine account of his friend Xu Xilin's liver and heart being eaten by En Ming's bodyguards. In a textbook about the Cultural Revolution there was a long description of the outdated tradition of *ko ku* – the pinnacle of filial piety, the act of boiling a piece of one's flesh into soup to rescue a beloved parent from sickness.

I picked up the three sheets of *kanji* – hunger, power, healing – went to the wall, pinned them on to the Tokyo skyline and looked at them thoughtfully. Japan's history was all coiled around China's: so many things had been transferred, why not this? If human flesh could be a medicine in China, then why not here in Japan? I returned to my textbooks. There *had* been something. I had a vague, vague recollection of something . . . Something I'd read in a module at university.

I pulled out a study of post-war Japan. Somewhere in it were transcripts of the Tokyo war trials. I quickly lit a cigarette, sat down cross-legged on the floor and leafed through it. I found what I was looking for two-thirds of the way through: the testimony of a young Japanese woman employed during the war by the notorious 731 unit. I sat there in the dim light, my hands and feet suddenly terribly cold, and read the chapter: 'Dubbed "maruta" (logs), allied servicemen POWs were subjected to vivisection and human experimentation.'

There was a picture of the assistant who had given evidence. She was young, pretty, and I could imagine the chill and absolute silence in the great military training auditorium, no one in the court moving – or even breathing – as she described in a small, clear voice the day she had eaten the liver of an American serviceman. 'For my health.'

I sat there for a long time, staring at the picture of this beautiful young cannibal. In 1944 at least one person in Japan had thought that cannibalism could help their health. It was time to take Fuyuki much more seriously than I ever could have imagined.

43

It took me a long time to fall asleep, the duvet wrapped round me like a shroud, and when I did I dreamed that everything in the room was laid out just as it was in real life. I was on the futon, exactly as I was in reality, in my pyjamas, lying on my side, one hand under the pillow, one on top, my knees drawn up. The only thing that differed was that in the dream my eyes were open – I was wide awake and listening. A steady rhythmic noise came from the corridor, muffled, like someone having a whispered conversation. From the other side, the window, there was the sound of something gnawing at the mosquito screen.

My dream self's first thought was that the gnawing was a cat, until with a wrench and a grinding of steel wire the screen gave, and some heavy thing like a bowling ball rolled into my room. When I squinted down I saw that it was a baby. It lay on the floor on its back, crying, its arms and legs agitating, going up and down like pistons. For a brilliant, exhilarating moment I thought it must be my baby girl, having made it at last across the continents to see me, but just as I was about to reach for her, the baby rolled on to its side and reached blindly for me. I felt hot breath and a little tongue licking the sole of my foot. Then, with horribly vicious speed, she snapped her gummy teeth round my toes.

I bolted from the bed, shaking her and batting at her, grabbing her by the head and trying to prise open her jaws, but she clung on, snarling and snapping and turning furious somersaults in the

251

air, saliva coming from her mouth. At last I gave a final kick and
the baby flew against the wall, screeching, and dissolved into a
shadow that slid to the floor and flowed out of the window. Shi
Chongming's voice seemed to come out of her as she disappeared:
What will a man do to live for ever? What won't he eat?

I woke with a start, the duvet tangled round me, my hair sticking to my face. It was five a.m. Outside the window I could hear
Tokyo bucking and tossing through the dying moments of a storm
and, for a moment, I thought I could still detect the screaming in
the undertones of the wind, as if the baby was rocketing through
the empty rooms downstairs. I sat very still, the duvet clutched in
my hands. The heating was chugging and the ventilation pipes
rattling, and the room was full of a strange, grey light. And, now
that I thought about it, there was another noise. An odd
noise that had nothing to do with my dream and nothing to do
with the storm. It was coming from somewhere on the other side
of the house.

44

Nanking, 20 December 1937

All knowledge comes with a price. Today Liu Runde and I have learned things we wish we could forget. Pushed up against the wall in the small room at the factory was a low army cot, a filthy blood-stained mattress thrown casually on it. A kerosene lamp, a Chinese make, stood unlit on it, as if someone had used it to light whatever diabolical procedure was performed there – whatever it was that had produced the copious amounts of blood that had congealed on the floor and walls. It seemed the only things not sticky with blood was a pile of belongings stacked against the wall – a pair of split-sole *tabi* overboots and a soldier's pack made of cow-hide so raw that there was still hair attached. On the small desk, next to the manager's old abacus, stood a row of small brown medicine bottles sealed with waxed paper, Japanese lettering on the labels; a handful of phials containing a variety of coarse powders; a pestle and mortar, alongside squares of folded apothecary paper. Behind these were arranged three army mess tins and a water canteen with an Imperial chrysanthemum stamped on it. Liu put a finger on one of the mess tins and tilted it. When I leaned over to look inside I saw rags floating in an indescribable mixture of blood and water.

'Good God.' Liu set the tin upright. 'What in heaven's name happens in here?'

'He's ill,' said the boy, sullenly indicating the medicine bottles. 'A fever.'

'I don't mean the bottles! I mean *this*. The blood. Where is the blood from?'

'The blood . . . the blood is . . . the boys on the street say that the blood is . . .'

'What?' Liu looked at him sternly. 'What do they say?'

He ran his tongue uncomfortably over his front teeth. He was suddenly pale. 'No, it must be a mistake.'

'What do they say?'

'They're older than me,' he said, lowering his eyes. 'The other boys are much older than I am. I think they must be telling me tales . . .'

'What do they say?'

His face twisted reluctantly, and when he spoke his voice was very quiet, no more than a whisper. 'They say that the women . . .'

'Yes? What about the women?'

'They say that he . . .' His voice became almost unintelligible. 'He takes shavings from them. Shavings of their skin. He scrapes them.'

The food in my stomach rolled and heaved. I sank down to my haunches, my face in my hands, dizzy and sick. Liu took a breath, then gripped the boy by his jacket and drew him away from the room. He led him straight out of the building without another word, and shortly I stumbled out after them, my stomach turning.

I caught up with them about a hundred yards away. Liu had his son in a doorway and was grilling him. 'Where did you hear this?'

'The boys on the streets are all talking about it.'

'Who is he? This *yanwangye*? Who is he?'

'I don't know.'

'He's a human being – of course he is. And what manner of human being? Japanese?'

'Yes. A lieutenant.' The boy gripped his collar where an IJA officer would wear a rank badge. 'The *yanwangye* in a lieutenant's uniform.' He looked at me. 'Did you hear the motor-cycle this morning?'

'Yes.'

'That's him. They say he'll be hungry for ever because nothing makes him stop. The other boys say he's on a search that will last for ever.'

I have to pause here as I write this because I am recalling a scene – a vivid scene – a conversation I had with Liu before the invasion. We are cramped in his reception room, some cups and a little dish of shredded Nanking salt duck between us, and he is telling me about bodies he saw in Shanghai, bodies desecrated by the Japanese. I can't help reliving the scenes he drew for me that night. In Shanghai, apparently, anything was taken as a trophy: an ear, a scalp, a kidney, a breast. The trophy was worn on the belt, or pinned to a cap – soldiers who could show off scalps or genitals had great power. They posed with their trophies, waiting for photographs to be taken by their comrades. Liu had heard rumours of a group of soldiers who had stitched Chinese scalps, shaved into old-fashioned Manchu queues, to the back of their caps as the badge of their unit. Among them moved a soldier from another unit who carried a cine-camera, probably stolen from a journalist, or looted from one of the big houses in the International Zone. The men showed off for him too, laughing and throwing the plaits over their shoulders, aping the walk of the girls in the cabarets on Avenue Edward VII. They were not ashamed of their unnatural behaviour, rather they were proud – eager to show off.

Now when I stop writing all I can hear is my heart thudding. The snow falls silently outside the window. What about skin? Scrapings of human skin? What sort of unspeakable trophy was the *yanwangye* harvesting?

'That's one of them.'

The child hadn't been very old. Maybe three or four years. Liu's son took us to see her. She lay at some distance from us, in the street at the side of the factory, face down, her hair spread round her, her hands tucked under her body.

I looked at the boy. 'When did this happen?'

He shrugged. 'She was there last night.'

'She needs to be buried.'

'Yes,' he said. 'Yes.' But he made no attempt to move.

I went a short way down the street to look at her. As soon as I got near I saw that her jacket, dust-silvered in the sun, was moving. She was breathing shallowly. 'She's alive,' I said, looking up at them.

'Alive?' Liu gave his son a fierce look. 'Did you know this?'

'No,' he said, backing away defensively. 'I promise – I promise I thought she was dead.'

Liu spat on the ground. He turned away from his son and came to stand next to me. We peered down at her. She wore a quilted jacket and cannot have weighed more than thirty *jin*, but no one had picked her up. Her feet were bound with a scrap of olive wool – the material of a Japanese army blanket.

I bent to her. 'Turn over,' I said. 'Roll on to your back.'

She remained motionless, only the shadows of a maple branch overhead moving across her back. I bent, took her by the arm, and turned her on to her back. She was as light as firewood, and once on her back her hair and arms lay where they fell, loose and spread out in the snow. I took a step back, choking a little. The front of her trousers had been cut away and a hole about the size of a rice bowl had been scraped in her right side, just below the ribs where her liver would be. I could see the blackish stain of gangrene around the edges of the wound, where she had been gouged at, and the smell made me grope instinctively for my sleeve, fumbling to hold it over my nose and mouth. It was the smell of the most vicious gangrene. Gas gangrene. Even if I could get her to a hospital she would not live.

I stood with my arm across my face, staring at the hole in the child's stomach, trying to imagine why it had been made. It was not accidental. It was not a stab wound. This hole had been carved out of her body with a purposefulness that made my blood run cold. 'What is this?' I muttered to Liu. 'Is it a trophy?' I couldn't think of any other reason for such a mutilation. 'Is this a trophy he's taking?'

'Shi Chongming, don't ask me this question. I have never seen anything like this . . .'

Just then the child's eyes opened and she saw me. I didn't have time to lower my arm. She caught the disgust in my face, she saw my sleeve held tightly against my mouth, trying to block out her smell. She understood that I was sickened by her. She blinked once, her eyes clear and alive. I dropped my arm and tried to breathe normally. I wouldn't allow my disgust to be one of the last impressions she had of herself in the world.

I turned to Liu in anguish. *What should I do? What can I do?*

He shook his head wearily, and went to the side of the road. When I saw where he was heading I understood. He was making his way to a place where a heavy paving-stone had come loose at the foot of a building.

When the act was complete, when the child was quite dead and the stone smeared with her blood, we cleaned our hands, re-buttoned our coats and rejoined the boy. Liu took his son in his arms and kissed his head over and over again until the boy became embarrassed and struggled to get away. The snow was falling again and we all headed in silence in the direction of our houses.

Old Father Heaven, forgive me. Forgive me for not having the energy to bury her. She is lying in the snow still, the reflections of clouds and branches and sky moving in her dead eyes. There are traces of her on the front of my greatcoat and under my nails. I am sure traces of her are sticking to my heart too, but I can't feel them. I don't feel a thing. Because this is Nanking, and it is not new, this death. One death is hardly worth mentioning in this city where the devil stalks the street.

45

Around me the room was emerging slowly from the darkness. On the futon I sat very still, my heart thudding, and waited for the noises outside to become recognizable. But every time I thought I'd got the tail of it between my fingers it faded under the racket of the storm. Shadows of leaves carried by the wind passed the window, and sitting in the semi-dark like that I began to imagine all manner of things: I hallucinated that the house was a little raft in the dark, juggled on the waves, that outside my room the city was gone, blasted away in an atomic attack.

The sound again. What was it? I turned to the door. My first thought was of the cats in the garden. I'd seen their kittens some-times, clinging like monkeys to the mosquito screens, screaming into our rooms like baby birds. Maybe a kitten was in one of the other rooms, crawling froglike up a screen. Or maybe it was . . .

'*Jason?*' I whispered, sitting up straight, my skin crawling. This time it was louder, an odd, ululating sound lisping round the house. I tipped on to my hands and knees and crawled to the door, opened it a little way, very silently, trying to take its weight so it didn't shriek on the runners. I peered out. Several of the shutters had been pulled back and opposite Jason's room a window stood open, as if he'd stopped there after our argument just long enough to smoke a cigarette. Outside, the garden was rearing and thrashing in the wind – branches had broken, and near the window a Lawson's Station carrier-bag, brought on the wind and caught in a tree, shifted and hissed and crackled, throwing its eerie shadow skittering round the corridor, up the walls and across the *tatami* matting.

But the storm wasn't what had woken me. The more I looked at the familiar passageway, the more I knew something was wrong. It was something about the light. Usually it wasn't this dark. Usually we left the overhead lamps on at night, but now the light coming under the doors from the Mickey Rourke poster was the only source of luminance, and instead of a row of lightbulbs, I could see jagged glitters of broken glass. I blinked a few times, my thoughts moving curiously slowly and calmly, allowing time for this to sink in. The lightbulbs in the corridor had been smashed in their fittings, just as if a giant hand had reached up and pinched them out.

Someone's in the house, I thought, still strangely calm. *There's someone else in the house.* I took a breath and stepped silently into the corridor. All the doors on this side of the house were closed – even the kitchen door. We usually left it open, in case someone was hungry or thirsty in the night. The toilet door, too, was shut tight, eerie in its blankness. I took a few steps up the corridor, stepping over the broken glass, trying to ignore the howling wind, trying to concentrate on the noise. It was coming from the third section of the corridor, where the gallery bent sideways and Jason's room lay. As I stood there, breathing carefully, the sound began to separate itself, detaching minutely from the wind, and when at last I recognized it my pulse leaped. It was the soft sound of someone whimpering in pain.

I stepped sideways and opened one of the windows a crack. Another noise was coming from the same part of the house: an odd, furtive rummaging, as if every rat in the house had converged on one room. The trees bent and whipped, but from here I had a view directly across the garden to the far corridor. When my eyes got used to the tree shadows bouncing off the glass, what I saw made me drop to a crouch, gripping the frame with trembling fingers, peering cautiously over the sill.

Jason's door was open. In the half-light I could see a shape in his room: a hideous, stooped shape, more a shadow than anything. Like a hyena crouching over a meal, intent on disjointing its prize, unnaturally crabbed, as if it had dropped straight down on to its prey from the ceiling. All the hairs went up on my skin at once. The Nurse. The Nurse was in the house . . . And then I saw another figure in the room, standing slightly to one side, half bent over as if he was looking at something on the floor. He was in shadows too, his back to me, but something about the shape of his shoulders told me that I was looking at the man who had sworn his allegiance to Fuyuki earlier that evening: the *chimpira*.

I blinked a few times, thinking in a surreal, fevered way: *What is this? Why are they here? Is it a joke?* I straightened a little, and now I could see the top of Jason's head and shoulders: he was face down, prone, pinioned to the ground by the *chimpira*, whose foot was planted directly on the back of his head. Just then the Nurse shifted a little, and settled herself in a sitting position, her big, muscular knees in the black nylons parted wide and high either side of her shoulders, her arms straight down between them. That thin, awful sound I'd heard was Jason pleading, struggling to get free. She wasn't listening to him – she was going about her business with unnerving concentration, her shoulders hunched, rocking herself calmly back and forth. Her hands, which were just below the frame of my vision, operated in small, controlled motions, as if she was performing a complex and delicate operation. I don't know how I knew, but I had a moment's rare clarity: *You're watching a rape. She's raping him.*

My trance fractured. A sweat broke out across my back and I stood up, opening my mouth to speak. As if she had smelt me on the wind, the Nurse looked up. She paused. Then her huge shoulders rose, the polished wig swayed round her great angular head, which she held back a little, as if she was rising from an interrupted meal. I froze: it was as if the whole world was a telescope, containing me at one end, the Nurse at the other. Even now I wonder how I must have looked to her, how much she saw: a moving shadow, a pair of eyes glinting in an unlit window at the far, lonely end of the house.

At that moment the wind made a ferocious lap of the garden,

screaming like a jet engine, filling the house with noise. The Nurse tilted her head and spoke in a low voice to the *chimpira*, who immediately became rigid. Slowly he straightened and turned to stare down the long corridor to where I stood. Then he pulled back his shoulders and flexed his hands. He began to amble casually towards me.

I lurched away from the window and bolted for my room, slamming the door and locking it, tripping and scuttling backwards like a crab, stumbling over the books and papers in the dark, banging into things blindly. I stood, pressed against the wall, staring at the door, my chest as tight as if I'd been thumped in the ribs. *Jason*, I thought, feverishly. *Jason, they've come back to get you. What games have you been playing with her?*

At first no one came. Minutes seemed to pass – time when they could have been doing anything to Jason, time when I thought I should open the door, get to the phone, call the police. Then, just as I thought the *chimpira* wasn't coming, that he and the Nurse must have left the house in silence, I distinctly heard, through the wind, his footstep creak in the corridor outside.

I shot to the side window, scrabbling crazily at the edges of the mosquito screen, breaking my nails. One of the catches gave. I flung away the screen, threw open the window and looked down. About four feet below, an air-conditioning unit that might hold my weight stuck out from the neighbouring building. From there it was another long drop into the tiny space between the buildings. I turned and stared at the door. The footsteps had stopped and, in the awful silence, the *chimpira* muttered something under his breath. Then a kick splintered the flimsy door. I heard him grab the frame, getting a hold so he could punch his foot straight through.

I scrambled on to the windowsill. I had time to see his arm splinter through the hole, his disembodied hand in the lavender suit groping in the dark for the doorlock, then I pushed myself out, landing noisily, the air conditioner shuddering under my weight, something ripping my foot. I dropped into a clumsy squat, scrambled on to my stomach, dangling my legs out into the darkness, the wind whipping my pyjamas around me. I pushed away and dropped straight to the ground with a soft thud, rocking forward a little so that my face slammed against the plastic weatherboarding on the neighbouring house with a painful *thuck*.

Another splintering sound came from above – the noise of something metallic – a screw or a hinge, maybe, ricocheting round the room. I hauled in a breath, sprang to my feet and flew out into the alley, diving into a gap between two buildings opposite where I crouched, the blood thundering in my veins. After a moment or two I dared to shuffle forward, my hands on the two buildings, and peer up at the house in mute horror.

The *chimpira* was in my room. Light coming from the corridor behind amplified every detail of him, as if through a magnifying-glass: individual hairs, the light shade swaying above his head. I pulled the collar of my pyjama jacket over my mouth, holding it there with both clenched fists, my teeth chattering, staring at him with eyes as hard and round as if I'd had adrenaline dropped into them. Would he guess how I'd escaped? Would he see me?

He hesitated, then his head appeared. I shrank back into the gap. He took long, patient minutes to study the drop from the window. When at last he pulled his head inside, his shadow wavered for a moment, then he disappeared from view, almost in slow motion, leaving the room blank save for the swinging light-bulb. I started to breathe again.

You can be as brave and confident as you like, you can convince yourself that you're invulnerable, that you know what you're dealing with. You think that it won't ever really get too serious – that there'll be some kind of a warning before it goes that far, danger music, maybe, playing offstage, the way you get in films. But it seems to me that disasters aren't like that. Disasters are life's great ambushers: they have a way of jumping on you when your eyes are fixed on something else.

The Nurse and the *chimpira* stayed in our house for over an hour. I watched them roaming through the corridors, slamming into rooms, throwing the shutters off their hinges. Glass smashed and doors were ripped away. They overturned furniture and ripped the telephone out of the wall. And all the time I sat squashed and frozen between the buildings, my pyjama top pulled up over my mouth, all I could think was: *Shi Chongming. You shouldn't have let me get into this. You shouldn't have let me get into things so dangerous.* Because this was more, much more, than I had ever bargained for.

46

The way I remember the rest of that night is like one of those time-lapse films you sometimes see of a flower opening, or the sun moving across a street – jerky, with people shooting suddenly from one place to another. Except my film is all lit in the electric cordite colour of disaster and the sound has a horrible sloweddown underwater quality, with the creaking noise that you imagine big ships make. *Zoom*, and there's the terrible shadow of the Nurse and Jason, making me think of something in a book, *beast with two backs/beast with two backs*, then *zoom!*, there's me crouched between the buildings, my eyes watering, the muscles in my flanks twitching with fatigue. I'm watching the Nurse and the *chimpira* leaving the house, stopping briefly at the door to cast a glance up the street, the *chimpira* swinging keys on his fingers, the Nurse tightening the belt on her raincoat, before melting away into the dark. I'm frozen and numb everywhere, and when I touch my face where I banged the wall, it doesn't hurt as much as it should. There's just a little blood coming out of my nose and a little more where I bit my tongue. Then *zoom* again, and the Nurse hasn't come back – the alley has been quiet for so long, and the front door is wide open, it's been popped out of its catch, so I'm creeping back up the staircase, shivering crazily, hesitating at each step. Then I'm in my room, staring in disbelief at the devastation – my clothes scattered on the floor, the door caved in and all the drawers open and rummaged through. Then *zoom* . . . into a terrible close-up of my face. I'm standing in the middle of the room, looking into an empty handbag, my heart sinking because this is the handbag where I store all the money I've earned in the last few months. It has never, until now, occurred to me to put it somewhere safe, but now I can see that the Nurse and the *chimpira* have not only come to torture Jason, but also to milk everything they possibly can from this rambling house.

I stood for a while outside my room and looked down the long corridor. It was dawn. The light coming through the broken gallery windows cast jagged shapes on the dusty *tatami* mat and everything was still and ominously silent, except for the *drip drip drip* of the tap in the kitchen. Every store room had been looted: they all stood open and silent, the air freezing, piles of dusty and decaying furniture lying all over the place. It was as if the developers' wrecking ball had come through early. Most of the doors were open. Except Jason's. It drew the eye, that door, all the way from the end of the corridor. There was something shamed and sinister about it, the way it was closed so tightly.

Instead of knocking I went to Irina's room. I'm that much of a coward. When I drew back the door two bodies recoiled in the dark: Svetlana and Irina, gibbering with fear, scuttling backwards as if they'd climb the walls like rats. 'It's me,' I whispered, holding up my hands to hush them. The room was musky with the smell of fear. 'It's me.'

It took them a moment to subside, sinking to the floor, holding each other. I dropped down next to them. Irina looked terrible – her cheeks were tear-streaked, her makeup everywhere. 'I want to go home,' she mouthed, her face twisting. 'I wanna go home.'

'What happened? What did she do?'

Svetlana stroked Irina's back. '*It*,' she hissed. '*It*, not she. It come in here – push us in here, and the other one take our money. Everythink.'

'Did she hurt you?'

She snorted loudly. I could tell it was an act. Her usual bravado was gone. 'No. But it don't gotta touch us to make us – *pssht*.'

She used her hand to mime the two of them flying into the corner in fear.

Irina wiped her eyes on her T-shirt, holding it up to her face and pressing it into her eyes. It came away with two black mascara smears on it. 'It is a monster, that one, I tellink you. A real *d'yavol*.'

'How they know we got money, hmm?' Svetlana was trying to light a cigarette, but her hands were trembling so hard that she couldn't control the flame. She gave up and looked at me. 'Did you tell to anyone how much money we make?'

'They didn't come because of the money,' I said.

'Of course they did. Everythink always about money.'

I didn't answer. I bit my fingers and looked back at the door, thinking: *No. You don't understand. Jason brought them here. Whatever he did or said to the Nurse at the party – we're paying the price now.* The silence coming from his room made my blood cold. What were we going to find when we opened his door? What if – I remembered the photograph in Shi Chongming's portfolio – what if we drew back the door and found . . .

I stood. 'We've got to go into Jason's room.'

Svetlana and Irina were silent. They looked back at me seriously.

'What is it?'

'You didn't hear the noise he make?'

'Some of it – I was asleep.'

'Well, we . . .' Svetlana had managed to light her cigarette. She held the smoke deep in her lungs, and blew it out through tight lips. '*We* hear everythink.' She glanced at Irina as if to confirm this. 'Mmmm. And it not *us* going in there now and look.'

Irina sniffed and shook her head. 'No. Not us.'

I looked from face to face, my heart sinking. 'No,' I said woodenly. 'Of course not.' I went to the doorway and stared along the corridor to Jason's room. 'Of course it should be me.'

Svetlana came to stand behind me, her hand on my shoulder. She peered out into the hallway. In front of Jason's room a suitcase lay up-ended against the wall, its contents spilling out on to the floor – his clothing scattered everywhere, his passport, an envelope stuffed with paperwork. 'My God,' she whispered into my ear. 'Look at mess.'

'I know.'

'You sure they gone?'

I looked across at the silent stairway. 'I'm sure.'

Irina joined us, still dabbing her face, and we stood in a huddle, looking timidly down the passageway. There was a smell – an unmissable smell that made me think, inexplicably, of offal in a butcher's window. I swallowed. 'Listen . . . we might have to . . .' I paused. 'What about a doctor? We might have to get a doctor.'

Svetlana chewed her lip uneasily, exchanging a look with Irina. 'We take him to doctor, Grey, and they gonna wanna know what happened and then the politsia gonna be here, looking snoopy-snoopy, and then—'

'Immigration,' Irina clicked her tongue against the roof of her mouth. 'Immigration.'

'And who gonna to pay for it, hmm?' Svetlana turned her cigarette and looked at the tip, as if it had spoken to her. 'No money left.' She nodded. 'No money left in whole house.'

'*Davai.*' Irina put her hand on the small of my back, and propelled me gently forward. 'You go see. Go see, then we talk.'

I went slowly, stepping over the suitcase, stopping in front of his door with my hands very stiff at my sides, staring at the doorhandle, the terrible silence ringing in my ears. What if I didn't find his body? What if I was right about Fuyuki and his medicine? The word 'hunt' came to my mind. Had the Nurse come here *hunting*? I glanced back down the corridor to where the Russians were huddled in the doorway, Irina with her hands over her ears as if she was about to hear an explosion.

'Right,' I murmured to myself. I turned, put a jittery hand on the door, and took a deep breath. 'Right.'

I tugged but the door wouldn't slide open.

'What is it?' hissed Svetlana.

'I don't know.' I shook it. 'It's locked.' I put my mouth to the door. '*Jason?*'

I waited, listening to the silence.

'*Jason – can you hear me?*' I tapped on the door with my knuckle. 'Jason, can you hear me? Are you—'

'*Fuck off.*' His voice was muffled. It sounded as if he was speaking from under a duvet. '*Get away from my door and fuck off.*'

I took a step back, putting a hand on the wall to steady myself, my knees trembling. 'Jason – you're . . .' I took a few deep breaths. 'Do you need a doctor? I'll take you to Roppongi if you like –'

'I *said* fuck off.'

'– we'll tell them we'll pay next week when—'

'Are you fucking *deaf*?'

'No,' I said, staring blankly at the door. 'No, I'm not deaf.'

'He okay?' hissed Svetlana.

I looked up at her. 'What?'

'He okay?'

'Um,' I said, wiping my face and looking dubiously at the door. 'Well, I think, yes, I think he is.'

It took us a long time to believe that the Nurse wasn't coming back. It took even longer to get up the courage to inspect the house. The damage was terrible. We tidied up a little and took it in turns to have baths. I washed in a daze, moving the flannel woodenly over my swollen face. There were scratches on my feet where I must have ripped them jumping out of the window. Coincidentally they were exactly where the dream baby had bitten me. They could have been the baby's toothmarks. I stared at them for a long, long time, shivering so hard that I couldn't stop my teeth chattering.

Irina had discovered some money in a coat pocket that the *chimpira* had overlooked and agreed to lend me a thousand yen. When I finished bathing I tidied my room, carefully sweeping up the broken glass and shattered door shards, stacking all the books into the wardrobe, arranging the notes and the paintings neatly, then put Irina's money in my pocket and took the Maranouchi line to Hongo.

The rain-soaked campus looked very different from the last time I'd been there. The thick leaf cover had gone and you could see all the way to the lake, the complex and ornately tiled roof of the gymnasium rising up behind the trees. It was early but Shi Chongming already had a student with him, a tall, spotty boy in an orange sweatshirt that said *Bathing Ape* on the front. Both of them stopped talking when I walked in, my coat buttoned up tightly. My face was bruised, blood still crusted my nostrils, my hands were in rigid fists at my sides, and I was shaking un-controllably. I stood dead in the middle of the room and pointed at Shi Chongming. 'You made me go a long way,' I said. 'You made me go a long way, but I can't go any further. It's time for you to give me the film.'

Shi Chongming got slowly to his feet. He steadied himself on his cane, then held up his hand to indicate the door to the student. 'Quick, quick,' he hissed, when the boy sat frozen in his seat staring at me. '*Come along now, quickly.*' The student got cautiously to his feet. His face was serious and his eyes were locked on mine as he sidestepped with great care to the door, slipping through and closing it behind him with a barely audible click.

Shi Chongming didn't turn immediately. He stood for a while with his hand on the door, his back to me. When we'd been alone for almost a minute, and there was no chance of interruption, he turned to me. 'Now, then, are you calm?'

'*Calm?* Yes, I'm calm. Very calm.'

'Sit down. Sit down and tell me what's happened.'

47

 Nanking, 20 December 1937

There is nothing so painful, so agonized, as a proud man admitting he has been mistaken. On our way back from the factory, leaving the dead child on the street, we reached the point where we would separate and Liu put his hand on my arm. 'Go home and wait for me,' he whispered. 'I will be with you as soon as I've seen young Liu back to the house. Things are going to change.'

Sure enough, less than twenty minutes after I'd arrived home, there was a coded series of knocks on the door and I opened it to find him standing on the threshold with a coarse bamboo-hemp folder under his arm.

'We need to talk,' he murmured, checking to make sure that Shujin wasn't listening. 'I've got a plan.'

He took off his shoes as a mark of respect and came into the small room on the ground floor that we use for formal occasions. Shujin keeps the room properly prepared at all times, set out with chairs and a red lacquered table, which is beautifully inlaid with peonies and dragons in mother-of-pearl. We seated ourselves at it, arranging our robes round us. Shujin didn't question old Liu's presence. She slipped upstairs to tidy her hair, and after a few minutes I heard her go out to the kitchen to boil some water.

'There's only tea and a few of your wife's buckwheat dumplings to offer you, Liu Runde,' I said. 'Nothing more. I am sorry.'

He bowed his head. 'There is no need to explain.'

In his folder he had a map of Nanking that he had prepared in great detail. He must have been working on it over the last few days. When the pot of tea was on the table, and our cups were full, he spread it out in front of me.

'This,' he said, circling a point outside Chalukou, 'is the house of an old friend. A salt trader, very wealthy – and the house is large, with a fresh well, pomegranate trees and well-stocked pantries. Not so very far from Purple Mountain. And this,' he put a cross a few *li* further into the city, 'this is Taiping gate. There are reports that the wall has been badly shelled in this area, and there is a chance, with the rush to the west, that the Japanese won't have assigned enough men to guard it here. Assuming we get through, we'll walk from there along back-streets, following the main Chalukou road, reaching the river a long way north of the city. Chalukou can be of no strategic importance to the Japanese, so if we're lucky we'll find a boat, and from the far shore we will disappear inland to Anhui province.' We were both silent for a while, thinking about taking our families through all those dangerous places. After a while, as if I'd expressed a doubt, Liu nodded. 'Yes, I know. It relies on the Japanese being concentrated upstream at Xiaguan and Meitan.'

'The radio says that any day now there'll be an announcement about the self-governing committee.'

He looked at me very seriously. It was the most unguarded expression I'd ever seen him wear. 'Dearest, dearest Master Shi. You know as well as I do that if we stay here we're like rats in a drain, waiting for the Japanese to find us.'

I put my fingers to my head. 'Yes, indeed,' I muttered. Tears were suddenly in my eyes, tears I didn't want old Liu to see. But he is too old and wise. He knew immediately what was wrong.

'Master Shi, do not take this blame too heavily – do you understand? I myself have done no better than you. I, too, have been guilty of pride.'

A tear ran down my face and fell on to the table, landing on the eye of a dragon. I stared at it numbly. 'What have I done?' I whispered. 'What have I done to my wife? My child?'

Old Liu sat forward in his chair and covered my hand with his. 'We have made a mistake. All we have done is to make a mistake. We have been ignorant little men, but that is all. Only a little ignorant, you and I.'

48

Sometimes people forget to be sympathetic and instead they blame you for everything, even for the things you did when you had no idea they were wrong. When I explained what had happened at the house, the first thing Shi Chongming wanted to know was had I jeopardized his research? Had I talked about what he was looking for? Even when I gave him an edited version, a vague explanation about what Jason had done, how he'd brought the Nurse to the house, Shi Chongming still wasn't as sympathetic as I'd hoped. He wanted to know more.

'What an odd thing for your friend to do. What was going on in his mind?'

I didn't answer. If I told him about Jason, about what had been going on between us, it would be like the hospital all over again, people tut-tutting over my behaviour, looking at me and thinking of mud-streaked savages mating in a forest.

'Did you hear me?'

'Look,' I said, standing up, 'I'm going to explain everything very carefully.' I went to the window. Outside it was still raining – the water dripped from the trees, soaking the straw target bales stacked outside the archery centre. 'What you asked me to do was very, very, *very* dangerous. One of us could have died, I'm not exaggerating. Now I'm going to tell you something very important . . .' I shivered, rubbing compulsively at the goosebumps on my arms. 'It's more serious than you ever guessed. I've been

273

finding things. Finding incredible things.' Shi Chongming sat
motionless at his desk listening to me, his face tight and intense.
'There are stories about human beings,' I said, lowering my voice,
'dead human bodies, cut up and used as a cure. Consumed. Do
you understand what I'm talking about? Do you?' I took a
breath. '*Cannibalism*.' I waited a moment to let it sink in.
Cannibalism. Cannibalism. You could feel the word spoken on its
own soaking into the walls and staining the carpet. 'You're going
to tell me I'm insane, I know you are, but I'm used to that and I
really don't care, because I'm telling you: *all this time the thing
you've been looking for, Professor Shi, is human flesh*.'

A look of immense discomfort spread slowly across Shi
Chongming's face. 'Cannibalism,' he said sharply, his fingers
moving compulsively on the desk. 'Is that what you said?'

'Yes.'

'An extraordinary suggestion.'

'I don't expect you to believe me – I mean, if the company in
Hong Kong heard, they'd—'

'You've got proof, I take it.'

'I've got what people have told me. Fuyuki used to run a black-
market. Have you heard of *zanpan*? Everyone in Tokyo used to
say that the stew they served in the market was—'

'What have you actually seen? Hmmm? Have you seen Fuyuki
drinking blood? Does he smell foul? Is his skin red? That's how
you recognize a cannibal, did you know?' Something bitter had
crept into his voice. 'I wonder . . .' he said. 'I wonder . . . Is his
apartment reminiscent of the terrible kitchens in *Outlaws of the
Marsh*? Are there limbs hanging everywhere? Human skins
stretched on the walls ready for the pot?'

'You're teasing me.'

There was sweat on his brow. His throat was working hard
under the high mandarin collar.

'Don't tease me,' I said. 'Please don't tease me.'

He took a deep breath and tilted back in his seat. 'No,' he said
tightly. 'No. Of course I mustn't. I mustn't.' He pushed back the
chair, got up, and went to the sink where he ran the tap and
scooped water into his mouth. He stood for a while with his back

to me, watching the running water. Then he turned off the tap, came back to his chair and sat down. His face had smoothed a little. 'I do apologize.' He looked for a while at his fragile hands resting on the table. They were twitching as if they had a life of their own. 'Well,' he said at length, '*cannibalism*, is it? If that's what you believe you'll bring me proof.'

'What? You can't want more. I've done *everything*. Everything you told me to do.' I thought about the house, the windows, the doors smashed, I thought about all the money that had been taken. I thought about the Nurse's shadow on the Salt Building – doing what to Jason? *The beast with two backs* . . . 'You're not keeping your promise. You've broken your promise. You've broken your promise again!'

'We had an agreement. I need proof, not speculation.'

'*That's not what you said!*' I went to the projector and pulled it out of the corner, ripping away the plastic cover, turning it on its castors, trying to find a hiding place. 'I need the film.' I went to the shelves, pulling out books, dropping them on the floor, pushing my hands into the cavities behind. I pushed piles of papers on to the floor, and wrenched aside the curtains. 'Where've you put it? *Where is it?*'

'Please, sit down and we'll talk.'

'No, you don't understand. You are a liar.' I clenched my hands at my sides and raised my voice. '*You* are a *liar*.'

'The film is locked away. I don't have the key here. We couldn't get to it even if I wanted to.'

'Give it to me.'

'*That's enough!*' He shot to his feet, flushed, breathing rapidly, and pointed his cane at me. '*Do not*,' he said, his chest rising and falling, 'do *not* insult me until you understand what you are dealing with. Now, sit down.'

'What?' I said, taken off-guard.

'Sit down. Sit down and listen carefully.'

I stared at him in silence. 'I don't understand *you*,' I whispered, wiping my face with the back of my sleeve and pointing a finger at him. '*You*. I don't understand *you*.'

'Of course you don't. Now, *sit*.'

I sat, glaring at him.

'Now, please.' Shi Chongming pushed back his chair and sat down, breathing hard, trying to compose himself, pulling his jacket into shape and smoothing it, as if the action might wipe away his anger. 'Please – you would do well to learn that sometimes it pays to consider things outside your immediate sphere of understanding . . .' He dabbed his forehead. 'Now, allow me to make you a small concession.'

I exhaled impatiently. 'I don't want a small concession, I want the—'

'*Listen*.' He held up a shaky hand. 'My *concession* . . . is to tell you that you are right. Or, rather, that you are almost right. When you suggest . . . when you suggest that Fuyuki is consuming . . .' He shovelled his handkerchief into his pocket and set his hands on the desk, looking from one to the other as if the action would help him concentrate. 'When you suggest . . .' he paused, then said, in a steady voice '. . . *cannibalism*, you are almost correct.'

'Not "almost"! I can see it in your face – I'm right, aren't I?'

He held up his hand. 'You are right about some things. But not everything. Maybe you are even correct about those dreadful rumours – human flesh for sale in the Tokyo markets! The gods know the *yakuza* did terrible things to the starving of this great city, and a corpse was not a difficult thing to find in Tokyo in those days. But to cannibalize for medicine?' He picked up a paperclip, twisting it distractedly. 'This is something different. If it exists in the Japanese underworld, then maybe it arrived in some parts of Japanese society centuries ago, and maybe again in the forties after the Pacific war.' He twisted the clip into the shape of a crane and set it on his desk, regarding it carefully. Then he put his hands together and looked at me. 'And this is why you need to listen carefully. I am going to tell you exactly why I *can't* give you the film yet.'

I made a noise and sat back, my arms folded. 'You know, your voice irritates me,' I said. 'Sometimes I really hate listening to it.'

Shi Chongming looked at me for a long time. Suddenly his face cleared and a small smile flickered around his mouth. He flicked the paperclip bird into the bin, pushed back his chair, stood up and fished out a bunch of keys from a desk tidy. From a locked drawer he pulled out a notebook. Bound in thin cowhide and held together with string, it looked ancient. He unwound the string and sheafs of yellowing paper fell on to the desk. They were covered in Chinese writing, tiny and unreadable. 'My memoirs,' he said. 'From the time I was in Nanking.'

'From Nanking?'

'What do you see?'

I leaned forward, wonderingly, squinting at the tiny calligraphy, trying to decipher a word or phrase.

'I said, what do you see?'

I glanced up at him. 'I see a memoir.' I reached out for it, but he pulled it back, crooking his arm round it protectively.

'No. No, you don't see a memoir. A memoir is a concept, like a story. You can't *see* a story.' He rubbed the first page between his veined fingers. 'What is this?'

'Paper. Can I read it now?'

'No. What is on the paper?'

'Are you going to let me have it?'

'Listen to me. I'm trying to help. What is on the paper?'

'Writing,' I said. 'Ink.'

'Exactly.' The strange grey light coming through the window made the skin on Shi Chongming's face almost transparent. 'You see paper, and you see ink. But they have become more than this – they have ceased to be just paper and ink. They have been transformed by my ideas and beliefs. They have become a memoir.'

'I don't know about memoirs and ink and paper,' I said, my eyes still locked on the diary. 'But I know I'm right. Fuyuki is experimenting with cannibalism.'

'I had forgotten that Westerners do not understand the art of listening. If you'd listened carefully, if you'd listened less in the manner of a Westerner, you'd know that I haven't disagreed with you.'

I looked at him blankly. I was about to say '*And?*' when what he was trying to say leaped at me, fully formed and quite clear. 'Oh,' I said faintly, lowering my hands. 'Oh, I think I . . .'

'You think?'

'I . . .' I trailed off and sat for a while, my head on one side, my mouth moving silently. I was seeing image after image of the Liberian Poro boys, squatting fearsomely over their enemies in the bush, of the Human Leopard Society, of all the people around the world who had eaten the flesh of their enemies, something transformed by their ideas and beliefs. The *kanji* for power that I had painted last night came back to me. 'I think,' I said slowly, 'I think . . . flesh can be transformed, can't it? Some human flesh can have a – a kind of power . . .'

'Indeed.'

'A kind of power – it can be transformed by . . . by a process? Or by . . .' And suddenly I had it. I looked at him sharply. 'It's not just any human being. You mean it's someone particular. It's someone special – special to Fuyuki. Isn't it?'

Shi Chongming shuffled the diary together and secured it with a rubber band, his mouth in a tight bud. 'That,' he said, not looking at me, 'is what you need to find out.'

49

I sat in silence, my fingers to my head as I rode back across Tokyo on the raised train tracks circling high above the city, among the neon advertising hoardings, the glinting white and chrome sky-scrapers, the blue sky and the madness, looking blankly into tenth-storey offices at the secretaries in their cookie-cutter blouses and tan tights who stared back out of the windows. Sometimes, I thought, Shi Chongming made me work too hard. Sometimes he gave me a headache. In Shinjuku the train rattled past a skyscraper covered with hundreds of TV monitors, each one bearing an image of a man in a gold tuxedo, belting out a song to the camera. I stared at it blankly for a while. Then it dawned on me.

Bison?

I got up, crossed the train and rested my hands on the window, looking up at the building. It was him, a much younger and thinner Bison than the one I knew, head on one side, holding his hand out to the camera, his image repeated and repeated, reminted and reminted, hundreds of times, until he covered the building, a thousand *doppelgängers* moving and talking in unison. In the bottom left of each screen was a logo that said *NHK Newswatch*. The news. Bison was on the news. Just as the train was about to pass the skyscraper his face was replaced by a hazy shot of a police car parked outside a nondescript Tokyo house. *Police*, I thought, pressing my hands flat on the window, gazing back at the skyscraper disappearing behind the train. My breath steamed up the glass. *Bison. Why are you on the news?*

It was getting dark when I got to the Takadanobaba house, and none of the lights was on, except in the stairwell. Svetlana was outside, staring at something on the ground, the door open behind her. She was wearing go-go boots and a knee-length fluffy pink coat, and was holding a dustbin-liner full of clothes.

'Have you seen the news?' I said. 'Have you been watching the television?'

'It's covered in flies.'

'What?'

'Look.'

The foliage that usually surrounded the house had been trampled. Maybe the Nurse and the *chimpira* had stood out there to watch our windows. Svetlana used the toe of her pink boot to hold it aside and point to where a dead kitten lay – the pattern of a shoe sole stamped into its squashed head. '*Suka*, bitch! It only leetle kitty. Nothink dangerous.' She dumped the bin-liners on the roadside and headed back up the stairs, brushing off her hands. 'Bitch.'

I followed her into the house, shivering involuntarily. The smashed lightbulbs and bits of shattered doors still lay on the floor. I looked warily along the silent corridors.

'Have you seen the news?' I asked again, going into the living room. 'Is the television still working?' The TV had been tipped on its side, but it came on when I righted it and tried the switch. 'Bai-san's just been on television.' I bent over the set and pressed the button that changed channels. There were cartoons, adverts for energy drinks, girls in bikinis. Even singing cartoon chipmunks. No Bison. I went through the channels again, getting impatient. 'Something's happened. I saw him twenty minutes ago. Haven't you been watching . . .' I looked over my shoulder. Svetlana was standing very quietly in the doorway, her arms folded. I straightened. 'What?'

'We getting out.' She waved her hand round the room. 'Look.' Grey and white Matsuya carrier-bags, belongings poking out of them, were propped everywhere. I could see a clutch of coat hangers, toilet rolls, a fan heater in one. There were more bin-liners full of clothes on the sofa. I hadn't even noticed. 'Me and Irina. We find new club. In Hiroo.'

Just then Irina appeared in the corridor, dragging a whole swathe of Cellophane-wrapped clothes. She was also wearing a coat and had a foul-smelling Russian cigarette in her free hand. She dropped the clothes and came to stand behind Svetlana, propping her chin on her shoulder, giving me a glum look. 'Nice club.'

I blinked. 'You're leaving the house? Where're you going to live?'

'The apartment we stay is, what you call it? In top of club?' She bunched up her fingers, kissed the tips and said, 'High class.'

'But how?' I said blankly. 'How did you . . .'

'My customer help. He take us there now.'

'Grey, you don't say *nuh-think* to no one, eh? You don't tell Mama Strawberry where we going, and not any of the girls neither. 'Kay?'

'Okay.'

There was a pause, then Svetlana bent towards me, put her hand on my shoulder and gazed into my eyes in a way that made me feel slightly threatened. 'Now listen, Grey. You better speak to him.' She jerked her head to where Jason's door was tightly closed. 'Something serious.'

Irina nodded. 'He tell us, "*Don't look at me*". But we seen 'im.'

'Yes. We see him trying to move around, trying to . . . how d'you call it? Krewl? Down on his hands? Like dog? Krewl?'

'Crawl?' A nasty sensation moved across my skin. 'You mean he's crawling?'

'Yeah, *crawl*. He been trying to crawl.' She gave Irina an uneasy look. 'Grey, listen.' She licked her lips. 'We think it true – he need a doctor. He say he don't wanna see one, but . . .' Her voice trailed off. 'Something bad wrong with him. Something bad bad.'

The girls went, chauffeured away by a nervous-looking man in a white Nissan, a blue tartan child-seat in the back. When they were gone the house seemed cold and abandoned, as if it was being closed down for the winter. Jason's door was shut, a chink of light coming from under it, but no sound. I stood, my hand raised to knock, trying to walk my mind through what I was supposed to say. It took a long time, and I still couldn't decide, so I knocked anyway. At first there was no answer. When I knocked again I heard a muffled '*What?*'

I drew back the door. The room was freezing, lit only by the flickering blue of his small TV up against the window. In the half-light I could see strange jumbles of things on the floor, empty bottles, discarded clothes, what looked like the tall aluminium pedal-bin from the kitchen. On the TV a Japanese girl in a cheerleader's outfit was jumping across floating islands in a swimming-pool, her miniskirt flicking up every time she jumped. She was the only sign of life. Pushed in front of the doorway, blocking the entrance, was Jason's desk.

'Climb over it,' he said. His voice seemed to be coming from the wardrobe.

I put my head into the room and craned my neck, trying to see him. 'Where are you?'

'Climb over it, for fuck's sake.'

I sat on the desk and pulled up my knees, swivelled round, then swung my feet on to the floor.

'Shut the door.'

I leaned over the desk and slid the door closed, then switched on the light.

'*No! Switch it off!*'

The floor was covered in handfuls of tissue and paper kitchen towels, all wadded and stuck down with blood. Soaking red tissues overflowed from the wastebasket. Poking out from under the bloodied futon, I could see the yellow handle of a carving knife, the tip of a screwdriver, a selection of chisels. I was looking at an *ad hoc* armoury. Jason was under siege.

'*I said, switch off the light. Do you want her to see us in here?*'

I did as he told me and there was a long, bleak silence. Then I said, 'Jason, let me get you a doctor. I'm going to call the International Clinic.'

'I said *no*! I'm not having some Nip doctor touching me.'

'I'll call your embassy.'

'No way.'

'Jason.' I took a step across the floor. I could feel the adhesive clack as my feet peeled from the sticky floor. 'You're bleeding.'

'So what?'

'Where are you bleeding from?'

'Where am I bleeding from? What sort of dumb fucking question is that?'

'Tell me where you're bleeding from. Maybe it's serious.'

'*What the fuck are you saying?*' He hammered on the wardrobe door, making the walls shudder. 'I don't know what you think happened, but whatever it is *you're imagining it.*' He broke off, breathing hard. 'You're making it up. You and your dumb-ass inventions. Your *weird* fucking head.'

'There's nothing wrong with my head,' I said steadily. 'I don't invent things.'

'Well, baby, you're imagining *this*. I wasn't *touched*, if that's what you're saying.' I could see him now, in the wardrobe, crunched up against the wall. I could just make out his outline, huddled under a duvet. He seemed to be lying on his side, as if he was trying to keep warm. It was spooky, standing there in the half-light, listening to his thickened voice coming from the wardrobe. 'I don't want to hear you even suggesting that – WHAT DO YOU THINK YOU'RE DOING? *DON'T STAND NEAR THE WARDROBE!*'

I took a step back.

'*Stay there. And don't fucking look at me.*' I could hear him breathing now, a laboured sound as if something was lodged in his airway. 'Now, listen,' he said, 'you've got to get someone to help me.'

'I'll take you to a doctor and—'

'No!' I could hear him trying to control his voice and get his thoughts in line. 'No. Listen. There's – there's a number written on the wall. Next to the light switch. See it? That's my – my mother. Call her. Go into a phone box and call collect, reverse the charges. Tell her to send someone for me. Tell her not someone from Boston, tell her it's got to be one of the men from the house in Palm Springs. They're nearer.'

Palm Springs? I stared at the wardrobe. Jason, part of a family where there were houses in California? Employees? I'd always imagined him as a real traveller, the sort I'd seen at the airport: a battered *Lonely Planet* under one arm, a toilet roll hooked on the back of a rucksack. I'd pictured him washing dishes, teaching English, sleeping on a beach with just a calor-gas stove and a patched bedroll. I'd always believed he had everything to lose – just like the rest of us.

'What is it? What don't you understand? Are you still there?'

An advert for Pocky chocolate wands came on the TV. I watched it for a moment or two. Then I sighed and turned for the door. 'Okay,' I said. 'I'll call.'

I'd never made a collect call before, and when the automated operator asked my name I almost said, 'Weirdo.' In the end I said, 'I'm calling for Jason.' When his mother answered the phone she listened in silence. I recited everything twice: the address, how to find the place, that he needed a doctor urgently and to please – I hesitated at this bit, thinking how odd it was talking about Jason like this – to please send someone from the west coast because it would be quicker. 'And who, may I ask, are you?' She had an English accent, although she was in Boston. 'Would you be polite enough to give me your name?'

'I'm being serious,' I said, and hung up.

It was dark now, and when I got back to the house I didn't switch on too many lights – I couldn't help thinking of what it would look like from outside, blazing over the darkened neighbourhood. I didn't know a customer who could lend me money, it was too cold to sleep in the parks, and I wasn't sure Mama Strawberry would give me a sub before payday, certainly not a big enough one to afford a hotel. I couldn't beg from Shi Chongming. After the club I might have to come back and sleep here. The thought made me cold.

It didn't take me long to find a selection of tools from the store rooms – there were a lot of things in that house if you'd decided you had to defend yourself: a mallet, a chisel, a heavy rice-cooker that you could probably throw if necessary. I weighed the mallet in my hand. It felt good and heavy. I took them all to my room, rested them against the skirting-board, then packed my holdall with a few things: a big sweater, all the notes and sketches of Nanking, my passport and the remainder of Irina's money. It reminded me of the earthquake kits we were all supposed to have – the few things you'd need in an emergency. I went to the window and, holding the strap, dangled it down, gently, gently, until my arm was straight. Then I let it drop the rest of the way. It fell with a very small *bump* behind the air-conditioning unit. From the alley no one would know it was there.

While I was standing at the window, suddenly, out of nowhere, it began to snow. Well, I thought, looking up, Christmas isn't far away. Soft flakes whirled against the thin slice of grey sky between the houses, obscuring Mickey Rourke's face. If Christmas was near then it wouldn't be long before my little girl had been dead ten years. Ten years. Amazing how time just gets packed away into nothing, like an accordion. After a long time I closed the window. I wrapped a plastic carrier-bag round my hand and went out into the snow. Using my fingernails inside the plastic I scraped up the dead kitten and took it to the garden where I buried it under a persimmon tree.

50

 Nanking, 20 December 1937

I am writing this by the light of a candle. My right hand is painful, a thin burn running diagonally across the palm, and I am cramped on the bed, my feet tucked under me, the bed curtains drawn tight to make sure that there is no possibility, absolutely no possibility, of any light escaping into the alley. Shujin sits opposite me, mortally terrified by what has happened tonight, clutching the curtains closed and shooting glances over her shoulder at the candle. I know she would rather I had no light at all, but tonight of all nights I have to write. I have an overwhelming sense that any history written in these days, however small and inconsequential, will one day be important. Every voice will count because no one person will ever contain or calibrate Nanking's story. History will fail, and there will be no definitive Nanking invasion.

Everything I thought I believed has fled – in my heart there is a hole as naked and rotten as in the body of the child outside the factory, and all I can think about is what this occupation has really cost us. It means the end of a China that I haven't valued for years. It is the death of all belief – the end of dialects, temples, moon cakes in the autumn and cormorant fishing at the feet of our mountains. It is the death of lovely bridges spreading over lotus ponds, the yellow stone reflected in the silent evening water. Shujin and I are the last links in the chain. We stand on the cliff-face, holding China back from a long fall into nothing and sometimes I startle, as if I've been awakened from a dream, thinking that I am falling and that all of China – the plains, the mountains, the deserts, the ancient tombs, the festivals of Pure Brightness and Corn Rain, the pagodas, the white dolphins in the Yangtze, and the Temple of Heaven – everything is falling with me.

Less than ten minutes after old Liu left our house, even before I'd found a way to tell Shujin we were leaving, the terrible screaming of motorcycle engines came from a street somewhere to the right of the house.

I went into the hall and grabbed the iron bar, positioning myself behind the spirit screen, my feet wide, the bar ready over my head. Shujin came from the kitchen to stand next to me, silently searching my face for answers. We stayed that way, my trembling arms raised, Shujin's eyes locked on mine, as the dreadful thunder of engines funnelled up the alley outside. The noise grew and grew, until it was so loud that the engine seemed to be almost inside our heads. Then, just as I thought it might drive straight through the door and into the house, there came a choked rattle, and it began to diminish.

Shujin and I stared at each other. The sound headed away to the south, gradually faded into the distance, and silence fell. Now the only thing disturbing the quiet was the unearthly echo of our own breathing, hard and hollow.

'What . . . ?' Shujin mouthed. 'What was that?'

'Ssh.' I gestured to her. 'Stay back.'

I stepped round the spirit screen and put my ear to the barricaded front door. The engines had faded, but I could hear something else in the distance – something faint but unmistakable: the pop and spit of fire. The *yanwangye* is going about his diabolical work, I thought. Somewhere, in one of the streets not far away, something was burning.

'Wait there. Don't go near the door.' I went up to the next storey, climbing two stairs at a time, still carrying the iron bar. In the front room I ripped away a loose slat of wood and peered out into the alley. The sky above the houses opposite was red: snarling flames leaping twenty and thirty feet into the air. Little black flecks floated down, pitted and scarred like black moths. The *yanwangye* must have come very close to our house.

'What is it?' Shujin asked. She had come up the stairs and was standing behind me, her eyes wide. 'What's happening?'

'I don't know,' I said distantly, my eyes fixed on the falling snow. The flakes were speckled with greasy soot and, riding on the tide of black smoke, came the smell again. The smell of meat cooking. The smell that had been haunting me for days. Earlier we'd filled our stomach with buckwheat noodles, but there had been no protein in the meal, no *cai* to balance the *fan* of the noodle, and I still craved meat. I drew in a lavish lungful of the smell, my mouth watering hopelessly. It was so much stronger this time – it coiled round the house, getting into everything, so pungent that it almost overpowered the smell of burning timbers.

'I don't understand,' I murmured. 'It can't be possible.'

'What can't be possible?'

'Someone's cooking.' I turned to her. 'How can this be? There's no one left in the neighbourhood – even the Lius don't have any meat to cook . . .' The words died in my mouth. The black smoke hung directly over the alley where Liu's house was. I stared at it in a trance, not speaking, not moving, hardly daring to breathe as a dreadful, unspeakable suspicion crawled into my throat.

51

When I got to the club that evening the crystal lift wasn't at street level, it was up on the fiftieth floor. I stood for a while in the empty socket it left, my handbag tucked up under my arm, staring up, waiting for it to come down. It was a long time before I noticed a sign printed on A4 paper and taped to the wall.

Some Like It Hot is open!!!!! We're waiting to see you!!!! Please call this number for access.

I went to the phone box opposite and dialled the number. As I waited for an answer I stared up at the club, watching snowflakes piling up on the front edge of Marilyn's extended leg. They built into a little ledge, until, every tenth swing or so, the movement dislodged them and they tumbled down, lit by the neon bubbles, glittering the way I imagined children's play snow did as it fell from Santa's sleigh.

'*Moshi moshi?*'

'Who's that?'

'Mama Strawberry. Who's that? Grey-san?'

'Yes.'

'Strawberry's sending the lift down now.'

On the fiftieth floor I got out cautiously. The hat-check girl, in her dinky yellow and black dress, was cheerful, but as soon as I got through the aluminium doors I knew something was very wrong. The heating was so low that the few girls dotted around the tables were shivering in their cocktail dresses and the flowers were suffering, drooping pitifully in the cold, the water in the vases smelling. All the customers were po-faced, and Strawberry was sitting hunched at her desk, dressed in a slim, calf-length white fur coat, a bottle of tequila at her elbow, staring distractedly at a list of hostesses' names. Under the little 1950s diamanté reading glasses, her makeup was blurred. She looked as if she'd been drinking for hours.

'What's going on?'

She blinked up at me. 'Some customers banned from this club. *Banned.* Understand, lady?'

'Who's banned?'

'Miss Ogawa.' She slammed a hand on the table, making the bottle jump and all the waiters and hostesses turn to look. 'I *tell* you, didn't I? What I say, huh?' She pointed her finger up at me, making an angry spitting sound behind her teeth. 'Remember I tell you Miss Ogawa have a *chin chin* in her panties, yes? Well, Grey-san, bad news! She got tail in back too. You take off Miss Ogawa panties and first—' She threw her knees apart and jabbed a finger between her legs. 'First, you gonna see a *chin chin* here. And round *here*,' turning her hips sideways in the chair she slapped her buttocks, 'you gonna see a tail. Because she *animal.* Simple. Ogawa, *animal.*' Her voice might have continued spiralling upwards, if something hadn't made her stop. She put down her pen, pulled the glasses to the end of her nose and peered at me over them. 'Your face? What happened to your face?'

'Strawberry, listen, Jason won't be coming to work. And the Russians too. They told me to say they've left. Gone somewhere, I don't know where.'

'My God.' Her eyes locked on my bruise. 'Now, tell Strawberry truth.' She checked that no one was listening. Then she leaned forward and said, 'Ogawa come to Grey-san too, didn't she?'

I blinked. 'Too?'

She poured another tequila and downed it in one. Her face was very pink under the makeup. 'Okay,' she said, patting her mouth with a lace handkerchief. 'Time to straight talk. Sit down. Sit down.' She motioned to the chair, flapping her hand bossily. I drew it back and sat, feeling numb, my feet together, clutching my bag on my knees. 'Grey-san, look around.' She raised her hand to indicate the empty tables. 'Look at Strawberry club. So many of my girls not here! You wanna know why, lady? Hmm? You wanna know why? Because they at home! Crying!' She held up the list of names, shaking it angrily at me, as if I was responsible for their absence. 'Every girl who go to Fuyuki party last night wake in middle of night, and look what they see – Miss Ogawa or one of Fuyuki's gorillas in the house. You the only girl who go to last night party and come to work tonight.'

'But . . .' I drifted off. I couldn't keep everything straight in my head. My thoughts and images were getting jumbled and coming out in a strange order. 'You have to explain things to me,' I said quietly. 'You have to explain them very slowly. What do you mean? It wasn't only our house, it wasn't only Jason—?'

'I told you! Ogawa *animal*,' she hissed, shooting her face forward at me. 'She go to *everyone* at party last night. Maybe she think she Santa Claus.'

'But . . . why? What did she want?'

'Strawberry don't know.' She picked up the old-fashioned pink and gold pedestal phone that sat on the desk and dialled a number. She held her hand across the mouthpiece and hissed to me, 'All evening I been trying to find out.'

At about ten o'clock that night, a flock of crows, blown off course, was flung against the club window by a gust of wind. I still think about those crows, even to this day. It was too late for them to be away from their roost, and it was one of those happenings that you count yourself too sensible to consider a sign. One hit the plate glass so hard that almost everyone in the club jumped. I didn't: I had been sitting in silence, vaguely watching the birds' course across the sky, wondering just who in Fuyuki's past might have had the transforming power that Shi Chongming had talked about. I must have been the only person in the club who wasn't shocked when the bird hit, and dropped from the air like a bullet.

Strawberry had helped me cover my bruise with makeup and had sent me out to the tables. I sat in a daze, not listening to anything, not speaking, only stirring if food arrived at the table. Then I would eat everything I could, very neatly and intently, holding a napkin to my mouth so nobody could see quite how fast I was eating. There was only a little money left after I'd paid my fares to Shi Chongming's, and all I'd eaten in twenty-four hours was a nibble of *shabu shabu* and a bowl of cheap noodles at a stand-up bar in Shinjuku.

There was a tense atmosphere in the club. A lot of the customers, even the regulars, felt it and didn't stay for long. Odd, icy silences seemed to flit round and at times it became so quiet that I could hear the squeak of the pulley system in Marilyn's swing. I was sure it wasn't just that so many of the hostesses were missing. I was sure that the stories of last night were getting round and making everyone anxious.

Strawberry spent most of the night on the phone, trawling her contacts for news. I thought of the strings of police officers who sometimes came into the club last thing at night – everyone knew she was well connected. But for long hours she seemed to be getting no information about what was happening, what had prompted the Nurse's attacks. It ended up being me who was the first person in the club to learn anything new.

It was the *kanji* that caught my eye, blazing out from the video screen on the opposite building. I recognized them immediately. *Satsujin-jiken*. A murder inquiry. Next to the characters was a blurred still of a familiar face: Bison smiling broadly into the night sky.

I stood up so quickly that I knocked over a glass. My customer jumped back in his chair, trying to dodge the whisky that rolled off the table on to his trousers. I didn't stop to give him a napkin. I stepped away from the table and walked in a trance to the plate-glass window where a youthful Bison, thinner and with more hair, was singing, his arm outstretched to the camera. Under the footage more *kanji* were superimposed. It took a long time for me to work them out, but eventually I understood: Bai-san had died at 8.30 p.m. Only a couple of hours ago. The cause? Serious internal injuries.

I put my hands on the glass, breath steaming in the cold air. The snow fell silently, catching the colours of the screen, which was dissolving into library pictures of Bison, one of him leaving a courthouse, another showing him as he'd been in his heyday – lean face above a microphone, ruffled shirt and good American teeth. Then a picture of a hospital appeared, a doctor addressing a crowd of reporters, the photographers' flashes reflecting off the smoked-glass doors. I watched with my mouth open, picking up the occasional *kanji* here and there. Singer – heart-throb – forty-seven years old – toured with the Spyders – number one in the Oricon charts – Bob Hope golf-club scandal. I put my head on one side. Bison? I thought. Murdered? And Fuyuki's men paid a visit to all the girls at the party last night . . .

Behind me a phone rang. I jumped. I hadn't noticed how silent the club had become, but when I looked over my shoulder there was no chatter, no conversation: every eye in the place was fixed on the video screen. Strawberry had got to her feet and was standing not far from me, staring out in silence, all the lights reflected in her face. For a moment she didn't notice the phone – it rang three times before her trance snapped and she went back to her desk. She snatched up the receiver and barked, '*Moshi moshi?*'

Every eye in the club was on her as she listened. Sometimes you can almost read the words a person is hearing from the way their expression tightens. It took her a long time to speak, and when she did her voice was blank and monotone. 'Are you sure?' she said. 'Are you sure?'

She listened a little longer, then dropped the receiver into the cradle, all the colour leaving her face. She put both hands on the table, as if she was trying to get her balance. Then she rubbed her temples wearily, unlocked a drawer in her desk, opened the cash tray and pulled out a wad of notes, which she stuffed into her pocket. I was about to move from the window when she straightened and clipped across the club towards me, so quickly that the white fur coat swung round her like a bell. There was a dramatic grey tinge round her mouth, a smudge of lipstick on the coat collar.

'This way.' Without missing a step she took my arm and pulled me away from the window, past all the tables, the staring faces.

'What's *she* done?' I heard a customer mutter. I was taken through the aluminium doors, where the hat-check girl was standing on tiptoe behind the desk, trying to see what was going on in the club. Strawberry guided me into the corridor that led to the stores and the toilets. She led me past the men's, where someone had tried to disguise the smell of vomit with a hopeful squirt of bleach, and into the little cloakroom we used to put on makeup. Then she drew the door shut behind her and we stood, face to face. She was trembling, breathing so heavily that her shoulders rose and fell under the white coat.

'Listen to me, lady.'

'What?'

'You got to get out.'

'What?'

'Get out of here.' She gripped my arm. 'You and Jason get out your house. Get out *Tokyo*. Don't speak to the police. Just go. Strawberry don't want to know where.'

'No,' I said, shaking my head. 'No, no. I'm not going anywhere.'

'Grey-san, this *very* important. Something bad happening in Tokyo. And something bad spreading – *spreading*.' She paused, studying my face curiously. 'Grey-san? You understand what's happening? You know the news?'

I glanced over my shoulder at the closed door. 'You mean Bai-san. You mean what happened to him.' A long shiver went up and down my arms. I was thinking about the *kanji*. Internal injuries. 'It was Ogawa, wasn't it?'

'Ssht!' She spoke in a rapid, low monologue: 'Listen to me. Bai-san got a visit. He was put into hospital, but he talked to police before he died. Maybe he crazy, talking to the police, or maybe he know he gonna die anyway . . .'

'A visit from Ogawa?'

She took off her glasses. 'Grey-san, at Mr Fuyuki's party last night there a thief.'

'A thief?'

'That why Ogawa going crazy. A worm go into Mr Fuyuki's house last night and now he not happy.'

A strange feeling washed over me. I had the uncanny sensation that some awful revelation was crouched just out of view, beyond the skyscrapers, Godzilla-like. 'What was taken?'

'What you think, Grey?' She dropped her chin to her chest and looked up at me from under knowing lids. 'Hmmm? What you think? Can't you guess?'

'Oh,' I whispered, all the colour draining from my face.

She nodded. 'Yes. Someone stole Fuyuki's medicine.'

I sat down on the nearest chair, all the breath forced out of me at once. 'Oh . . . no. This is – this is . . . It isn't what I expected.'

'And listen.' Strawberry leaned very close to me. I could smell the tequila mingling with her lemony perfume. 'The thief is some-one at the party last night. The Nurse went to everybody's house last night, she look everywhere, but Bai-san tell police he think she *still* don't find her *sagashimono*. The thing she is looking for.' She licked her fingers, patted her hair, and glanced over her shoulder, as if someone might have come in behind us. 'You know,' she said, very quietly, bending even closer, her face point-ing in the same direction as mine, so our cheeks were touching and I could look down and see her red mouth moving close to my own, 'if I Ogawa, and I hear what come out of your big mouth sometimes . . .' Somewhere, fifty floors below, a siren wailed. '. . . I'm gonna think, Grey-san, I'm gonna think you the thief . . .'

'*Nobody knows I was asking questions*,' I hissed, turning my eyes up to hers. 'Only you.'

She straightened and raised her eyebrows sarcastically. 'Really? Really, Grey? That true?'

I stared at her, suddenly very cold. I remembered how defensive Fuyuki had been when I wanted to look round his apartment. I remembered the Nurse coming down the corridor. She'd caught me trying to slip away when Fuyuki was having his choking attack. When you look back at the things you do, sometimes you can't believe that you were ever so brazen or stupid. 'Yes,' I said tremulously. 'Yes. I mean I—' I put my hand distractedly to my head. 'Nobody knows. I'm – I'm sure.'

'Grey-san, listen, Miss Ogawa going *crazy*. She gonna go back to every house again until she find the thief. *Every single house.* And this time she not gonna be so kind.'

'But I . . .' I stared blankly at the lipstick on Strawberry's collar. It made me think of blood, of animals being trapped, of the foxes that would come screaming past my parents' back door in the hunting season. I thought of how silently the Nurse had crept into our house. I thought of the hand with the watch sticking out of the car boot. I rubbed my arms because goosebumps were breaking out on my skin. 'I can't leave Tokyo. I can't. You don't understand—'

'Strawberry telling you now. You leave Tokyo. You fired. Hear? You fired. Don't come back.' She reached into her pocket, pulled out the wad of money and held it under my nose with her index and middle finger. 'This goodbye from Strawberry. Give some to Jason too.' I reached for it, but the moment my fingers were on it she tightened her grip. 'Grey-san.' Her eyes met mine and I could see my face reflected in the ice-blue contact lenses. When she spoke it was in Japanese, a very musical Japanese that would have sounded beautiful under different circumstances. 'You understand me when I speak Japanese?'

'Yes.'

'Make me a promise, will you? Promise me that one day I'll get a letter from you. A nice letter, telling me how happy you are. Written by you, safe in another country—' She broke off and studied my reaction. 'Promise?'

I didn't answer.

'Yes,' she said, still staring at me intently, as if she was reading my mind. 'I think you promise.' She released the money and held open the door for me. 'Now go on. Get out. Get your coat and leave. And, Grey . . .'

'Yes?'

'Don't take the glass lift. It's better you use the one at the back.'

52

史 **Nanking, 20 December 1937**

The fire didn't take long to die, its furious dragon-like glow drifting away across the sky. Almost immediately the snow came back, angelic and forgiving, drifting drowsily past me as I stood bedraggled and weak outside the remains of Liu Runde's house, a handkerchief to my mouth, tears in my eyes. The fire had eaten everything in its path, leaving only smouldering rubble, a terrible skeleton of blackened timbers. Now it was finished the inferno had dropped with a whimper, dwindling to nothing but a small steady flame, very straight and controlled, on the floor in the centre of the building.

The alley was silent. I was the only soul who had come to look at these charred remains. Maybe Shujin and I are the only two souls left in Nanking.

The scent of kerosene lingered, the *yanwangye* must have doused the house before he torched it, but there was the other smell too – the smell that had been lingering in our alley, tantalizing me all these days, the smell that I now recognized with a sinking heart. I wiped the tears from my face and picked my way round to the side of the house. The Lius must still be in there, I thought. If they had managed to escape we would know – they would have come straight to our house. They must have been trapped inside: the *yanwangye* would have made sure of it.

A breath of smoke floated across the house, obscuring it for a short time. When it cleared I saw them. Two objects, lined up like

297

blackened tree-trunks after a forest fire, their human shapes melted down so that they had no recognizable angles, only the charred silhouettes of hooded figures. They were upright, huddled in the little vestibule behind the back door as if they'd been trying to escape. One was large, one small. I didn't have to look too closely to know it was Liu and his son. I recognized the buttons on the burned *zhongshan* jacket. Liu's wife wouldn't be there – she would have been taken from the house for the *yanwangye*'s own purposes.

I pushed the handkerchief into my nostrils and stepped forward for a closer look. The smell was stronger, unbearable for the craving it started in me. Under the bodies puddles of fat had collected, already growing a thin white skin on the surface where it was cooling, like the fat I sometimes see cooling in the wok when Shujin has been preparing meat. I pushed the handkerchief harder into my nose and knew I would, from that moment on, be eternally afraid of one thing: I knew I would always be afraid of what I am eating. Swallowing will never again be comfortable for me.

Now, only an hour later, here I sit and shiver on the bed, clutching in one hand my pen, and in the other all I dared take of Liu Runde: a scrap of his hair, which came crisp away in my hand when I bent to touch his cooling body. It was still so hot that it burned all the way through my glove and left a scorchmark on my palm. And yet curiously the hair remains intact – eerily perfect.

I put a shaky hand to my head, my whole body trembling. 'What is it?' whispers Shujin, but I cannot answer because I am recalling, time and time again, the smell of Liu and his son burning. From nowhere a picture comes to me of a Japanese officer's face, grinning dimly by the firelight in the camp at night. The officer's face is greasy from army-issue amphetamines and some nameless meat. I think about the flesh taken from the little girl next to the factory. As a trophy, I'd imagined, or are there other reasons to remove human flesh? But the Imperial Army is well fed – fed and muscled and nourished. They've no reason to peck and scavenge like the bearded vultures of the Gobi. And something else is on my mind – something about the medicine bottles in the silk factory . . .

Enough. For now it's enough to ponder. Here I sit, my journal on my knee, Shujin watching me wordlessly with the eyes that blame me for everything. The time has come. The time has come to tell her what will happen next.

'Shujin.' I finished the entry and set down the quill, pushed aside the ink stone and crawled across the bed to where she sat. Her face was white and expressionless, the candlelight flickering on it. She hadn't asked about old Liu, but I am sure she knew – from my face, and from the smell of him on my clothes. I knelt facing her, only a few inches away, my hands on my knees. 'Shujin?' Tentatively I put my hand to her hair – it was as rough, as heavy as bark against my palm.

She didn't recoil. She met my eyes steadily. 'What do you want to say to me, Chongming?'

I want to say that I love you, I want to talk to you the way men talk to their wives in Europe. I want to say I'm sorry. I want to take the hands of the clock and wind them backwards.

'Please don't look at me like that.' She tried to move my hand away. 'What do you want to say?'

'I . . .'

'Yes?'

I sighed and dropped my hand, lowering my eyes. 'Shujin.' My voice was hushed. 'Shujin. You were right. We should have left Nanking a long time ago. I am sorry.'

'I see.'

'And . . .' I hesitated '. . . and I think that now we should do our best. We should try to escape.'

She looked at me steadily, and this time I could hide nothing. I stood undisguised, desperate and apologetic, letting her read every ounce of fear in my eyes. Eventually she closed her mouth and reached across the bed, took the candle and snuffed it out. 'Good,' she said evenly, putting her hand on mine. 'Thank you, Chongming, thank you.' She opened the curtains and swung her legs off the bed. 'I'll make *guoba* and noodles. We'll eat some now. Then I'll pack for the journey.'

My heart is heavy. She has forgiven me. And yet I am afraid, mortally afraid, that this will be the last time I write in my journal. I am afraid that I am her murderer. What hope have we got? May the gods protect us. May the gods protect us.

53

Outside it was freezing. The snow was coming fast now, almost a blizzard, and in the short time I'd been in the club it had settled on the pavement, on the roofs of parked cars. I stood in the lee of the building, huddled as close to the lift doors as I could, and peered up and down the street. I could see only about twenty yards into the swirling flakes, but I could tell that the street was unusually quiet. There was no one on the pavements, no cars on the street, only the snow-covered form of the dead crow in the gutter. It was just as if Mama Strawberry was right – as if something bad was creeping through Tokyo.

I fumbled out the money and counted it. My hands were trembling and it took me two goes to get it right, and even then I thought I must be wrong. I stood for a moment, staring down at what was in my hands. It wasn't the week's wages I'd expected. Strawberry had given me three hundred thousand yen, five times what she owed me. I looked up fifty floors through the swirling snow, to the club, to where Marilyn swung. I wondered about Strawberry, in her replica Monroe dresses, spending her life among young waiters and gangsters. I realized that I knew absolutely nothing about her. She had a dead mother and a dead husband, but apart from that she could have been all alone in the world, for all I knew. I had done nothing to make her like me. Maybe you're never really aware of the ones who are looking out for you until they're gone.

At the crossroads a car went by cautiously, catching the snow in its headlights, making it appear to swirl faster. I shrank back against the wall, pulling up my collar, wrapping the thin coat tightly round me, shivering. What had Strawberry meant, don't leave in the glass lift? Did she really think Fuyuki's men were prowling the streets? The car disappeared behind the buildings and the street was quiet again. I peered out. It was important to think slowly. To think in stages. My passport, all my books and notes were in the alley next to the house. I couldn't call Jason on the phone – the Nurse had ripped out the wires. I had to go back to the house. Just once.

I hurriedly counted out Strawberry's money, divided it between my two coat pockets, a hundred and fifty thousand yen in both rolls. Then I pushed my hands into my pockets, and began to walk. I ducked into back-streets to keep from the main routes and found myself moving through a magical world – the snow falling silently on the air-conditioner units, piling on the lacquered bento boxes stacked outside back doors waiting to be collected by the takeaway drivers. I wasn't dressed properly: my coat was too thin and my stilettos left funny exclamation-mark tracks behind me. I'd never walked in the snow in high heels before.

I went quietly, cutting over the crossing near the Hanazono shrine, with its ghostly red lanterns, and back into the alleys again. I passed lighted windows, steaming heating vents. I heard television sets and conversations, but in all the time I walked I only saw one or two other people. Tokyo seemed to have shut down its doors. Someone in this city, I thought, someone behind one of these doors, had the thing I was searching for. Something not very big. Small enough to fit into a glass tank. Flesh. But not an entire body. So, a piece of a body, maybe? Where would some-one hide a piece of flesh? And why? Why would someone steal it? A line from a long-ago book came back to me, Robert Louis Stevenson maybe: 'The body-snatcher, far from being repelled by natural respect, was attracted by the ease and safety of the task . . .'

I traced an arc across Takadanobaba so that I arrived back at the house via a small passageway between two apartment buildings. I stopped, half hidden behind a Calpis drinks machine, its blue light flickering spectrally, and cautiously put my head round the corner. The alley was deserted. The snow fell silently, lit by the lanterns outside the *ramen* restaurant. On my left rose the house, dark and cold, blotting out the sky. I'd never seen it from this angle – it seemed even bigger than I remembered, monolithic, its curved, pantiled roof almost monstrous. I saw I had left the curtains open in my bedroom and I thought of my futon all laid out in the silence, my painting of Tokyo on the wall, the silent image of Jason and me standing under the bead galaxies.

I dug in my pocket for the keys. I checked once over my shoulder, then slipped silently into the alley, staying close to the buildings. I stopped at the cleft between the two houses and peered over the air-conditioner. My holdall was still there, tucked in the dark, snow piling on it. I continued along the edge of the house, under my window. Ten yards away from the corner, something made me stop. I looked down at my feet.

I was standing in a gap in the snow, a long black groove of wet Tarmac. I blinked at it. Why had instinct halted me here? Then I saw, of course, it was a tyre track. I was standing in the greyed-out shadow left by a car, recently parked. Adrenaline bolted through my veins. The print stretched out all round me. The car must have sat there for a long time because the outline was clear, and there was a pile of soggy cigarette ends exactly where the driver's window would have been, as if they'd been waiting for something. I backed hastily into the shadows of the house, my blood pressure spiking. The tyre tracks led straight ahead, all the way to Waseda Street, where I could make out one or two cars passing as usual, silent, muffled by the snow. The rest of the alley was deserted. I let out a nervy breath, and glanced up at the windows in the tumbledown old shacks, some lit yellow, shapes moving in them. Everything was as normal. *This doesn't mean anything* . . . I told myself, licking my sore lips, and staring at the car print. *It means nothing.* People were always parking in alleys, privacy was so difficult to find in Tokyo.

I moved on cautiously, avoiding the car shadow, as if it might be a trick trap-door, and keeping close to the house, my shoulders brushing the snow from the security grilles on the ground floor. At the corner I leaned round and peered at the front door. It was closed, as if it hadn't moved since I'd left, a snowdrift already piled up against it, perfect and downy. I glanced once more up the alley. Although it was deserted I was trembling as I stepped forward and hastily fumbled my key into the lock.

Jason's TV was on. A flickering blue light was coming from under his door, but the bulb on the landing had been shattered by the Nurse and the house was unusually dark. I climbed the steps slowly, jumpily, all the time imagining something shadowy and rapid hurtling down the corridor towards me. At the top I stood in the dim light, breathing hard, the memories of last night like shadows racing away from me along the walls. The house was silent. Not a creak of floor or a breath. Even the usual sound of the trees rustling in the garden was muffled by the snow.

My teeth chattering now, I went to Jason's room. I could hear him breathing inside the wardrobe, a congested, bloody sound that quickened when I pulled back the door. 'Jason?' I whispered. The room was freezing and there was an unpleasant organic smell in the air, like animal dung. 'Can you hear me?'

'Yeah.' I could hear him shifting painfully in the wardrobe. 'Did you speak to someone?'

'They're on their way,' I hissed, scrambling over the dressing-table and dropping silently to the floor. 'But you can't wait, Jason, you've got to get out now. The Nurse is coming back.' I stood next to the wardrobe, put my hand on the door. 'Come on, I'm going to help you downstairs and—'

'*What're you doing?* What the fu— *Stay back!* Stay away from the wardrobe.'

'*Jason!* You've got to get out *now*—'

'*You think I didn't hear you? I HEARD. Now get away from the fucking door.*'

'I won't go anywhere if you shout. I'm trying to help.'

He made an irritated sound, and I heard him sink back in the wardrobe, breathing fast. After a moment, when he had calmed a little, he put his mouth to the wardrobe door. 'Listen to me. Listen carefully—'

'We haven't got time to—'

'I said *listen*! I want you to go into the kitchen. There are rags under the sink. Bring me as many as you can find – and get towels from the bathroom too, anything you can get hold of.' He was struggling to get up. From inside the wardrobe a pool of something viscid, matted with hair, had crept a short way across the floor and congealed. I couldn't take my eyes off it. 'Then get my holdall from the peg, and my suitcase – is it still outside the door?'

'Yes.'

'Bring me everything from the suitcase and then I want you to switch off the lights and leave the house. I'll take care of the rest.'

'Switch off the lights?'

'This isn't a fucking freak show. I don't need you staring at me.'

My God, I thought, clambering back over the desk into the corridor, *what has she done to you? Is it what she did to Bison? He died. Bison died from what she did*. The shutters were all open and in the garden the snow was still falling, huge fat grey flakes the size of hands, circling and batting into one another, their shadows skittering across the floor. The carrier-bag in the tree sent a long, lantern-like shape on to the wall. I couldn't remember the house ever being so cold – it was as if the air had frozen in blocks. In the kitchen I grabbed an armful of rags, then some towels from the bathroom. I climbed shakily back over the desk.

'Put them near the wardrobe. *I said don't look at me!*'

'And *I* said *don't shout*.' I clambered back into the hallway, pulled his suitcase to the door, lifted it over the desk and pushed it down on to the floor. Then I went to the row of pegs at the top of the stairs to get his holdall from where it hung under the coats. As I pulled aside the coats and jackets I kept my ears trained on the alley, all the time imagining the Nurse silently sidewinding down the streets towards us, standing outside the house looking up at the windows and trying to decide how she would—

I came to a halt.

Jason's holdall.

I stood absolutely still, staring at it, only my ribs rising and falling under the coat. An odd idea was whorling through me. The house was silent, only the *click click click* of the floorboards contracting in the cold and the muffled sound of Jason shuffling around in the wardrobe. He had been carrying that holdall the night of Fuyuki's party. Slowly, dazedly, I looked along the silent corridor stretching into darkness, then I turned stiffly and stared at his door. Jason? I thought, the blood in my veins like ice. *Jason?*

I placed my hands on the holdall, looking at it thoughtfully. *Listen*, he'd said, when he'd come to my room after the party. He'd been holding this bag. I remembered it all clearly. *We've both got exactly what the other needs. I'm going to tell you something you're really going to love.* Suddenly I wasn't imagining the Nurse lingering outside in the alley – instead I was imagining her hurrying past a black pool with the sky reflected in it, a red emergency light flashing on and off above her head. Last night I hadn't seen Jason reappear with the Nurse when Fuyuki was choking. There had been a few minutes, just a few, when in the confusion anything could have happened . . .

Gingerly, moving slowly, painful inch by painful inch, I unzipped the bag and put my fingers inside. I could feel tissues and cigarette cartons and a pair of socks. I pushed my hands in deeper. A set of keys and a cigarette lighter. And in the corner of the bag something furred. I stopped. It was something furred and cold, and the size of a rat. I became very still, the skin on the back of my neck twitching. *Jason? What's this?* I brushed my fingers over it, felt the fibrous tug of old dead animal skin, and a memory came to me. I took a breath and pulled the object out and stared at it in dumb surprise. It was a model of a bear – about five inches tall. There was a long red and gold braided string tied to a ring in its nose, and the moment I saw it I knew it was Irina's lost fighting bear. *He a strange one, that one*, I remembered her muttering one day so long ago. *He watch the bad video and he thief too. You know that? Stole my bear, my glove, even stole picture of my grandmama, my grandpapa . . .*

'Hey!' Jason called suddenly. 'What the fuck's going on out there?'

I didn't answer. Moving woodenly, I took the holdall off the peg and went back to his room. I stopped outside the door, and stared at the suitcase lying on the floor. I was thinking of him weeks ago, throwing his hand into my face, mimicking Shi Chongming's exploding dragon. He'd known I was looking for something. But – *I had no idea how perfect you were, not until tonight* . . .

Of course, Jason, I thought, my knees weak. *Of course. If you found Fuyuki's medicine it would be exactly the sort of thing you'd like . . . You're a thief, aren't you? Someone who'd steal for nothing but the thrill.*

The suitcase wasn't closed properly – his belongings were hanging out of it, a pair of trainers, jeans, a belt. 'Yes,' I said, under my breath, as things began to fit into place. 'Yes – I see.' All the questions and answers were knitting dreamily together. Something else had been nagging at me since that morning, something about all the other objects that had been strewn around the corridor: a camera, paperwork, some photos. His passport. *His passport?*

'Jason,' I murmured, 'why were all those – those things . . .' I lifted my hand, pointing vaguely at the suitcase. 'Those—You were *packing* last night, weren't you? Packing. Why would you have been packing if you hadn't known –'

'What the fuck're you talking about?'

'– *if you hadn't known* . . . that she might come?'

'Just put everything on the floor and go.'

'That's it, isn't it? You realized what you'd done. You suddenly realized how serious it was, that she might come because you'd stolen—'

'I *said* put everything—'

'Because you'd stolen,' I raised my voice. 'You'd stolen from Fuyuki. You had. Hadn't you?'

I could almost hear his indecision, his lips moving silently, muttering his fury. For a moment I thought he was going to leap out at me, full of aggression. But he didn't. Instead he said irritably, 'So? Don't start lecturing me. I'm choking with it, believe me. Choking with you and all your weird fucking issues and obsessions.'

I dropped the holdall and put my hands to my head. 'You . . .' I had to breathe in and out very quickly. I was shaking all over. 'You – you . . . *Why? Why did you* . . .'

'*Because!*' he said, exasperated. 'Just *because*. Because it was *there*. Suddenly this fucking thing you'd been . . .' He caught his breath. 'It was *there*. Right in front of my eyes and, believe me, I had *no idea* of the fucking hell-fire that was going to rain down on my head if I took it, and now is *not* the time to be giving *me* judgement, so just put the *stuff* on the *fucking floor* and—'

'Oh, Jason,' I said dazedly, 'what is it?'

'You really don't want to know. Now put the—'

'Please, please, tell me what it is, where you've hidden it.' I turned and looked up the empty corridor, stretching into the darkness. 'Please, it's so important to me. Where is it?'

'Put the holdall on the floor—'

'Where is it?'

'And move the towels nearer the wardrobe.'

'*Jason*, where is it?'

'I said move the towels to the wardrobe and—'

'Tell me now or I'll—'

'*Shut up!*' He hammered on the doors, making them bounce in the runners. 'Fuck you, *fuck you*, and *fuck* your shitsucking little treasure hunt. If you're not going to help me then either fight me – because I *will* fight you, I'm not afraid to hit you – or *go* and *screw* yourself.'

I stood for a moment, looking at the wardrobe door, my heart racing. Then I turned and stared back down the corridor. Most of the doors were closed. It was still littered with broken glass and fabric from the walls. 'Okay,' I said. 'It's okay.' I put out my hands blindly in front of me, moving the fingers, as if the air texture would hold the answer. 'I'm going to find it. I don't need you. You brought it back last night and it's still here somewhere.'

'*Just shut up and switch the fucking lights off!*'

My trance cleared. A sweat broke across the back of my neck. I pulled the roll of money from my right pocket and threw it into

Jason's room. It broke and notes floated down in the semi-darkness. 'There,' I said. 'Strawberry sent you some money. And, Jason—'

'*What?*'

'Good luck.'

54

One morning, a few days before the Nurse had come to the house, I'd woken, pulled back the window and there, standing in the alley below, dressed in a hard hat and a suit, clipboard in hand, had been a surveyor, or an engineer, looking up at the house. It had made me so sad to think of the house, after war and earthquake and famine, after everything, giving in to the property developers. Its paper-slim walls and wooden structure were designed to fall in a quake, to fall like matchsticks so that the occupants had a chance to escape. When the men came to pull it down, when they wrapped a thin blue cover round it and took their demolition ball to it, it would go without a whisper, taking with it all its memories and trapped secrets.

The surveyor and I had regarded each other for a long time – he in the cold, me standing warm and wrapped in my duvet – until eventually my hands grew cold, my cheeks red, and I closed the window. At the time I had thought vaguely that his presence meant the end of our lives in the house was near. It hadn't occurred to me that the end might come in a different, totally unexpected way.

I grabbed a torch from the kitchen and went silently down the corridor, switching off all the lights as I went. One or two doors were open and there were no shutters or curtains at most of the windows – from the street the Mickey Rourke light illuminated everything that happened in those soft, silent rooms. Someone watching from outside would see everything, so I moved swiftly, bent into a crouch. In my room I crept to the side window and leaned out as far as I dared, until I could crane my neck round and see through the gap into the alleyway. It was deserted, the snow falling silently, no sounds of cars or voices. The tyre tracks and my footprints had already disappeared under the new snow. I grabbed the money from my coat pocket and threw it on top of the bag. It landed with a silent flutter and a puff of snow. I turned and changed hurriedly, fumbling in the dark, throwing off my club dress and pulling on trousers, flat shoes, a sweater, a jacket zipped up to the neck.

Where did you put it, Jason? Where? Where am I supposed to start?

I crouched in the doorway, clutching the torch, my teeth chattering. From his room I could hear a series of muffled thumps – I didn't want to imagine the secret, painful manoeuvre he was going through. *But no. It's not in your room – Jason, that would be too easy.* The torchbeam played over the other silent doors. I let it rest on the store room next to mine. Even when you haven't got a map, when you haven't got a clue, you have to start somewhere. Stooped awkwardly, I crept to the door, sliding it back in fractions, careful not to make a noise. I peered inside. The room was in chaos. The Nurse and the *chimpira* had gone into everything, into all the decomposing futons, the fragmenting piles of ageing, insect-chewed silks, a case of framed photos, posed black-and-white portraits of an elderly woman in a formal kimono under splintered glass. I squatted in the middle of the room and began to tear at things, a rice-cooker, a box of yellowing paperbacks, here was a silk *obi*, once silver and blue, now stained brown in places and riddled with moth holes. When I touched it, it crumbled in my hand and iridescent flakes of silk, like butterfly scales, moved in a cloud, upwards through the cold air.

I went through everything, my panic building, sweat dampening my clothes. I had almost worked across the entire room when something made me stop and raise my eyes. Headlights were sweeping across the ceiling.

Fear lit up across my skin. I clicked off the torch and put it into my pocket, resting my fingers on the floor in a runner's crouch, every muscle twitching. My ears crawled out of the room, out into the alley, trying to guess what was happening out there. The beams ran down the wall, then moved quickly in a straight line, sideways like lights from a spaceship. From the alleyway came a long silence. Then, just as I thought I would stop breathing, I heard the car change gear and move off. Brake lights appeared, reflected in the window, an orange indicator flashed. The car had stopped in the snow, waiting to turn left on to Waseda. I closed my eyes and sank to my haunches against the wall. 'My God, Jason,' I murmured, my fingers to my forehead. 'This is going to kill me.'

It was pointless searching blindly like this. The Nurse had been through these rooms and hadn't found anything. Why would I be able to do any better? But I was clever and I was determined. I was going to think my way through the walls, the ceilings and the fabric of the house. I was going to look where she hadn't. *Try*, I thought, putting my fingers to my eyelids, *try to picture this house through different eyes*. Picture it through Jason's eyes last night. Picture its skeleton. What had he been thinking? What had been the first thing he looked at when he came home last night?

The image of the house rotated in my mind. I saw through its skin, I saw beams and joinery, a timber frame laced with wires. I saw the windows. *The windows*. The windows in the gallery were saying something important. They were saying – *think carefully now* – they were saying: *Remember Jason last night. Remember him outside your room*. We are having an argument. Then what? He walks away. He's furious and he's still drunk, and he's banging on all the shutters. He stops for a while looking out at the garden – one of the windows had been open when I came out of my room – he stands there, smoking a cigarette. Then he turns and he's going to his room and starting to pack . . .

I opened my eyes. Through the opened shutter, snow was blizzarding in the garden, frosting and glittering as far as I could see, making a white topiary of the haphazard shapes. The plastic bag hanging in the branches was frosted almost solid. I backed up a little in my thoughts and came at it again. Jason had stood at the window, holding what he'd stolen and . . .

I saw him clearly now – opening the window, reaching his hand back and throwing a plastic bag into the stormy night. It flew out above the branches, spinning and pirouetting in the wind, and landed where it hung now, twisted and frozen. *Oh, Jason,* I thought, tipping forward on to my knees, staring up at the bag. *Of course.* I know where it is. It's in that bag.

I got to my feet and stepped to the window, putting my numb hands against the pane, my skin pricking up in wonder, just as, from the staircase, came the discreet but distinctive popping sound of the front door being forced open.

55

史 Nanking, 21 December 1937 (the nineteenth day of
the eleventh month)

In Nanking nothing is moving except the snowclouds – everything, every stream, every mountain, every tree, is exhausted by
this Japanese winter and lies limp and uncomprehending. Even
the coiled dragon Yangtze river is stalled, stagnant and motionless, clogged behind a hundred thousand bodies. And yet here it
is, the entry I thought I would never make. Made on a bright
afternoon in the peace of my house, when everything is over.
Really it is a miracle to see it being made, my hand brown and
strong, the thin line of paling ink flowing from the ends of my
fingers. It is a miracle to put my hand inside my jacket and find
that my heart is still beating.

In our cargo Shujin included a folded cloth that she had packed
with cutlery: chopsticks, a few spoons, one or two knives. She
placed it in a small sandalwood money chest and added a black
baby's bracelet, with an image of Buddha dangling on it. I had to
dissuade her from putting in the red-painted eggs. 'Shujin,' I told
her, trying to be gentle, 'there won't be *zuoyuezi* or *man yue.*'

She didn't answer. But she did take the eggs out of the bags and
into our bedroom, where she arranged the quilts round them, so
they lay in a little nest on the bed, waiting for the day when we
would come home.

'Are you all right?' I asked, looking anxiously at her white face
when she came downstairs. 'Do you feel well?'

314

She nodded silently, and pulled on a pair of gloves. She was wearing several layers of clothing: two ordinary cheongsams, a pair of my woollen pants underneath and fur-lined boots. Our faces were blackened, our refugee certificates pinned to our clothing. At the door we stopped and stared at each other. We looked like strangers. At length I took a deep breath and said, 'Come on, then. It's time.'

'Yes,' she replied soberly. 'It's time.'

Outside a light snow was falling, but the moon was bright, shining through the flakes so that they appeared to dance merrily. We got as far as Zhongyang Road and stopped. Without Liu Runde, the old horse who knew its way, I was unsure. About a hundred yards away I could see a dog, lying on its back in the snow, bloated so that its four legs were forced open as wide as could be, like an overturned stool. One or two of the houses had been burned since I was last here, but there were no tracks in the snow and the street was deserted. I had no idea how Liu had planned to break through the Taiping gate, no instinctive compass or intuition of what had been in his head. The lock of his hair was inside my glove. It lay against the burn on my palm and I tightened my hand on it. 'Yes,' I said steadily, pulling the collar of my jacket up round my ears to keep out the whirling snow. 'Yes, this way. This is the right way.'

We walked in silence, Purple Mountain rising ahead of us, terrible and beautiful against the stars. The streets were deserted, nevertheless every new corner deserved our suspicion. We went slowly, keeping near the walls, ready to abandon the cart and shrink into the gaps between the buildings. Shujin was absolutely silent, and for a long time all I could hear were our footsteps and my heart pounding. Once in the distance I heard the rumble of a truck going past on Zhongshan Road, but it wasn't until we had passed the Xuanwu area that we saw our first human being: a bent old man, struggling towards us out of the snow, carrying two heavy baskets on a bamboo yoke. He seemed to be headed in the direction we'd come, and in each of his baskets was a child, asleep, arms collapsed and dangling out of the basket, snow settling on their sleeping heads. He didn't appear to register us at all, he didn't blink or nod or focus on us, he only kept coming towards us. When he got very near we saw he was crying.

Shujin stopped in her tracks as he approached.

'Hello, sir,' she whispered, as he drew parallel with us. 'Are you well?'

He didn't answer. He didn't slow down or look at her.

'Hello?' she repeated. 'Are your children well?'

It was as if she hadn't spoken. The old man continued limping down the street, his eyes fixed on a point somewhere in the distance.

'Hello!' she said loudly. 'Did you hear me? Are the children well?'

'Sssssh!' I touched her arm and pulled her to the side of the road, afraid that she had spoken too loudly. 'Come away.'

The old man was shuffling away into the snow flurries. We stood, pressed into a doorway, watching him stagger along under his cargo, a spectre in an old coat.

'I wanted to know if the little ones were well,' she murmured.

'I know, I know.'

We both stood in silence then, not meeting each other's eyes, because from behind, the answer to the question was clear. One of the children was asleep, but the other, a boy, slumped in the right-hand basket, was not asleep at all. He had been dead for some time. You could tell that from just one look.

Midnight found us creeping through the alleys near the military academy. I knew the area well. I used to go through it as a student on my way to view the Xuanwu lakes and I knew how close to the wall we were. In an abandoned house I discovered a scorched rosewood clothes trunk, and found that if I climbed up on it and peered through the gaps in the burned houses, I could just glimpse the Taiping gate.

I put my finger to my lips and leaned forward a little further, until I could see a two-hundred-yard stretch of the wall. Liu had been right. The wall had been shelled and broken in several places and in both directions I could see piles of bricks and rubble stretching off into the night. Where the gate had been, two sentries in khaki caps stood erect, lit only by army lamps balanced on piled-up sandbags. Beyond them, outside the wall, a Japanese tank was parked among the rubble, its flag dirty with ash.

I slid off the chest. 'We're going north.' I brushed off my gloves and pointed out beyond the houses. 'That way. We're going to find a breach further up the wall.'

And so we crept up a side-street, moving parallel to the wall. This was the most dangerous part of our journey. If we could get through the wall we'd have achieved the greatest hurdle. If we could just get through the wall . . .

'Here. This is the place.' A hundred yards up from the gate I happened to peer through a fence and saw, beyond a burned and devastated patch of land, a valley-shaped notch in the wall, stones tumbling into a scree below it. I took Shujin's arm. 'This is it.'

We slid between the houses on to the main road and pushed our heads out from the gap, peering up and down the length of the wall. Nothing moved. We could see the dim glow of the sentries' lanterns to the south. To the north the snow fell in darkness, only the moonlight illuminating it.

'They'll be on the other side,' Shujin whispered. Her hands were fluttering unconsciously round her stomach. 'What happens if they're waiting on the other side?'

'No,' I said, trying to keep my voice steady, trying to keep my eyes on hers and not look down at her hands. Did she sense an urgency that she wasn't communicating to me? 'I make you this promise. They are not. We must get through here.'

Half bent to the ground we hurried across the open patch of land, the handcart skidding in the churned-up snow and earth, causing us both to slip and almost lose our balance several times. When we got to the wall we instinctively dropped to a crouch behind the cart, breathing hard and peering out into the silent snow. Nothing moved. The snow swirled and shifted, but no one shouted to us or came running.

I put my hand on her arm and pointed up the slope of rubble. It was a small climb, and I covered it easily, turning back and reaching down for the handle of the cart. She did her best, trying to lift it, trying to push it up the scree to me, but it was almost impossible for her, and I had to double back and drag it up with all my strength, my feet sliding hopelessly on the rubble, the stones avalanching down and making a noise I was sure would wake every Japanese soldier in Nanking.

Eventually I reached the top of the scree. There, I let the cart roll as far down the other side as possible, until I couldn't lean any further and had to let it topple away, bouncing down the stones and falling on its side, all our belongings tumbling out into the snow. I held out a hand to Shujin, hauling her up, her ponderous weight coming slowly, so slowly, her eyes all the time on mine. We half scrambled, half slid down the other side of the wall, where we fell on to our belongings, grabbing them up in armfuls, throwing what we could into the cart, then racing blindly into a group of maple trees, me bumping the cart wildly behind me, Shujin doubled over as she ran, a bundle of clothing clasped to her chest.

'We've done it,' I panted. We huddled in the shadows under the trees. 'I think we've done it.' I squinted out into the darkness. On our right I could just make out a few slum dwellings, unlit and probably uninhabited. A track ran in the shadow of the wall and about twenty yards along it, in the direction of Taiping gate, a goat was tethered under a tree. Apart from that there was not a soul to be seen. I put my head back against the tree and breathed out, 'Yes, we have. We have.'

Shujin didn't answer. Her face seemed not sullen, but unnaturally tight and drawn. It wasn't the fear alone. She had hardly spoken in the last few hours.

'Shujin? Are you well?'

She nodded, but I noted she would not meet my eyes. My sense of unease increased. It was clear to me that we couldn't rest here – that we needed to get to the salt dealer's house as soon as possible. 'Come along,' I said, offering her my hand. 'We must keep going.'

We loaded up the cart, stepped out of the clump of trees and began to walk, looking around ourselves in disbelief, astonished to be here, as if we were children stepping through a magic world. The streets grew narrower, the houses more sparse, the road underfoot giving way to a dirt track. Purple Mountain rose up silently on our right, blotting out the stars, while on the left the land fell away, leading back down to the blackened ruins of our city. The relief was exhilarating: it drove me along, intoxicated. We were free of Nanking!

We walked rapidly, stopping every now and then to listen to the silence. Beyond the five islets on the Xuanwu lakes a fire was glowing in the trees. We took it for a Japanese camp and decided to cut off the path and head across the foot of the mountain, moving along one of the many storm gullies. From time to time I would leave Shujin and slither down the small embankment to check that we were keeping parallel with the road. If we stuck to this course we would reach Chalukou eventually.

We saw no one – not a man, not an animal – but now something else was on my mind. Increasingly I was concerned for Shujin. She looked more tense than ever. From time to time she would allow a hand to float down to her stomach.

'Listen,' I said, slowing to whisper to her. 'The next time the snow clears for a moment, look to where the road bends.'

'What is it?'

'There. Do you see? The trees?'

She squinted into the snow. In the torched remains of a wild sugar-cane field stood a ghostly snow-covered windlass, spidery above a well. Next to it was a border – a row of bushes.

'A mulberry orchard. If we reach that we'll be able to see the outskirts of Chalukou. We're nearly there. That's all you have to do, these few last yards . . .'

I broke off.

'Chongming?'

I held my finger to my lips, looking down at the land sloping into the darkness. 'Did you hear anything?'

She frowned, bending forward and concentrating on the silence. After a while she looked back up at me. 'What? What did you think you heard?'

I didn't answer. I couldn't tell her that I thought I had heard the sound of the devil touching down in the dark countryside nearby.

'What is it?'

From out of the trees to the left of the track came a sweep of headlights, and an ear-shattering roar. About two hundred yards away a motorcycle leaped up over the lip of a bank, found its balance on the higher land, and pivoted round, sending up a plume of snow. It stopped, seeming to come to a rest facing us directly.

'Run!' I grabbed Shujin's arm and threw her bodily into the trees above the track. I grabbed the handcart and stumbled up the slope behind her. 'Run! Run!'

Behind me the rider throttled the engine, making it roar. I didn't know if he'd seen us, but he seemed to aim the motorcycle at the track we were on. 'Keep going. Keep going.' I stumbled through the thick snow, the cart twisting behind me, threatening to shed its load.

'Which way?' Shujin hissed from above. 'Which way?'

'Up! Keep going up the mountain.'

56

When the footsteps began their stealthy progress up the metal stairs, I could have kept quiet. I could have gone silently to my room, crawled out of the window, disappeared into the muffling snow and never found out what was in the plastic bag. But I didn't. Instead I hammered on Jason's door, yelling at the top of my voice: '*Jason! JASON, GO!*' As the Nurse's horrible shadow appeared out of the gloom of the staircase, I launched myself away, skidding, still shouting, bounding down the corridor in a way that was so frantic it must have looked like exuberance, not fear, all the way to the garden staircase – '*JASON!*' – throwing myself down the steps, half sliding, half falling, slamming into the screen at the bottom, diving out into the snowy night.

Outside I paused, just for a second, breathing hard.

The garden was silent. I glanced through the branches at the gates to the street, then back to the plastic bag, which hung only a few tantalizing yards to my left, just above the do-not-go-here stone. I looked back to the gates, then to the bag, then up at the gallery. A light came on, glaring across the garden.

Do it—

I launched myself sideways from the doorway, not through the wisteria tunnel but away from the gates, towards the bag, scurrying crablike into the undergrowth, hugging the wall where it was darkest. Overhead the branches bounced, throwing snow everywhere. The shadow of the carrier-bag flickered across my head.

When I got to the deep shadows and the undergrowth was too thick to go any further, I sank down on to my haunches, panting silently, my pulse rocketing in my temples.

The bag swayed lazily overhead, and beyond it the silvered windowpanes outside Jason's room sent back a reflection of the trees and swirling snowflakes. A few beats of silence passed, then something in the house splintered deafeningly – a door flying back on its hinges, or furniture being overturned – and almost immediately came a sound I will never forget. It was the sort of sound the rats in the garden sometimes made at midnight when a cat had them skewered. It unravelled through the house like a whip. Jason was screaming, a terrible, penetrating sound that raced round the garden and lodged in my chest. I clamped my hands over my ears, shuddering, unable to listen to it. *My God. My God.* I had to open my mouth and gulp in air: big, panicked lungfuls because for the first time in my life I thought I might faint.

The bag in the tree shifted in a small breeze and a little snow shook out of its soft hollows. I looked up at it, my eyes watering with fear. There was something inside it, something wrapped in paper. I could see it clearly now. Jason's cries crescendoed, echoing into the night, bouncing off the walls. I didn't have long – it had to be now. Concentrate . . . *concentrate.* Sweating, trembling uncontrollably, I stood on tiptoe, groped for the branch, pulling it down and reaching cold fingertips up to the bag. A little ice fell off it, the plastic crackled under my fingers, and for a moment I pulled my hand back instinctively, startled that I'd actually touched it. The bag swayed a little. I took a deep breath, stretched up and grabbed it more firmly, just as Jason stopped screaming and the house fell into silence.

I shot back, pulling the bag along the branch with a series of shuddery jerks. When it came off the end the branch leaped away from me, whipping back and forward. Icicles cascaded on to me as I tumbled backwards into the dark, huddling in the undergrowth – the frozen bag tight in my numb hands. *Did you hear me?* I thought, staring up at the gallery, wondering where she was, why the house was so silent. *Jason – why so quiet? Are you quiet because she's stopped? Because you've told her where to look?*

A window flew open. The Nurse's horrible horse-like form appeared in the gallery, her face indistinct through the trees. I could tell by the intent, motionless way she stood that she was thinking about the garden – maybe thinking about the echoes of me, ricocheting down the stairs. Or maybe she was looking at the trees, wondering where a plastic bag might be hanging. I rotated my head slowly and saw the shadow of the branch I'd moved, magnified ten times and projected up on to the Salt Building, whipping and bouncing across the white stretches on the wall. The Nurse put her nose into the air and sniffed, the odd sightless eyes only two blurry points of shade. I shuffled further back in the undergrowth, breaking sticks, groping blindly for something heavy to hold.

She turned, stiffly, and walked slowly along the corridor, tapping her long fingernail on each window as she passed it. She was coming in the direction of the garden staircase. A second shadowy figure moved behind her – the *chimpira*. Next to my foot a stepping-stone was sunk into the wet ground. I clawed at it frantically, making my fingers bleed, dragging it out and clasping it, with the bag, against my chest. I tried to picture the garden around me. Even if I could get through the twisted branches, the gates were a fifteen-second sprint from there, straight across the naked garden. I'd be safer in here, where my tracks couldn't be seen for the undergrowth, and if I . . .

I stopped breathing. They'd found the staircase. I could hear their footsteps echoing on the stairs. *They're coming for me*, I thought, all the bones in my body turning to water. *I'm next.* Then someone was pulling open the screen door, and before I could scramble away the Nurse's dark profile emerged through the frozen filigree of snow-covered branches. She dipped a little to enter the wisteria tunnel then travelled quickly, smoothly, as if running on invisible tracks, to the end where she emerged, standing straight and dark in the snow-covered rock garden, twitching her huge head in tiny movements, like a stallion sniffing the air. Her breath was white – she was steaming as if from some exertion.

I didn't breathe. She'd sense it if I did – she was so attuned she'd sense my hairs going up, the infinitesimal widening of an artery, maybe even the crackle of my thoughts. The *chimpira* hovered in the doorway, peering out at the Nurse, who turned her head first in my direction, then to scan the trees, and then in the opposite direction – to the gates. After a moment's hesitation, she continued across the garden, every now and then stopping to look around herself with great deliberation. For a moment, as she went into the tunnel, she was lost in a swirl of snow, then I heard her trying the gate, I heard it opening with a long, slow creak. The snow cleared and I could see her, standing very still, contemplating, her hand resting on the latch.

'What is it?' hissed the *chimpira*, and I thought I heard nervousness in his voice. 'Can you see anything?'

The Nurse didn't answer. She rubbed her fingers on the latch, then lifted them to her nose and sniffed, her mouth a little open as if to let the scent roam round her mouth. She pushed her head through the gates and looked out into the street and it hit me like lightning: *no tracks – no tracks in the snow. She'll know I haven't gone out there . . .*

I shoved the package inside my jacket, zipped it up, pushed the stone into my pocket and edged silently, just another shadow slipping round the trees, to where the broken security grille hung on its hinges. The window was just as I remembered it, slightly open, the glass rather mossed. I leaned over as far as I dared, gripping the frame for balance, and hauled myself across the blank stretch of snow, up onto a toppled branch that lay against the wall. I stood for a moment, wobbling, my hot, terrified breath coming back at me, steaming up the pane. When I wiped it my own face met me in the glass and in my shock I almost stepped back. *Slowly, slowly, concentrate.* I turned and squinted through the undergrowth. She hadn't moved – her back was still towards me, she was still considering the street in her detached, unhurried way. The *chimpira* had stepped out of the doorway and was watching her, his back to me.

I pulled the window open in tiny increments, lifting the pane to stop it squealing and at that moment, as if she had heard me, she turned from the gate and looked back in the direction she'd come, her head rotating very slowly.

I didn't wait. I hooked my leg through the gap and with one push levered myself into the house, dropping down into a crouch in the dark. I stayed there, shocked by the noise I'd made, my hands on the floor, waiting until the sound had spent itself, echoing around the closed-off old rooms. Somewhere in the darkness to my left I could hear the scattering footsteps of rats. I fumbled in my pocket, switched on the torch and, holding my hand over it, allowed a timid beam to creep across the floor. The room leaped into flickering life around me – small, with a cold, flagged floor and piles of rubbish everywhere. A few feet ahead was an empty doorway. The beam extended into it, smooth and featureless, far down into the depths of the house. I clicked off the torch and crawled like a dog, pushing through cobwebs and dust, head first into the doorway, then on into the next, going deeper and deeper into the house until I had gone so far into the warren of rooms that I was sure they would never find me.

I stopped and looked back the way I'd come. The only thing I could hear was the thudding of my heart. *Did you see me? Did you see me?* Only silence answered. From somewhere in the darkness came a steady *drip drip drip* and there was a smell, too, rich and peaty, the mineral smell of trapped water and decay.

I crouched there, breathing hard, until, when an age seemed to have gone by and I could hear nothing, I dared to switch on the torch. The beam played over piles of furniture, timbers that had broken from the ceiling, a confetti of plaster and wiring. I could hide here for ever if I had to. My hands quivering, I pulled the package out from my jacket. I'd expected something weighty, something dull and clay-like, but this was too light, as if it contained balsawood or dried bone. I put my fingers inside and found something wrapped in tape, a smooth surface that had exactly the quality of butcher's paper – thick and shiny. Blood wouldn't settle long on its waxed surface. I had to stand for a while supported against the wall, breathing hard through my mouth because the thought of what I was holding was too much. I picked at the tape, got hold of the end and pulled at it, when from behind me, a long way back in the darkness, I heard an unmistakable sound. Metal screeching against metal. Someone was pushing open the window I'd climbed through.

57

I shoved the package inside my jacket and scrambled forward blindly, banging into things, my panicky sounds echoing off the walls. Through one room into the next, then the next, not thinking about what I was passing – the rows of kimonos hanging in the corner, as quiet as corpses, the low table in the shadows of one room, still set for a dinner, as if everything had frozen when the landlord's mother died. I was deep, deep inside the bowels of the house, in endless darkness, when I realized I couldn't go any further. I was standing in a kitchen, with a sink and a western-style cooker on one wall. On the other wall, unlike the previous rooms, there was a blank where there should have been a doorway leading onwards. No way out. I was trapped.

Fear scuttling up under my hair I whipped the torch round the walls, over the cobwebs, the peeling plaster ceiling. The beam played over a flimsy cupboard panel in the side of the room and I lurched at it, scrabbling at the catch, gouging my fingertips, my feet tattooing on the floor in frantic fear. The panel clicked open with a noise that echoed away into the rooms behind.

I thrust the torch in and saw that it wasn't a cupboard but a doorway that opened on to the top of a rotting staircase and led away into the darkness. I stepped straight into the opening, carefully pulled the door closed behind me, and went down two steps, clinging to the rickety banister. Dropping to my haunches I shone the torch around. It was a small cellar, maybe a foodstore, about five foot by ten, the walls of thick stone. At head height ran shelving on rusting brackets, upon which crowded dozens of old glass jars, their contents browning. Below that lay a silent, thickened skin of pale pink algae. The stairs led straight down into a stagnant indoor lake.

I looked back up at the closed panel door, stretching my ears out into the unlit rooms I'd come through. Silence. I'd stood on a branch – I couldn't have left any tracks under the window, and my trail would be impossible to see through all the undergrowth. Maybe they hadn't heard me at all. Maybe they were just checking all the windows out of routine. *Please yes*, I thought. *Please.* I turned and played the beam around the cellar. From a small crack in the rendering of the right-hand wall trickled a weak rivulet of brown water – this was what Jason had told me about: the pipes in the street that had cracked in an earthquake and filled up the basement: green and copper tidemarks marked the changing water levels over the years. The beam skimmed a low, bricked arch. I bent close to the skin on the water, and held the torch out, angling the light upwards. It was a tunnel, flooded to within an inch of the ceiling, leading away into the depths of the house. It would be impossible to—

I stiffened. A loud boom echoed through the rooms behind, as if the loose grille on the window had been wrenched from its moorings.

I began to pant with fear, my mouth open like a dog's. Holding the torch in front of me like a weapon I lurched into the water, making it rock around me as if I'd prodded the belly of something sleeping, disturbing things that had been motionless for years. It was freezing. It set my jaw tight and made me think of teeth, mysterious fins and mouths, and the possibility that this was something's home. I thought of the Japanese vampire goblin, Kappa, the swimming predator who would pluck down unwary swimmers by the heels, suck them dry of blood and discard their empty, bleached husks on the riverbank. Tears of fear sprang to my eyes as I waded on.

I stopped at the far wall and turned to look back the way I'd come. Around me the water slowly stopped sloshing, and silence descended. The only sound was the panicky *shush shush* of my breathing bouncing back off the walls.

Then another crash came through the silence. More furniture being overturned. I scanned the cellar desperately, the wavery torchbeam bringing the yellowing ceiling swooping in and out of focus. There was nowhere to hide, nowhere to . . . *The archway!* I bent my knees and sank down until my shoulders were submerged and my chin was almost touching the surface of the water. Some of the jars around me broke the skin with an elastic glooping noise, and disappeared out of memory into the water below, taking their darkened pellets of pickled plums, rice and small sightless fish with them. I pushed my hand into the dark insides of the tunnel, rolling it sideways, opening and closing my fingers so they scraped against the slimy roof. Only when I'd straightened my arm and my cheek was pressed tight against the wall could I feel the ceiling rise, my hand emerge into air. I pulled my arm out and shone the torch at it. How long was it? Twenty-five, thirty inches maybe? *Not far. Not that far.* Shivering frantically I looked back up at the staircase, at the flimsy panel door.

From somewhere close, maybe even the kitchen, there came another crash. I had no choice. I pulled out the parcel and tied the handles of the bag tightly, sealing it completely, then pushed it back into my jacket, which I zipped up to the neck. As I did I lost my grip on the torch. It slipped from my numb fingers and landed on top of the skin, the beam hitting the nearby wall in a distorted oval. I grabbed for it, got it, began to lift but lost my grip and dropped it again. The skin tilted this time, tipping the torch forward, plopping it down into the water, its beam seesawing up through the rotting pink colonies of organisms, sending their lacy shadows swirling up on to the walls. I plunged after it, swinging for it, my hand moving in slow motion under the water, swirling up dustclouds under the surface, but the torch sank silently away, pirouetting lazily, its faint yellow glow thinning to just a glimmer. Then – *gloop*. Quite near me something small but weighty dropped into the water and swam.

Tears of terror welled in my eyes. The torch. The torch. *Don't need it. Don't need it. You can manage without it.* What's that in the water? *Nothing. A rat. Don't think about it.* At the top of the staircase, a thin light filtered round the cracks in the panel. I heard a man's voice, low and serious, and above it the Nurse's hot equine breath moving round the kitchen, as if she was inspecting it, trying to smell what had come through it.

Stop to think and you'll die. I sucked in a breath, put my hands on the wall, bent my knees and dropped face down into the pitchy tunnel.

The freezing water filled my ears, my nose. I thrust my hands out and tried to stand, crashing into bricks, grazing my elbows, stumbling around in the floating murk. An unearthly noise reverberated inside me, my own voice, moaning in fear. *Which way? Which way?* Where did the arch end? Where? It seemed to go on for ever. Just as I thought my breath would run out and it would all be over, my hand shot up from the ceiling, clear above the water, and I went after it, scraping my head, pushing desperately forward, after the hope of air. I surfaced, retching, spitting, my head jammed painfully into the ceiling. I couldn't stand up straight, but if I bent my knees and held my neck sideways, there was just enough room – a four- or five-inch gap between the water and the brickwork – to breathe.

Breathe. Breathe!

I don't know how long I was there, or what state of crisis my body entered – maybe I fainted, or went into a fugue state – but as I stood, shaking, only the insistent life-beat of my heart for company, so loud it sounded several hundred times its size, as big as the house itself, something, the cold or the fear, picked up my consciousness and siphoned it slowly out of my reach down a long, silent tunnel, until I was nothing, nothing except a thudding, hollow pulse in a place with no geography, no boundaries and no physical laws. I floated in a vacuum, no awareness of time or existence, bobbing lazily like an astronaut in eternity and even when, after a millennium had rolled by and I became aware of a faint pinkish light coming through the water to my left – the Nurse shining the torch along it – I didn't panic. I watched myself from a different place, seeing my frozen face floating on the algae, my lips blue, my eyelids half lowered. Even when the light left and eventually, after an eternity, retreating footsteps sounded in the rooms upstairs, I stayed absolutely still, a modern Alice, my head canted to one side, cramped and so desperately cold that I thought my heart would freeze closed and fossilize me there, metres under the ground.

58

At dawn, as the first light was moving over the garden, when the house had been silent for hours, I reached the open window. I was so numb with cold that it had taken hours to crawl back. Every inch was a fight with the seductive lethargy of cold, but at last I was here. I peered out cautiously, my heart thudding dully, sure that the Nurse would come charging down on me from some hidden lair. But the garden was silent, an eerie, crystalline world, as still and quiet as a ship marooned in ice. Everything was covered in little diamonds of frozen drops, surreal against the snow like necklaces strewn among the trees.

Climbing out of the window exhausted me. I dropped into the snow and, for a long time, I was too numb to do anything except sit where I'd landed, slumped drunkenly against the branch with the carrier-bag at my feet, and stare distantly at this silent winter world.

What had happened here? What had happened? Every one of the windows in the gallery had been smashed, the branches on the trees had been snapped, a shutter hung on its hinges, squeaking occasionally.

The drops in the branches are so beautiful . . . In the dawn light my mind moved slowly. *So beautiful.* I looked at the trees round the stone lantern, at the area of the garden that had so fascinated Shi Chongming. A slow bud of recognition was opening dreamily inside me. Frozen drops of blood and tissue were sprayed in the branches, as if something had exploded there. Draped across the stone lantern, like a faded paper chain, was . . . A hazy memory of a newspaper photograph – a nameless Japanese victim, his viscera spooling below the car.

Jason . . .

I stared at what was left of him for what seemed like hours, astonished by the patterns – the braids and furbelows, the little scrolls like Christmas decorations. *How could it look so beautiful?* A wind came, buffeting and pirouetting the snowflakes, springing the blood from the branches. The wind rattled through the broken panes in the gallery and whirled along the corridor. I imagined myself from above, I imagined looking down at the garden, at all the vermiform paths and the thickets, I imagined the way the blood would look, a halo round the stone lantern, and then as I drew further away I saw the roof of the house, its red tiles all gleaming in the melting snow, I saw the little alleyway with a solitary old woman clipping down it in clogs, I saw the poster of Mickey Rourke, then the whole of Takadanobaba, the 'high horse field', and Tokyo glittering and glinting next to the bay, Japan like a dragonfly clinging to the flank of China. Great China. On I went, on and on, until I was dizzy and the clouds came over and I closed my eyes and let the sky or the wind or the moon pick me up and drift me away.

59

 Nanking, 21 December 1937

I don't know how long we stumbled through the trees in our desperate flight, the snow flurrying behind us. We went on and on. I had to pull Shujin much of the way because she was quickly exhausted and pleaded with me to stop. But I was remorseless, dragging her with one hand, the cart with the other. On and on we went, into the forest, the stars flashing between the trees overhead. Within a few minutes the sound of the motorbike had died away and we were left with only the sounds of our breathing on the deserted mountain, as quiet as a ghost mountain. But I wasn't prepared to stop. We passed hulking presences in the darkness, the burned and abandoned remains of the beautiful villas, the vast, plundered sasanaqua-covered terraces destroyed, the faint smell of their cinders hanging between the trees. On we went, wading through the snow, wondering if the dead, too, lay out there in the dark.

Then, after a long time, when we seemed to have scrambled half-way to the heavens, and the sun was already sending up red dawn rays above the mountain, Shujin called out behind me. I turned to find her leaning against a camphor tree, her hands on her stomach. 'Please,' she whispered. 'Please. I can't.'

I slid down the slope to her, catching her by the elbow as her knees gave way and she sank into the snow. 'Shujin?' I hissed. 'What is it? Is this the beginning?'

She closed her eyes. 'I can't say.'

'Please.' I shook her arm. 'This is no time to be shy. Tell me –
is this it?'

'I can't say,' she said fiercely, her eyes flying open and fixing on
mine. 'Because I don't know. You are not the only person, my
husband, who has never had a child before.' Her forehead was
damp with perspiration, her breath steamed in the air. She moved
her arms round herself in the snow, creating an odd little nest,
curling into it. 'I want to lie down,' she said. 'Please let me lie
down.'

I dropped the cart. We had come so high up that the fires of
Nanking were no more than a red stain in the dawn sky. We had
reached a small level area, hidden from the lower slopes by dense
walnut, chestnut and evergreen oaks. I walked a few yards back
and listened. I could hear nothing. No motorcycle engine, no soft
footfall in the snow, only the air whistling in my nostrils and the
clicking of my jaw as I worked my teeth together. I climbed
the slope, and walked in a great circle, every few paces stopping
to listen to the great gulping silences among the leafless branches.
It was already getting light, and the weak rays filtering through
the trees alighted on something about twenty feet further
down the slope, half buried in leaves, forgotten and moss-
covered. It was an enormous stone statue of a tortoise, its snout
and shell covered in snow. The great symbol of male longevity.

My heart rose. We must be near Linggu temple! Even the
Japanese hold a shrine sacred – no bombs had dropped on our
places of worship. If this was to be the place our child emerged
into the world then it was an auspicious one. Maybe a safe one.

'Come here, behind these trees. I'm going to build you a
shelter.' I turned the handcart on to its side and pulled out all the
blankets, packing them tightly under the cart. I led Shujin inside,
lodging her into the bed, giving her broken icicles from the trees
to quench her thirst. Then I went to the other side and kicked
snow up against the cart so that it would be invisible. When she
was settled I squatted next to it for a while, biting my fingers and
staring out of the trees to where the sky was growing lighter by
the second. The mountainside was utterly silent.

'Shujin?' I whispered, after a while. 'Are you well?'

She didn't respond. I shuffled nearer the cart and listened. She was breathing fast, a tiny whistle of air, muffled in her forest bed. I took off my cap and shuffled closer to the cart, cursing myself for knowing so little about childbirth. When I was growing up it was the province of the matriarchs, the stern sisters of my mother. I was told nothing. I am ignorant. The brilliant modern linguist who knows nothing about birth. I put my hand on the cart and whispered, 'Please, tell me. Do you think that our baby is—' I broke off. The words had come out of my mouth without thinking. *Our baby*, I had said. Our baby.

Instantly Shujin seized on it. She let out a long, drawn-out cry. 'No!' she sobbed. 'No – you have said it. You have said it!' She hauled the cart upwards and pushed her head out: her hair wild, tears standing in her eyes. 'Leave!' she cried feverishly. 'Leave me. Stand now and walk away. Walk away.'

'But I—'

'No! What ill luck you have invited on our moon soul!'

'Shujin, I didn't intend—'

'Walk away now!'

'Please! Keep your voice down.'

But she wasn't listening. '*Walk away with your dangerous words! Take your curses away from me.*'

'But—'

'Now!'

I dug my nails into my hands and bit my lip. What a fool I had been. How thoughtless, to have infuriated her! And at such a time! At length I sighed. 'Very well, very well.' I backed away a few feet through the trees. 'I will stand here, just here, should you need me.' I turned, so my back was towards her, and I was facing the dawn sky.

'No! Further! Go further. I don't want to see you.'

'Very well!'

Reluctantly I took a few more clumsy steps through the snow, until the slope of the mountain put me just out of her sight. I sank dejectedly to the ground, knocking my knuckles against my forehead. The forest was so quiet, so silent. I dropped my hand and looked around. Should I try to find help? Maybe there would be someone in one of the houses who could offer shelter. But the radio reports had said that all these houses had been looted, even before the eastern gate had been breached. The only people I might encounter would be Japanese army officers, lording it in the deserted mansions, drunk on plundered wine stores.

I straightened, and stepped a little way out of the trees to get a sense of what else was nearby. I pushed aside a branch, took a pace forward, and my breath caught in my throat. For a moment Shujin was forgotten. We had climbed so high! The sun was coming up behind the mountain, pink and flecked with cinders from distant fires, and further down the slopes, perched among the trees, the intense, glazed blue of Sun Yat-sen's mausoleum shone against the snow. If I turned to the east, between the mountains I could see glimpses of the thirsty yellow plains of the delta stretching away into misty horizons. Below me the city basin was smouldering like a volcano, a black pall of smoke hung over the Yangtze, and I saw, with a sinking heart, that it was all as I had guessed: the river at Meitan was in chaos – I could see bombed boats and sampans listing in the mud. Old Liu had been right when he said east was the direction to go.

As I stood there, with the sun on my shoulders and all of Jiangsu stretched out beneath me, I had a sudden surge of defiance, a sudden furious determination that China must survive as the China I grew up in. That the silly superstitious Festivals of White Dew and Corn Rain would live on, that ducks would always be driven across fields at dusk, that every summer the lotus leaves would appear, so thick you would believe it possible to walk across the ponds balancing on the slabbed leaves alone. That the Chinese people would continue – that my child's heart would be for ever Chinese. As I stood on the mountain, in the first rays of dawn, with a rush of pride and fury, I raised my hand to the sky, daring any evil spirit who cared to come and take my son. My son, who would fight like a tiger to preserve his country. My son, who would be stronger than I had ever been.

'I dare you,' I whispered to the sky. 'Yes, I dare you.'

60

You can never tell what's going to make the headlines. Most of the evidence surrounding the crime scene in Takadanobaba pointed to one guilty party: Ogawa, the so-called Beast of Saitama. And yet for one reason or another (perhaps you could forgive the nervousness of the journalists involved) this detail was never widely publicized by the newspapers. She was brought in for questioning, but quickly and mysteriously released, and to this day lives free, somewhere in Tokyo, occasionally glimpsed behind the smoked glass of a fast-moving limousine, or entering a building at dead of night. It's a mistake to underestimate the links between the *yakuza* and the Japanese police.

Meanwhile the murder of Jason Wainwright, as I later discovered he was called, hit the news and stayed there for months. It was because he had been well educated and was a good-looking Westerner in Japan. Hysteria gripped his mother's state of Massachusetts. There were accusations of police incompetence, of corruption and mob influence, but nothing that ever led anywhere, least of all to Fuyuki and the Beast of Saitama. Suit-wearing teams of family lawyers jetted in on Thai Air jumbos, but no matter what strings they tried to pull, what money was offered, no one would talk about Jason's life in the months before the killing. Nor was the mystery female who had called his mother a day before his death ever found.

But probably what caught the public's imagination more than

anything was the horror of the crime scene. It was what the Nurse had used to decorate the stone lantern. It was the image of the Wainwright family man arriving fresh off a plane from California, knocking on the door, still clutching his Samsonite travel bag, an aeroplane toothbrush and a taxi receipt in his pocket, snow falling on to his suit. It was the thought of what he saw when he got no answer and decided to walk a few feet down the alley, where two rusty garden gates stood open.

I had been gone from the house only half an hour. I had crept through the gates, taken my bag from the alley and gone to the public baths on the other side of Waseda Street. As the Wainwrights' man was making sense of the serpentine coils round the stone lantern, as the blood left his face, as he sank to his knees, fumbling for a handkerchief, I was only a hundred yards away, squatting on the little green rubber stool in front of the knee-high showers, shivering so hard that my knees were knocking. Ten minutes later, when he staggered out on to the street, his hand up to hail a taxi, I was in another taxi on the way to Hongo, perched on the edge of the seat, my hair wet, a cardigan clasped round me.

I stared out of the taxi window, at the piled-up snow, at the strange light it reflected into the faces of the women as they picked their way carefully along the pavements under pastel-coloured umbrellas. I had an overwhelming sense of the loneliness of this city – a trillion souls in their bedrooms, high in the cliffs of windows. I thought of what was underneath it all – I thought of the electricity cables, steam, water, fire, subway trains and lava in the city's guts, the subterranean rumbling of trains and earth-quakes. I thought of the dead souls from the war, concreted over. The tallest, most-visited building in Tokyo, the Sunshine Building, stood over the spot where Japan's prime minister and all her war criminals had been executed. It seemed to me so odd that no one knew what had just happened to me. No one had come up to me and said, 'Where have you been all night? What's that in your rucksack? Why haven't you gone to the police?' I watched the taxi driver's eyes in the rear-view mirror, certain that he was studying my face.

I got to Todai just after nine. The blizzard had picked up and the snow was settling on all the parked cars and the tops of lampposts. The *Akamon*, the huge red lacquered gate at the entrance of Todai, was visible only as a wavering red splash in the white, an intermittent blaze in the snowstorm. A guard wearing a black slicker ushered me through the gate and the taxi nosed along the driveway until, out of the white, a light appeared, then more, and at last the Institute of Social Sciences, rising up in front of us, lit and gilded like a fairy castle.

I asked the driver to stop. I tucked in my coat collar and got out, standing for a while, looking up at the building. It was four months since I'd first come here. Four months, and I knew so much more now. I knew everything – I knew the whole world.

Slowly I became aware of a dark figure not far away from me, small as a child, standing perfectly still in the snow, as insubstantial and wavery as a ghost. I peered at it. Shi Chongming. It was as if my thoughts had conjured him, but done the job half-heartedly so instead of the real flesh and blood Shi Chongming I'd created only this watery half-person.

'Shi Chongming,' I whispered, and he turned and looked and smiled. He came towards me, slowly materializing from the white, like a ghost evolving. He was wearing a coat and his plastic fisherman's hat pulled down over his hair.

'I was waiting for you,' he said. His skin in the odd light looked papery and insufficient: there were penny-sized liver spots on his face and neck. I saw that his jacket was fastened tightly round his neck.

'How did you know?'

He held up his hand to hush me. 'I don't know. Now, come and get warm. It's not good to stay out in the snow for a long time.'

I followed him up the steps. Inside, the institute was warm, overheated, and we trailed melting snowflakes across the floor. He closed the office door, put on his glasses and began to make the room comfortable. He plugged in a heater, and made me a bowl of steaming tea. 'Your eyes,' he said, as I put down the holdall and knelt on the floor, instinctively adopting the *seiza* position, as if it would warm me to be so contained, cupping the hot tea in both hands. 'Are you unwell?'

'I'm . . . I'm alive.' I couldn't stop my teeth chattering. I held my face into the sweet steam. The popcorny smell of rice tea. It smelt of Japan. I sat for several minutes until the shivering subsided, then I looked up at him and said, 'I've found out.'

Shi Chongming paused, a spoon raised above the teapot. 'Please – say it again.'

'I've found out. I know.'

He let the spoon drop into the teapot. He took off his glasses and sat down at his desk. 'Yes,' he said wearily. 'Yes, I thought you had.'

'You were right. Everything you told me was right. You must have known all the time. But I didn't. It's not what I was expecting. Not at all.'

'No?'

'No, it's something Fuyuki's had for a long time. Maybe for years.' My voice grew quieter and quieter. 'It's a baby. A mummified baby.'

Shi Chongming fell silent. He turned his head to the side and, for a moment, his mouth moved up and down as if he was reciting a mantra. At last he coughed and put away his glasses in a battered blue case. 'Yes,' he said eventually. 'Yes, I know. It's my daughter.'

61

And it is unbearable now to think of it: to think of that one moment of clear peace, of clear hope. How very still everything was in those few seconds before Shujin's screams echoed through the forest.

I looked round vaguely, as if someone had casually mentioned my name, frowning into the air, as if I didn't know what I'd heard. Then she screamed again, a short yelp, like a dog being beaten.

'Shujin?' I turned in a trance, pushing aside the branches and moving back through the trees. Maybe the birth was closer than I'd expected. 'Shujin?'

No reply. I began to walk. I crested a slope and picked up speed, breaking into a numb trot back to the place I had been sitting. 'Shujin?' Silence. 'Shujin?' My voice was louder now, a note of panic creeping in. 'Shujin. Answer me.'

There was no reply, and now real fear hit me. I broke into a run, leaping up the slope. 'Shujin!' My feet slid, pine trees dropped their soft snow loads on to me. '*Shujin!*'

At the base of the tree the handcart had been set upright, our blankets and belongings scattered around it. A set of muffled tracks led away into the trees. I swerved into them, my eyes watering, ducking as the bare branches whipped against my face. The track led on for a few more yards, then changed. I skidded to a halt in a flurry of snow, breathing hard, my heart racing.

The tracks had become wider here. An area of disturbed snow stretched around me for several feet, as if she had fallen to the ground in pain. Or as if there had been a struggle. Something lay half buried at my feet. I fell to a crouch and snatched it up, turning it over in my hands. A thin piece of tape, frayed and torn. My thoughts slowed, a terrible dread creeping over me. Attached to the tape were two Imperial Japanese Army dogtags.

'*Shujin!*' I leaped up. 'SHU-JIN?'

I waited. Nothing came back to me. I was alone in the trees with just the sound of my panting and my pulse. '*SHUJIN!*' The word reverberated into the trees and slowly folded away into the forests. I spun round, searching for a clue. They were out there somewhere, the Japanese, holding Shujin, crouching and sharpening their bayonets, framing me with their blood-filled eyes, somewhere, behind one of those trees . . .

Very close behind me someone released their breath into the silence.

I whipped round in a crouch, my hands out, ready to leap. But there was nothing, only the trees, black and mossy, icicles dripping in the branches. I breathed in and out through my nose, my ears straining for any sound. Someone was there. Very near. I heard a whisper of dry leaf, a rustle from about ten feet away where the ground dipped, then the crack of a branch, a sudden, mechanical sound, and a Japanese soldier stepped out from behind a tree.

He wasn't dressed for combat – his webbed steel helmet hung on his belt with the ammunition pouches, and his badges of rank were still in place. He held up not a rifle but a cine-camera, the lens pointed directly into my face. It was whirring, the crank handle whipping round and round. The Shanghai cameraman. I knew him instantly. The man who had filmed the soldiers' exploits in Shanghai. He was filming me.

We stood for a few seconds in silence, me staring at him, the lens staring unflinchingly at me. Then I lunged forward. '*Where is she?*' He took a step back, the camera steady on his shoulder, and at that moment, from further down the trail, I heard Shujin's voice, as sweet and breakable as porcelain.

'Chongming!'

Years and years from now I will recall that sound. I'll dream about it, I'll hear it in the cold white spaces of my future dreams.

'Chongming!'

I stumbled away from the cameraman into the trees, the snow almost up to my knees now, blindly following her voice. 'SHUJIN!'

I waded on, tears in my eyes, ready for a bullet to come whistling through the air. But death would have been easy when compared with what happened next. From ahead came the distinctive jangle of a bayonet frog in the frosty air. And then I saw them. They stood a hundred feet further down the goat track, two of them in their mustard greatcoats, their backs to me, looking at something on the ground. A motorcycle leaned against an old black pine tree. One of the men turned and glanced nervously at me. His hood was pulled over a field cap: he, too, was not dressed for battle, and yet his bayonet was slotted into his rifle. There was a line of blood on his face, as if Shujin had scratched him during the struggle. As I stared at him he lowered his eyes with shame. I had a brief flash of what he was, not much more than a teenager kept awake on amphetamines, worn down to nothing but skeins of naked nerves. He didn't want to be there.

But then there was the other man. At first he didn't turn. Beyond him, against a tree, Shujin lay on her back in the snow. One of her shoes had come loose, the naked foot blue against the snow. She was clutching a small, lacquer-handled knife against her breast. It was a sharp little fruit knife for dicing mango, and she was holding it in both hands, pointing up at the men.

'Leave her,' I shouted. 'Stand back.'

At my voice the other man became very still. His back appeared to grow – to gain in stature. Very slowly he turned to face me. He wasn't tall, only my height, but his eyes seemed to me very terrible. I slowed to a trot and then to a walk. The single gilt star on his cap flashed in the sun, his fur-collared greatcoat was open, his shirt ripped, and now I saw that it must have been his dogtags I'd found. He was close enough for me to smell last night's sweet *sake* in his sweat and the odour of something trapped and old

344

coming from his clothing. His face was damp, a sick, sweaty grey. And in that moment I knew all about him. All about the stained bottles lined up in the silk factory. The pestle, the mortar, the endless search . . . For a cure. This was the sick man who couldn't be cured by army-issue medicine, the sick man who was desperate enough to try anything – even cannibalism. The *yanwangye* of Nanking.

62

The baby hadn't been very old when she'd died. She still had a centimetre of umbilical cord attached to her. Dried and brown and mummified, she was so light that I held her easily, across the palms of my hand, light as a bird. She was tiny. Pitifully under-sized. A crumpled, brown newborn's face. Her hands were frozen – stretched out above her head as if she had been reaching for someone at the moment her world halted.

Her legs had gone and so had most of her lower half. What remained had been cut at, hacked and scraped at by Fuyuki and his Nurse. Most of her had been worn away because a wealthy old man insisted on his fantasy of immortality. She couldn't choose who looked at her or handled her. She couldn't stop herself being kept in a tank, facing a blank wall, helpless to move and waiting . . . for what? For someone to come and turn her to face the light?

If I hadn't found her the garden might have been the place she'd stayed for ever, alone in the dark, with only the rats and the changing leaf cover for company, frozen in eternity – reaching in the wrong direction. She'd have disappeared under the demolished house, and a skyscraper would have grown over her instead of a tree, and it would have been her final grave. The moment I unwrapped the carrier-bag and opened the parcel, I learned for sure that Shi Chongming was right: the past is an explosive, and once its splinters are in you they will always, always work their way to the surface.

*

I sat in his office with my mouth open, and stared at a point just above his head. The air in the room seemed stale and dead. 'Your *daughter*?'

'Taken by him in the war. In Nanking.' He cleared his throat. 'Who do you think is shown on the film if not Junzo Fuyuki and my wife?'

'Your wife?'

'Of course.'

'Fuyuki? He was *there*? He was in Nanking?'

Shi Chongming opened his desk drawer and threw something on to the table. Two flat engraved tags, fastened on an ageing, yellowing strip of tailor's tape. Because they weren't on a chain it took me a moment or two to recognize them as soldier's dogtags. I picked them up and rubbed the surface under my thumb. The *kanji* was clear. Winter and a tree. I looked up at him. 'Junzo Fuyuki.'

Shi Chongming didn't answer. He opened the cupboards that ran across the walls and pointed at them. Every shelf was crammed with stacks and stacks of paper, yellowing, torn and wedged together, secured with ribbon, string, tape and paperclips. 'My life's work. My only preoccupation for the last fifty years. On the outside I am a professor of sociology. On the inside I work only to find my daughter.'

'You didn't forget,' I murmured, gazing at the piles of paper. 'You never did forget Nanking.'

'Never. Why do you suppose I speak English so well, if not to find my daughter and one day tell the world?' He pulled out a stack of papers and dropped it with a thud on the table. 'Can you imagine the convolutions I have been through, the time it took me to track Fuyuki down? Think of the thousands of old men in Japan named Junzo Fuyuki. Here I stand, a little man, respected internationally for my work in a field that holds no interest for me, none whatsoever, a field that has only the distinction of being the one area that would adequately cover my true purpose and allow me access to these records.' He handed the top paper to me. A photocopy stamped by the National Defence Agency's war

347

history library. Now I recalled seeing the logo stamped on some of the papers in his portfolio weeks ago. 'Imperial Army unit records. Copies. The originals – at least, those that survived transfer between here and the United States during the occupation – are very well protected. But I was lucky – after years of appeals I was at last granted access to the records, and then I found what I needed.' He nodded. 'Yes. There was only one Lieutenant Junzo Fuyuki in Nanking in 1937. Only one. The *yanwangye* of Nanking. The devil – the guardian of hell. The man who hunted for human flesh to cure himself.' He rubbed his forehead, corrugating his skin. 'Like all the other soldiers, like almost every Japanese citizen who returned from China after the war, Fuyuki brought with him a box.' Shi Chongming held out his hands to indicate the shape and the size. 'Hanging round his neck.'

'Yes,' I said faintly. I remembered it. A white ceremonial box, lit and displayed in the corridor of the apartment next to Tokyo Tower. It should have brought back to Japan the ashes of a fellow soldier, but Fuyuki's had been used for something else.

'And with that baby he brought something else.' Shi Chongming gazed sadly at the reams and reams of paper. 'He brought the grief of a parent. He dragged with him a line . . . a line from here,' he put his hand on his heart, 'from this place to eternity. A line that could never be cut or shaken off. Never.'

We were both silent for a long time. The only sounds were of the trees outside the window, moving in the wind, occasionally bending to run their fingers lightly across the glass pane. At length Shi Chongming wiped his eyes and got to his feet, moving slowly, slightly bent, across the familiar spaces, the well-worn paths between the few pieces of furniture. He wheeled the film projector into the centre of the room, plugged it in and crossed awkwardly, without his stick, to where a small portable screen stood near the window. He rolled it down and secured it to the base of the stand. 'Here it is,' he said, as he unlocked a lower drawer and took out a rusting film can. He eased it open. 'The first time anyone has seen it. I am sure to this day that the man who filmed this was repentant. I am sure that he would have distributed this on his return to Japan – even if it meant his death. And yet he is dead and here is the film. Protected to this day by me.' He shook his head and smiled wryly. 'Such irony.'

When I didn't speak he stepped forward and held out the canister for me to look inside.

'You're going to show it to me,' I whispered, staring at the film. This was it: the manifestation of the words in the orange book, the testimony I'd been looking for all these years, the proof that I hadn't invented something – hadn't invented one detail, one exquisitely important detail.

'Yes. You think you know what you're going to feel about this film, don't you? You've researched Nanking for years, and you've read every account of it. You've played this film in your head a hundred times. You think you know what you're going to see and you think that will be horror enough. Don't you?'

I nodded numbly.

'Well, you're wrong. You're going to see something more than that.' He put on his glasses and laced the film into the projector, bending close to the machine to inch the film through its complex gears. 'You're going to see that *and* more. As ugly as you imagine that act, as ugly as the *yanwangye* of Nanking is, someone on this film is more ugly still.'

'Who?' I said faintly. 'Who is worse?'

'I am. Me. You will see me, uglier by far than Fuyuki.' He cleared his throat, crossed to the wall and switched off the lights. In the darkness I heard him fumble for the projector. 'This is one of the true reasons no one has ever seen this film. Because an old man who has spoken a thousand wise words about facing the past cannot, *cannot*, accept his own.'

The mechanism trundled into life, and the room was filled with the *flik flik flik flik* of the film rattling through the gate.

Shi Chongming had known how to store his film: there was no decomposition, no peeling and liquefying of polymers. No shadow and swirl on the image to hide your eyes behind.

The first frames came through, the screen cleared and a man appeared: thin, scared-looking, standing in the middle of a snowy

349

forest. He was half bent, staring into the camera with wild eyes as if he would leap at it. The hairs went up on my neck. This was Shi Chongming. Shi Chongming as a young man. A world away. He took a step towards the camera and shouted soundlessly at the lens. He seemed about to leap forward, when something off-screen distracted him. He turned and ran in the opposite direction. The camera followed, jolting silently down a path, Shi Chongming's arms flailing as he leaped over branches and gullies. He was so thin, I saw now, a stick-like man, no bigger than a maquette in his baggy, quilted clothes. Ahead of him, at the bottom of the path, two blurred figures appeared, muffled in fur-lined greatcoats, their backs to the camera. They were standing quite close together, looking down at a shape on the ground.

The projector rattled noisily, and, as the camera drew closer to the figure, the picture jolting, one of the men looked round in surprise. With pinched, expressionless eyes he took in, first, the tiny Chinese man running to him with his arms out, then the camera. Shi Chongming slowed and the cameraman must have lowered the camera as he ran because for the next few frames I saw only snow and leaves and feet.

Above the clattering of the projector I could imagine the noise on the mountainside, the panting, the rattling of equipment, the snapping of branches underfoot. Then the camera was raised again and this time it was closer. It was only a foot or so behind the second man. There was a pause, a distinct hesitation. The camera inched challengingly forwards, creeping up on him and suddenly he turned, horribly swiftly, and stared directly into the lens. A star on his cap caught the sun and flared briefly.

I held my breath. It was so easy to recognize a person across more than fifty years. A youthful face, cut out of wood, it seemed, and ill, very ill. Grey and sweating. But the eyes were the same. The eyes, and the miniature cat's teeth when he grimaced.

The camera crank mechanism must have wound to a halt then, because the picture disappeared, a jumpy join in the film rattled through the projector like a train on the brink of derailment, and suddenly we were at a different angle, looking at Fuyuki who stood, sweating, breathing hard, little puffs of steam issuing from him. He was a little bent, and when the camera drew back I could see that he was fitting a bayonet into his rifle. At his feet a woman lay on her back, her *qipao* pulled up above her waist, her trousers torn away to show the dark slant of her stomach.

'My wife,' Shi Chongming said quietly, his eyes locked on the film as if he was watching a dream. 'That was my wife.'

Fuyuki was shouting something at the camera. He waved and grinned, revealing his cat's teeth. The camera seemed to sag, as if wilting under his gaze. It backed slowly away, and the screen yawned wider, taking in the slope of the ground, more trees, a motorbike propped against one. In the corner of the frame I saw the second soldier. He had taken off his coat and his big arms were wrapped round Shi Chongming, whose mouth was open in a silent, anguished howl. He twisted and fought, but the soldier held him firm. No one was interested in his pleading. Everyone was watching Fuyuki.

What happened next had been living inside me for years. It had started as just a sentence on a page in my parents' house, but now I was seeing the reality. The thing everyone said was in my imagination was now a grainy truth crawling across the screen in flecks of black and white. It was all so different from the way I'd pictured it: in my version the edges had been clear-cut, the figures weren't blurred and jumpy, bleeding into the scenery behind them. In my version the act itself had been swift and ornate – a *samurai* dance: a trademark flick of the sword afterwards to clean it of blood. A dark, peacock tail splatter on the snow.

But this was something different. This was ungainly and fumbled. This was Fuyuki's bayonet locked and twisted into his rifle; he was holding the weapon in two hands like a spade, elbows seesawing up behind his body, thick and black against the snow, and this was him, the man trained in bayoneting since boyhood, plunging it into the woman's unprotected stomach with all his strength.

It took two vigorous movements. She jerked the first time, lifting her arms in a strange, casual way, the way a woman sometimes moves her arms to ease a tight shoulder muscle, dropping the knife she was holding into the snow. With the second

351

thrust she seemed to sit up, her arms out in front of her like a puppet. But before she could raise herself completely her strength left and she fell back abruptly, rolling slightly to the side. Then she was still, the only movement a darkening stain spreading its wings round her like an angel.

It was so sudden, so unexpectedly cruel, that I could feel the shock that descended on the forest even fifty-three years later. The second soldier's face became slack, and the cameraman must have fallen to his knees, because the picture jolted. When he regained control and managed to straighten, Lieutenant Fuyuki was reaching into the messy hole he'd made. He tugged out an arm, then the whole baby, slipping it out intact, steaming, a bloated clot of placenta coming with it. He dropped it a few feet away in the snow, and stood over the mother's body, poking his bayonet idly into her empty stomach, biting his lip thoughtfully as if there might be something else in there. The junior soldier had had enough, he put his hands to his throat and stumbled away, releasing Shi Chongming, who shot forward, throwing himself into the blackening snow. He dropped down on to all fours, grabbed his daughter into his quilted jacket and crawled clumsily to his wife. He was inches from her, shouting into her face, into her lifeless eyes. Then the cameraman moved a little, sideways, revealing Fuyuki standing above Shi Chongming, holding a small handgun, a 'baby *nambu*', pointed directly at his head.

It took a moment or two for Shi Chongming to realize what was happening. When he felt the shadow fall on him he looked up in slow, creaky stages. Fuyuki released the pistol's safety catch and extended his free hand in a simple gesture known across the globe. *Give me.*

Give me.

Shi Chongming struggled to his knees, the baby clasped to his chest, never taking his eyes off that extended hand. Slowly, slowly, Fuyuki cocked the *nambu*, and squeezed the trigger. Shi Chongming flinched, his body sagged, and two feet behind him the snow leaped once. He wasn't hit, it was only a warning, but his knees buckled – he began to shake visibly. Fuyuki took a step forward, putting the muzzle of the gun against his head.

Trembling, weeping, Shi Chongming looked up at his captor's face. Everything was there in his eyes, everything was there among the reflection of the trees, the long twisting story of his wife and their baby, the question 'Why us, why now, why here?' His history stringing back into the past.

Somehow I knew what was going to happen next. I felt it all about to accelerate. Suddenly I understood why Shi Chongming had kept this film secret for so many years. What I was watching, I realized, was him measuring and weighing his life against the value of the baby in his arms.

He stared at the hand for so long that the camera wound down, another film join went through, and when the picture came back he was still staring. A tear ran down his face. I put my fingers to my forehead, hardly daring to breathe, conscious of the old Shi Chongming sitting in silence behind me. With a single sentence that seemed to mean nothing to anyone but himself, Shi Chongming raised the baby and rested it gently across Fuyuki's arms. He bowed his head, then struggled to his feet and walked wearily into the trees. No one stopped him. He walked slowly, limping slightly, every few paces his hand going up to steady himself against a tree.

No one moved. The second soldier stood a few yards away in the snow, his head bowed, his face in his hands. Even Fuyuki was motionless. Then he turned, said something to the camera, and picked up the baby by a foot – holding her for inspection like a skinned rabbit.

I didn't breathe. This was it. This was the crucial moment. Fuyuki looked at the baby, with a strange, intense expression, as if she held the answer to an important question. Then, with his free hand, he pulled out his rubber belt and knotted it round her ankles, lashing her tightly round his waist, letting her swing down, hanging upside-down, facing his leg. She twisted there for a few moments. Then her hands flexed.

I sat forward, gripping the chair arms. Yes. I had been right. Her hands were moving. Her mouth opened a few times, her chest rose and fell and her face crumpled in a wail. She was alive. She twisted and reached out blindly, instinctively trying to grasp

Fuyuki's leg. When he turned she lost her grip and flared in an arc from his waist like a dancer's skirt. He did it once, twice, showing off for the camera, letting her weight bump against his uniformed thigh, smiling and saying something. When he stopped and let the baby come to a rest, her instinctive grasping resumed.

The film ran through its guides and at last sputtered out, I felt as if the breath had been punched out of me. I fell forward, on to my knees like a supplicant. The screen was empty, only a few amoebic squiggles and hairs left in the gate. Shi Chongming reached over, switched off the projector and stood looking down at me on the floor. The only sound in the office was the dull *thock thock thock* of the clumsy old timepiece on the mantelpiece.

'Is it what you expected?'

I wiped my face with my sleeve. 'Yes,' I said. 'She lived. It's what the book said. The babies were living when they came out.'

'Oh, yes,' said Shi Chongming, in a hushed voice. 'Yes, she was alive.'

'For years . . .' I lifted my arm to wipe my eyes '. . . for years I thought I'd – I'd imagined that part. Everyone said I was insane, that I'd made it up, that no baby could live through – through that.' I dug in my pocket for a tissue, balled it up and dabbed at my eyes. 'I know now I didn't imagine it. It was all I wanted to know.'

I heard him sit down at the desk. When I looked up he was staring at the window. Outside the snowflakes seemed suddenly bright, as if lit from below. I remember thinking that they looked like tiny angels falling to earth.

'I'll never be sure how long she survived,' he said. 'I pray it wasn't long.' He rubbed his forehead and shrugged, looking blankly around the office as if searching for something safe to rest his eyes on. 'I am told that Fuyuki became well after this. He killed my daughter and I am told that, shortly afterwards, his symptoms disappeared. It was a placebo effect, quite coincidental. The malaria would have left him eventually, and over the years the attacks would have lessened whether or not he had my . . .'

His eyes stopped roving and met mine, and we looked at each other for a long time. There and then, as I was, prone on the floor of Shi Chongming's office, something terrible and inescapable stood up in me: the knowledge that there wasn't going to be a quiet escape. Alive or dead, our children would hold us. Just like Shi Chongming I was going to be eternally connected to my dead baby girl. Shi Chongming was in his seventies, I was in my twenties. She would be with me for ever.

I got to my feet and picked up the holdall. I put it on the desk in front of him and stood with my hands resting on it, my head lowered. 'My little girl died too,' I said quietly. 'That's why I'm here. Did you know?'

Slowly Shi Chongming took his eyes off the holdall and raised them to me. 'I have never known why you came to me.'

'Because I did it, you see. It was me.' I pushed at the tears with the heel of my hand. 'I killed her myself – my little girl – with a knife.'

Shi Chongming didn't speak. An awful puzzlement crept into his eyes.

I nodded. 'I know. It's terrible, and I've got no excuse for – for crying about it. I know that. But I didn't mean to – to kill her. I thought she would live. I'd read about the Nanking babies, in the orange book, and I – I don't know why, but I thought maybe my baby would live, too, and so I—' I sank into the chair, staring down at my shaky hands. 'I thought she'd be okay and they'd take her away and hide her somewhere, somewhere my . . . my parents couldn't find her.'

Shi Chongming shuffled round the table and put his hands on my back. After a long time he sighed and said, 'Do you know something? I consider myself a man who knows sadness very well. But I – I have no words for this. No words.'

'Don't worry. You were kind, you were so kind because you kept telling me ignorance wasn't the same as evil, but I know.' I wiped my eyes and tried to smile up at him. 'I know. You can't ever really forgive someone like me.'

63

How can you measure the power that the mind exerts over the body? Fuyuki would never have believed that the tiny mummified corpse of Shi Chongming's baby didn't hold the secret of immortality. He would never have believed that what he had carefully saved and protected over the years, slowly nibbling away at, was only a placebo, and that what had really kept him alive was his own powerful belief. Those who surrounded him believed it too. When he died in his sleep, only two weeks after the theft of Shi Chongming's baby, they believed wholeheartedly that it was because he'd lost his secret elixir. But there were others, the sceptics, who wondered secretly whether Fuyuki's death was brought on by the strain of the sudden interest paid him by a working group based within the USA Department of Justice.

It was a small, dedicated team specializing in the investigation of war criminals, and the team members were delighted to hear from one Professor Shi Chongming formerly of Jiangsu and Todai universities. Now that he had his daughter's remains safe, Shi Chongming had opened up like a shell in warm water. For fifty-three years he'd been working towards it, trying to get permission to travel to Japan, struggling with the bureaucracy of the Land Defence Agency, but now that he had her everything came out: his notes; the soldier's ID tags; a collection of unit logs from 1937; photographs of Lieutenant Fuyuki. Everything was packaged up and couriered to Pennsylvania Avenue,

Washington DC. A little later a 16mm film followed across the Pacific, a grainy black-and-white film from which the team were able to get a positive identification of Fuyuki.

Some whispered that something was missing from the film, and pointed to some very modern-looking edit points. They said sections must have been removed from it recently. It had been my idea to take out the few frames that showed Shi Chongming giving up his baby. I'd done the splicing myself in a hotel room in Nanking, crudely, with scissors and Scotchtape. I had made a decision for him, overruled him. I had decided that he wasn't going to martyr himself. It was as simple as that.

I didn't copy the film before I packed it in bubble-wrap, carefully addressing the parcel with black marker pen. *Dr Michael Burana, IWG, Department of Justice.* I could have sent it to the doctors in England, I suppose, maybe a copy to the nurse who used to crouch next to my bed in the dark. Maybe a copy, with a dried flower pressed inside, to the jigging girl. But I didn't need to – because something had happened. I was older now, I knew lots and lots of things. I knew so much that I was heavy with it. I knew instinctively what was born of ignorance and what of madness. I no longer needed to prove anything to anyone. Not even myself.

'But now it is over,' Shi Chongming said. 'And, really, I see my wife was right to say that time circles constantly, because here we are. We have come all the way back to the beginning.'

It was a blue and white December morning, the sun reflecting blindingly from the snow, and we stood among the trees on Purple Mountain above Nanking. At our feet was a fresh, shallow hole and in his arms Shi Chongming held a small bundle wrapped in linen. It hadn't taken him long to find it, the place where he had given up his daughter. Some things on the mountainside had changed in those fifty-three years: now, little trams flashed red through the trees, taking tourists up to the mausoleum; the city below us was a grown-up twentieth-century city, extraordinary with its hazy skyscrapers and electronic signs. But other things were so unchanged that Shi Chongming became silent when he looked at them: the sun glinting on the bronze azimuth, the black pines drooping under the weight of snow, the great stone tortoise still standing in the shadows, staring impassively at the trees that grew and seeded on the slopes, died and re-sprouted, died and resprouted.

We had shrouded the baby's remains in white, and across the bundle I'd tied a little sprig of yellow winter jasmine. In a shop on the Flower Rain Terrace, I'd bought a white *qipao* so I could dress traditionally for the burial. It was the first time I'd worn white in my life and I thought I looked nice in it. Shi Chongming was wearing a suit with a black armband. He said that no Chinese parent should come to their child's funeral. He said, as he stepped into the hole, that he shouldn't be here and he certainly shouldn't be standing in the grave, placing this small bundle in the ground. He should be following etiquette, standing to the left of the grave, averting his eyes. 'But,' he said, under his breath, as he scraped dirt down on the tiny shroud, 'what is as it should be any more?'

I was silent. A dragonfly was watching us. It seemed so strange to me that a little animal that shouldn't have been alive in the middle of winter had come and rested on a branch near the grave to watch us bury a baby. I stared at it until Shi Chongming touched my arm, said something in a low voice, and I turned back to the grave. He lit a small incense stick, stuck it in the ground, and I made the Christian sign of the cross because I didn't know what else to do. Then, together, we walked through the trees back to the car. Behind us the dragonfly took off from the branch and the incense smoke floated up out of the fatsia, trailing in a slow bloom up the edge of the mountain across the sycamore trees and into the blue.

Shi Chongming died six weeks later in a hospital on Zhongshan Road. I was at his bedside.

In his last days he kept asking me one question over and over again: 'Tell me, what do you think she felt?' I didn't know what to say in reply. It's always been clear to me that the human heart turns itself inside out to belong, it reaches and strains for the first and nearest warmth, so why should a baby's heart be any differ-ent? But I didn't tell Shi Chongming this, because I was sure that in his darkest moments he must have wondered if the only human his daughter had reached out to, if the only person she'd felt love for, was Junzo Fuyuki.

And, if I couldn't answer Shi Chongming, do I have any hope of answering you, my unnamed daughter, except to say that I acted in ignorance, except to say that I think about you every day, even though I'll never know how to measure your life, your existence? Maybe you weren't ever a soul – maybe you didn't get that far. Maybe you were a spectre, or a flash of light. Maybe a little moon soul.

I'll never stop wondering where you are – if you will re-emerge in a different world, if you have already, if you live now in peace, in love, in a faraway country that I will never visit. But I am sure of one thing: I am sure that if you have returned, the first thing you will do is tilt your face towards the sun. Because, my missing baby, if you have learned anything at all, you have learned that in this world none of us has very long.

Author's Note

In 1937, four years before the USA was drawn into the Pacific war with the attack on Pearl Harbor, Japanese forces advanced into mainland China and stormed the capital, Nanking. The events that followed exceeded every Chinese citizen's worst fears, as the invading army embarked on a month-long frenzy of rape, torture and mutilation.

What prompted an otherwise disciplined army to behave in this way has been long debated (for an excellent exploration of the Japanese soldier's psyche, see Ruth Benedict's classic *The Chrysanthemum and the Sword*). But perhaps the most contentious issue concerns the numbers of casualties involved. Some in China say as many as four hundred thousand died that winter; some in Japan insist it was no more than a handful. History, we are repeatedly reminded, is written by the victors, but history is *rewritten* by many other parties: revisionists; politicians; fame-hungry academics; and even to some degree the Americans who sought to mollify Japan, recognizing in its geographical position a strategic advantage in the fight against communism. History can change like a chameleon, reflecting back the answer required of it: and with every concerned agency claiming something different, there may be little hope of ever finding an internationally agreed casualty tally.

In a partially opened mass grave at the official Jiangdongmen memorial site, visitors to Nanking can inspect the mingled remains of unidentified citizens killed in the 1937 invasion. Looking at these bones, attempting to appreciate the real extent of the massacre, it struck me that, whatever the true number of casualties, however great or small, four hundred thousand or ten, each of those unremembered and uncelebrated citizens deserves our recognition for what they represent: the large tragedy of the small human life.

Evidence of the massacre has come down to us in fragments: witness reports, photographs, a few feet of blurred 16mm film shot by the Reverend John Magee. Shi Chongming's film is fictional, but it is entirely possible that more footage does exist and has not surfaced for fear of reprisals from Japanese holocaust deniers – certainly a print of Magee's film, which was taken by a civilian to Japan with the intention of distributing it, quickly and mysteriously disappeared without trace. Given this scattered and anecdotal evidence, it is no easy task, when building a fictionalized account of the massacre, to steer a course between the sensationalists and the obfuscators. For a steadying hand in this matter I relied extensively on the work of two people: the late Iris Chang, whose book *The Rape of Nanking* was the first serious attempt to alert a wider public to the massacre, and, rather less well known outside Japan, Katsuichi Honda.

Honda, a Japanese journalist, has been working since 1971 to bring the truth to his sceptical nation. In spite of the fact that there has been a recent sea change in the Japanese appreciation of their past – the Nanking invasion has been cautiously reintroduced to the school curriculum, and no one who witnessed the event will forget the shocked and baffled tears of middle-aged Japanese parents learning the truth from their children – Honda Katsuichi nevertheless lives anonymously for fear of right-wing attacks. His 1999 collection of testimonies *The Nanjing Massacre* contains several witness accounts of the 'corpse mountain' somewhere in the region of Tiger Mountain, including the living human column attempting to climb to safety on thin air. It also contains an almost unbearable first-hand account of an unborn child being cut from its mother's womb by a Japanese officer.

In addition to Honda's work, I also plundered the scholarship of the following: John Blake; Annie Blunt of the Bright Futures Mental Health Foundation; Jim Breen at Monash University (whose excellent *kanji* database can be found at csse.monash.edu.au); Nick Burton; John Dower (*Embracing Defeat*); George Forty (*Japanese Army Handbook*); Hiro Hitomi; Hiroaki Kobayashi; Alistair Morrison; Chigusa Ogino; Anna Valdinger; and all at the British Council, Tokyo. Any remaining errors I claim as my own.

Thank you to the city of Tokyo for permitting me to tinker with its remarkable geography, also to Selina Walker and Broo Doherty, for their faith and energy. The usual resounding howl of gratitude goes out to: Linda and Laura Downing; Jane Gregory; Patrick Janson-Smith; Margaret O.W.O. Murphy; Lisanne Radice; Gilly Vaulkhard. A special smile to Mairi the great. And most of all, thank you to my constants, the best constants a heart could hope for: Keith and Lotte Quinn.

For the sake of clarity all Japanese names have been presented according to the Western tradition: personal name followed by family name. Chinese names, however, are represented traditionally, the family name preceding the personal. Chinese names and terms have been mostly transcribed in the official *pinyin* system of the People's Republic of China. Exceptions are names or terms that are well known in the West in their Wade-Giles form. These include (with *pinyin* in brackets) the Daoist classic the I-Ching (Yijing), Sun Yat-sen (Sun Yixian), the Kuomintang (Guomindang), the Yangtze (Yangzi), Chiang Kai-shek (Jiang Jieshi), and most importantly the city of Nanking as it was known in the 1930s, now known in *pinyin* as Nanjing.

Read on for the opening pages of *Gone* by Mo Hayder, winner of the Edgar Award for Best Novel.

"Artfully constructed . . . chilling . . . Shocks are in store."
—Marilyn Stasio, *The New York Times Book Review*

Available Now

1

Detective Inspector Jack Caffery of Bristol's Major Crime Investigation Unit spent ten minutes in the centre of Frome looking at the crime scene. He walked past the road blocks, the flashing blue lights, the police tape, the onlookers gathered in huddles with their Saturday-afternoon shopping bags peering to catch a glimpse of the forensics guys with their brushes and bags, and stood for a long time where the whole thing had happened, among the oil leaks and abandoned shopping trolleys of the underground car park, trying to soak up the place and decide how anxious he should be. Then, already cold in spite of his overcoat, he went upstairs to the manager's tiny office where the local officers and the forensics guys were watching CCTV footage on a small colour monitor.

They stood in a semicircle, holding cups of machine coffee, some of them still in their Tyvek suits with the hoods down. Everyone glanced up as Caffery entered, but he shook his head, opened his hands to show he had no news, and they turned back to the TV, their expressions closed and serious.

The picture had the typical graininess of a low-end CCTV system, the camera trained on the entrance ramp of the car park. The opaque timecode graduated from black to white and back again. The screen showed cars ranked in painted bays, winter sunlight coming through the entrance ramp beyond them, bright as a floodlight. At the back of one of the vehicles – a Toyota Yaris – a woman stood with her back to the camera, loading groceries from a trolley. Jack Caffery was an inspector with eighteen years of the hardest policing in his pocket – Murder Squad, in some of the country's toughest inner-city forces. Even so, he couldn't fight the cold pinch of dread the image gave him, knowing what was going to happen next on the film.

From the statements taken by the local officers he knew a lot already: the woman's name was Rose Bradley. She was the wife of a C of E minister and she was in her late forties, though on screen she looked older. She was dressed in a short dark jacket made of something heavy – chenille maybe – with a calf-length tweed skirt and low pumps. Her hair was short and neat. She was the type who would be sensible enough to carry an umbrella or tie a scarf around her head if it was raining, but it was a clear, cold day and her head was bare. Rose had spent the afternoon browsing the clothes boutiques in the centre of Frome, and had finished the excursion with the family's weekly food shop in Somerfield. Before she'd begun loading the bags, she'd put her keys and the ticket to the car park on the front seat of the Yaris.

The sunlight behind her flickered and she lifted her head to see a man running fast down the ramp. He was tall and broad, in jeans and a Puffa jacket. Over his head he wore a rubber mask. A Santa Claus mask. To Caffery that was the creepiest part of it – the rubber mask bobbing along as the man raced towards Rose. The grin didn't change or fade as he got close to her.

'He said three words.' The local inspector – a tall, austere guy in uniform who must also have been standing outside in the cold, judging by his red nostrils – nodded at the monitor. 'Just here – as he comes up to her. He says, "Get down, bitch." She didn't recognize the voice and she's not sure if he had an accent or not because he was shouting.'

The man grabbed Rose's arm, cartwheeling her away from the car. Her right arm flew up, a piece of jewellery snapped and beads scattered, catching the light. Her hip slammed into the boot of the neighbouring car, catapulting her upper torso sideways over it, as if she was made of rubber. Her hair flew up from the scalp, her elbow made contact with the roof and she rebounded, whip-like, falling away from the car and landing on her knees. By now the man in the mask was in the driver's seat of the Yaris. Rose saw what he was doing and scrambled to her feet. She got to the car window and was tugging frantically at the door as the guy got the keys into the ignition. The car gave a small jolt as the handbrake came off, and shot backwards with a jerk. Rose staggered along next to it, half falling, half dragged, then the car braked abruptly, changed gear and skidded forwards. The movement loosened her grip and she fell away clumsily, rolling once, legs and arms in an ungainly crabbed position until she came to a halt. She recovered herself and raised her head just in time to see the car speed towards the exit.

'What next?' said Caffery.

'Not much. We pick him up on another camera.' The inspector aimed the remote control at the DVR box and shuffled through the different camera inputs. 'Here – leaving the car park. He uses her ticket to get out. But the picture's not so good on this feed.'

The screen showed the Yaris from behind. The brake lights came on as it slowed at the barrier. The driver's window opened and the man's hand came out, put the ticket into the slot. There was a pause and the barrier opened. The brake lights went off and the Yaris pulled away.

'No prints on the barrier,' said the inspector. 'He's wearing gloves. See them?'

'Freeze it there,' Caffery said.

The inspector paused the picture. Caffery bent closer to the screen, turning his head sideways to study the back window above the lit-up numberplate. When the case had been called in to MCIU, the unit superintendent, an unforgiving bastard who would screw an old woman to the floor if she had information that would improve his clear-up rates, told Caffery the first thing to check was whether or not the report was genuine. Caffery searched the shadows and reflective parts of the back windscreen. He could see something on the seat. Something pale and blurry.

'Is that her?'

'Yes.'

'You sure?'

The inspector turned and gave him a long look, as if he thought he was being tested. 'Yes,' he said slowly. 'Why?'

Caffery didn't answer. He wasn't going to say out loud that the superintendent was worried about all the dickheads out there who'd been known, in the past, to invent a child on the back seat when their car had been jacked, thinking they'd get a higher alert attached to the police hunt for the vehicle. These things happened. But it didn't look as if that was what Rose Bradley was up to.

'Let me see her. Earlier.'

The inspector aimed the remote control at the TV and flipped through the menu to the previous clip, to a point ninety seconds before the attack on Rose. The car park was empty. Just the sunlight in the entrance and the cars. As the time code flicked round to 4:31 the doors to the supermarket opened and Rose Bradley emerged, pushing the trolley. At her side came a small girl in a brown duffel coat. Pale, with blonde hair cut in a fringe, she wore pastel-coloured Mary Jane shoes, pink tights, and walked with her hands in her pockets. Rose unlocked the Yaris and the little girl opened the back door and crawled inside. Rose closed the door on her, put the keys and her car-park ticket on the front seat and went to the boot.

'OK. You can stop it there.'

The inspector clicked off the TV and straightened. 'Major Crime's here. Whose case does that make it? Yours? Mine?'

'No one's.' Caffery pulled his keys out of his pocket. 'Because it's never going to get that far.'

The inspector raised an eyebrow. 'Says who?'

'Says the statistics. He's made a mistake – didn't know she was in the car. He'll dump her first chance he has. He's probably already dropped her and the phone call's just working its way through the system.'

'It's been almost three hours.'

Caffery held his eyes. The inspector was right – those three hours were outside what the statistics said, and he disliked that.

But he'd been in the job long enough to expect the wide balls that came from time to time. The sudden swerves, the mould breakers. Yes, the three hours felt wrong, but there was probably a good reason. The guy might be trying to get a good distance. Find somewhere he was sure he wouldn't be seen to dump her.

'She'll be back. You have my word.'

'Really?'

'Really.'

Caffery buttoned his coat as he left the room, pulled his car keys out of his pocket. He'd been due to knock off work in half an hour. There were a couple of things he'd been considering doing with his evening – a Police Social Club pub quiz at the Staple Hill bar, a meat raffle at the Coach and Horses near the offices, or a night at home on his own. Dismal choices. But not as dismal as what he had to do now. What he had to do now was go and speak to the Bradley family. Find out if, apart from the statistical blip, there was any other reason their younger daughter, Martha, wasn't back yet.